D0962019

HAMMER
—— OF ——
WITCHES

HAMMER
—— OF ——
WITCHES

SHANA MLAWSKI

Tu Books

AN IMPRINT OF
LEE & LOW BOOKS
New York

Text copyright © 2013 by Shana Mlawski
Jacket art © 2013 by Andrew Mar

Map in back cover illustration based on Vinckeboons, Joan. Map of the islands of Hispaniola and Puerto Rico. Map. ca. 1639. Library of Congress, Geography and Map Division, call number G3291.S12 coll .H3. 1 ms. map : col., paper backing ; 50 x 71 cm., http://www.loc.gov/item/2003623402 (accessed September 2012).

TU BOOKS, an imprint of LEE & LOW BOOKS Inc.
95 Madison Avenue, New York, NY 10016
leeandlow.com

Manufactured in the United States of America
by Worzalla Publishing Company, April 2013

Book design by Isaac Stewart
Book production by The Kids at Our House
The text is set in Adobe Garamond Pro

10 9 8 7 6 5 4 3 2 1
First Edition

Library of Congress Cataloging-in-Publication Data
Mlawski, Shana.
Hammer of witches / by Shana Mlawski. — First edition.
pages cm
Summary: "Fourteen-year-old bookmaker's apprentice Baltasar, pursued by a secret witch-hunting arm of the Inquisition, escapes by joining Columbus' expedition and discovers magical secrets about his own past that his family had tried to keep hidden"—Provided by publisher.
ISBN 978-1-60060-987-9 (hardcover : alk. paper) —
ISBN 978-1-60060-988-6 (e-book)
[1. Magic—Fiction. 2. Wizards—Fiction. 3. Explorers—Fiction.
4. Storytelling—Fiction. 5. Columbus, Christopher—Fiction. 6. America—Discovery and exploration—Spanish—Fiction.] I. Title.
PZ7.M7123Ham 2013
[Fic]—dc23
2012048627

To my parents,
who gave me life,
love,
and a lot of books

Prologue

My uncle Diego always said there was magic in a story. Of course, I never really believed him when he said it. My uncle was an old man to me for as long as I can remember, and a bookmaker, too, so his head was always full of one story or another. You could never be sure if he was telling some truth from his past or some legend he had heard along the way. Half the time he probably wasn't sure himself.

Now I know my uncle was right. There *is* magic in a story. Real magic. Only when I was a little older and sitting on a shore at the edge of the world did I understand how right my uncle was.

He had almost convinced me one time before. Back then I was seven, an olive-skinned child with thick black hair and a big mouth that was learning to tell lies. We were back in Palos de la Frontera in Spain, in a candlelit closet they called my bedroom. It was summer. The night was sweaty and raw with the smell of tallow and burning wicks.

"Wait, Uncle," I murmured as I peeked up at him through half-closed eyes. The old man bent in shadows in the doorway. A ball of warm light pulsed on the candle in his hand. "Don't leave yet. You didn't tell me a story."

The ball of light bobbed on the candle as my uncle laughed, and his long shadow laughed across the wooden beams of my ceiling. "All right, Bali. All right." Each syllable bounced across his tongue. Uncle Diego had always had the perfect voice for stories. He had grown up in Turkey, so his Castilian was stained with shades of his native Greek.

My uncle placed his candle on the floor and lowered himself onto the stool next to my bed. "And what kind of story does His Majesty want to hear tonight?"

"One about Amir al-Katib, of course!"

Of course! My poor uncle had spent the last seven years telling me stories of Amir al-Katib, the noble warrior who fought against his own Moorish people for the freedom of Christian Europe. Best of all, the stories were true. My uncle had known the man in the old times, in Constantinople.

"So His Majesty wants another story about Amir al-Katib. And which one does He want to hear this time?"

"One about the siege of the city. The one where he saved your life."

"Didn't I tell you that one last night, Baltasar?"

"Tell the one where he brought you and Father to Palos. No, tell me a new one. Tell me one I haven't heard before."

2

The old man yawned, picked up his candle from the floor, and stuck a hasty kiss on the top of my forehead. "I'm sorry, Bali. It's late. I'll come up with a good story for you tomorrow. I promise."

And he turned to leave. But as he did, a shrill caw like a hawk's or an eagle's tore through my bedroom's open window. The flame of my uncle's candle seemed to shrink at the sound, and a ragged shadow like a bird of prey trembled across his wrinkled face.

"You know, Baltasar. There is another story about al-Katib, now that I think about it. But if I tell it, you must promise not to tell your aunt Serena. I mean it. There is magic in this story."

And for some reason, that night, I almost believed him when he said it. "I won't tell, Uncle. I promise." So my uncle returned to his seat and began his story:

"Once in Arabia there were two men who killed another. The slain man was innocent, the deed done out of jealousy and spite. The man they had killed was their brother. The two men had coveted his wife.

"When the act was done the elder brother looked down at the slain man and said, 'Leave him here on the road, where his blood will color the earth. Tomorrow when the sun rises the vultures will come and eat his flesh.'

"Now in Arabia, Baltasar, it is a dreadful sin to murder and a grave dishonor not to bury the dead. But the younger man heard violence in his brother's voice, so he did not argue. The

3

brothers took a last look at their kinsman, wiped their daggers of his blood, and returned to their homes certain they were safe.

"But they were not safe. For that night, the blood of the slain man clawed toward the heavens, screaming for revenge. And its call was answered. That night a beast sprang from that crimson pool, howling the name of its ancient god. It was the beast known only as the hameh."

Hameh. I shuddered as the word slithered up my chest. "What is it?" I said almost voicelessly.

"The hameh is a bird, Bali. Black as the sea on a moonless night. Its scream can drive a man to madness, and it leaves a bloody trail in its wake. And it never forgets its sacred charge. From that moment on the hameh pursued the two men until it delivered justice unto them."

Somewhere in the distance I thought I heard another hideous shriek, and my fingers curled themselves around the edge of my quilt. Somewhere, I knew, a hellish black hawk was circling the skies, searching, waiting to rend me with its claws and judge me for my sins. Hameh. It sounded like a curse. Like a deadly spell. Like the last warm breath in the mouth of a dead man.

"Uncle," I whispered, "you said you would tell me a true story. You said you would tell me about Amir al-Katib—"

"I did, Baltasar," my uncle said, and I heard the sorrow in his answer. I couldn't yet understand what he meant by that, nor why he told me that story that night. I didn't yet know that my destiny and the destiny of the hameh had been entangled for many years and would be so for many years to come. And although I suspected it, I didn't yet know that every word my uncle had said was perfectly true.

"But maybe he's right," I remember thinking that night. "Maybe there is magic in a story. Dark magic. Magic that can steal your soul."

Soon my uncle left and closed the door behind him, and I kissed the Lord's Prayer into the wooden cross that hung around my neck. It wasn't long before I fell asleep. And in my dream I thought I heard my aunt's voice, muffled and distant. "You shouldn't have told him, Diego. It's better if he doesn't know."

And in my dream my uncle answered, "Do not worry, my love. It is just a story. Meaningless . . ."

Part One

PALOS DE LA FRONTERA, SPAIN
July 1492

One

EYES IN THE WINDOW

There were eyes in my bedroom window. Yellow ones— bodiless and surrounded by smoke. I was fourteen, and it was summer. I had been dreaming about the war.

Hundreds of years ago Moorish armies had taken Granada from its Christian rulers, and from the time I was born our King Fernando and Queen Isabel tried to reconquer it. In my dream I was there at the final battle, surrounded by grim men on tall black horses that stomped, impatient, on the sun-baked ground. Tangled beards hid the men's dark faces. Splashes of blood defiled their robes. Behind them I saw mountains and burning trees, and the red fortress Alhambra waiting silently for battle.

And it came. The Moorish soldiers raised their voices in one ululating chorus and whirled their sabers above their heads. At once their horses pounded, screaming, past me. I ran from them. I tripped. I felt a sword slicing through my neck—

Then a sudden shriek ripped me from my nightmare, and

I awoke to see a pair of yellow eyes shining through my bedroom window. Eyes. Long black pupils bled vertically within them— and beyond them, I could see nothing, nothing.

I groped behind me for the quill lying on the stool next to my bed. As sharp as it was, it was the closest thing I had to a weapon. I grasped the thing in my fist as if it were a dagger, but before I could do anything with it, a whispery voice drifted in from outside.

"Be calm, my shadow," the whispery voice said. "*Shh.* Now, do you see him?"

The yellow eyes twitched up and to the side as if listening, not to their questioner but something farther in the distance. Holding my breath, I listened too. Over the sound of my heartbeat throbbing in my ears, over the light trills of humming crickets, I could hear urgent shouting. The yellow eyes listened to them intently, floating bodiless in gray wisps of smoke.

I pushed myself upright on my woolen mattress. "Who are you?" I said in what was supposed to be a whisper.

But the question came out louder than I had meant it, and the yellow eyes snuffed out like two candles. A gust of wind sent a nearby lemon tree into a tumult. Heavy footsteps clanged down the dirt road near my house.

"They've found us!" the whispery voice cried from outside. "Quick! Quick! We must go!"

"No, wait!" I exclaimed. I flung my quilt from my legs and lunged for the window. A puff of smoke burst in front of me, filling my nose and the back of my mouth with the scents of cinnamon and incense. I tried to cough the smoke away, but no use. In an instant the smells overpowered me, made me dizzy. I fell back against my pillow.

"No," I think I murmured. The sound of birds' wings beat in my ears. "No. Please. Wait. Come back."

The last thing I saw as the world darkened was the wild image of a bearded man whispering a sentence in a foreign tongue. In vain my mind grasped at his words. Then I plunged into a restless sleep, unsure if I had ever been awake or not.

By the next morning my memory of the night had faded, as dreams do. I spent most of the day napping in my Uncle Diego's bookmaking workshop, slumped over the manuscript I was supposed to be ruling for him. Dream or not, my experience with the yellow-eyed demon had exhausted me. Even if it hadn't, the workshop's stagnant air—hot from summer and vinegary from curing—could fatigue even the world's most energetic apprentice.

Of course, I had never been the world's most energetic apprentice.

"Bali."

Still dull with sleep, I mumbled some insult and covered my head with my arms.

"Bali. Baltasar. Your ink."

I opened my eyes just in time to see my inkwell sliding off

the edge of my slanted desk. In a moment of insanity I threw myself sideways to catch it. Mistake. The sound of my stool's legs scraping against ceramic tiles was the last thing I heard before I, my inkwell, and all my papers went crashing down onto the tiled workshop floor.

My uncle Diego appeared above me, his smiling face outlined by the brown boughs that supported the roof above him. Though his white head was balding and his green eyes hidden by wrinkles and spectacles, he always gave the impression of an overgrown child.

"This is good, Nephew!" My uncle put his hand on my head, supporting most of his arthritic weight on my skull. "If you don't make it as a bookmaker, you can always become an acrobat."

Underneath him I rubbed my bashed elbow with the bony base of my hand. "Make sure it doesn't stain the grout," my uncle said. He took a damp cloth from his desk and dropped it onto my face.

Frowning, I peeled the rag off my face so I could see how much grout there was for me to clean. It wasn't pretty. The workshop's tiles, once white and hand-painted with blue and red floral patterns, were now covered with splotches of sooty ink. Worse yet, the papers I had spent the last week painstakingly ruling by hand now lay crumpled and ink-spattered under my stool.

"What a mess," my uncle agreed as I bent over to start

cleaning. "You're worse than Titivillus. You know that, Bali?"

"Titivillus?" I said with a false innocence. In reality, my uncle had told me that story maybe a thousand times—maybe a thousand times that week.

"Titivillus is an imp, Bali. A demon who would sneak into scribes' workshops and ruin their work when they weren't looking. And whenever a monk wrote the wrong word in a manuscript, he'd know that Titivillus was to blame!" My uncle put his hand around his chin. "But I may have told you this story before."

"Maybe." I smiled. "Once or twice."

Chuckling, the old man picked up a quill and returned to his slanted desk, where a long piece of parchment waited for him. Hundreds of ornate black letters shimmered, wet, across the page, and a gold-leafed letter T gilded the upper left corner. A wooden contraption used to stretch leather book covers hid most of the table next to him, along with various awls, brushes, and lacquered boxes. This was the future Diego was preparing me for—the aproned future of the bookbinder and scribe. It wasn't the most exciting future, to be sure, and it all but guaranteed that my old age would be as hunched and nearsighted as my uncle's. But I supposed crooked hands and boredom were a small price to pay for not having to toil in the fields or on a fishing ship slaving in the river that connected Palos to the sea.

When I was done cleaning up the mess I had made, I said,

"Tell me this, then. If the demon Titivillus made me spill my ink, why didn't *he* have to clean it up?"

My uncle didn't even glance up from his work. His face was so close to the page he was inking that I could see a white whisker from his nose scraping against the parchment. "That is a good question, Bali. It must be one of the advantages of being a demon."

I smirked at him. "You ought to tell the demon I saw last night. It'll be glad to hear it."

"I hope you're not talking about your aunt Serena, Nephew."

"No! It was a hameh, actually. You know: scary yellow eyes, 'a scream that can drive a man to madness'—"

My head snapped up at the sound of a sudden, splintery *crack*. My uncle had driven his quill right through the page he was working on; part of the tip had snapped off near the end.

The man squeezed the pen harder into his fist, then realized what he was doing and placed it on the table with both hands. "'Hameh'?" he said in a carefully measured tone. "Where did you ever pick up that word?"

I scratched a spot of ink off my face. "You told me, Uncle. Remember?"

The old man's hands relaxed noticeably around his quill. "Yes. Yes, of course. So what did this hameh of yours do?"

"Not much." I got up from my place on the floor and walked to the window to wring out my now-filthy rag. "It was probably just a dream. Except . . . " I crumpled the rag into a ball and patted my other hand against it. "Except I could smell spices. Cinnamon, maybe. And I thought I saw someone." I replaced the damp rag on my uncle's desk. "Never mind. Forget it."

My uncle, however, was clearly not going to forget it. In a twitchy, arrhythmic manner, he tapped his broken quill against the side of his desk. Finally he said, "Go inside the house, Baltasar. I think we're done for today."

Done? It took my mind a moment to recognize the word. "Done? You mean with work?"

"Yes. That is exactly what I mean."

My uncle vaulted off his stool like a much younger man, and before I could figure out how to respond, he was pushing me out the workshop door. Now I was outside, overwhelmed by sunlight, and slouching on the clay steps that led down into our garden. A pure blue sky filled most of my sight. My uncle's gaze arced over it, as if searching for a hameh.

"Go in the house, Baltasar. And don't leave until I tell you to. And don't speak a word of this to your aunt. Promise me you won't speak of this to her."

There is magic in this story, I thought I heard him say from somewhere in my memory. "Now you're asking me to lie to a family member?"

With a hurried sarcasm he answered, "Yes, I know it will be difficult for you. Now please, Bali. Promise. Promise me you won't tell her."

"All right, I promise. But—"

"Then have a good afternoon, Bali."

And the door clicked shut in front of me.

I couldn't believe it. Go on, leave your work early? Stay inside the house, and don't tell your Aunt Serena?

But what did he . . . ? Why did he . . . ?

I made a move to reenter the workshop, but as I did I felt something crack beneath my foot. And when I lifted my shoe, I saw that I had stepped on a single black feather, bent in the middle where my foot had snapped it. Its black quills splayed in every direction, caked with some grimy substance I couldn't name. I knelt and lifted the thing to the sky. White sunlight haloed each fraying quill, and black ooze—maybe ink, maybe tar—sweated from the feather's surface and out the bottom of its tip.

I rubbed the ink off my fingers, feeling it damp and sticky on my skin. Oh, something strange was going on, all right. Something that linked hamehs and Amir al-Katib and cinnamon that tasted tangy on the back of your tongue when you smelled it.

But what?

CAPTURED

Not knowing what to do about my uncle, I stuffed the feather into the leather pouch hanging from my belt and hopped down the crumbling clay stairs that led into our garden. My aunt Serena knelt there under the blazing summer sun, knee-deep in a bed of parsley and fennel. Her long, graying hair was a nest of sweat and tangles. Rivers of soily sweat snaked down her burly, sunburned arms. Beyond her, a dirt road meandered up a scrub-covered hill, winding its way past more off-white terracotta-roofed houses. Eventually that dirt road would lead into town, around the public fountain where we collected our water every morning, past the town church where I'd be confirmed later this year, and all the way to the alley where my friends loitered each midday break with cheap wine, dirty jokes, and a well-used deck of cards.

The few coins in my pouch called out to them, chattering each time I took a step. *Ignore your uncle, Baltasar,* the coins seemed to say. *Why care about dreams and feathers when there are more important matters to attend to? Like Tristán's compulsion to bet on the worst hands possible and Ruy's inability to bluff!*

My coins were right. I wasn't going to waste such a nice day fretting over my uncle's lunacy—or imaginary demon-birds, come to think of it. At least, not when there was a card game waiting for me.

So carefully, quietly, I tiptoed around my aunt. "Wherever you're going," Serena said as I passed her, "could you at least *try* to be home before dinner?"

"Absolutely!" I said, flashing her my most dashing grin. We both knew I would never keep that promise. I didn't see a reason to tell her I'd been ordered to stay inside the house. After all, Diego *had* told me to keep quiet.

After giving her a final wave, I headed into downtown Palos, that maze of craggy buildings and narrow cobblestone streets made narrower by the legions of housewives who shuffled through them. Before long I was in the marketplace, surrounded by the stench of fish and red-capped merchants who hollered sales at me from all sides. Tired of the crowds, I darted down a side street. Within minutes I was running through the port. The sun beat harder on me out here where there was no shade from crowded houses to protect me, but my dusky skin had always shrugged off the harmful effects of the sun. According to my uncle, I'd inherited my dark skin from his side, from my long-deceased Mediterranean-Jewish father. It was about the only thing I had left of my Jewish heritage; my family had converted and had me baptized shortly after I was born.

I ran through the port, breathing in the summer air deeply. Ah, the smell of seaweed and ale—the smell of home. With a row of flophouses on one side and a gleaming river on the other, what more could a young man ask for? Other than a card game with friends, of course. And today I wasn't going to be late.

Well, maybe a little late. I just had to get a better look at the three unfamiliar ships moored near the docks. Three masts stood at attention atop each of them, but with their sails so tightly furled the ships looked fairly plain. They didn't seem to be new ships either. With so many scratches and barnacles marring their hulls, they appeared as worn as the sailors milling about them.

"Beauties, ain't they? I'll be on the Dirty Mary myself."

I spun around, startled. To my side stood a thickset, grizzled man who seemed to have more scraggly hair on his face than on his head. The man's eyes were a happy, milky blue, and they stuck out slightly from his red, puffy face. His accent sounded Northern to my untrained ears, but it was a common, pleasant Northern, not the lofty staccato I'd heard spoken by bejeweled merchants who occasionally passed through town. No, this man was one of the regular folk for sure. He wore the short slops of a sailor and drummed a wooden hammer against his thigh. A ship's carpenter, I gathered—and a drunkard, if his breath and complexion were any indication.

"An absolute beauty!" the carpenter went on. "Bet a young buck like you would love to be on top of a woman like that!" With a thick, well-callused finger the carpenter pointed at the largest of the three vessels, the one that was moored closest to us. "But Dirty Mary's only what we call her, see. Her real name, my boy, is *Santa María*."

Santa María. Unlike her namesake she was a sturdy old thing and definitely no virgin to the high seas. Clearly her worn, round belly had been filled many times before—with barrels of spices, Valencian silks, or even African slaves.

"Looks like a trading boat," I pointed out, and the carpenter clapped me on the back so hard most of the air whizzed right out of me.

"Well done, boy! That she is! A trading boat called a carrack. Sailing on her, we'll be rich in no time. You know, you should join us! With a mind like that you'd make one hell of a cabin boy."

I coughed away a laugh. Me? A sailor on a trading vessel? Oh, Aunt Serena would love that idea.

Nevertheless I laced my fingers together and stretched out my arms. "I might be up for it. Where are you going?"

The man's milky eyes nearly bulged out of his head. "Haven't you heard? To the Indies, of course! To an entirely new world of profit. We'll meet the Grand Khan, load *María* here up with spices, perfumes. And gold—gold, of course! With Admiral Colón at the helm we'll make a bundle in no time! And history, too." The carpenter moved in close to my face so I could better smell the booze on his breath. "You see, this time we're going west. Around one side of the world to the other." Tracing his finger around the circumference of his hammer, the man illustrated the concept.

I raised my eyebrows. By this time in my life, I knew the world was round; it was common knowledge in Palos, where that information had practical applications for our sailors.

But a trip from one side of the globe to the other?

"Isn't that . . . I don't know. Dangerous?" I ventured.

"Well, of course it's dangerous! What would an adventure be without danger? And isn't that what a boy your age wants most of all? Adventure?"

I glanced past the carpenter in the direction that would lead to my friends. I supposed adventure sounded fine and all, but right now I had a card game to get to.

"So what do you say? Interested in being the admiral's new cabin boy?"

I gingerly extracted myself from the carpenter's grip. "I say I'll think about it."

"Sure! You think about it. The name's de Cuellar—Antonio de Cuellar. When you're ready, come look for me at the Dark Sea Inn. You will consider it, won't you?"

"Absolutely!" I lied. Tossing a final glance at the disappointed de Cuellar, I hurried on my way.

Pushing away any thoughts of hamehs or my uncle or mad voyages around the world, I swerved around the corner past the house that once belonged to Amir al-Katib. For as long as I could remember, this house had been abandoned. Tattered shutters hung limply from the windows. Some tiles from the roof had long ago fallen and shattered. Time had muted the brick-red doors into a threadbare, muddy pink, and the iron bolts that striped that entrance were now crudded over with rust.

I thumbed an itch off my nose and slowed my pace as I passed the building. When I was a boy I'd often played in this house, pretending to be Amir al-Katib, the Moorish hero of Spain. One time my friends Ruy and Tristán found me inside, waving an invisible cutlass at the rats that had taken up residence within. My friends laughed and told me I couldn't play al-Katib—that Moors were always villains and tyrants and sneaks. I calmly countered that al-Katib was different. Despite his Moorish name he was a Spaniard—a hero through and through. The legends even called him the Eagle of Castile for the services he had rendered the crown.

So you can imagine how I felt when I learned that al-Katib had betrayed us, had run off to fight for the Moors in Granada. I was twelve, rambling around town with Tristán and Ruy, when we saw eight-year-old Luis de Torres and his mother sobbing in each other's arms.

"What happened?" I said.

"His brothers died," was Tristán's answer.

"What? All four of them? How?"

"In Granada. The Eagle of Castile cut them down in one big swoop. You know, your old hero. Amir al-Katib."

And my cheeks flushed so hot I thought they'd melt off right there. "No, he couldn't have. He wouldn't. If he did it would make him—"

"A traitor."

"Yes. It would make him a traitor." Amir al-Katib, my childhood hero. My friends had been right about him all along.

Fortunately this January, news arrived that the kingdom of Granada was ours, and Amir al-Katib had died in battle. The citizens of Palos rejoiced that day, and my aunt and uncle grieved for their lost friend. But all I felt was relief. Now the abandoned house I was standing next to was my only reminder of my childish stupidity.

"Stop it, you thief! Gonzalo, give it back!"

The sound tugged me out of my memory, and quickly I peeked around the corner. Down the street Luis, Ruy, and Tristán were sitting on rotting barrels in our hideout, an alley full of empty wine jugs and vomit. They were currently being terrorized by five of our local bullies, Gonzalo Brasa and his four sadistic friends.

"It's not fair!" the same young voice cried. It was Luis de Torres, now ten years old. For the past two years I had invited him to our daily card games as a penance for once idolizing his brothers' killer.

"Please, Gonzalo!" Luis de Torres begged. "My mother gave me that money. Now give it back or I'll—"

"Or you'll what?" a bored voice drawled. "Or you'll run home? Call your brothers to save you?"

Expectant hoots rang out behind Gonzalo. No doubt about it; he and his friends were itching for a fight.

"You just wait," Luis sniffled at his lap. "You just wait till Baltasar gets here."

Oh, no. I slouched back against the nearest wall. I didn't mind inviting Luis to our midday card games, but I *did* mind that he had started to look to me for protection after his brothers' deaths. How in the world did he expect *me* to deal with Gonzalo? Didn't he realize I had trouble just lifting the heavier books in my uncle's workshop? I had a hard enough time avoiding Gonzalo's attention. His favorite pastime was harassing *conversos* like me for sport.

"Infante?" I heard Gonzalo laugh. "That scrawny Jew couldn't beat up a cat. Talk about Baltasar Infante like he's some hero. He's probably never even kissed a girl."

Exactly. Leave it to Gonzalo Brasa to get to the heart of the matter. Now he would flex his muscles, and Luis would cave like he always did. Then Gonzalo would return home, victorious, and I could finally walk around the corner without getting involved in this nonsense.

But today luck was not with me. Because today Luis—Luis, Luis, that baby-faced half-wit Luis!—finally discovered his courage. "That's not true!" the little boy cried. "Baltasar has *so* kissed a girl! I saw him kissing Elena Hernández in the market yesterday!"

Uh-oh. I quickly swiveled on one foot, ready to quickstep it back home.

Or at least that's what I tried to do. What actually happened was that I slipped over a cobblestone and fell chin-first into a muddy puddle. A cry of pain fell from my mouth before I could catch it, and within moments, finely-made shoes surrounded me on all sides. A sizable hand dragged me to my feet, and I found myself facing a giant with a broad snout and bull-necked snarl.

"Ah, afternoon, Gonzalo!" I exclaimed. "Thanks for helping me out of that puddle—"

Gonzalo pinned me hard against the outer wall of Amir al-Katib's house. Gonzalo Brasa was the son of a powerful local merchant, and he spent most of his free hours lording his power over the rest of us. Despite his fine clothing, he looked more like a farmer's son than a trader's, with his rocklike muscles bursting through the sleeves of his doublet. With little effort he held me against the wall, pressing only one forearm up against my throat.

"What were you doing with my girl, Marrano?"

You can see the level of Gonzalo's delusion here. Thought he owned everything, everyone. *His* girl! Since when was Elena Hernández *his* girl? The last time Gonzalo had tried to make a move on her, Elena had actually kicked him in the shins.

His girl! If Elena Hernández was *his* girl, then I was the queen of France!

Pointing this out, however, would surely lead to my murder, so I simply raised my hands as much as I could, considering I was trapped against a wall.

"'Marrano'?" I said as innocently as I could manage. "Oh, 'Jewish pig,' right? Because my parents were Jewish! I get it."

Gonzalo slammed me harder into the wall. "Answer the question, Marrano! What were you doing with my girl?"

"What girl, Gonzalo? Dirty Mary, that flower girl near the docks? Dark hair, big lips, hips like the bow of a carrack? That's why the sailors love her, you know. She reminds them of the sea!"

But Gonzalo didn't appreciate my stories. My words met a punch in the jaw. A slab of hurt smashed against my cheek and temple and dropped me down into the mud.

"You son of a whore!" Gonzalo blustered. "You want a story? Well, here's a story for you: You knew Elena Hernández was my girl, and you went after her anyway! You're a goddamned traitor!" Gonzalo tromped up to me and sent a swift kick into my gut.

"Gonzalo, listen," I croaked out.

Gonzalo didn't listen. He seemed to have a thought, and he laughed to himself above me. "But what did I expect? Treachery's in your blood." Gonzalo grabbed a handful of Luis's coins from a pouch on his belt, and shook them slightly in his hand. He pressed the coins into his fist for a moment before chucking the lot at my face. "Well? Go ahead, Christ-killer! Jew banker. Go on and buy something for my woman, pig— or do you want to keep the coins for yourself?"

It's funny how words can sting worse than coins thrown with full force at your face. And it's funny how a punch in the jaw wasn't enough to rile me, but being called a banker was. My breaths became quick and labored, and I felt heat rising on my cheeks where the coins had hit them.

"Oh, he's angry now!" Gonzalo mocked me. "What, piggy doesn't like that name? Is 'pig' not kosher enough for you, Jew boy?"

Sitting up in the mud, I drew in a painful, livid breath and bent my fingers into a shaking fist.

"Oh, the scrawny piggy wants to fight me! Aw, what are you doing, piggy?"

"Don't listen to him!" Luis de Torres blurted out.

Ruy and Tristán joined him. "Come on, Infante!" "Punch him in the face!"

Yes. Yes, I would fight! I clenched my teeth, full of resolve.

But as I did, the tip of my tongue caught on the gap where one of my canines used to be. It was cold reminder of my fighting abilities: The last time I'd gotten into a scrape with Gonzalo, he'd smashed that tooth right out of my face. The merchant's son had eighty pounds on me, easy. If he wanted, he could rip off my arms without a second thought.

Gonzalo laughed. "Right, like you're going to fight me. Come on. Everyone knows that you're a coward."

"Coward, coward," one of Gonzalo's noble buddies cried, and the others added their voices to the choir. Behind them, my friends seemed to have shrunk. I slumped down in my puddle, feeling the word weighing down on my shoulders.

Coward. Coward.

Worst of all, I knew it was true.

I let my fist fall pitifully beside me. And I knew exactly what I had to do. I would hate myself for it later—I knew that, too—but it seemed I had no other choice. If I tried to fight, they'd probably take their anger out not only on me, but on my friends, too. We were outnumbered, and Luis was only ten.

So I did the only thing I could do. I said, "You're right, Gonzalo."

Whatever reaction Gonzalo had been expecting from me, it clearly wasn't this one. "What did you say?" he said, inching closer to me.

I reached back for the closest wall and rose painfully from my spot in the puddle. "I said you're right, Gonzalo. I *am* a coward. I'm nothing more than a Foolish Cohen."

My words had the effect I'd desired. Gonzalo loosened his fist and scrunched up his eyes. Around us the chants of "coward" fizzled to nothing. I wiped the dirt from my chin with my sleeve and forced a swollen, wretched smile.

"Don't tell me you've never heard the story of Foolish Cohen," I willed myself to say. "It's about Cohen, a Jew, so of course he wants some money. So Cohen sneaks over to his neighbor's yard and steals a goat so he can sell some milk. Later that day, *Bang! Bang!* The neighbor's banging like crazy on Foolish Cohen's door. The neighbor screams, 'Where's my goat, Cohen? Where's my goat?' Cohen says, 'Goat? What goat? I haven't seen any goat.' The neighbor screams, 'You know damn well, you dirty Jew! Now bring her out here before I shove my fist down your throat! And trust me, my fist ain't kosher!'"

Gonzalo and his gang shared a few snickers. I forced myself down on all-fours in the mud.

"Just then the goat pops his head out Cohen's window, braying, '*MAAA! MAAA!*'" I shot to my feet. "The neighbor takes Cohen by the collar, screaming, 'I knew it! You treacherous swine! I knew you had her all along!'

"And can you believe it? What does Foolish Cohen do? He says, 'Now who are you going to believe? Me or a goat?'"

I stretched another fake smile across my face as Gonzalo's gang hollered, and I tried to ignore the pain I felt when I saw my own friends hiding their own laughter. But I couldn't blame them for laughing, not really. Everyone always laughed at my stories and howled when I made a fool of myself. That was my role, after all—the Jewish jester.

Gonzalo crossed his bulky arms and shook his head at me.

"All right, Infante. This I want to hear. What does any of this have to do with Elena Hernández?"

I smiled wider, feeling my lips rip at the corners. "You said it yourself, Gonzalo. Me and Foolish Cohen? We've got the same blood. I knew Elena Hernández would never go for someone like that. I only tried to kiss her as a joke."

A joke. Gonzalo's jaw relaxed as the idea took hold of him. "And you should have seen it!" I went on. "I move in real close—romantic, like this. And *bam!* She cracks me right across the face! She screams, 'Ew, get off me, Baltasar! Like I'd want to kiss some big-nose like you!' Luis was there. Tell him, Luis."

Luis avoided my gaze but got the idea. "That's what happened, Gonzalo. It was . . . it was pretty funny."

Gonzalo's crew muttered to one another, not sure what to believe. I put a muddy arm around their leader. "Come on, Gonzalo! You know I'd never *really* go after your girl. I swear on the name of my foolish Jewish God."

Gonzalo considered me, the muddy Marrano standing next to him, as the facts of my case clicked together in his head. Finally a wry grin formed between his jowls, and he choked me in the crook of his elbow.

"I should have known." I flinched as Gonzalo gave me a playful punch in the stomach. "You dumb bastard! Did you actually think she'd kiss you back? I mean, if the stories didn't scare her off, your ugly mug would!"

"Exactly," I said. I put my hand out in a symbol of truce and waited. "Friends?"

Gonzalo took my hand, and I knew I was forgiven. Behind him, Luis gathered up the coins Gonzalo had thrown at me—the coins Gonzalo had stolen from him earlier. And Gonzalo said to me, "You're mad, you know that, Marrano?"

I just nodded and smiled like a fool.

When I entered my house, I marched straight into my room and slammed the door behind me. The scent of my aunt's eggplant and onion stew followed me inside. As nice as it smelled, I couldn't deal with her kitchen lectures now. Thinking of the fuss she'd make when she saw my bruised face, I buried it into my pillow and hoped sleep would take me soon.

No such luck. The sound of a door opening and closing told me my uncle had entered the kitchen. "Was that Baltasar?" I heard him say with some urgency.

"Hmph," was Aunt Serena's answer. "Sounded more like the Behemoth with all that stomping."

"But he's home," Diego said, relieved. Then, "Stomping? What happened? Is something wrong?"

"Why don't you go ask him?"

Bracing myself for my uncle's inevitable entrance, I tossed myself onto my side and crossed my arms at the open window. Even someone as old and scatterbrained as Diego could understand that signal.

Or maybe not. Before long I heard the door to my room open. Soon a muffled creak told me that my uncle had settled on the stool next to my bed, the one he used to sit on to tell me stories.

"Bali, I told you not to leave the house." I winced as he pressed a finger against my bruised face. "Another fight with Gonzalo, I see. What did he say about your parents this time?"

"Nothing."

"I know it's hard, Bali, but you mustn't be ashamed of them! Your parents were heroes! They died for what they believed in."

Frowning out the window, I toyed idly with the cross hanging from my neck. My parents. Not long after I was born they'd converted and changed their name from Mizrahi to Infante, hoping to protect me from Palos's anti-Jewish mobs. Then King Fernando and Queen Isabel introduced a new inquisition meant to free their kingdoms of false Christian converts. My aunt and uncle thankfully escaped trial and execution, but my parents were not so lucky. The Inquisition tried them and put them to death after they refused to publicly renounce their Jewish beliefs.

According to Diego that refusal made them heroes. Heroes. The word always put me in a silent fury. If my parents were heroes, they would have forsworn their faith, gone to church on Sundays like they were supposed to! Heroes didn't leave their children orphans. Heroes didn't die.

Diego and I were quiet for some time, and eventually I thought he might leave without saying anything more. But then he raised a bent finger and said the words I'd been dreading most: "You know, Bali, I know exactly what you need. A golem."

I moaned, knowing it was no use. Once my uncle started a story, it was unstoppable, like a volcano or a flood.

"'What is a golem?' you might ask. One of my favorite stories. It's a wonder I didn't tell you about him sooner. The golem is a giant beast made out of clay. But the best part of the golem—to an old bookmaker, anyway—is that he comes to life through the power of the written word. Must have been an invention of bookmakers. They're creative fellows, you know. Philosopher kings, if they wanted the power—"

"But moving on," I grumbled.

"Now, to give a golem life, you write the word truth, which is *ameth*, like this." With a finger, my uncle traced out some invisible runes on my quilt. "You write it on a tablet and put it into the creature's mouth. And to stop the golem, simple enough. You erase the first letter." My uncle covered the first invisible symbol with a veiny hand. "Now it says *meth*, which means death, and voilà—the golem stops."

"Please, Uncle. No more stories."

"But I haven't even gotten to the point of it yet. You see, Bali, the golem is a protector. Brute strength, pure loyalty. In fact, he is the Jewish people's greatest protector—"

My uncle couldn't have known that was the exact wrong thing to say, but he must have realized when I jumped up so our noses nearly touched. "I said *enough,* Uncle! You don't know when to stop! I've had enough of you, enough of your Jews, and enough of your boring old stories! They aren't real! They are a complete waste of time!"

"Bali."

No. I didn't want to hear it. I pushed my uncle away and stormed out of my room, past my aunt, and out the door.

"Baltasar, come back!" my uncle yelled after me, and I heard his footsteps as he tried to follow me outside. But I was too fast for him. I ran up the hill that led into the lonely streets of Palos.

I spent the rest of the afternoon storming through town, trying to force Gonzalo's insults and my own shameful story out of my head. *Coward. Traitor. Christ-killer. Foolish Cohen.* No matter how much I walked I couldn't escape those words.

Eventually I returned to my friends' hangout by Amir al-Katib's house. Except for a few dragonflies, it was empty. A ceramic bottle lay on a barrel, dripping a small puddle of wine. Not enough, though. Not if I wanted to forget.

The sun was starting to set now; the candle in the iron lamp on the wall beside me had already been lit. Fog was filtering up from the cobblestones, covering them with an eerie golden mist. I paced back and forth through it, feeling my insides burn.

Damn Diego, damn Gonzalo, damn my parents, damn the Jews! And damn myself most of all. I sat on the nearest barrel and and banged a fist lightly against my knee. A crumpled piece of paper stuck with mud to the sole of my shoe. It was a copy of the Alhambra Decree, signed by the king and queen in March of this year. "Knowing they are trying to subvert our Catholic faith," one of its paragraphs began, "it is resolved that all Jews and Jewesses leave our kingdoms under penalty of death."

I crushed the page into a ball and chucked it at the nearest wall. Then I bent my head into my hands.

Two shadows, long from dusk, spread over the golden puddles in front of me. "Good evening," said a man's voice, lean, dark, and oddly amused. I removed my hands from my head. Two figures waited in the entrance to the alley, blanketed by the shade of Amir al-Katib's house. A cowl hid the face of the first man. A helmet hid the face of the other. The second man was decked in armor, and he carried a shining spear. Agents of the Inquisition, maybe. I didn't want to wait to find out.

Slowly I rose from my barrel. "We are looking for someone," the cloaked man said. "A Baltasar Infante of Palos."

My fingers twitched at the sound of my own name. "I don't know any Infante. I'm sorry, but I can't help you."

I held back the tremors ready to race across my body so I could push my way past the two men. But the soldier swung his spear in front of me, and I danced back to avoid its shining edge.

"I'm sorry," I repeated somewhat breathlessly. "But I really don't know who you're talking about! Listen, this is all some big misunderstanding!"

"That is correct," the cloaked man replied. "We know you are Baltasar Infante. And you will be coming with us. Now."

My horrified reflection stared back at me, warped in the soldier's tarnished helmet. The cloaked man made a quick motion at the soldier, and I tried to make a run for it. The cloaked man caught me from behind by both arms. With all my strength I stomped on his foot and tried to wrest myself out of his grip. The man cursed but held on. The soldier swung the flat of his spear across the side of my skull. With stars in my eyes, I doubled over. The soldier rammed the dull end of his spear into my back, and I fell into endless darkness.

INQUISITION

My body was pitched forward. I tasted some animal's mane. Rain pattered against my back, reins rattled, and hooves clopped in my ears. Although it took my bashed brain some time to fit the pieces together, soon enough I understood.

The men had put me on a horse.

The top half of my body was slumped forward in a twisted position that squished my face up against the horse's head. When I tried to move my arms, I found they'd been tied behind my back with a thick and splintery rope. "No need to struggle," the cloaked man said behind me. He snapped our horse's reins above my shoulders. "You're not going anywhere, so you may as well enjoy the ride."

I was in no state to argue, so I lifted my aching head off the horse's and squinted through the downpour. Already the landscape around us had changed. The sunny skylines of Palos and nearby Huelva had given way to barren, storm-swept marshes covered in unending night. Rain whipped down on us, strict and blinding, but I could distinguish the outlines of pines twisting toward the sky on either side of us. Every so often our horses would slosh through shallow black water, and tall, creeping reeds would brush against their haunches. In daytime, maybe, this land would be beautiful. But now, in darkness and rain, it was a world of nightmare.

At last the cloaked man pulled our horse to a whinnying stop, and the soldier slowed his own horse beside us. In the distance we could see a jagged, moss-covered building that appeared to have grown out of the black hill in front of us.

"Strange place to have an interrogation," the cloaked man behind me said. "What is it? Some kind of old monastery?" When the soldier didn't answer, the cloaked man snorted. "And here I'd thought the Inquisition was flush with coin. Didn't they just build a fancy new courthouse up in Cuenca?"

The soldier answered gruffly in his helmet. "The Inquisition and Malleus Maleficarum are no long affiliated. And if you want to keep working for us, you'll keep your questions to yourself."

Rain plinked against the soldier's helmet as he dismounted his horse. He trudged up to us through the mud, pulled me off my horse by my tunic, and hurled me to the ground. I had only a moment to shiver in the dirt before he lugged me to my feet. Then he shoved me into the wooden mouth of the monastery door and down a spiral staircase.

Down and down we went. We descended into gloom and

finally blindness. From out of nowhere, it seemed, the cloaked man lit a torch, a burning parody of the fire back home in Aunt Serena's kitchen. The thought of it put a half-smile on my face, but the smile trembled under its own weight and shattered.

I was going to die here.

A dim orange light throbbed below us now, leading us to our destination. The narrow throat we had been traveling through gave way to the expansive bowels of the monastery's underworld. To my relief the torches on this basement's damp walls revealed no shackles, no metal spikes, no open-mouthed skeletons. Only huge stone blocks cowering in neat rows over the floor, each roughly the size of my bed back home. Nothing more in this cellar but a single chair and its shadow, which shifted spectrally under the torchlight.

There was a priest, too—or at least, a balding man in the garments of priest. Above his long robe and short cape was a plain, pudgy face that might have been pleasant if it didn't try to smile. But it did, and the sight of the man's lizard teeth churned acid through my gut.

The soldier removed the rope from my worn wrists, shoved me into the room's only seat, and tied my arms firmly to the chair. "There is no need for roughness," the man dressed as a priest said. His accent sounded German—quiet, high-pitched, and lyrical. "Allow me to apologize, Baltasar. Normally we wouldn't have arrested you this way or brought you to such a distasteful place as this one. But due to the lack of insight of the current Inquistional administration, we are nowadays forced to do our work, shall we say, underground."

The frigid air of the basement clutched at my lungs, and my head was still ringing with pain. Through the agony and the wheezes I was somehow able to mutter, "Who are you? Why did you bring me here?"

The priest rifled through a pile of papers sitting on the massive stone block behind him. "There is no need to worry, Baltasar. This is not a trial. You are not under arrest, officially. I will simply be asking you some questions, that is all. Now where is that—ah, yes."

The priest reached a ringed hand into his robes and removed a roll of parchment sealed shut with red wax. An image of a hammer was imprinted on that seal—printed on the diagonal, as if ready to strike. As the priest opened the scroll I noticed the golden signet ring he wore bore the same symbol. He plucked a quill from the block of granite behind him and dipped it into the inkwell next to his papers.

"But first we must handle some paperwork," the priest said. "So if you don't mind, please state your full name for the record."

He had to be joking. "But you already know my na—"

The priest cut me short by taking my swollen jaw in one hand and crushing it in his fingers. The pressure of his grasp sent pain stabbing through the insides of my teeth.

The priest knelt in front of me and shook my head lovingly.

"Oh, Baltasar, Baltasar! There is no time for arguments! Do you realize that at this very moment your country is in grave danger, and that you, my dear boy, are the only one with the information to save it? And I'm sure you're in a hurry, too, to leave this place. So please. State your full name."

He let go of my face, and I cracked the pain out of my jaw. "Baltasar Infante. Are you happy now?"

The priest must have been; his quill frolicked across his paper as he scribbled down my response. "Very good, Baltasar! I thank you. And what are the full names of your parents?"

It was the wrong question to ask me—definitely the wrong one. "Parents!" I hissed. "You know who my parents were! My parents were Abram and Marina Infante, converted Jews from Palos. And the Inquisition killed them! *You* killed them!"

Fourteen years ago a man like this had captured them, stolen them away from me. I glared up at the priest with a sharp desire to murder him, too, to crack open his stupid face and watch the blood spill from his blubber.

Unfazed, the priest scratched some more words into his parchment. "As I said before, Baltasar, we are not part of the Inquisition. But I thank you for answering my question. And would you please tell me the names of your guardians? Your closest relatives?"

As quickly as my hatred took me it set me loose. Uncle Diego. Aunt Serena. Had they been captured too? Were they trapped in their own dank cellars, being tortured by their own awful priests? I had to escape, somehow, find them, save them! We could flee to Portugal, maybe. Genoa! Or to Constantinople, where my father and uncle had lived in their youths.

The priest prodded my chair with a velvet shoe. "Baltasar. I am becoming impatient. I thought we agreed it was in your best interest to answer my questions as quickly as possible."

But I couldn't answer them—I wouldn't!—and the man's mouth wrinkled sternly at my silence. "Very well. I wish it hadn't had to come to this, Baltasar. But time is running out, and if you will not help us . . ."

The priest raised his roll of parchment up near his face so the cloaked man and the soldier could see it more clearly. "I do not wish to use torture, Baltasar, but all I need to do is sign this warrant before two witnesses to use it. Do you know that upstairs we have a device made of ropes and pulleys that allows us to hang you by your arms and rip your bones from their sockets?" The priest picked up two wooden blocks from the stone behind him and shook them before my eyes. "And did you know that we can place your feet within this contraption and smash nails through each of your toes?"

My own toes cringed inside my shoes, but I thought of my aunt and uncle and said nothing.

"And if that method fails, we will move on to the heretic's fork." The priest replaced the pieces of wood on the stone behind him and picked up a long metal object with a two-pronged fork at either end of it. It clanged as its tip bounced off the edge of the stone, and it burned red and gold under the torchlight. With one end of the metal tool he poked me lightly above my collarbone, pricking my skin with dots of cold. "We will bend your head back and stick the bottom prong through your flesh, here." The priest then flicked up the heretic's fork so it chilled the underside of my chin. "The other end we will thrust through here, taking care to avoid splitting the tongue."

By now my breathing had become fast and shallow. I could feel my stomach seizing at the thought. "Would you like to hear more, Baltasar?" the priest said. "We also have a rack in the other room. I'm sure you would like to hear about how that device works. We'll attach you to the wood, and then we'll crank it, little by little. First you'll hear your bones start to pop, but that's not all. We'll crank it a little more until you—"

"Stop," I breathed against my will. "Please. Stop." I shut my eyes. My shoulders were sharply convulsing. I had heard rumors of the Inquisition's foul methods, but never this. Never this.

The priest dug his own nails into the backs of my hands. "I will stop if you answer my questions, Baltasar! Your closest relatives. Tell me their names!"

I tried not to respond. I did my best, I swear. But when I saw the light sparking off the heretic's fork in his hand, the words ran out of my mouth of their own accord: "Diego and Serena Infante. Please! Their names are Diego and Serena Infante!"

I had never before, and have never since, felt the amount of guilt that I felt at that moment. I thought I could feel my aunt and uncle's souls pulling me down to Hell, and the feeling was so horrific I almost begged the priest's forgiveness.

But for his part, his expression was blank. "Very good, Baltasar. I thank you for telling the, ah, truth. For I am certain you answered those questions with perfect honesty." He leaned back against the giant stone block behind him and reexamined his parchment. "Unfortunately my records indicate that some of your answers are less than accurate. It appears our organization knows more about you than you know about yourself. I will go through the questions one by one. You will see what I mean."

The priest trod softly around the room as he read from his paper. "Question one," he read. "'What is the accused's full name?' Your answer was 'Baltasar Infante.' That answer is correct—for all intents and purposes.

"Ah, but question two! 'What are the names of the accused's parents?' You said, 'Abram and Marina Infante, killed in the Inquisition.'" The priest tut-tutted. "I'm afraid that answer is incorrect."

The priest's lips rolled into a frown—one that looked strangely like a smile. "And finally, question three. 'What are the names of the accused's closest relatives?' You answered, 'Diego and Serena Infante.'" The priest knelt in front of me, his lizard teeth gleaming like daggers.

"I'm sorry to tell you this, Baltasar, but that answer is also incorrect."

It took me a moment to understand what the man thought he was saying. Was he saying the Inquisition *hadn't* killed my parents? That they were alive somewhere, and my aunt and uncle were fakes? It was impossible, part of the torture. The priest was lying—he had to be—trying to disorient me and loosen my tongue.

"So quiet, Baltasar," my interrogator said. "Funny. Your priest—Father Joaquín, was it?" The priest took hold of the wooden cross I wore and with a swift jerk yanked it off my neck. "He told me you could talk all day. Always had a good story, he said."

"Are we done here?" I said between my teeth.

The priest placed my cross on the block of granite behind him. "Soon enough. But there's one question left for you to answer. The man licked the tip of his quill and held it at the ready over his parchment. "Question four," he started, but I knew this question would not be like the others. Because slowly the priest's plain face was transforming into that of a gargoyle. His beady eyes smoldered with torchlight, filled to the brim with a mix of glee and loathing.

And then, very carefully, he said four words I never thought anyone would ever ask me.

"Where is Amir al-Katib?"

I actually laughed. He had to be kidding. The Amir al-Katib I had heard of was long dead, killed last year by Spanish armies in Granada. And even if the man *were* alive, how would I, of all people, know where he was? The question made

45

no sense. Absolutely no sense at all.

The priest's eyes narrowed in on me. "This is no joke, boy. If you want to see morning, you will tell us where he is. Now."

Good. The man was angry. That meant he was serious now, which meant I had leverage. "All right," I said. "You want to know about Amir al-Katib? Untie these ropes, and I'll tell you everything I know."

The priest instead motioned over his shoulder, beckoning his friend the soldier toward me. As the armored giant advanced in my direction, the edge of his spear caught the light of the torches, sending chills flitting down my arms and legs.

And the words flew out of my mouth before I could even think them: "Wait, I'll tell you! Amir al-Katib. They call him the Eagle of Castile. They say he looks like a rukh. They say he can cut down fifty men in one swoop. And they say that—"

The priest's fingernails cut into my forearms. "Don't you play games with me, boy! That man is an enemy of Spain, a traitor fighting on the side of the Infidel! We know you know where he is! And you will tell us. Now!"

"How should I know where he is? I've never seen him before in my life!"

The priest dug his nails deeper into my skin. "You dare take me for a fool? Never seen him! Al-Katib was outside your house last night!"

And the night tumbled back to me in an instant. The smell of cinnamon and incense. Yellow eyes glowing in the window. Hameh.

46

I searched for a way out, any way. The one entrance was the one exit, and the cloaked man and soldier's spear barred my path. Nothing more around here but those mysterious rectangular stones.

No. Not stones. Coffins.

Coffins. I was sitting in a tomb.

My heart rushing up in my throat, I raged against my bonds.

"Where is Amir al-Katib?" the priest demanded.

"I don't know!"

"Where is Amir al-Katib?"

"I said I don't know! He's dead! He's only a story! He's not real! *Please!"*

By this point I was completely broken, and the priest must have realized it as well. With a wave of one finger he stopped the soldier from his slow path toward me.

"Enough," the priest said to the soldier. "We're done here. The boy is telling us the truth."

I let out a breath that sounded almost like a sob. Finally. Finally, they believed me. Finally, finally, I could go home.

"Give me your torch," the priest directed the cloaked man behind him. "The boy must not leave this place. We will burn him. There must be no evidence we were here."

Burn! I squeezed my eyes shut. Serena. Diego. I had been so unkind to them earlier. Now I would never have a chance to apologize.

Oh, if only I had a golem now! It occurred to me that I really was a child, and that my uncle, eccentric as he was, had always been my protector, my golem. At this moment, the last moment, I yearned to be back home, safe in bed, protected by Diego and his stories. Stories that, like a golem, came to life with a single word.

It's hard for me to explain what happened next. The closest I can get is to say I felt like some deep part of myself, somewhere beyond the backs of my eyes, was reaching toward another. As if the words "Diego," "golem," "protect," and "word" unlocked something within me I didn't understand. In front of my closed eyelids something was glimmering, and my eyes flicked beneath them like I was watching a dream. I felt warmth caressing my cheeks and fingers, warmth like a fire embracing you on a stormy day. And somehow, for an instant, I felt safe.

I opened my eyes.

A series of fiery letters in an unknown language flared before me. Though I had never seen those symbols before, the word *ameth* escaped my lips, and I knew they stood for truth. Several inches tall, the letters browned the atmosphere around them as if the world were nothing more than paper that could burn away to nothing. Around the edges of the symbols rebellious flames fluttered about, moths with fraying wings of charring paper.

The priest's head twitched sideways so he could watch the flames. "It is as we had feared. A lukmani." He choked out the word with palpable disgust. "No matter. Your sorcery won't save you today, boy!" He seized the cloaked man's torch and swung it down to meet me.

But the room lurched, and his hand swept past its target. As the priest hit the ground the torch flew from his grasp and clattered, extinguished, across the floor. The room lurched again. The soldier and cloaked man grasped one of the stone coffins. I clung to the arms of my chair and waited for it all to end.

With a thunderous crash the entrance to the basement exploded. Dust and rubble filled my mouth, my lungs. My vision blurred—I felt weak. Beyond the dust I could make out the outline of a ten-foot-tall earthen beast. Its coal eyes blazed red as it barged through the exploded doorway. With a howl it shoved away the cloaked man and the soldier as if they were nothing more than toys.

The priest's face flashed red as he scrambled to his feet. "Don't think you've won, lukmani!" he screamed. "The Malleus Maleficarum doesn't sleep! We will find you, lukmani! We will find you!"

In answer the rocky monster let loose another primal roar. Lifting both arms above his head it ran at my interrogator. But I didn't get to see any more—the beast's last monstrous step sent another tremor surging through the ground. My chair and I crashed and tumbled past the stone coffins. Then pain smashed into my shoulders, my knees, and my head as they collided with the floor. I lay sideways, trying to hang onto consciousness, but my last bits of energy drained out of me with every breath.

It was then that I realized this might be the last thing I ever thought. But my last thought wasn't about the pain or my family or even Amir al-Katib. No, my last thought was a plain and simple one, full of a plain and simple wonder.

I don't know how I did it, but somehow, I've created a golem.

DIEGO'S STORY

I dreamed the golem heaved me onto his shoulder and bounded from hill to hill over the Spanish countryside. Or maybe that's what really happened—I'm not sure. The next thing I remember was my uncle's voice: "Say you release him, Baltasar. Quickly."

"I release him," I think I mumbled.

When next I awoke it was around dawn, and I was stunned to find myself in my own bed. My uncle was sitting next to me, poring over my bruises with an expression of dire worry etched into his face. "I'm sorry to wake you again, Bali. But they will be here soon. Can you sit?"

This man who looked like my uncle but spoke with such heartache was unknown to me, but I did as he asked. Were those tears in his eyes? No. No, they couldn't be.

"So a golem, Baltasar? And here I thought you'd had enough of my 'boring old stories.'"

Oh, right. That. "Uncle, I am so sorry. I was such an ass. I just—"

My uncle put up a hand. "As much as I appreciate your groveling, there isn't time. And I expect you'll have plenty of questions to ask about this."

To my surprise my uncle raised the priest's parchment, the one with all of those dreadful questions in it. The document crackled as my uncle flattened it against my covers, revealing hundreds of lines of script flowing crisply across its surface.

"Where did you . . . ?"

"The golem brought it along when he dropped you here. Quite a smart one you made there. I'd always thought they were all fools with heads full of clay and dirt, but life would be no fun if nothing could surprise you."

I swear I almost leaped through the ceiling. "You mean you *knew* that golems were real?"

Twining his fingers together my uncle said, "'Real' is a relative term, Baltasar. Quite the tricky word you have there."

I opened my mouth and shut it again. "You're mad."

"That's another relative term, Nephew."

My gaze trailed across the parchment lying in front of me. *Amir al-Katib . . . last known sighting near Alhambra Palace, Granada . . . known accomplices currently operating under the aliases Diego and Serena Infante . . .*

"'Relative'?" I said, breathing heavily. "All right: let's talk about that word, 'relative.' Question three: 'What are the names of your closest relatives?' Sounds like an easy question, doesn't it, Uncle?"

"Baltasar."

"That's what I thought, but it's not so easy, is it, *Uncle*? 'Who are your closest relatives?' I said, 'Diego and Serena Infante.' Or was I wrong about those names?"

"Bali."

"So I have a question of my own, Diego! Question one: *Who the hell are you?!*"

By this point the room was cartwheeling around me, so I sank back, drained, against my pillow. With calm hands Diego brought my quilt over my torso.

"Bali, there's a story about this. And believe me, this is one you're going to want to pay attention to. All right?"

I took a breath and smelled the remains of Serena's stew in the kitchen, the vinegar on Diego's hands. Those were real, still. I was real. So I nodded at my uncle, and he began his story.

"A long time ago—well, not *that* long ago—I lived in Constantinople, in the East. Back then the city was much like Palos once was. It was a Christian city, but many Jewish families lived there too. Even some Muslims lived there—or Moors, as you call them. Not everyone got along all the time, certainly, but it was a good place to grow up, and full of history.

"Then when I was about your age a group of Moors known as the Ottomans laid siege to my homeland. The siege lasted for nearly two months, a terrible time. No food was allowed in from the countryside. Many people died of disease and starvation, including most of my family.

"At the end of May, the Ottomans began their final assault.

53

Our armies were small, and though I was just a boy, I was sent to the front lines. The Pope had sent aid in the form of soldiers from across Europe, but it was not enough to defeat the Ottomans. The city fell to the Moors. I was left without a family, without a home. With nothing."

I considered the story. It was the same one my uncle used to tell me when I was a child. But back then it had been a tale of adventure and excitement, of swashbuckling heroes and daring escapes. "This story was different when you used to tell it," I murmured.

"Yes, I admit I may have . . . embellished things slightly. But one part about those old stories was true. During the war I met a young man not much older than myself, a foreigner who had answered the Vatican's call to protect Constantinople. And although he, like the Ottomans, was born and raised a Muslim, to him the conflict wasn't about religion. It was about what was right and what was wrong."

I remembered the story. "You're talking about Amir al-Katib. He saved your life."

"And gave me a new one. When the war was over, he said, 'You will come with me to Castile, my brother, to my home in Palos de la Frontera.' I didn't have any reason not to, so I did. It didn't take long for me to make a new life here. I began speaking Castilian, and I apprenticed myself with a book-maker. Before long I met your aunt and we married. The two of us were very happy.

"The same couldn't be said for al-Katib. The man was a traveler. The people of Castile sometimes call the Moors the *mudejares*, 'the ones who stayed.' But it was against Amir's nature to stay in one place for long. He would disappear from Palos for years at a time, only to return like a lost dog. Your Aunt Serena had a solution to the problem. 'You need to get married!' she'd say. She'd actually grab the books from his hands and throw them out the window. 'You're not going to find a wife in there!' You know your aunt has never been scared of anyone, warrior or not.

"Just when we were beginning to think it was hopeless, al-Katib met a woman. It was amazing to see this warrior's heart slain by such a creature. They were fiercely in love, but it had to be secret, as were many loves at the time, for she was Christian and he a Moor. They soon had a child, and I have never seen a man—and a warrior, no less—dote so on an infant. But it was a child of his old age, so I supposed I could not fault him.

"Back then many secret marriages were performed, and few were persecuted for such loves. But that was before the Inquisition, and before the Malleus Maleficarum." Uncle Diego took a deep breath and shook his head. "Al-Katib and his wife were among the first to be captured."

There was that term again, that "Malleus Maleficarum." But something about what Diego said bothered me even more. "That doesn't make sense, Uncle. Al-Katib couldn't have been captured. He was seen at Granada last year."

"I said 'captured,' not 'killed,' Baltasar. And he was not killed, though sadly his wife was." Diego paused and said, "Do you remember that story I told you when you were a boy? The one about the hameh and three Arabian brothers? Al-Katib told me that story the day I met him in Constantinople. He said it was a story about men from his family who lived centuries ago, and it was passed down to him through a thousand generations. Al-Katib told me the story was about the evils of revenge, about how hatred can turn you into a monster. But the night the Inquisition killed his wife, he showed up at our door with blood splattered over his clothes and a black bird with yellow eyes sitting on his shoulder. And that night, Amir wore a look so desperate and hateful that I feared he had turned into a hameh himself.

"He said to me, 'I must go, old friend. I don't know when I will return here again.' He thrust something into my arms and said, 'I leave this in your care, my brother.' Before I could ask him what had happened or where he was going, he dashed off like a madman." My uncle's meaningful stare pierced right through me. "Dashed off, leaving a child in my arms."

By that time in my life, I'd heard enough fairy tales to know what a sentence like that meant. Until then, though, I'd never known what it felt like to be part of such a story. The end of my uncle's tale was so obvious, so inevitable, and yet I could hardly believe the words. I said—or maybe I didn't, I don't know— "Amir al-Katib is my *father*?"

My uncle clasped his hands firmly on his lap. "Yes, Baltasar. You are his son."

I couldn't believe it. My gaze scrolled across the priest's parchment once more. *Amir al-Katib . . . last seen in Palos, Spain at the home of Baltasar Infante . . . believed to be his only living relation . . .*

"But you told me my parents were Abram and Marina Infante!"

"Your mother *was* named Marina," Diego explained. "And as for 'Abram,' well, that was my idea of a joke. After Serena and I married, she invited Amir over for Shabbat dinner every Friday night. He joined us so many times that after a while we started to call him 'the honorary Jew.' And your father would laugh and say, 'Yes, call me Abram.'"

As Diego chuckled at the memory, I lowered my head into my hands. "None of this makes any sense, Uncle."

"Why not?"

Why not? I opened my mouth a few times trying to sputter out an answer. Why not? "For one thing, he's a Moor!"

My uncle removed the spectacles from his nose and cleaned the lenses with the bottom of his gown. "Yes. He is a Moor. And so are you. That is something you will have to make peace with for yourself, in time.

"But there is more you do not know. When your father left you that night, he left to wage war on Spain, on all of Christendom. And though I do not agree with his decision, I understand it. Al-Katib had spent his whole life fighting for the safety of Europe, and now Europe was coming after him and his family. They took his wife from him, his dearest love. And I knew they'd be after us next. We would have to hide, all of us.

"Your aunt and I were Jews back then. And we still are, though we'd never say so aloud. Your aunt and I were known as David and Sara Mizrahi once, but to avoid the Inquisition and Malleus Maleficarum, we became Catholics and were baptized under new names. Diego and Serena because they are sturdy Spanish names, and Infante because with new names and new lives we were like infants again."

I said, "You keep bringing up this 'Malleus Maleficarum.'"

"A renegade offshoot of the Inquisition founded in Germany. Both the Inquisition and Malleus Maleficarum were charged with protecting the purity of Christian Europe, but they do so from different angles and with different tools. The Inquisition, as you know, is tasked with rooting out secret practitioners of Judaism and Islam. And as for the Malleus Maleficarum. . . . Well, you know your Latin."

I ran a finger across the crumbling scarlet wax that had once sealed shut the priest's parchment. The wax had been marked with a hammer. "Malleus Maleficarum—the Hammer of Witches," I translated. "So the Malleus Maleficarum's job is to find witches and kill them?"

"That is correct."

The fiery letters burned through my memory. *Ameth.* Truth.

"You mean witches . . . like me."

My uncle's eyes twinkled behind their spectacles. "And me. And your Aunt Serena. And your father."

There was that word again. Father. Why did I taste bile whenever he said that word?

"Is that why the priest last night called me lukmani?" I asked.

My uncle clapped his hands on his knees. "He did, did he? I haven't heard that word for a long time. I've always called us 'Storytellers,' but the meanings are about the same."

"Why Storytellers?"

"Come now, Bali! You don't think I told you all those stories for my health, do you? Not that I don't like them, of course. I wouldn't be a good Storyteller if I didn't. But there was another reason too. I wanted you to be prepared, just in case. Perhaps I should have taught you to harness your powers when you were younger, but I didn't want to risk raising suspicions with the neighbors."

Before he could continue, three huge bangs pounded at the front of our house. "What's all this noise?" I heard my aunt announce from inside the kitchen.

A man's voice boomed back at her. "Open the door in the name of Their Majesties King Fernando and Queen Isabel!"

"Did you say the king and queen?" Aunt Serena called back. "How nice! Just give me a moment to move this stew before it bubbles over. Then I'll be right with you."

Diego glanced at my bedroom door. "I thought we had more time. The Malleus Maleficarum. For all their ranting about the sins of sorcerers, they always seem to have some magic up their sleeves whenever it's convenient for them. Come, Bali. It's time to go."

The old man helped me stand, but I felt like a golem who had come to life before the clay had set and had to grasp my headboard to support myself on wobbly feet. "What do you mean, 'go'?" I said. "You just said we're sorcerers. Let's go out there and fight them!"

My uncle breathed out some air in a kind of bleak chuckle, and his eyes went very wide. "No. They now know you are a Storyteller, which means they will have sent far more men than we can handle. And I will not risk your being captured again. Their methods of torture are too brutal to think about. They say they have perfected a way of drowning a man so that he does not die, only languishes in the agony between life and death, wishing that his lungs would burst. And they say—"

But Diego could not continue. He closed his eyes briefly, shook his head, and stole a leather bag from beside his chair. He stuffed the priest's parchment into that bag and thrust the thing into my hands. "You must go. There's a coin purse in here, and the scroll you can finish reading later. Some of your aunt's bread is in here too. Not enough for a long journey, but that's what the coins are for."

"What journey? Where are we going?"

"Not 'we.' You. Don't worry about us. You just worry about running."

The banging at the front of the house was growing louder now, as was Serena's scolding of the soldiers. "Run?" I said as if the word were unknown to me. "What do you mean? Run where?"

"Anywhere. Your aunt and I will hold them off as long as we can. Just run. Spain is no longer safe for you."

With one hand my uncle pushed me toward the window, and with the other he swiped my hat from the foot of my bed and shoved it under my arm. He checked out the window and saw the way was clear. Then he ruffled my hair around my ear.

"I'm so sorry, Bali. I had hoped we could spare you of this. But in real life stories don't always go the way we hope. Still, one good thing might come of this. You can find your father. There must be a reason he came here—not just here, but to *your* room, to *your* window. You must find him. You must find out—"

"*Cariño,*" Aunt Serena called from outside my door. "There are some nice men here to see you!"

"I believe your aunt is calling me," Diego said. "Quick, out the window. Oh, I nearly forgot." He removed a thin golden strand from around his neck and pressed it into my hand. "It's from your father. For your protection, he said." Diego paused as if remembering some joke from long ago, and he exhaled a dark laugh. "Although now that I think about it, maybe he said *you* should protect *it*. That would make more sense. At any rate, do not lose it. Now go. Go and find him."

I stuffed the necklace into Diego's bag, secured its strap over my chest, and clambered out the window. "But how?" I asked him. "If the Malleus Maleficarum can't find al-Katib, how can *I* find him?"

"I know you'll find a way. The necklace will help you. But there's no more time for questions." My uncle seized me through the window and held me close. "Please, Bali. Get as far away from here as possible. No matter what you hear, do not look back. Remember the story of Lot's wife. She looked back at her home when she was running away, and look what happened to her. She turned into a pillar of salt."

I could hardly believe what my uncle was saying. "That's just a story. I'm not leaving without you."

Distantly my uncle stared out the window, past me and through the neighbors' nearby wall. "Maybe it is just a story," he said, very quiet. "But it is true nonetheless. Now, please. Run. I promise we will find you."

"What? No. I—"

Out in the kitchen I heard the metallic scrape of armor, and the heavy sound of boots tumbling over the floor. "No more stalling!" shouted one of the guards. "We know you have the boy."

"Don't go in there!" Aunt Serena exclaimed. "My husband does alchemical experiments in there. The chemicals, they're very dangerous! You shouldn't—!"

There was the sound of a struggle, and I heard Serena scream. The door to my room banged open. My aunt was sagging against it, holding her stomach, now shredded red with blood. Wet webs of scarlet crisscrossed down the sword in front of her and dripped heavily onto the tile floor.

"Aunt Serena!" I cried, and Diego dived forward to push back the blades inching toward her neck.

"Run, Baltasar!" my uncle shouted, but a soldier grabbed him from behind and plunged a knife straight into his side. His eyes wide with pain or shock, my uncle groped for the doorframe to keep himself steady. Then he simply collapsed to the floor.

"Run, Baltasar!" he wheezed to me as he fell. "Don't look back! Run!"

One of the soldiers yelled, "He's on the side of the house! Get him!"

"Oh, no, you don't," Aunt Serena grunted. Her long hair flew in cascades behind her as a series of letters flared up before her hands. "Come to me, Behemoth!"

At the same time my uncle shouted, "Go, Baltasar!" I gave him a last look and fled.

I tore up the hill that would lead into town, feeling a series of vibrations buzzing up against my feet. Then came a sound like an explosion. The force of it threw me up the hill. *Don't look back*, my uncle had said. But I couldn't obey that command. Spitting the dirt out of my mouth, I flipped onto my back so

I could face my childhood home.

What I saw flooded me with horror. In the valley below me, our little cottage lay in ruins. My uncle slumped among the debris—alive or dead, I couldn't say. A dozen soldiers ducked in front of him, gaping at the monster my aunt had summoned.

It was the Behemoth, a clomping black reptile the size of several houses. It had the black face of a lion. Spikes the width of tree trunks shot out from its stout body and atop its scaly head. Its tail whipped this way and that, sending rocky chunks of what used to be my house flying at the heads of the soldiers.

"Go, Behemoth!" my aunt cried, and the black lizard surged forward. Its teeth snapping at the soldiers, the beast ripped through the remains of the workshop's floor, tossing up shards of tile and parchment as it went. The soldiers shielded themselves and scattered, throwing spears at the Behemoth's armored back. A couple of them stuck in the monster's skin. Most glanced off and rained back down on the soldiers.

They continued fighting each other, I'm sure, but I couldn't concentrate on the battle. All I could see was my aunt staggering toward my uncle, cradling her bloody belly, and dropping to her knees. Finally she fell forward, reaching one bloody hand toward Diego's.

Don't look back, I thought I heard my uncle say. *Run! Run, Baltasar!*

So with tears in my eyes I ran, knowing that they had saved me.

five

THE NECKLACE

My feet pounded over cobblestones; the muscles in my legs tightened and burned. But I couldn't stop running—not now, not yet. In another minute I was tearing through the port. Over my winded breaths I could hear soldiers shouting "Fan out this way!" and "He can't be far!" My uncle's voice still drummed through my head. *Run, Baltasar! Go! Spain is no longer safe for you!*

Run. Yes, yes—but where? Portugal and France were too close; Diego had said I must run far. The Malleus Maleficarum was formed in Germany, and the Inquisition started in Rome.

Oh, then where else was there to go? The only other places I'd heard of were the imaginary ones listed in stories. Cathay, Arabia, Cipango, Zanzibar. But those were just names, weren't they? Fairy tales. Even if those places were real, how could I hope to get to one with those men following two steps behind?

And how could I leave my aunt and uncle dying on the floor?

65

"Check near the ships!" I heard another Malleus soldier yell in the distance, and I ducked behind an overturned rowboat. My gaze ticked up and down the port, searching for something friendly, something safe. To my right stooped Palos's salt-encrusted houses of ill repute. To my left the *Santa María* and her sisters waited to sail off on a suicide mission.

The *Santa María*.

At once the face of Antonio de Cuellar flew up in my memory. *We're going west,* the ruddy carpenter had said just yesterday. Suddenly that route didn't seem so dangerous at all. The Malleus Maleficarum would never send their men that way. *Look for me at the Dark Sea Inn,* de Cuellar had said, so I fled across the street and into the tavern.

Once inside I slammed my uncle's coin purse on the bar in front of the innkeeper, who took in the sight with gleaming, greedy eyes. A few coins bought me a tray of greasy soup, a lit candle, a painted pitcher of water—but most important, they bought me secrecy. The innkeeper said I could hide up in his attic, and no one would know I was staying there as long as the coins kept coming. And as for Antonio de Cuellar, the *Santa María*'s carpenter? I would be alerted the second he returned.

So I flew up the inn's rickety back staircase and into my attic sanctuary: a room only large enough to fit a broken-down dresser, a few anxious moths, and a single lumpy bed. Some dusty light pushed in from under the slats of the window's shutters. They barely made a dent in the shadows that blanketed the slanted ceiling.

I placed my lit candle on the broken dresser and peered through the sliver of light that shone between the attic's closed shutters. From up here I could see three helmeted figures gathered below near the *Santa María*, pointing back and forth, furious for information.

I gasped through my nose and jumped away from the window. But my heel stuck on a raised floorboard that sent me flying sideways. As I crashed onto the floor, soup sloshed across my tunic and water sprayed across my cheek. And when I next looked up, I saw my bag had spit its contents across the floor.

I couldn't take it anymore. I tore my bag from across my chest and threw it across the room. As I did, I smashed my elbow against the bedframe. "Goddamn it!" I shouted, clutching at my throbbing elbow. I gritted my teeth and cringed, hugging my shaking shoulders. And then I could hold it in no longer. I beat my head with my wrists and wept and howled, thinking of Serena and Diego, and cursing them for leaving me lost and scared and alone. And I cursed myself for crying, and God and the Malleus Maleficarum too. But most of all, I cursed Amir al-Katib. For getting my family into this mess, for being a traitor and a Moor. For everything.

When I was done, I slumped against the side of the bed and rubbed the tears from my face with the heel of my hand. Distantly I looked upon my few remaining possessions. My last piece of Serena's bread had rolled into a pile of dust near the attic door. I brushed it clean and squeezed it in my hands before replacing it in my bag. I picked up my tray with the half-full pitcher and the remains of my soup and tossed it with a clatter onto the dresser.

Not far from the foot of the bed I found the Malleus Maleficarum scroll the priest had read to me in the monastery. Curious, I opened it. But the words "son of Amir al-Katib, the Moor" jumped out at me, and I flung the page from my hands as if it were on fire. Amir al-Katib—my father. No. No, I couldn't deal with that information right now. First I would find that necklace that Diego had given me. It had to have landed around here somewhere.

I found it under the bed, a mess of glittering gold tangles that I unsnarled with my fingernails. In a fist I raised the necklace to eye level and watched drips of sunlight trickle down its chain. At the bottom of that chain shivered a golden charm in the shape similar to a teardrop or one of the flasks in our workshop back home. And like a flask, it appeared the charm could be opened. The top of the teardrop could be clicked back so you could put something inside it: a piece of a loved one's hair, the relic of a saint, or even a drop of someone's blood.

I touched the charm with the tips of my fingers, feeling the shallow scratches in its dull surface. Oddly enough, the charm felt warm to the touch—bizarrely warm, even on such a hot summer's day.

A disturbing thought flew up in my mind. This was Amir

al-Katib's necklace—my *father's* necklace. That man had touched this charm with *his* fingers, had worn this necklace around his own neck. What if this warmth I was feeling was *his* warmth, a warmth that had been trapped there for the last fourteen years?

It was an irrational thought, but all the same I let the chain jangle back to the floor. This necklace. It was proof. Amir al-Katib was no legend, no myth. He was my father—a Storyteller and a traitor and a Moor. I looked down with horror at the dark skin on the back of my hands. A Storyteller and a traitor and a Moor. Now I was all those things too.

I rubbed my face, stretching back the skin around my long Moorish nose. Every time I closed my eyes I saw a terrible bearded man, his face splattered with the blood of innocents. That was the way al-Katib looked the night he had abandoned me, after the Inquisition came and killed my mother. At least, that was the story al-Katib had told Diego—but who knew if that story was true? Everyone knew Amir al-Katib was a deft and savage warrior. In a fit of rage, he could have killed my mother himself, just as he killed Luis de Torres's brothers in Granada.

I could feel my uncle's gaze pushing against me, as if he were standing right behind me, just out of sight. *It's from your father,* Diego had said of the necklace. *For your protection,* he said. *It will help you.* And my uncle had laughed, too, though I could hardly figure out why.

I sat on the edge of the bed and again lifted the necklace

before my eyes. I didn't get it. Gold was worthy of protection, sure. But how could a necklace possibly protect *me*?

Unless . . .

Unless there was something inside that gold charm. Only one way to find out. I clicked open the necklace.

And was blasted back against the wall. My head thunked against the wall behind me, and most of the breath shot out of my lungs. The golden charm jumped out of my hands, its glittering chain waving behind it—and then I knew I had gone completely mad.

Because it appeared to me that the charm was bouncing across the floor with purpose, as if it were trying to get from one place to another. In fact, it was trying to get to the exact center of the room. Once there it stopped short and sat itself upright, as if someone were balancing it there with the tip of an invisible finger. When the charm was perfectly perpendicular to the floor, a stream of gas began hissing out, filling the room with plumes of purplish smoke.

In a panic I covered my face with an arm and threw open the attic window. With a stubborn *bang* the shutters slammed themselves back shut. Above me, purple clouds swirled about the ceiling, sending jagged bolts of violet light toward the charm vibrating on the floor. Every moment, the vibrations grew more urgent, and the clouds above the charm swirled faster. Until—

An unnameable mass spewed out of the necklace. I ducked as it bounced off the wall right next to me. It flew past me so quickly that a gust of wind blew up the hair around my ears.

Still ducking, I watched the glob zoom around the attic. It banged off the dresser, the shutters, the attic door, the opposite wall. As it flew, the glob spasmed and squelched, raging against itself, writhing. At last, it reached its dizzying peak in the center of the room, spinning faster and faster until it was a purplish blur.

And then, of course, it exploded.

Tears stung my eyes. I squeezed them shut. The popping sound of the explosion had temporarily deafened me. I could hear nothing but the dulled sound of my barking coughs. But gradually, I thought I heard something else, too. Something like girlish sneezes. I waved the smoke away from my eyes and was astonished by what I saw.

A slight girl sat on her knees in the middle of the room, surrounded by dissolving puffs of smoke. That fact alone was enough to make my pulse stop short, but when the smoke finally cleared that's not what surprised me most.

What surprised me most was that the girl's head was on fire.

The girl sat frozen in the center of the room, a lithe reddish-brown figure with black flames ravaging her skull. The girl sneezed again—a series of three quick, short *achoo*s that together sounded something like a birdsong. "Excuse me," the girl said. Her voice chimed, nymphlike, through the attic.

From my place on the bed I took in this spectacle, my back perfectly flush against the wall. The girl swept her flaming head from side to side. "You're not Amir. What is this place?"

71

My hands gripped the bedspread, my only link to reality. Obviously the girl in front of me was a demon. At the same time she appeared to be a girl of eleven or ten. Her eyes were violet, friendly and warm, and her mouth soft with the loving amusement of a grandmother. Glittering jewels of every color covered her fingers and bare toes, and half a dozen diamonds hung in neat rows under her batlike ears. The ivory dress she wore was cut from some rich material too, something like whatever flower petals are made of.

The girl-demon raised herself up on tiptoes. Soon I realized her feet were no longer touching the floor. Now the girl was floating above the floorboards, her violet eyes calm and inquiring. Finally she alighted in a graceful squat on the edge of the mattress, sending me scrambling toward the foot of the bed so quickly that I nearly fell off.

With a delicate finger the girl cracked open the window so she could peep down at the marina below. Her bat ears perked up at the sight. "Oh, good, good, good!" the girl said. "At least we're still in Palos."

Were we? At the moment it seemed like I had been transported into one of my uncle's old stories—one where a mischievous spirit tries to steal a young man's soul.

My own mischievous spirit cocked her head at me. "Who are you, anyway? How do you know Amir?"

This time I at least tried to answer, but my voice came out in little crackles that disintegrated in my mouth. The demon's ears twitched happily as she raised her chin toward the room's only exit.

"Is Amir down there?" she asked. She hopped off the bed and flounced toward the attic door.

I threw myself in front of her. "Don't go out there!"

Again the girl cocked her head at me. The way she hung there, her bare feet pointed vaguely inward, she looked like a young child waiting for a parent's return. "Why?" she asked me in that way only a child can. When I couldn't answer she reached out to open the attic door.

Again I jumped in front of her. "No, I mean it! You *cannot* go out there!"

The girl floated slowly to the floor. "Why?" she asked me again, but this time her voice was heavy with suspicion. The black bonfire that was her hair was growing larger now, swirling closer and closer to the ceiling. Little black sparks, I noticed, were springing onto the girl's bony bare shoulders.

"Why do you keep telling me what to do?" The girl flew in close to me so her flat chest was an inch away from my own. "You can't do that. Only Amir can do that!"

"I'm sorry," I said, backing away from her toward the bed. "But there's no reason to go downstairs. Amir isn't down there. Really!"

The girl flew toward me faster now, at such a steep angle that her bare feet were nearly over her head. "Then where is he? Huh?" The girl poked me hard in the chest, sending me falling into a sitting position on the bed. "Huh? Tell me! Where is Amir?"

Rubbing my chest, I scooted away from her toward the pillow. "Ouch! Look, I swear to you! I have no idea where Amir is. No one does!"

The girl's hair erupted in a black fireball. "Liar!" she cried. "You're a liar, liar, *liar!*"

By this point there was nowhere left for me to run. I had backed all the way into the corner of the bed, with a wall on one side of me and the window on the other. The girl flew in closer, her hair roiling. I shrunk back so my skin wouldn't be burned off by the flames.

Because the flames were growing larger now—much larger. In fact, they were cascading down the girl's entire body. "Liar!" the girl shouted, and the black flames lapped down her neck. "Liar! Liar!" And they swallowed her arms and stomach. I cowered at the sight of her. This girl was a demon, no doubt about it—a white-eyed demon of pure black flame.

I had to do something. At this rate, she was going to set the whole inn on fire! That's when I noticed something in the corner of my vision. Of course—the pitcher! The ceramic pitcher the innkeeper had given me! I covered my eyes with a forearm and, in one wild motion, snatched up the container and flung the liquid inside at the girl.

I heard a splash, which I expected, and a fizz, which I ex-pected too. But what I didn't expect was the horrible, strangled yelp that came out of the demon's mouth when I splashed her. I heard a couple of thumps and then silence. The girl had crashed onto the floor.

My God.

I had killed her! My heart gasped at the thought. I threw myself on my hands and knees so I could look over the side of the bed. "Are you all right?" I said, but it was clear the girl was anything but. She was curled into a ball on the floor, her head completely bare except for a fizzing black splatter that covered most of her brown scalp. It was a burn—a deep, black burn. The water had branded it into her skin where it hit her. More burns, black and dry as charcoal, snaked down the girl's once-flawless neck and arms. Clouds of steam sizzled out from her skin, and her blackened toes bent inward, petrified in pain.

"I'm sorry!" I whispered to the poor corpse below me. "I didn't mean to— I didn't want— Look, I'm sorry!"

In response, the corpse whimpered and hugged her cracking arms. "That really hurt," the girl croaked. She sat up and sulked down at her broiled arms. "Oh, look what you did. Now I'll have to change."

Which is exactly what she did. With a *whoosh*, the black flames rekindled on her skull. The girl winced as the burns gradually disappeared from her body, and the wet spots on her ivory dress slowly faded away. In a few more seconds the girl had completely transformed. She now looked exactly the way she had looked before.

"Amir didn't tell you I'm an ifritah," the girl said sadly, as if that explained what I had done to her.

I didn't know the word, so I shook my head.

"You really don't know where he is, do you?"

I shook my head once more, jaw slack. The girl floated up from the floorboards and landed beside me on the mattress. This time I tried not to flinch away from her as she came near.

"Who are you?" the girl said to me at last.

"Baltasar," I answered, and I offered her a timid handshake.

She didn't take it. Distress or something like it was wrinkling her brow, and tears were forming in the corners of her eyes, singeing the skin near the bridge of her nose.

The girl reached out hesitantly and touched my cheek with one of her thin hands. "You can't be Baltasar. It's a joke. Tell me it's a joke."

Feeling uncomfortable, I turned my face away from the girl's hand. "Here," I said. "Look, I can prove it." I bent over the side of the bed so I could pick up the scroll from the floor. I unrolled it between us on the bedspread. "It's from the Malleus Maleficarum. It should have my name on it somewhere."

The girl dragged a ringed finger across the parchment as she read to herself in a whisper. "Warrant for the arrest of Baltasar Infante, son of Amir al-Katib, the Moor. Should be treated as an enemy of the Spanish crown." The girl looked up at me with those huge violet eyes. "What is this? When was this written?"

"There's probably a date on it somewhere. Here—the thirtieth of July, the year of our Lord fourteen-hundred and ninety-two—"

The girl, stiff and unblinking, shook her head. "No. Read it again."

Not sure of what she'd do if I refused, I reread, very carefully, "Warrant for the arrest of—"

"No, the year! The year! Tell me the year!"

"1492?" I said, shocked that I bothered to repeat it.

"No." The girl's body quaked in terror or rage. "No, it can't be!" The girl grabbed the top of my tunic and yanked me roughly toward her. "If you really are Baltasar, you must know where Amir is! Where is he? Tell me! Where is your father?"

I tried to back away, but the girl's hold on my shirt was too strong. "I already told you. I have no idea where he is!"

"And I already told you to stop lying!"

"I'm not!"

"Yes, you are! You're a liar! So just stop it, Baltasar! Bal—! Amir . . ."

Though the girl's words were fierce, I heard pain twinging in every syllable. It was a pain I knew all too well. This girl, this little demon—she was just as alone as I was.

"He left me," the girl said. She let go of my tunic and slumped against the attic wall. Silent tears burned down her eyelids and onto her cheeks.

I crawled closer to her on the bed. "Hey," I said to her,

softly. Demon or no, this person beside me was a little girl, and right now, this little girl was crying. "Hey, no. Please. Please don't cry. *Shh*. What's your name?"

"Jinniyah," the girl answered. She hiccuped back a new batch of tears. "How could he, Baltasar? Fourteen years! Fourteen years, and he left me all alone. Fourteen years, and I . . . I . . . I hate him!"

And the girl collapsed into new sobs.

Not knowing what else to do, I held onto the girl and let her cry. Amir al-Katib. Jinniyah's necklace had once been in the man's possession, maybe even forty years ago when Amir met Diego in Constantinople. And then, at the same time he left his son as an orphan on Diego's doorstep, Amir had left this girl—this Jinniyah—too. That time, when my father had abandoned me, he had abandoned Jinniyah, as well.

An odd sensation worked its way up my body. If that was true, then this girl was as good as my sister. Not knowing what to do with this information I shut my mouth and held her close, like I thought a brother should.

Six

JINNIYAH

The next time I awoke, it was dusk. Sidelong shadows prowled the slanted lines of architecture above me, and music thumped in from under the floorboards: guitars and drums playing some gypsy dance I had heard once before.

Jinniyah was bent in a bow on the floor, chanting something under her breath with her hands flat against the ground. Her knees rested on my bag, which she used as a pillow. Her flaming black hair waved gently on her head as she chanted, casting blackish lights across the attic's walls.

I kept watching her strange ritual as I reached for the tray waiting for me on the dresser. Despite my previous accident, there was still some cold, greasy soup left in my bowl, and for that I was grateful. I hadn't eaten for more than a day now, and my stomach was quick to remind me of it.

"I can warm it for you," Jinniyah said, referring to my bowl of soup.

I sat with it on the edge of the bed. "What were you doing?"

"Praying," was the answer. The girl floated over to me and

79

cupped her hands under my bowl, her rings clinking against the ceramic as she touched it. Within seconds I could feel heat traveling from the bowl to my hands, and greasy yellow bubbles popped across the soup's surface.

"Thanks," I said, blinking back my surprise. Careful not to drip any soup on to the covers, I balanced the warm bowl on my legs so I could remove the loaf of Serena's bread from my bag. I ripped off a hunk for myself and handed a piece to Jinniyah. She sniffed it, picked a crumb off the top, and popped it into her mouth.

"What *are* you?" I said at last, unable to think of a better way to ask it.

The girl smiled in her grandmotherly way and pointed at her fiery black hair. "Ifritah. God made us out of subtle flame and smokeless fire. In Europe they sometimes call us genies. Like 'genius,' you know, because we're all very smart." The girl wagged a ringed finger at my face. "But don't think I'm going to start granting you wishes! Only attention-starved genies do that, and I am *not* attention-starved!"

"A fire genie," I said, trying to make sense of it. "And that's why the water hurt you before. Because you're a fire spirit, and fire and water—"

"Don't mix," Jinniyah finished. She picked another piece of bread off my loaf. "But don't worry about all that water business. I'm fine now! We ifritah aren't fragile like humans." The girl put her arms in front of her with her wrists facing the ceiling. The skin on the undersides of her arms was completely clear, with no signs of the burns that had previously scarred them.

"So you're immortal," I remarked, and I slurped up some soup.

"Uh-uh." The girl shook her head at me. "We ifritah are good at healing, but you *can* kill us. Actually humans have killed genies a bunch of times. But Allah—praised be His name—gave them magic swords to do it, so that made things easier for them."

With difficulty I choked down the piece of bread I was chewing on. Allah? Wasn't he the Moorish god? And he sent warriors to slaughter genies—innocent little girls like this one? The Moorish horse riders of my nightmares returned to me then, their features growing grotesque as they rattled their curved blades. And with them, Amir al-Katib rode across Granada, cutting down Spaniards in the name of his vengeful god.

"But those genies were evil," Jinniyah continued dismissively. "Anyway, I can heal, and I can fly a little, and I can change shape if I want to. Not into objects or anything like that. And not animals—ick, so dirty. But I can make myself look like a human if I need to! Not a specific human, of course, but human enough."

Skeptical, I munched on my bread. "I guess that sounds helpful."

"It is! Why? What can you do, *Baltasar*?"

I laughed as I brushed the crumbs off my tunic. "Not much. My Uncle Diego's been teaching me to make books." Suddenly I fell quiet. "I mean, he *was* teaching me to make books . . ."

I trailed off, unable to speak of the man any longer.

"What happened to him?" Jinniyah said in small, sad voice. "What happened to *you*?"

I shook my head, unable to say a word. But I supposed it was my duty to tell her everything I knew. We were in this thing together now, whatever it was. So, unsure of where to start, I told her about the eyes at the window, the golem and the capture, Diego's story, and the gift of the necklace. And when I reached the part where I had to leave my aunt and uncle behind, I plunged through as if it were a fable, a myth—a fairy tale that had happened to someone else and not to me. And Jinniyah, who had been so talkative before, fell mute as tears fizzled down her face.

"Did David really say that Amir left my necklace for your protection?" the girl said after a time.

It took me a moment to place the name. "You mean Diego. Yes, that's what he said."

A huge, fang-toothed grin broke out in Jinniyah's tear-burned face. "Baltasar! Do you know what this means? Amir didn't abandon me after all! He left me to protect you, to help you!" The girl knocked herself in the head with a tiny fist as the tear-burns faded from her cheeks. "Stupid, stupid Jinniyah! I should have known he had a good reason! Amir is the best person. The very best person in the world!"

"So I take it you don't hate him anymore?" I said, dubious.

"Hate Amir? Never!"

I tried to smile, but there was little joy in it. If only I could forgive as easily as Jinniyah could. Maybe if you're near-immortal, being abandoned for fourteen years isn't a big deal in the scheme of things. But I was fourteen years old, and I could never forgive Amir al-Katib.

Done with her bread, Jinniyah patted the crumbs from her hands, planted her bare feet on the floor, and pushed herself up to face me. "Well, that settles it! We have to find him. Right now."

Find Amir? I swallowed my last bit of soup with difficulty. "Uncle Diego said that too. But—"

Jinniyah jumped up in the air and stayed there. "But nothing! He's your *father*!"

I shrugged, not willing to agree with that one.

"And he's in trouble!" Jinniyah went on. "Why else would he come to your house the other night? He must need you for something—something important!"

I placed my empty bowl of soup on the dresser, took the girl by the shoulders, and pushed her gently to the ground. "Even if that were true, how are we supposed to find him? Even the Malleus Maleficarum can't figure out where he is. For all we know the man's in Africa by now."

I was glad to see that my question had Jinniyah stumped. Unfortunately she was only stumped for three seconds. "That's easy!" the girl said with a grin. "We'll ask the Baba Yaga."

I frowned. This sounded like the beginning of another story, and I was getting sick of stories by this point. Being part of my own was about more than I could take.

"She's a Storyteller," Jinniyah explained. "A very powerful Storyteller! The Baba Yaga's so famous that people in Russia even make up stories about *her*. They say she's an evil old witch, and Amir says she's a kind of a ghul. You do know what ghuls are, don't you?"

"No . . ."

"Arabian desert demons. The men live around cemeteries and dig up the graves to eat the corpses. And the women, the ghulah, lure men to the desert so they can eat them all up."

My face pulled itself back at the thought. "And you want to go visit one of these people?"

Jinniyah nodded with vigor, sending black sparkles springing from her hair. "Oh, yes, yes, yes! The Baba Yaga knows the answers to all sorts of questions. She can see the past, the future. She'll know where Amir is, easy!"

Exactly what I was afraid of. I turned away from Jinniyah toward the closed window shutters. How could I tell her that I had no interest in finding Amir al-Katib, that I had liked the man a lot better when I thought he was dead—and not my father?

On the other hand, a meeting with this Baba Yaga did sound tempting. A wise fortune-teller who could answer any question? Maybe it was exactly what I needed. Lately everything I knew as true was disappearing, melting away. What I needed most was answers, someone who could help me separate the truth from all the stories. A person who could tell me, without qualification or doubt, exactly what I needed to do.

Jinniyah took one of my hands in both of hers. "Come see the Baba Yaga with me, Bal. Please?"

I looked down at the girl and sighed. Oh, how could I say no to that guileless face, that hopeful smile? I took Jinniyah's hand and led her toward the attic door.

"So, 'Bal,' huh?" I said, smirking at her.

The girl grinned back at me. "Baltasar's too long."

"All right, but I'm going to have to call you Jinni."

Jinni made a face but didn't seem too put out over it. "That's what your *mom* used to call me." Before my eyes the ifritah transformed into a human girl with curly black hair and the threadbare clothes of a peasant. And before I knew it, we were galloping down the inn's staircase, pushing our way through the crowded tavern—where there was still no sign of Antonio de Cuellar—and bursting out onto the dusky pier.

Outside the sky had changed to a lilac-indigo hue. Above the *Santa María* and its sisters, the first stars began to twinkle. Jinniyah stopped us short in front of the ships and raised her head to the sky.

She started sniffing.

I followed her lead but found I couldn't smell anything at all—only the normal salty-fishy aromas of Palos's port.

"Is this some kind of genie thing?" I asked her.

"I'm trying to find an entrance to the Baba Yaga's house. People from all over the world always want to visit her and ask her questions about the future, but she lives very very far away. So the Baba Yaga created magic doors all over the world so people could come visit her more easily. There used to be a door in Palos that she created for Amir. But that was before . . ."

Though Jinniyah trailed off, I knew exactly what she meant. She meant before Amir had trapped her in the necklace. Before he had abandoned us.

But Jinniyah got over the thought quickly—much quicker than I did, anyway. "I can sense magic, you know," the girl said, out of nowhere. "It makes my skin all prickly. Especially right here, on my nose." She tapped the tip of her nose and went cross-eyed. "The entrances to Baba Yaga's house are highly, highly magical, so it's always easy for me to find one. In fact, they're so magical, they even make me sneeze sometimes!"

I chuckled through my own nose at the thought of Jinniyah sneezing her way through Palos, but quickly my face hardened. Not far away, three Malleus soldiers were gathered, holding spears, sharing information—searching. For me.

"Whatever you're doing, make it fast," I said to Jinni.

"Got her!" the girl cried, and she raced off through the port with me still attached to her.

The girl scurried down the road and into the empty market, zipping this way and that with such certainty that an on-looker would have been sure that she was the Palos native. By the time we reached Amir al-Katib's house, I hoped she'd take a second to pay her respects and catch her breath. Instead she darted forward even faster, propelling me on at speeds I hadn't felt since being tied to the back of a horse. At least at this rate the soldiers would have a hard time keeping up with us.

Jinniyah stopped us abruptly in front of a crumbling hovel not far from the edge of town. I bent over and gulped down as much air as I could. Drab, moth-eaten curtains covered the hovel's tiny window, and tortured branches like chicken feet poked out from under the building's grimy walls.

"This is the entrance to the Baba Yaga's house?" I said. I gave the hovel door a light knock. No answer. I tried again, knocking a little harder. This time the door yawned open to reveal a dark, cobwebbed room devoid of human presence.

"Looks like no one's home," I said into the shadows.

"Looks like," Jinniyah said with the haughtiness of knowledge.

"Well, we came this far. We might as well go inside and wait for her."

With a final glance at Jinniyah, I strode into the building.

Seven

THE SEER

I was overwhelmed by a wall of heat—not the humid heat of Palos but the roasting heat of a fire. The door to the house slammed shut behind Jinni, and instantly the interior transformed. No longer were we standing in a dusty, empty hovel, but a cozy one-room cabin, walls bright with the orange light of a fireplace. About a million dripping candles covered the cabin floor, along with piles of books and scrolls and crumpled pieces of parchment. In the middle of the room sat a large table carved from a single piece of wood, and in the corner lounged a fur-covered bed.

Impressed by the transformation, I stepped farther into the house, then flipped through one of the cabin's many books. "Do you think the Baba Yaga will be back soon?" I asked Jinni.

The cabin door immediately squealed the answer. A freezing gust of wind brushed up against the back of my neck from outside. That was when I saw her, a dwarf of an old woman made larger by the pile of scarves and shawls draped over her rounded back. The woman hobbled into the room with a gnarly oak cane. "Come in, come in," the dwarf said as she shut the door behind her, letting a final gust of wind blow in from outside. The wind was biting cold, as if the woman had entered not from Palos in the summer but some far-off mountain town in December. I stretched my neck to see out the cabin's only cloudy window, which was almost completely obscured by a pile of books. Sure enough, I could see no hint of the buildings of my hometown, nor could I hear crickets, nor could I see the sea. All I could see through the window was a gloomy pine forest and flurries of gray snow swirling through the trees.

The dwarfish woman hummed in disapproval as she un-bandaged the shawls from her head and neck. "I would have been here when you arrived," she said, "if only you had arrived on time." Pressing one of her bent hands against my back, she pushed me farther into the cabin, the tips of her nails prick-ing me through my tunic as she did. I allowed the woman to push me forward; I moved as if walking through a dream. It was as if I had stepped into another fairy tale—but I wasn't sure whether it was one about a helpful old wizard or an evil hag who gobbled up visitors.

"Just like your father," the old woman complained as she pushed me. "No sense of punctuality."

Her scolding broke me out of my trance. "How can I be late?" I said over my shoulder. "I've never even met you before!"

In answer the woman wiped the bottom of her large nose

with one of her curled fingers. She unwrapped the final scarf from her head, revealing white, corkscrewing hair that gave her the look of an elderly medusa. Sniffling, she motioned toward one of the chairs around her table and said, "Have a seat, have a seat."

I obliged, and she sat in the chair across from me, the dwarf with liver spots on her drooping cheeks. "Are you the Baba Yaga?" I asked her.

"I see you brought the ifritah with you," she answered, her voice both sympathetic and teasing. "You poor dear," she said to Jinniyah. "Did Amir leave you behind *again*?"

Behind me Jinniyah sat on the ground on her knees, focusing tearfully on a knot in the wood floor. "Please don't say that," I said in a low voice to the Baba Yaga. "She's really sensitive about him. It hurts her feelings."

When the Baba Yaga laughed, her neck inflated like a frog's. "Feelings! What feelings? That girl is a figment, my boy! A mere wisp of air, a daydream! Oh, I've no doubt she's *told* you she's a genie. But she's not even that. A half-genie. Half-human. Can't even grant her own wishes."

The witch's voice was so mocking, so easily cruel, that I shot right up from my seat. And before I knew what I was saying, I heard myself shout, "Well, you're not anything special, you jealous old witch!"

Regret immediately took me by the throat and pushed me back down in my chair. Why had I done that? The woman sitting in front of me was supposedly a master of Storytelling. Who knew what awful spell she was about to cast on me?

But the crone's sea-green eyes merely flashed at me. "'Jealous'?" she repeated, carefully weighing the word. "Interesting. Young men usually ask me to answer their questions, not the other way around. Tell me, boy. What is it, exactly, that I am jealous of?"

I didn't know what would be worse: to answer or not to answer. I glanced back at Jinniyah, cleared my throat, and mumbled, "Her youth."

The Baba Yaga's eyes became narrower, and the thin line on her face ticked up into a wide, evil V. "So you are clever, son of al-Katib. Take care that your cleverness is not your ruin."

In punctuation, a strong gust of wind threw open one of the cabin's windows and brushed away the light of the nearest candles. "There is a story from my village about cleverness," the Baba Yaga said. "It is about a king who had three daughters, and on their thirteenth birthday, he asked each of them to make a wish. The first daughter, a raven-haired girl, wished for beauty, and she grew up to be the most beautiful woman in the land. The second daughter, a fair-haired girl, wished for love. When she was older she married a prince and had many children, each of whom loved her more than anything in the world.

"But the third daughter, the scarlet-haired child . . . she was like you, son of al-Katib. She wished for cleverness. When she was older people would come from all over the kingdom to ask her questions, and she would always have the perfect answer for them.

"One day a prince came from afar, seeking a bride. Every woman he met he would ask, 'Fair lady, what is the fastest thing in the world?' Many beautiful women considered the question and gave answers such as 'a horse' or 'an eagle.' But the scarlet-haired daughter knew the real answer. 'The fastest thing in the world,' she said, 'is the human mind.' The prince married her then and there, and they enjoyed several happy years together.

"Little did the scarlet-haired princess know that her wish had also been a curse. Soon she realized that, every time she was asked a question, a new wrinkle would appear on her face, and a new spot would appear on her skin. By the time she was married five years, she already looked like an old woman.

"Her husband, the prince, was a wise man too. He knew it would not do for a king to have a crone as his queen. So he banished his wife to the forests, to a crumbling old hut where she would never be seen again. And the villagers called her names and told stories about her, and she became a wicked witch to live up to their stories."

It took a moment for me to understand what the woman was saying. Then, realizing, I said, "You were that girl."

The old woman removed one of her shawls from the back of her chair and wrapped it back around her shoulders. "You children! When you are young, oh, you ask so many questions!

But as you age, you have fewer and fewer of them. Before long all you have is answers.

"But those who wish to be wise are forever plagued with questions, questions that eat their flesh from the inside out. 'How should I live?' 'Why must we die?' 'What is right, and what is wrong?' Whether or not they look so on the outside, the wise age quicker than most, and their lives are filled with heartache." The Baba Yaga adjusted her shawl around her. "You came here to ask me a question or two, I think."

I gulped down my fear and said, "Jinniyah said you're a powerful Storyteller. She said you would know where Amir is, and where I need to go. To be honest I have no idea what I'm doing. I know I have to leave Spain. Diego said so. But I don't know what to do next. I don't—"

"You are so like your father," the crone said, bowing her head deeper into the candlelight. "I saw him a few weeks ago. He came in through the door in North Africa. He was much older this time. On the run. In search of direction." The Baba Yaga reached under the table. "I used the tarot." The old woman brought up a deck of decaying cards from the floor and spread the cards faceup in front of her. Spades, clubs, diamonds, hearts . . .

"Playing cards?" I said, disbelieving. "I thought Jinniyah said you were a Storyteller."

The Baba Yaga gathered the cards in a neat stack and placed it in the center of the table. "The cards tell a story, son of al-Katib. If you know how to read them properly, you can summon images: of what has passed, of what you seek, of what will befall you in times to come. Over the centuries Storytellers have consulted the cards to discover the direction in which they must travel. Shall we consult them now, Baltasar ibn Amir?"

The name sent a shiver dripping down my back. All the same I nodded. With shaking but nimble hands, the seer shuffled the deck of cards three times. Then she dealt the top card between us.

"This is you," she said.

I examined the card. "It looks like the jack of spades."

"Impertinent boy. The jack of spades is a *symbol*. It *symbolizes* you." She placed a curled hand on top of the card, which began to glow red underneath it. A near-transparent image flashed up above the card: a shadow in the shape of a young page striding toward an unknown future.

"The jack of spades," the Baba Yaga explained. "The symbol of a young man seeking information from afar." The crone removed her hand from the card, letting the ghostly image fade above the table. "It also means someone who talks too much, doesn't listen. Each card, you'll see, has several significances."

I couldn't help myself. "Is one of those significances the jack of spades?"

"One who talks too much," the Baba Yaga repeated, leaving a hint of a smile on her withered face. She dealt a few more

cards and placed both of her hands over them. The image of
an opening book appeared between us. "An unknown past,
recently revealed." The image of the book swirled in the air
and shifted into the shadow of a flame-haired girl. "New meet-
ings,"—here the Baba Yaga's gaze jumped to Jinniyah—"new
losses."

The silhouettes of Diego and Serena darkened the air in
front of me. They screamed in silence before shriveling into
nothing.

"Losses," I repeated to myself. "So my aunt and uncle . . .
they're . . . they're definitely . . ."

The Baba Yaga's face filled with sorrow. "They have gone
to a place you cannot follow."

I turned away from her toward the fireplace. Deep inside
me I'd known it was true. But I'd been keeping a grain of hope
they'd somehow escaped that fate.

And now that grain was gone. For some reason I imagined
Amir al-Katib cackling at the knowledge.

The Baba Yaga removed another card from her pile—the
eight of hearts—summoning the image of three ships racing
across a choppy black ocean. "This is your present. The shed-
ding of familiar things. A journey to an unknown land. This
card is a heart, Baltasar: the suit of water and the west."

"A journey by sea to the west," I said to myself. "So I was
right to seek Antonio de Cuellar." To the Baba Yaga I continued,
"If that's the story of my present, then what about my future?

95

What about Amir al-Katib? And the Malleus Maleficarum! Even if I find Antonio de Cuellar and travel west, who knows if they'll try and follow me? And what am I supposed to do once I reach Cathay? Will I be safe there? What language do they even speak in Cathay?"

"You ask many questions, son of al-Katib, but never the right ones. The Malleus Maleficarum, Antonio de Cuellar— these are pieces in a much larger game. Your true quest is far more dire than you imagine. I do not need to read the cards to know that the winds are shifting. They move west, bringing with it a terrible force. A force more powerful than I have seen in my lifetime."

The ancient woman spread her hands over the meaningless arrangement of cards between us. The candles around us shrank and darkened, and the wind from the open window shivered across my skin.

A black shadow towered over the playing cards, a horned colossus wearing a cape that billowed malevolently over the table. The horned man grinned as he picked up a globe and crushed it in his hands.

"What does it mean?" I asked the Baba Yaga.

"It is a prophecy," the old woman said. "A great power travels west: a being who will destroy the world as we know it."

The vengeful eyes of the hameh flashed in my memory, and the fiendish warriors from Jinniyah's tale.

"This is my future?"

"No. This your quest. The same quest foretold in your father's reading."

That made Jinniyah jump up from her seat on the floor. Before she could speak, I asked, "What did Amir say when you told him the prophecy?"

The Baba Yaga leaned back in her chair. "Exactly what I expected. Your father vowed to travel west, to find this being and destroy it."

Jinniyah flew over to me as the Baba Yaga bit down on her last syllable. "Bal, that's it!" the girl cried. "It all makes sense now! Your father goes to the Baba Yaga from Africa. She tells him his fortune. Then he comes to Palos to get you! Don't you see? He must have wanted us to come with him out west so we could help him find this evil being and destroy it together! It's the only thing that makes sense!"

Between me and the Baba Yaga, the horned man let the pieces of the globe sprinkle to the ground before dissolving into nothing. As much as I didn't want to admit it, Jinniyah was right. Her story did make sense. Except . . .

I swiveled around in my chair to face Jinniyah. "Except why would Amir al-Katib come to my room if he needed help? *He's* the great warrior. What would he need me for? I don't know anything about destroying evil spirits."

"He came to you because you are one of us," the Baba Yaga interrupted. "One of the people of Story."

I swiveled back around to face the Baba Yaga. "You mean I'm a Storyteller. But I didn't even know that until yesterday. How could Amir know?"

"He knows because you are his son."

Oh. That.

"I can't help him," I murmured down at the table. "I know I summoned that golem, but I don't know how I did it."

"You will learn."

I turned away from the Baba Yaga's humor-filled eyes. "Look," I said, as delicately as I was able, "I didn't come here to learn about any prophecies. I need to know how to get away from these Malleus people. That's it."

"You seek escape, Baltasar. But there is none. You wish to run from your shadow, but a shadow will follow you no matter where you turn."

A shadow?

What did she . . . ?

No. Enough of this. I had better things to do than listen to some batty old woman who thought she knew the future. There were people after me. Real people, not shadows. I pushed back my chair with my feet. "Come on, Jinni. We have to go." I fumbled in my coin purse for some of the copper coins Diego had given me and tossed them on the table. "Thanks for your help."

The Baba Yaga bubbled up with laughter. "I do not require money, Baltasar! I tell you this for your own sake. For the sake of the world."

"Right, the world. The thing is, the world doesn't really interest me right now." I picked my coins off the table and put them back in my pocket. If the woman didn't want them, I wasn't going to let them go to waste. "I know that probably sounds unfair, but my life is kind of complicated right now. Maybe when everything settles down a little, I'll be able to help you."

I took a step backward and bumped into one of the woman's piles of books, knocking several onto the floor. "Sorry," I said automatically as I replaced them on the pile.

"I am sorry too, Baltasar," the Baba Yaga said. "It is unfortunate that you would leave without allowing me to answer your original question. You wanted to know the story of your future, did you not? I have told you your past, your present, your quest, your fears. But I have not yet told you about your future."

I wrapped my hands around the back of the chair I had been sitting in, my heart beating syncopation in my fingers. "Go on, then. Tell me."

The Baba Yaga pressed her hand against the final card in the top-right corner. The shadow of a tall, stately man with a pointed beard and a crown rose up in the air above her fingers. "Your future: the king of spades."

"What does it mean?"

"The tarot tells a story, Baltasar. A beginning: a past. A middle: a present. An end. Like every story, it has many significances. Many different interpretations."

Over the palpitations of my heart, I could barely hear the seer's words. "But what does it *mean*?"

"Impertinent boy. The king of spades represents your future. It represents a dark man, full of wisdom and purpose—"

"Amir!" Jinniyah piped in. "It has to be!"

I agreed with her. "Because if I'm the jack of spades, then the king of spades has to be my . . . my father."

The Baba Yaga removed her hand from the table and shrugged, letting the image of the tall king shrink into nothing. "It is possible," the Baba Yaga said, her voice uncharacteristically high. "With the cards, anything is possible."

Ignoring her, I took Jinniyah's hand. "Come on, Jinni. We have to go."

The Baba Yaga swept her cards into a pile. "Be outside tomorrow at dawn. The man you seek, the carpenter. You will find him there. And Baltasar? Remember what I told you."

"Oh, I will," I said as I dragged Jinniyah back out into Palos. But to tell you the truth, as I crossed through the threshold, for the life of me I couldn't figure out what it was she wanted me to remember.

THE INTERPRETER

Jinniyah and I somehow managed to make our way back to the inn without being noticed by any Malleus men. Still exhausted, I soon fell asleep. It was a restless sleep, though, full of golems and Malleus soldiers and those glowing yellow eyes I had seen in my window two nights ago, and the next morning I awoke clammy and fatigued.

A din was roaring outside—surprising, given that it was newly dawn. I pushed my battered body upright, opened the window a crack, and peered down at the port. Dozens, maybe hundreds of colorful figures were muddling through morning fog, rolling barrels up long ramps onto the three ships anchored across the way.

The sight threw me into a minor frenzy. I kicked off the sheets that had knotted themselves around my ankles and slung my bag over my chest. "It's the *Santa María*!" I said to Jinniyah, who was busy praying on the floor. I yanked her up by her elbow. "Come on! They're going to leave without us!"

As we ran out of the attic, Jinniyah transformed into a curly-haired peasant boy wearing a simple linen gown and feathered cap. "Oh, Bal," she said in her chiming voice, "they won't leave without us. The Baba Yaga said we're going west, so we're going west!"

I wondered if things could be that simple. It would only work if we weren't too late. The Baba Yaga had said we'd meet Antonio de Cuellar at dawn, but once outside, I had no idea how we would find him. On every side of us men were rushing about in a blur, barely giving us a moment to catch a glimpse of their faces. Many I could tell had been sailors for years; others appeared to be servant boys who had never even seen a ship before. While most of the men wore linen shirts and plain cloth hats, there were others too, wearing embroidered doublets, silk gowns, and fur-lined mantles. And it seemed that everyone was barking some order to the poor man just below him in rank.

"Load that one on the *Pinta*!"

"Dry up the deck, you lout!"

"Get the cabin ready for the admiral's arrival!"

Somehow one command managed to stand out from the rest: "You tell your brother the next time he makes an ass of you in public, he'll have to have a long conversation with Antonio de Cuellar!"

And sure enough, not too far from where I was standing, a stout, grizzled man was clapping a hand over his belly. Antonio de Cuellar. Sure, the man was rough, drunk, and possibly a criminal, but I couldn't be happier to see that mottled, bearded face. Here was my ticket out of Spain, my balding savior from the Malleus Maleficarum!

Antonio was currently guffawing with a handsome young nobleman with shoulder-length black hair. "Speaking of that brother of yours," Antonio said as Jinniyah and I made our approach, "he and Colón still at each other's throats?"

Traces of pity and amusement lined the nobleman's voice as he answered. "More than ever. I don't understand it. They were on such good terms to begin with! But Martín refuses to believe that Colón's calculations are anything but faulty. According to him, we're all going to die of thirst in the middle of the Atlantic unless Colón starts doing things Martín's way. My brother's just lost the adventure in his heart! I keep telling him, even if he's right and the trip is longer than Colón thinks, who's to say there's only sea in the way? Marco Polo spoke of far-off islands east of Cathay, filled with all manner of food and jewelry and drink!"

"Knowing our luck, we'll run into man-eating barbarians," Antonio said.

"And beautiful women with bones pierced through their noses!"

As excited as the nobleman sounded when he said that, I was growing more and more concerned. Faulty calculations? Man-eating barbarians? Dying of thirst in the middle of the ocean?

Just what kind of mission was this, anyway?

But I didn't have the luxury of worrying about it, so I stepped up to the old carpenter and said, "Excuse me. Señor de Cuellar?"

The carpenter's eyes smiled under ratty eyebrows. "Now, looky here, Vicente!" he said to the nobleman. "A native of dear Palos if there ever was one." The carpenter clapped a sturdy hand against my back and said, "Now if I could only remember where I know you from!"

"We met the other day by the *Santa María*," I said. "You said I should look for you at the Dark Sea Inn?"

"Yes, of course! My young friend from the docks. Sorry I didn't see you at the Dark Sea. I checked in at one of Palos's other fine establishments. One with a better selection of, *ahem*, barmaids." De Cuellar scratched his graying beard. "Can't say I remember your name, though."

"Luis. De Torres. And this is my friend, uh, Juan." If Jinniyah's expression protested against her new name, I didn't notice it. Instead I stayed focused on Antonio and Vicente.

"So did you consider my offer, Luis?" Antonio asked me. "Of being Admiral Colón's new cabin boy?"

"Actually," I said with a bit of pride, "Juan and I would like to join you."

The carpenter whacked the back of his hand against the nobleman's upper arm. "You hear that, Vicente? More members of our splendid crew!"

Vicente didn't seem as thrilled by the news as Antonio did.

"You'll have to see Martín about that. He's the one in charge of that sort of thing."

"That brother of yours. Always a pain in everyone's side." To me Antonio said, "Don't let it worry you, Luis. It's just a formality. You know how these rich folk like to stand on ceremony. Come on. I'll take you to him now."

So Jinniyah and I followed Antonio through the chattering crowds in the direction of the *Santa María*. We passed a swarthy, short-bearded man, and Antonio said, "That's our master-at-arms, Juan de la Cosa." Next, we passed a heavy, extremely hairy man. "That's Bartolome. He escaped from prison back in Portugal."

As I hastened past the felon, Jinni inquired, "Who are we going to see now?"

"Captain Martín Alonso Pinzón, the one and only! He's captaining one of the other ships—the *Pinta*, they're calling it now. And his brother Vicente's the captain of the *Niña*, that little stack of splinters over there."

I could hardly believe my ears. These men were *the* Pinzón brothers? But they were local heroes in Palos, who had served as sailors in a recent war against Portugal. Their family had always been one of the wealthiest in town, and as fishermen and shipping magnates the brothers had amassed even more wealth. The fact that men as influential as the Pinzóns were involved in this mission was an encouraging sign. This trip had to be important if they had signed on.

"Now look, Martín's a bit of a grouch, I'll tell you that now," Antonio said. "But he's the best captain there is, and good to his crew. Every man you see here would follow him to the ends of the Earth. And they're going to, in less than an hour."

We found Martín Pinzón standing near the base of the *Pinta*. A man of about fifty, Martín sported the same rich clothing and dark hair as his brother. Unfortunately for Martín, he did not enjoy Vicente's handsome features. Where the young Vicente enjoyed a fair but healthy complexion, Martín's skin had a greenish undertone and dry red spots around his nostrils. Where Vicente's mouth was mischievous, seeming to hold back an untold joke, Martín's lips were thin from being pulled into a grimace. And where Vicente's dark eyes twinkled with hopes for adventure, Martín's were sunken, heavy from adventures past.

Currently Martín was being waylaid by a gangling man of about eighteen with an upturned nose, lank brown hair, and a chaotic pile of papers balanced on his forearms.

"I need you to sign here, initial here, and another signature goes here," the gangling man said, and he attempted to adjust the papers so Martín could read the fine print.

Martín looked down on this tornado of a man with half-lidded eyes. "And what would you like me to sign them *with*, Señor Sanchez?"

The young Sanchez quailed when he heard that, and he

sputtered something incomprehensible as he stuck his papers under his chin and hastily patted himself down in search of a quill. At last he appeared to find one in one of the many bags drooping from his belt, but as he reached for it he somehow lost his balance, twisted his foot, and went crashing down onto his elbows. His papers, needless to say, went flying in all directions. Martín turned away from Sanchez without another word.

While Sanchez chased down his errant papers, Martín threw his hand out toward Antonio. "This is what the queen sends me," the captain said. "Some idiot accountant to report on every last *maravedí* we spend!"

"Aw, give the kid a break," Antonio said about Sanchez. "Rodrigo's a good lad." Glancing in my direction, Antonio went on, "And speaking of good lads, I have two more for you and the admiral. So I'll be taking my *maravedíes* now, if you don't mind."

Martín's thin lips curled up slightly at the edges. "Looking for money again, de Cuellar? What, your girlfriends raise their rates again?"

The way Antonio flashed his teeth, you'd think the captain had given him a compliment. "That's what I like about you, Martín. Always such a good sense of humor."

"Yes, I am hilarious," Martín said dryly. "And you know what else is funny, de Cuellar? The fact that *I've already paid you your salary.*"

"I'm not talking about my salary! I'm talking about the bonus! The ten extra *maravedíes* for supplying a spry young cabin boy for Admiral Colón. And I brought an extra boy if he needs one. Juan could be a servant or something." Antonio moved aside to reveal Jinniyah and me to the captain. I gave the man an awkward bow; Jinniyah, a kind of curtsy.

Martín appraised us like we were part of a recent catch. "This is all very nice, de Cuellar, but you're too late."

The carpenter eyed the captain. "What do you mean 'too late'? The ships aren't leaving for another hour—"

"I mean we already have a cabin boy. A Don Pedro Terreros, the first son of a very eminent—and highly unpleasant—family from Burgos."

"Well, I'm sure you have room for Luis and Juan somewhere. There must be some job these boys can do."

Martín's body grew rigid as he whipped an angry hand toward the *Santa María*. "Room? Have you been on these ships, de Cuellar? We've barely enough room for our supplies as it is, let alone two more street urchins. We're about to die of thirst and starvation in the middle of the Atlantic, and Antonio de Cuellar brings me two more mouths to feed!"

"Aw, come on, Martín—"

"'Captain,' de Cuellar! I am a captain, which means *I* make the decisions! And those boys are *not* coming with us, and that is *final!* Send them home, or I will send you home with them!"

And Martín stormed off, leaving me and Jinni alone with Antonio.

"But that's not fair," the carpenter mumbled as he went. And it *wasn't* fair, not at all. The *Niña*. The *Pinta*. The *Santa María*. In less than an hour, these ships would be leaving without me, leaving me to deal with the Malleus Maleficarum on my own. The Baba Yaga's prophecy would unravel itself without me, and whatever Amir al-Katib wanted from me would remain a mystery forever.

"No," Antonio said, reaching back to anxiously pat the front of my tunic. "No, don't you go anywhere, Luis. God as my witness, I am getting you on that ship! It's a matter of honor . . . and . . . integrity . . . and . . . and . . ."

"The admiral's bonus?" I tried for him.

Antonio shoved his sleeves up his brawny arms. "You stay here, Luis. The admiral will hear about this." Continuing to mutter to himself, Antonio lumbered past me toward the *Santa María*.

I smiled weakly as he left. Though his heart was in the right place, I didn't expect any success out of him. "I guess we go back now," I said to Jinni.

The girl's lips barely moved. "Go back? Where?"

"I don't know." To the inn? To the Baba Yaga? "Maybe we can get onto another ship. There has to be another one around here that—"

"No!" Jinni exclaimed. A layer of tears glazed over her huge, currently-brown eyes. "These are the only ships going west, Bal! The Baba Yaga said we have to go west to find Amir! If we don't . . ."

"No, Jinni," I said in a low voice, hoping no one would hear. "The Baba Yaga just threw a bunch of cards on a table and told us what she thought they meant. The fact is, the Baba Yaga's not helping us get on the *Santa María*, and neither are her cards. If we have to go west, you're going to have to think of a way to do it, because I'm all out of ideas."

Jinniyah, however, didn't seem to be listening to me. She was standing on her tiptoes and listing to one side. When I opened my mouth again, she shoved a finger against my lips. As hard as I strained to hear what she was hearing, all I could make out above the roar of the crowds was the conversation of the two fair-haired men standing next to us on the dock.

Jinniyah shot a glance in their direction. "Bal, can you hear them? Those two blond men."

"Well, sure, but—"

"What are they saying?"

"I don't know." I didn't really understand why Jinniyah couldn't hear them—or why she cared. "They're talking about some other sea voyage, down to the Horn of Africa. Why?"

A cunning grin surfaced on Jinniyah's boyish face. And before I could understand what she was doing, I found myself being dragged through the crowds over to the *Pinta*. Martín Pinzón stood before it, rubbing his eyes as a sailor holding a heavy-looking barrel wasted his precious time.

Jinniyah burst in between them. "Captain Pinzón!"

Martín removed his fingers from his eyelids. "You two? Didn't I just send you away?"

Jinniyah nodded up at him. "Captain Pinzón, I know you don't need a cabin boy, but do you need an interpreter?"

At first I thought nothing of the question. Then I snapped my attention to Jinniyah.

An interpreter? What in God's name was she doing?

"We have one," Martín said, but Vicente, who must have overheard, slipped in front of him.

"Yes, and he's awful. Why? Can you translate?"

Jinniyah shoved her hands proudly against her hips. "Bal . . . Lui . . . My friend here is able to read at least ten different languages."

"Really?" Martín appeared skeptical, a look that fit him well.

"Don't pay any attention to her—him!" I said, jumping in front of Jinniyah. "He's exaggerating about my, er, abilities."

Jinniyah nuzzled her boyish face on my arm. "Oh, Luis is so humble. Humble and *handsome*." I pushed her away. This wasn't helping!

Martín pinched the bridge of his nose with two bony fingers. "Enough. If you must waste my time." He thrust the pile of yellowed papers he was carrying forward and jammed a finger toward it. "Read this."

I took a hold of the top sheet, wondering if I should risk another lie. Then I exhaled, relieved. "It's Latin." As an apprentice

111

bookmaker and scribe, I had known the language most of my life. "It's a list of supplies: fresh water, vinegar, cod, wine. Cheese, honey, and lentils—"

"Yes, yes, that's enough." Martín whisked the paper away and substituted it with another. "Now this one."

My confidence growing, I meditated over the second paper. Hmm. Although I couldn't speak the language sprawled across this page, I definitely could recognize it. Portuguese. It was funny, but the more I pored over the text, the more I thought I could read it all the same. And why not? It wasn't that far off from Latin or my own Castilian tongue.

"It's a contract," I said to Martín with conviction. "It says you will pay the undersigned a salary of a thousand *maravedíes* per month for his services on the *Pinta*, the first half of which shall be paid before the voyage and the remainder to be paid upon our return."

"Hmm," Martín said, but his disappointed tone told me I had read it correctly. Unsurprisingly Martín Pinzón was a hard man to impress, and he demanded that I read passages in Italian, French, Arabic, and even Ottoman Turkish. To my shock and his rising chagrin, I could read them all. It was impossible, but . . .

But . . .

By then Antonio de Cuellar had returned to see what all the fuss was about, since it seemed half the crew had gathered around to watch the show. Antonio, I gathered, had not found his admiral. "Luis," he said, a mix of worry and awe infusing his voice. "How are you doing that?"

I would have liked to know that myself.

"He is splendid," Vicente agreed. "Just perfect for the expedition."

"Mmm," was Martín's answer. He tapped his quill against his palm. And then, for no reason at all, he vanished into the crowd. Jinniyah and I exchanged glances but didn't say a word.

A minute later: "Make way! The admiral approaches!"

The waves of men standing before me parted, revealing Martín Pinzón and a sturdy gray-haired man with a navy cape draped over his shoulders. Admiral Colón. He looked down his Roman nose at me, his blue eyes piercing right through mine.

"Is this what you wanted me to see about, Martín?" The admiral's voice was very deep, with a trace of an unfamiliar accent.

"Yes." Martín stepped in front of me, holding a cover-worn book in his hands. Without ceremony he tossed it open to a random page. "Read this."

I squinted down at the unfamiliar text. The letters were angular, and their points and serifs were decorated with inkblots. My gaze trailed along the lines. And barely aware of what I was saying, I recited, "'Consider three things, and thou wilt not fall into transgression: know whence thou comest, whither thou art going, and before whom thou art about to give account and reckoning—'"

"That's enough." Martín stole the text away before I could finish and clapped the book closed with the force of judgment. "It's as I suspected."

"As I suspected as well, Brother," said Vicente. "He's perfect! With talent like this, we'd be able to speak with the Grand Khan!"

Admiral Colón peered down at me. "I'm wondering if you could tell me something, Señor . . . ?"

"Luis de Torres," I said.

"I was wondering, Señor de Torres, if you could tell me where you became so skillful in reading these languages?"

Always ready to unsheathe a new story, I said, "Oh, here and there. I've done a lot of traveling over the years—"

"And where would you say you picked up this particular language?" Colón took the book from Martín Pinzón's hands and held it up in front of me.

"That one? From my uncle. He was a bookmaker."

I thought that answer was as good as any, and it was very nearly true. At any rate Colón seemed placated as he handed the book back to Martín. But the look on Martín's face, a look of distrust and scorn, told me my lie had not worked on him.

"Don't listen to a word this boy says, Admiral," Martín said, taking a menacing step closer to me. Was he always this tall and commanding? Was his face always so ghoulish and gray?

"You, Señor de Torres, are a liar. And I do not like being lied to. I think de Torres isn't your real name at all."

I could hardly believe anyone could be so perceptive. Where had I gone wrong? Did my voice waver? Did I leave a hole in my story that Martín worked his way through? Or maybe Martín was an agent of the Malleus Maleficarum who knew my true identity.

"He's a Jew."

The statement stopped sailors in their tracks. The admiral said, "What are you talking about, Martín?"

Martín slapped the fateful book against Colón's chest. "I'm talking about this. It's in Aramaic. A Jewish text. Not something any boy off the street is going to understand. That is, unless he's a Jewish converso—a Marrano, as people so rudely call them. Am I right, de Torres?"

I bowed my head as low as it could go. "That's right, sir."

"I knew it!" It was amazing what an effect being right had on Martín. A light kindled his features, transforming him in an instant from a sallow, sad-looking man into a being vibrant with youth.

Antonio de Cuellar scowled. "So he's a Jew! What difference does that make? He could out-translate the Pope. God as my witness, he could!" For a moment I wondered if Antonio would hit the captain even if it meant losing his job.

Fortunately the carpenter failed to faze the captain. "If you were paying attention," Martín said, "you would realize that I borrowed this copy of the Talmud from a sailor on the *Pinta* who happens to be Jewish. And there are three converted Jews on this voyage, as well, including your friend Sanchez over there. It makes no difference to me if this boy is Jewish, pagan, or one of the Mohammedan peoples. If the boy can help us find gold in the Indies, he can be Moses, for all I care. Gold is the only religion to me, Carpenter."

"So he's got the job?" Antonio looked up at Colón expectantly.

"Yes," the admiral said. "He and the other boy will be coming with me on the *Santa María*. The rest of you ready yourselves. We will depart in a half an hour."

And all of a sudden the show was over. The crowd around me dispersed, and Antonio ran after Martín, ready to collect his bonus.

As for me? I just stood there, completely and utterly bewildered.

What had happened just now? What did I just *do*?

Lost in these thoughts, I barely noticed when Admiral Colón stepped up next to me. "You will see me later, in my cabin," he said in a very low voice. "You and I need to talk." And he swept past, leaving me to wonder what in the world he wanted.

I needed Jinniyah. She had wandered off near the base of the *Santa María*, probably to get a better look at the ships. I tramped up to her and said, "How did you do it?"

Jinniyah was busy twirling locks of her frizzy black hair around her fingers, clearly entertained by the novelty of appearing human. "Do what?"

I lowered my voice so no one would hear. "Make me able to translate all that stuff! I mean, Latin's all right. Italian, *maybe*. But Aramaic? I've never even *seen* it before, let alone read it! But you saw. I understood it. I . . . I . . ."

The old-adult look resurfaced on the little boy's face. "You're scared, aren't you?" Jinniyah said. "Well, don't be! You're a Storyteller. You take the stories and make them real. But first you have to read the stories. It only makes sense that you'd be able to understand other languages. I thought you knew that."

"I didn't."

"That's why Storytellers are called lukmani, after the sage Luqman. He was so wise, he was able to speak with anyone and anything—even the flowers and the trees and the earth!"

"You're saying I can speak with flowers and trees?"

"No, silly! But you can speak with people! Remember those two men who were talking about the Horn of Africa before? They were speaking English, Bal! Do you speak English?"

"No." Not before today, anyway. Nearby, one of the two tow-headed men by the *Santa María*'s gangway was telling a joke to the other, something about the promiscuity of Andalusian women. But the real punchline was that I could understand every single word.

"Anyway, Amir could do it, so I figured you could too," Jinniyah said, and she gave me a warm smile.

I returned it. "Thanks, Jinni." While I didn't always understand the girl, now I owed her big-time.

"You're very welcome! And remember this the next time I tell you to trust me."

"I do trust you."

"Then promise when we get to Cathay we'll look for Amir."

I groaned. This again?

The girl shoved her hands onto her hips. "No, Bal! This is important! We have to stop that evil being the Baba Yaga told us about, and we need to find Amir to do it. I don't know why you hate him so much—"

"I don't," I said, not really believing the words.

"—but when I say Amir's a good person, I mean it! He's a hero! When you were younger, you must have wanted to meet your father. Both your parents. Didn't you?"

I turned away from her. "More than anything. But I thought they were different people. I thought they were—"

"No! No more buts! You said you trusted me. Now tell me the truth! Do you mean it or not?"

So I considered her, the skinny sort-of-boy standing in front of me. It was hard not to think of her as a child, with that undeveloped body and those huge shiny eyes. But I did trust her, and she'd been around far longer than I had. If it weren't for her, I would probably never get out of Spain alive. She was right about the Baba Yaga, and she was right about my being a translator.

Maybe she was right about Amir al-Katib too. She said the man was a hero, and so did the Baba Yaga. And Diego. So what if . . .

118

It was an uncomfortable thought, but it kept coming back no matter how hard I tried to shake it. What if they were right? What if Amir al-Katib wasn't the bloodthirsty Moor I had taken him for? When I was a child, my friends always called him a villain. But what if they were wrong? What if my parents really were heroes, like my uncle said they were? And when Father Joaquín said the Moors were all devils, what if he was wrong about them, too?

I took a breath, feeling the beginnings of something—maybe confidence, maybe destiny—burning within me. As I looked out over the mighty Atlantic I thought I could see the outlines of a new future forming on the horizon, a future where I was a hero like the Baba Yaga said, with my legendary father standing beside me. A shadowy figure, a monster bent on destroying the world, would rear up above us, baring its terrible claws. But we'd strike it down, my father and I, and start a new life on the other side of the world.

"What do you say, Bal?" Jinniyah said. "We'll find him, won't we?"

I took her hand. "Of course we will."

She leaped up and rung me around the neck with a hug. "Oh, Bal! You mean it?"

I laughed. Oh, what had I gotten myself into?

"And one more thing." I opened my bag, pulled out Jinniyah's necklace, and held it out to her. "You can have it."

Jinniyah bit her lip and said, "You mean you're not going to trap me in there anymore?"

"It means I trust you. From now on you only have to go in that necklace when you want to. We're a team now. Equals."

Jinniyah's growing smile could barely contain her joy. She put the necklace around her neck and tucked it into her shirt so no one could see it. "Of course we're a team!" She hopped up and smothered me with another hug. "We're the best team in the world!"

Laughing, I led her up the gangplank to the *Santa María*. "No time to dawdle, Luis!" Antonio said, coming up behind me. He was grinning like a fool—most likely he had received his bonus. "On the deck, sailor! Time for us to make history!"

I stopped on the gangplank to take one last look at my home. Palos, the village by the sea. Palos, the place where I was born.

Good-bye, Diego, I thought. *Serena.* I would make them proud. I took a deep breath of salty air and raised my head to the sky. Above me, pink clouds were flowering in the purpling dawn. Today would be a good day to sail.

Before I knew it the anchors were raised and we were departing. Men shouted from ship to ship as gulls sang over their cries. Soon Palos was nothing more than a blurry apparition in the morning haze. The sea came up to greet us, a blanket of endless watery sky.

A voice drifted up beside me. "Uqba," it said, and it was a moment before I realized it was Jinniyah. Her voice sounded lower than usual, solemn. "He was a warrior who traveled farther than any living man, until finally he reached the seas on the western shore. He said, 'Allah, if it were not for thine ocean, in thy holy name I would conquer the earth.'"

Before us the seas spread themselves into the horizon, waiting to be conquered.

Part Two

THE ATLANTIC OCEAN

Nine

THE SPY

The open sea. From my spot on the deck of the *Santa María*, I could see why people used to think you could sail off the edge of it. The way that sparkling blue seemed to go on forever, you had to convince yourself that it would end somewhere or you would quickly go insane.

Taking a breath of sea air, I rested back against the starboard rail and held my gurgling stomach. Jinniyah and the other boys had gathered up on the forecastle next to me, waiting for Juan de la Cosa to assign them their duties. Six weeks, I thought. That's what Antonio had told me. Six weeks of living on this ship and we would land in Cathay.

All right. Six weeks I could handle. The heroes in the old stories always went on journeys, always endured some minor trials before they got their happy endings. I could deal with six weeks of that if it meant getting my own holy grail. In six weeks Jinniyah and I would build new lives in the Orient, far away from the Malleus Maleficarum. In six weeks we would be free again.

I contemplated this happy future, letting the sounds of a nautical life wash over me. There was the creaking of the bow, the flaps of the sails, the ever-present *swish* of the ocean. Suddenly a gust of wind sent the deck pitching underneath me, and I heard a very different sound, a strangled voice braying, *"Look out!"*

I raised my head just in time to see a gawky figure flying at me headfirst. The man crashed into me with about as much force as a cannonball, and I went stumbling backward into the rail. In fact, if I hadn't shifted my weight just in time, I might have tumbled overboard. That sea, that sea, that infinite, sparkling sea . . .

One wrong move, and it might have been my graveyard.

"Ay, cielos. Are you all right?" said the man who had crashed into me. It was Rodrigo Sanchez, the accountant who had annoyed Martín Pinzón back in Palos. Rodrigo's hands were currently half-hidden under his lank brown bangs. He held his heart-shaped head and waited for the world to settle around him. "I almost killed you there, didn't I?"

I gulped down another breath but said, "Don't worry about it."

The accountant squeezed one of my hands tightly with both of his. "Well, you have my deepest apologies! I'm still very much the landlubber, I'm sorry to say. Walking across a deck isn't easy, especially when the ship is swaying to and fro. And those rails! They're here to make you feel safe, but it's really easy to fall over one. I did it myself, back when we were still moored. Dislocated both of my shoulders." The accountant fell silent for a moment, lost in the memory. I stood there awkwardly, unsure how to respond. "I'm Rodrigo Sanchez, by the way. Her Majesty's inspector and controller."

"Luis de Torres," I said, massaging the knuckles of my crushed hand.

"Oh, I know! The new interpreter! Everyone's been talking about you, how you translated those documents on the pier. They're saying you're a miracle, Luis. An absolute miracle!"

An image of Diego and Serena flashed across my mind—eyes glassy and blood dripping from their sides. They wouldn't say I was a miracle, if they were here now. A miracle? A curse was more like it.

"Do you know what the men are calling you, Luis? 'Martín Pinzón's Miraculous Jew!' Pretty nice, don't you think?"

"Yes," I said, feeling suddenly exhausted. "Yes, that's just great."

Rodrigo jumped a little. "Ah, I was supposed to bring you to the cabin, wasn't I? The admiral wanted to see you."

I forced myself to gulp down my worsening nausea. *You and I need to talk,* the admiral had said back in Palos—and it didn't sound like a friendly suggestion.

But it wasn't like I had a choice in the matter. "This way, Luis," Rodrigo said, so I adjusted the strap of my bag over my chest and followed him across the heaving deck toward the aftcastle.

We found Colón standing outside the cabin door, appearing

taller than I remembered him, and broader. While I continually had to shift my weight to keep balance on the deck, Colón seemed completely still, as if his boots were attached to the *Santa María*. Steps away from him stood a very young tawny-haired noble, speaking to him in a clipped but cultured tone.

"It was my father's idea to bring him along, actually. Captain Pinzón said it wouldn't be a problem. After all, we wouldn't want to be without him if any rodents happened to stow their way aboard."

For an instant I thought the boy was talking about me and Jinniyah. Colón directed his attention to a spot not far from his boots. "I must admit this is a first," he said. "I've never had the privilege of traveling with a cat."

In fact not far from the admiral plopped a large, golden-eyed tomcat, who seemed to be wearing the same condescending expression as his tawny-haired owner.

The admiral went on, "But when I said I was glad your father changed his mind, I wasn't talking about your feline companion. I was talking about you, Don Terreros. Back in Granada, the count didn't seem too eager to send his only son on a voyage to Cathay."

The young nobleman was inspecting his fingernails. "My father had hoped that I would honor his good name by winning a victory on the field of battle. Unfortunately our kingdom is at peace for the moment, so the Terreros name will have to win glory on the seas."

The sound of the name made Rodrigo's muscles jolt within his skin. "Did you say 'Terreros'?" the accountant interrupted. "But you couldn't be one of the Terreroses from Burgos?"

That made the tawny-haired noble look up from his fingernails. "I am," the boy said guardedly.

Rodrigo swooped in and shook the young man's hand as if using it to paint the side of a barn. "Why, this is an honor! You must allow me to congratulate you, Don Terreros. I just heard about your sister! To win a betrothal to the Duke of Alba's son—why, your family must feel so honored!"

Don Terreros's face went bright scarlet. "I'm sorry, Señor . . . ?"

"Rodrigo Sanchez of Segovia." The accountant arched his lanky body over the deck in a stiff bow. "I am Her Majesty's inspector and—"

"Yes, Señor Sanchez, and where, exactly, did you obtain the information about my sister's impending nuptials?"

Rodrigo's raised fingers twiddled away the question. "Oh, it's about the biggest news in Segovia these days. Everyone's talking about it. Everyone." Rodrigo's hand then snapped up to his mouth. "Oh. It wasn't supposed to be a secret, was it?"

I didn't think it was possible, but Don Terreros's face seemed to grow even redder at that question. Obviously the news of his sister's betrothal *was* supposed to be a secret.

"I must applaud your rumormongers, Señor Sanchez!" the boy said shrilly. "I did not realize how quickly news travels these days. At this rate I am certain by the end of the month the Khan of Cathay will know all about my family's private affairs! And it will be thanks to you, Señor Sanchez! Thanks to you, the ever-noble accountant!"

Rodrigo blanched at the outburst and even seemed to cower a bit. Terreros, though muscular, was not all that large, but I'd no doubt he could re-dislocate Rodrigo's spindly arms out of sheer ferocity.

Fortunately Colón stepped between them. "Have you met Luis yet, Pedro?" Colón said, giving Rodrigo the opportunity to scurry away. "Luis, let me introduce Pedro Terreros, our ship's cabin boy."

Ah, so that's where I'd heard the name Terreros before! This was the person Martín mentioned back in Palos, the one with the unpleasant family who had beaten me to the cabin boy job.

"Pedro," Colón went on, "Luis here is our new interpreter. Our very gifted new interpreter, I should say."

I inadvertently snorted at the statement. Gifted? I'd been called a lot of things in my life: coward, lukmani, Marrano. But gifted? I'd never been called that before, and never by an admiral either. Grinning dopily at the compliment, I put my hand in front of Pedro Terreros. "Pleased to make your acquaintance."

"A pleasure." Pedro took my hand and gave me a good look-over, and I returned the favor. Pedro's athletic figure was overburdened by fineries of all kinds: an emerald clasp held a black sable-lined cape in place over one shoulder; underneath it, I saw a brocaded ochre jerkin covering a doublet of patterned forest green silk. Yes, Pedro was a nobleman if ever there was one. Or at least a nobleboy. He seemed about my age, maybe fifteen at the most. Not one curl of his tawny hair was out of place under his smart brimless hat. His delicate features, offset by thick eyebrows and a severe chin, were growing more and more crinkled by the second. He appeared to have smelled something particularly acrid—and that something, I could easily guess, was me.

"He is quite young, is he not?" Pedro said to the admiral.

"As are you," Colón pointed out.

"I meant for an interpreter." From the haughty way Terreros spoke to the admiral, it seemed Terreros held the senior position.

"Perhaps. But Luis here is a marvel. He can translate anything put in front of him: Italian, Portuguese. Even Aramaic and Turkish. The crew's taken to calling him 'The Miraculous Jew.' Isn't that right, Luis?"

"Yes, sir," I said, still grinning at Colón's compliment. For all the pain it had brought me, this Storytelling business was turning out to have its perks.

Pedro Terreros was not as impressed with me as I was with myself, however. The red-faced noble ran his gaze up and down my body once more. "But Admiral, this is absurd! This voyage is far too important to place in the hands of a child!"

In a patient tone Colón said, "What would you suggest I do, Don Terreros?"

"Return to Palos. We can find a new translator there—an educated translator. What you do with this . . . *boy* is up to your discretion."

As Pedro spoke I remained silent, examining Colón's face for a clue of my fate. If Pedro's father really was a count, he was probably funding this voyage. No, I was thinking small. For all I knew the Terreroses were related to royalty! If it came down to a choice between me and some royal, it was obvious how Colón would choose.

Or maybe not. Colón put on a fatherly tone and said, "I appreciate your suggestions, Pedro. But I cannot in good conscience abandon any member of our crew. Please trust me when I say I am certain Luis will live up to your high expectations. And who knows? I have a feeling that once you and Luis get to know each other, you two will become fast friends. But right now you must excuse me. I must see Luis in my office."

And like that the conversation was over. Having asserted his authority, Colón entered his quarters, leaving his cabin boy to sputter outside on his own. Smiling, I turned to follow the man inside. A hand clasped around my upper arm from behind.

"You stay away from me," Pedro breathed into my ear. He roughly released my arm, sending me tripping into the cabin's outer wall. "And watch your step."

Pedro's threats didn't worry me very much. If dealing with him was the extent of my heroic trials, this journey was going to be easier than I'd thought. I was sure I'd win him over to my side sooner or later. If six weeks of my dumb jokes and stories didn't turn him into a friend, well, that was his problem, not mine.

I entered the admiral's cabin, a cramped, dim room with only two meager portholes—one in the door, and one in the back behind the admiral's desk. The desk itself was a sight to see, not due to its workmanship, but because of the mess of papers that spilled over it. The papers were an expensive luxury, and the bed behind that desk was, too. The rest of the men on this ship would sleep out on the deck in rain or shine.

"Have a seat," Colón said, gesturing to the chair across from him. A long-barreled gun sat on that chair—an arquebus, I later learned it was called. I moved it to the bed and sat in the now-empty place, listening to the *Santa María*'s bow creak below and beside us.

For a while Colón and I regarded each other in silence. The man was much whiter than anyone I'd seen on deck, and quite sunburned in places from the noonday sun. His bushy gray mane was streaked with the remains of a more youthful strawberry blond—not a particularly Spanish color, to be sure—and many of the papers on his desk had mysterious symbols scribbled in the margins. No wonder the crew questioned the admiral's origins. Colón was like no man I'd ever seen before.

"So," the admiral said at last. "'Martín Pinzón's Miraculous Jew.'" Colón picked up a nearby quill and rolled it between his fingers. "At least, that's what that fool thinks you are. Yes, I said, 'fool.' Oh, Pinzón's an able captain, to be sure"—the way Colón grimaced suggested that this was a main point of contention between the two—"but he cannot see past his sails and his tables to the truth. That you are what the stories speak of. A lukmani."

I caught my breath at the word.

"Yes, I know what you are," the admiral said, eyes twinkling. "There was talk that your kind did battle in Granada, and although I did not see them for myself, I know it is God's truth. And that you, who can understand any language, are one of them. Tell me I am mistaken." The admiral's pale blue eyes bored into me, reading me as if I were one of his papers. "Do not lie to me, de Torres. I swear I will not harm you."

I don't know why, but I believed him when he said it. It could have been the way he held himself or the calm power of his voice. It could have been the way he never seemed to blink. But whatever the reason I trusted this man. There was something straightforward about him, something strong. Maybe Martín was right. Maybe Colón's calculations *were* incorrect. Maybe we'd all starve to death before we reached Cathay. But right now, if I had to believe one man over the other, I'd choose the one sitting in front of me without question. I would bet this man could get us to the Indies by force of will alone.

So I said, "You're right, Admiral. I am a Storyteller."

Colón clasped his hands together on his desk. "I appreciate your honesty. And I will not lie to you, either. So let me be upfront. I would not have chosen to have a sorcerer on my ship. I am a Christian, and some say the lukmani do the work of the Devil."

I cast my eyes down at his papers. Until now I'd not had time to consider where my Storytelling abilities had come from, but it was common knowledge that witches got their powers from Satan. Everyone knew witches traded their souls and any chance at happiness in the afterlife in order to lay curses on their enemies—or summon demons from the underworld. The sight of Colón's papers lying before me filled me with unease. Castilian, Portuguese, Aragonese, Latin: I was able to read them all.

It reminded me of a story Father Joaquín used to tell when I was a boy. In ancient times the people of the world could speak the same language, and they joined together to build a tower that would reach up to Heaven. The Lord, seeing this as arrogance, destroyed their tower and made it so they were unable to understand one another's tongues. The moral of the story, the priest said, was this: The people of the world were not meant to understand one another.

But I could. I could understand them all. Maybe Colón was right about me. Maybe I had sold my soul for these powers.

Colón must have noticed how upset I was, because his

normally-steely voice turned gentle. "My apologies, Luis. I should not have said that. Where your powers come from makes no difference to me. Now that you are here I wish to keep you. When we reach the Indies I will have need for an interpreter, and a lukmani will be a certain boon for us.

"But if you will remain on this ship, you must do two things for me. First I would know what your business is here. It is clear you are no sailor, so that means one of two things. Either you are running to something, or you are running from something. So which is it?"

The answer, of course, was both. "I'm looking for someone," I mumbled. "I'm trying to find my father."

Colón's clasped fingers relaxed noticeably at the answer. "As for the second thing: You must make me a promise. You must vow to keep yourself secret from the men. You must not use your magic. No one is to know you are a lukmani. Not the Pinzón brothers, not your friend Antonio de Cuellar. No one. Do you understand? Should someone learn of your powers, it will spell doom for this mission."

I couldn't help but fidget under the word "doom." It sounded like another of the Baba Yaga's prophecies. "May I ask why, sir?" I said.

Colón walked to the porthole in the door to size up his men. "They are good men, Luis. Sturdy. Strong. But they are not educated men like us. They are simple people, who live not by God's word but by the dark whisperings of superstition.

And they will fear your powers. I've no doubt they will mutiny if they know of them."

I stretched my neck to get a better look out the window. There was the carpenter Antonio de Cuellar, joking with some of his sailor friends. Uneducated? Maybe. But I would hardly call him "simple."

All the same I said, "I won't tell them, Admiral. You have my word."

"Good," Colón said, and he smiled a real smile. "I think we'll get along fine, you and I. Something about you. It reminds me of my son."

The conversation apparently over, I got up to leave. But before I could reach for the cabin door the admiral's voice rose up hesitantly. "There was one more thing I was meaning to tell you, Luis. Have you ever heard the term 'Malleus Maleficarum'?"

I stopped reaching for the door and brought my hand back to my side. "I see that you have," Colón went on. "Back in Spain your Queen Isabel told me she was concerned that we might run across lukmani over the course of our travels. Officially the Malleus Maleficarum is not supposed to exist. But your queen intimated that she might send a man from that organization on this voyage to report on magic use abroad."

My inquisitor's lizard teeth glinted at me in my memory, and the heretic's fork in his hand. *You think you've won, lukmani! But we will find you! We will find you!*

"I do not want to worry you unnecessarily," Colón said, "but there may be a spy on this ship. I thought perhaps you should know."

I looked back out the cabin window. Outside, dozens of sailors were ambling across the deck, ready to begin their watch. How many men lived on this ship now? More than forty, if I had to guess, and nearly forty more on the *Niña* and *Pinta* combined. That made eighty men. Eighty men who could be my assassin.

"Thank you, sir," I said, and I left the cabin with eyes unfocused. The Malleus Maleficarum. They were here, waiting to capture me and punish me for my sins. The shadow of the mainsail fell coldly over me, and I looked up to see Pedro Terreros resting against the ship's rail. He tilted back his head, and his brown eyes flashed red in the summer sun. Then my body started shaking from top to bottom, and there was nothing I could do to stop it.

Ten

TITIVILLUS

"What?!"

Jinniyah and I had locked ourselves down in the damp, creaky hold, having come here so she could pray in privacy before dinner. Tons of supplies had been stuffed within the room's bowed walls: barrels of water, crates of trade goods, a hodgepodge of plain-sheathed swords. Off to one side a thick ladder, eroded in places by years of climbing hands and heavy boots, led up to the hatch that opened out onto the main deck. Jinniyah and I had been sitting here, legs dangling over one of the hold's stale-smelling barrels, when I'd made the mistake of revealing what Colón said to me in the cabin.

"There's a *spy*?!" Jinniyah exclaimed, and she flew up and around me so she could shove me off my barrel. "Well, that settles it! You're going to learn to be a Storyteller. Right now."

I waved her away with a halfhearted swat, then picked at my half-eaten bowl of lentils with a piece of hardtack. Of course Jinniyah would demand I learn magic now, mere hours after

I'd sworn to Colón that I wouldn't. Even more importantly, I had promised myself.

"But you have to learn to protect yourself!" Jinniyah insisted. "Go on. Make a creature—quick, quick!"

Her words barely registered. I was still lost in an ancient world of collapsing towers. "You heard what I said at the Baba Yaga's. I'm not interested in being a Storyteller."

"Why not?" Jinniyah said, and I found I couldn't answer. Why not? Because Colón was right, that was why not. Because sorcerers were evil beings who got their powers from the Devil. No, I hadn't actually made any pacts with Satan, to the best of my knowledge, but that didn't mean that my powers weren't demonic, somehow.

Why not, indeed. "Come on, Jinni. Haven't you read the Bible?"

Jinniyah crossed her arms and looked down on me, her eyes mildly scolding. "Oh, right," I muttered. Jinniyah was a Moor—a fact I had to constantly remind myself of.

I pointed my piece of hardtack at the girl. "Well, I'm sure it says the same thing in *your* Bible. Doing magic is a sin, and I'm not going to do it."

Jinniyah glided closer to me and plucked a hair out of my head. "But *I'm* magic," she said with a tone of mischief. "Do you think *I'm* a sin?"

I rubbed my head. "That's completely different."

"Exactly the same," Jinniyah all but sang. "Lots of people

140

think genies are evil, you know. They say we're all sinners, that we're demons, blah, blah, blah. But we're not! At least, not all of us. It's the same thing with Storytellers. Storytelling can be good or bad, depending on how you use it."

I shrugged, and the girl glided onto my barrel. "I'm sorry, Bal," she said more quietly, "but you don't have time to waste! The Malleus Maleficarum is here, and they're coming after you whether you like it or not. You have to learn how to defend yourself against them! Or would you rather die?"

It's funny to say so, but I didn't know how to answer that question. Would I rather die than go against my religion? Yes, I decided. Yes, of course I'd rather die! I would be a martyr like Jeanne d'Arc, like Saint Stephen—hell, like Jesus Christ himself! I would . . .

I would . . .

I sighed. Who was I kidding? "All right. What do I have to do?"

Jinniyah crossed her legs in front of her, grinning one of her lupine grins. "Well, first you need to think of a story."

A story. For some reason, the first one that popped into my head was a fairy tale my aunt had told me when I was young. "There's always the story of the unicorn, I guess."

"Ooh, what's that?"

"A kind of white horse with a horn growing on its head."

"Like a karkadann," Jinniyah said. "It has a horn on its head too. But it's not a horse—more like a mix between a lion and a rhinoceros. And also it eats people!"

As usual, she sounded a little too excited when she said that. I made a face and went on, "The unicorn doesn't do that. And it only lets girls ride it for some reason."

"Same as the karkadann! Only A'isha, the prettiest and purest of the Prophet's wives, was able to charm the karkadann with a magic flute. Then she was able to ride it over the countryside and all the way to India!"

I raised my eyebrows. Maybe my unicorn and her karkadann weren't that different after all. "Actually, summoning a unicorn is probably a bad idea." Leaving my bowl of lentils on my barrel, I stood and knocked on the hold's nearest wall. "There isn't much room in here. Not enough for a horse, anyway."

"Then make something smaller. There are other stories out there, you know."

True. I lifted my eyes up at the ceiling, rifling through the mess of stories Diego had deposited in my head over the course of my lifetime. Hmm. The golem was too big, and so was the Behemoth. The hameh was much smaller—only the size of a hawk or eagle. But the thought of it made me shiver against my will and think of Moors and revenge, all the aspects of Amir al-Katib I didn't want to consider.

So I said, "I guess there's always Titivillus."

Jinniyah sat up straighter at the word. "What's that?"

"He's an imp who makes you mess up when you're copying down a text."

The girl crinkled her nose at the thought. "That's tricky.

What if all the books people read are all messed up? Like the history books! Or the stuff Admiral Colón writes down so the boats go in the right direction?"

Ready to one-up her I said, "You think that's bad? Most scribes are clerics. What if Titivillus messed up the Bible?"

Jinniyah covered her head and ears to block out the idea. "Or the Qur'an! I don't even want to think about that! Tricky, tricky beast!"

"You mean like you?"

"Never!"

Feeling tricky myself, I paced around the hold. "How about I summon him? Then we'll see who's trickier."

I closed my eyes and tried to picture an imp causing mayhem in a scribe's workshop. I rubbed my hands together and said, "Come out, Titivillus."

I waited for a moment, and then a moment more. But there was nothing. I opened my eyes.

"I have no idea what I'm doing."

Jinniyah flew off her barrel and around me. "How did you do it the first time?"

Distracted, I combed back my bangs with my fingers. "I was down in the crypt in the monastery. I was thinking about my Uncle Diego. I can't explain. It was a certain state of mind. I was thinking about the story of the golem, but I wasn't only thinking about the story. It was like I was thinking about the meaning of it too . . ."

I wasn't making any sense, I knew that. Then all at once

half-a-dozen thoughts flashed before me:

Diego telling me about Titivillus for the first time when I accidentally skipped a line in my first transcription.

Father Joaquín reading his sermon every Sunday from a Bible a tricky demon might have rewritten.

Colón's crisp notes on the papers on his desk, written in half-words and knotted sentences that only he could understand.

How maybe a scribe writing a history about this first voyage around the globe would base it on that jumble of notes.

And how Titivillus could mess up that story too, so that every historian from now until the end of time would make his apprentices memorize things that weren't true, things that never really happened.

And then came the thought that unsettled me the most: that everything I'd ever read could have been invented, a demon's joke—and that I'd never be able to parse out what was true from what wasn't.

I opened my eyes. Before them an invisible quill wrote over the air in impossibly dark ink the word TITIVILLUS. We heard a crash like that of glass or ceramic, and Jinniyah and I jumped backward. A black figure about a foot high burst through the lettering and tumbled to the floor near our feet. It scampered up a nearby barrel and cocked its head at us.

The thing was all points, black and skinny, with white slits for eyes. It looked like it had been made out of the strokes of a brush, each of which tapered off at the ends. Something about the creature recalled my old priest, Father Joaquín, but before

I could figure out what it was, the creature came at us with claws outstretched. The motion was so sudden that I ducked, and Jinniyah poofed back into her true genie form before she could help herself.

Titivillus landed on the floor by our feet and cackled at us.

"I did it, I guess," I said, rising from my crouch. Titivillus bared his claws at Jinni, who squeaked and jumped up in the air. "What are you so scared for? He's kind of cute."

"He looks like you," Jinniyah said as she circled above me. And maybe she was right. Although my first thought had been of my old priest, I saw my own long face mirrored in the Titivillus's.

And like Titivillus, I loved to play with words . . .

"I have an idea," I said. "Wait here."

"With him?" Jinniyah said, scrunching her nose up at Titivillus.

"I really don't think he's going to hurt you. He looks scary, but he's just a trickster—he only plays with words. Just make sure he doesn't go upstairs."

I climbed up to the main deck and sneaked into Colón's empty cabin, where I filched one of the millions of papers covering his bed. I folded it so it could fit into the bag on my belt and sneaked back down to the hold before anyone could notice.

I jumped off the hold's ladder and knelt so I could flatten the page I had stolen across the floor. From the top of the barrel he was perching on, Titivillus looked at me inquisitively.

Jinniyah floated down next to me so she could better see my paper. "What are you doing?"

"Just watch." I nodded up at Titivillus. "The story says you ruin scribes' work. Go on. Show us what you can do."

Titivillus skittered down his barrel and over to me and Jinni, his sharp fingers ticking against the floor as he went. On all fours he sniffed at the paper with his pointed face, circling the page like a dog searching for a bone. Finally he jumped up, cackled, and clicked one of his fingers against a phrase on the paper. I knelt closer to the page. The imp was pointing at the words ALMIRANTE COLÓN—Admiral Colón. The imp put his hands against the letters and—yes, I'm saying this right— lifted the words off the paper.

Titivillus mashed the letters together with his angled claws and spread them across the air as if they were a pack of Baba Yaga's prophetic cards. With a sharp finger he tapped the tip of his chin. Then he thinned the L in COLÓN into an I and dealt the letters, one at a time, in the air before us. Now Jinniyah and I could see that ALMIRANTE COLÓN had become ALMIRANTE, ICONO.

"'Admiral, icon,'" I read aloud. "That sounds right. When Colón gets back from Cathay, he'll definitely be an icon. He'll be rich—probably famous, too."

But Titivillus wasn't finished yet. He reformed the I into an L, re-mashed together the letters of Colón's name, and re- placed them in the air. Before we knew it ALMIRANTE, ICONO had become COLÓN LA MENTIRA.

"Colón the lie," I read to Jinniyah, not sure what to make of it. I looked over at the girl and said, "Want to try one?"

Jinniyah bent closer to the stolen paper. "Hmm. Why don't we try . . . this one?" She pointed at the words PEDRO TER-REROS. Titivillus cackled voicelessly at the choice and juggled the letters of the name. He spread the letters across the air twice. First they read PRESO DE TERROR—"prisoner of fear." Next they read, PERDERE ROSTRO.

"'I will lose a face'?" I read, not understanding.

Jinniyah pouted. "But that doesn't make sense!"

Titivillus just stuck his tongue out at her.

"One more," I said to the imp, and I mulled over the admiral's paper. "Here, Titivillus. Do this one."

I pointed at the words SANTA MARÍA. The imp galloped over on all fours. This time, he studied the letters much more carefully. At last he picked up the letters and spread them across the air with one hand. The imp looked at me somberly, standing under the words MATARÁN ASÍ.

"What does it mean?" I asked him. "It says, 'They will kill this way.' What does it mean? Who are 'they'?"

But Titivillus had no voice to answer. He hid behind one of the hold's barrels and only peeked out at intervals.

"I guess we're done," I said, puzzling over the words in front of me.

"See? You did it!" Jinniyah said brightly. "Now you know how to summon creatures."

I leaned back against the barrel behind me as the words

MATARÁN ASÍ faded from view. "I guess I am getting the hang of this Storytelling business. You have to think differently to do it. Deeper, almost . . ." Then I looked up and snapped, "Hey, stop that!"

While I was busy talking, Titivillus had made his way back to Colón's paper and was picking up more words from the page and flinging them in random directions. Splotches of ink were staining the hold's walls, mislabeling barrels and boxes of supplies.

"Hey, stop!" I ordered Titivillus. I sprinted across the room to catch him before he caused any more damage. He was too fast. Colón's paper in hand, he scurried between two barrels and receded into the shadows.

"Would you come back here?" I lay on the floor to find him, only to see a glob of ink flying at my face. My hand shot up to my cheek, and when I removed it again I found my fingers completely covered in black. Laughing his voiceless laugh, Titivillus scurried up a barrel to admire his handiwork from above.

"Jinni, how do you get rid of this thing?" I begged, wiping the ink off my face with my sleeve.

Jinniyah was hovering near the ceiling to avoid being soiled with Titivillus's inky weaponry. "When Amir was done with a creature, he would always say 'I release you from my service.'"

I watched with horror as Titivillus hopped up the ladder rungs and pushed his tiny body against the hatch that led out onto the *Santa María*'s deck. "I release you from my service!" I cried. "Go back where you came from! Don't you dare open that door!"

I was relieved to hear Titivillus make a disappointed squeak. Leaving the hatch closed above him he stuck out his tongue, wrapped his hands around his knees, and vanished. Colón's paper, now mostly blank, dropped back to the hold's floor by my feet.

I flopped down next to it and caught my breath. "Remind me never to summon *him* again," I said.

"You never know, Bal," Jinni said as she floated down beside me. "Maybe when we find Amir, Titivillus will help you fight that evil power the Baba Yaga told us about!"

I wiped some more ink off my face and frowned down at my blackened hand. "I think I'll learn some better stories first."

HAMEH

Heretical or not, conjuring Titivillus gave me a sense of power, a sense of pride. Let the Malleus Maleficarum come, I thought. If they called me a sinner, so be it. I felt with every muscle in my body that the Almighty had made me to do this. Why would He make me feel that way if he didn't want me using magic at all?

Unless it was some kind of test.

I ignored the thought and spent every free moment sneaking down to the hold to practice my new skills. First I worked on summoning Titivillus over and over, trying each time to summon him more quickly. When I'd finally gotten the hang of it, I moved on to the story of El Cid, the ever-honorable Castilian hero who brought down entire armies of Moors. But when the summoned man saw me and the color of my skin, he pulled out his sword and honorably swung it at my head. Luckily I was able to send him away before he decapitated me, and I shakily vowed that I would never summon him again.

About a week into our journey I thought I might try something harder, so when Jinni was busy with her chores I sneaked downstairs to summon a real genie. I'd hoped I could wish our way to the Orient or, even better, wish my aunt and uncle back to life. But when the black spirit of fire finally appeared before me, he crossed his huge arms over his chest and shook his head at each of my wishes. An hour of wishing later, I released the good-for-nothing from my service, and I climbed out of the hold miserably disappointed.

The next day I tried to summon two creatures at the same time, but this was another power that was beyond my ability. Summoning just one story was difficult enough for me, and keeping two stories in my head at once was, for the moment, impossible.

Then one day after Storytelling I emerged onto the main deck, only to see Admiral Colón glaring at me from up on the aftcastle. *You swore you would not use your powers*, his glare seemed to say. I pretended not to see him and ran off with my heart pounding. For the rest of the afternoon I hid down in the hold where I re-swore my old oath: I would not use my magic again until we reached the Indies, not until I was far away from Colón and the Malleus spy.

Being stuck on a ship without being able to use magic soon became mind-numbing, so I decided to spend my days helping Jinniyah and the other servants with their chores. We made stews, checked knots, caught fish off the side of the boat. The deck was in constant need of sweeping; occasionally we took latitude off the stars. It was a tiring life under the brutal autumn sun, but at least it kept my mind off the Malleus Maleficarum.

And it wasn't all sunburns and backbreaking labor. Every night at supper, Jinniyah and I would sit with Antonio de Cuellar and his friends, who were quickly becoming our friends too. We'd laugh together over our hardtack and salted cod, listening to Martín Pinzón argue with Colón in the cabin while Diego Salcedo strummed his guitar.

Later at night we'd sing bawdy songs and tell stories from home, trying to forget how much we missed Spain and its women. The snub-nosed Pérez would regale us with tales of his crazy wife, and Bartolome spoke in a hushed tone about the girl he wrote letters to while in prison. I, of course, was not one to waste an opportunity to spin my own yarns: "So there was this flower girl, Dirty Mary, that I used to know back in Palos . . ."

The men listened raptly as I described the girl's increasingly debauched deeds, and before long they were guffawing and hooting at my descriptions of her. "Oh, I wish I had a girl like her back home," Antonio said with a far-off look in his eyes. He extended his arm around Jinniyah, and led her around the deck in a kind of two-person jig. "I'd dance with that Dirty Mary until we could barely feel our feet. Then I'd take her home and water her flowers, if you know what I mean!"

Everyone laughed, and Salcedo strummed his guitar louder,

and before long most of the crew had joined in with Antonio's dance. Even the sailors who were on duty were singing along and clapping their hands like castanets. The only one who wouldn't join in the fun was Pedro Terreros, but I supposed he was too sophisticated to enjoy such a low-class dance.

Nevertheless I jigged over to Colón's cabin boy and said, "You don't have to sit alone all the time, you know. Come join us." The boy glared at me, scooped up his cat, and strutted away.

Work, prayers, supper, stories. It was the same, day after scorching day. Then finally one night I realized six weeks had passed, and we'd arrive in the Orient any day now. I found a place on the deck next to the already-snoozing Jinniyah and watched the clouds slide through the misty night above us. For the first time in a month and a half, I felt safe. Soon my new friends and I would arrive in the Indies, and the Malleus spy still hadn't materialized. Colón, I decided, had been mistaken all along. I pulled my hat over my face and nestled back against the ship's rail, ready to get a good night's sleep.

"Looks like a bird to me."

"Probably just a seagull."

"Seagull? A harpy, more like."

I pushed my hat back on my head and opened my eyes. A group of my crew-mates had gathered not far from me, their necks craned up so they could watch the midnight sky.

"I'll get Colón," Antonio's friend Pérez said. "He'll want to

153

write it down in that damn log of his."

"Forget Colón. Get Sanchez." Salcedo brushed his fingers lightly across his guitar strings. "He'll tell you how much it costs and report it back to the queen."

As the sailors around him dissolved into laughter, I shielded my eyes and looked up at the sky. But I could see nothing up there—no bird, no harpy. Just clouds and darkness and a hidden moon.

Suddenly an awful scream pierced the night. That scream. I bolted to my feet.

The floor rumbled under my shoes as dozens of sailors stampeded across the deck, shouting.

"What was that noise?"

"I told you, it's a seagull!"

"A seagull! What kind of seagull sounds like that?"

Juan de la Cosa barged down the stairs of the aftcastle. "What in heaven's name is going on here? Why aren't you at your stations?"

Rodrigo Sanchez came up beside him, holding his knobby arms. "We saw something. In the sky. Some of the crew's saying it's a demon." Rodrigo's voice sounded thin and warbly, his laughter loud and brittle. "To tell you the truth, another scream like that and I might start to agree with them!"

Behind him Pedro Terreros hmphed, and Colón pursed his mouth with the same scorn. "Superstition on top of superstition," the admiral muttered. "No demons will come near these ships. This journey has been blessed by God Himself."

Another tattered shriek ripped across the sky, and I felt Jinniyah's fingernails digging into my forearm. "Bal, did you hear that? It's a . . . it's a . . ."

She couldn't say it, but I knew. I knew that cry. It was the same one I heard in my bedroom that night. Two yellow eyes in my window. The smell of incense and cinnamon.

"Uncle," I said. "You said you would tell me a true story. You said you would tell me about Amir al-Katib."

"I did, Baltasar."

Antonio de Cuellar barreled down the forecastle stairs and swung his tree trunk of an arm upward. "There she is!"

And there she was. The hameh: a ragged black hawk with a scimitar of a beak and piercing gold eyes surrounded by smoke. It loosed its horrendous shriek—the sound of women murdered in their beds or spirits clawing in vain as the earth swallowed them. It threw open its wings. Though the night was clear, its feathers were slick and shining, even from a distance.

My insides shook, and a jerky laugh escaped my mouth. "It's blood," I said, realizing.

A dozen heads snapped to look at me. Jinniyah tugged on my arm. "Luis, don't talk like that. It scares me."

I stared down at my fingers. Once they were stained black from a feather found on the steps of my uncle's workshop. At the time I'd thought it was ink on the feather. But it wasn't.

It was blood. Black blood.

"Look out!"

The full force of Jinniyah's slight body smashed into my side, and it was moments before I realized we were both on the floor.

"Sorry," Jinniyah said under her breath. Blood dribbled through her tunic where the hameh had buried its claws.

I opened my eyes wide. "Jinni!" I said, in my panic forgetting to call her by her false name.

"Bal, above you!" she cried.

I only had a fraction of a second to look with horror at the eyes of the hameh. Smoldering with some unknown fire, they aimed at me with unwavering hatred. That look told me everything. The hameh wasn't here for just anyone. It wasn't here for the crew. No.

It was here for me.

The bird sliced through the sky, lunging at its prey. I dived sideways and threw my arms across my face.

"Luis!"

A bone-crunching noise sounded over the din.

"Get away from him, you bastard!"

Loosing a muted squawk, the hameh reared up and shook its head against the blow. Behind it Antonio de Cuellar clenched his teeth as he finished the follow-through of his carpenter's hammer, now damp with black blood. "Go back where you came from, demon!"

The hameh flapped higher, crowing in defiance. Then the bird stopped in its place and cocked its head toward the southwest as if hearing a voiceless call. It reeled around and raced off into the western horizon, dripping a trail of bloody feathers behind it. Rodrigo Sanchez ran out of the admiral's cabin, Colón's arquebus in hand. He aimed the gun at the demon and fired—too little, too late.

"Are you all right, Luis?" Antonio asked me. I barely heard the question. I was staring down at the puddle right in front of me. Hameh. Cinnamon. Blood. Black blood.

A whimper broke me out of my stupor. Then I remembered. "Jinni!"

I rushed up to the ruined heap that was Jinniyah. Quickly I fumbled at her belt and servant's tunic toward the wounds those deadly talons had inflicted.

"No no no. Jinni. Come on. You can't leave me now."

From her place on the floor, Jinniyah gave me a sad smile. "Silly boy. Don't cry." She cringed to a seated position and motioned at her bloody side. "Look. I'm not even hurt."

I could hardly bring myself to look at her. But she was right. Under her tunic, under the drying black blood, Jinniyah's brown skin was as smooth and whole as ever.

Murmurs were beginning to buzz around me—angry, frightened murmurs. I looked around and found myself surrounded by the men of the *Santa María*. Colón and Juan de la Cosa broke into the circle. "It's over," the master-at-arms said.

"Now get some sleep. We've had enough excitement for one day."

"Sleep!" Bartolome exclaimed in his Portuguese accent. "How are we supposed to sleep when there's demons—"

Colón cut him off before he could finish. "That was no demon. It is a type of Oriental bird described in Marco Polo's writings of the Indies. It is called a black heron or somesuch. It is a good sign. It is a sign of land."

"Bullshit!" I heard Salcedo whisper.

Colón continued, "And if I hear the word 'demon' again, whoever says it will spend the remainder of the journey locked down in the hold. Do you understand?"

As the crowd broke out into new arguments, I noticed the *Pinta* and *Niña* sidling up beside the *Santa María*. Vicente probably wanted to see what the fuss was about, but I knew Martín would use the opportunity to pick another fight with Colón. Now was my chance to get away before anyone noticed, so I hooked my arm around Jinniyah's and brought her down into the hold.

It was pitch black down here, so Jinniyah briefly changed into her genie form so we could see each other under the eerie light of her fiery hair.

"Are you all right?" was the first thing I asked her.

"I'm fine," she said. "I told you."

I pushed one hand against the side of my forehead. "You scared the hell out of me."

"I know. I'm sorry. But I told you genies are hard to kill.

What was it he used to call me back then? 'Durable,' I think."

"Who?" I asked her, but the answer announced itself the moment I spoke the word.

Embarrassed, Jinniyah avoided my eyes. "Well, Amir, obviously."

We stood there a while without speaking. "That was his hameh, wasn't it? Amir's."

Jinniyah sat on a nearby crate and brought her knees up to her chin. "I think so."

My vision caught on my forearm. Under the black light of Jinniyah's fire, I could see maroon dots beading around three scratches the hameh had left above my wrist. My eyes locked on them, unable to look away.

I lifted my arm so Jinniyah could see the wound. "All right, Jinni," I said, very carefully. "Why does my father . . . why does Amir al-Katib want me dead?"

Twelve

LOST AT SEA

When a person first discovers that his father is trying to kill him, he will be overcome by a variety of emotions. First comes surprise—that one's only natural—which defers to anger, confusion, and fear.

But that night when I climbed up the ladder that led out of the *Santa María*'s hold, I found myself overtaken by a different emotion: vindication. This whole time I had been right about my father, while Jinni, Diego, and the Baba Yaga were dead wrong. If I was the hero of this story, Amir al-Katib was clearly the villain. I had known it in my gut from the first time I held his necklace.

As for what I was going to do when I confronted this villain . . . well, I hadn't made a decision about that yet.

Rodrigo Sanchez awaited me as I climbed out of the hold. Under the moonlight his face was pasty, and his neck seemed very long.

"The admiral wants to talk to you." Rodrigo's Adam's apple

bobbled in his neck. "He seems angry? I could be wrong."

Something told me he wasn't wrong about this. But Colón's anger was about the least of my worries, so I crossed the deck and entered the admiral's cabin. Colón's back faced me as he stood behind his desk staring out the porthole that pointed home.

"Tell me, Interpreter," Colón said into that porthole. "Have you ever heard the story of Job?"

"Yes, sir."

"Then tell it to me."

Although I didn't quite grasp the point of this exercise, I did as he ordered. "It's about Job, a Jew. He was the most righteous man in the world. God pointed him out to Lucifer and said, 'Here is a pious man even you cannot corrupt.' Satan replied that it was easy for Job to be pious. He was rich, had a family, many friends. Without those things, the Devil argued, Job would never stay faithful."

I stopped there, not knowing if I should continue. "Go on," Colón said in a cold monotone.

Looking away from him I continued, "God took Satan's bet. He tested Job. He took everything from him: killed his family, destroyed his home. After a while, Job's friends left him. They thought he was cursed." The faces of my dying aunt and uncle passed quickly before me then. In my mind I saw their blood seeping onto my bedroom floor. In a quieter voice I added, "They were right. He *was* cursed."

"Go on, Storyteller," the admiral said with some malice. "What happened to Job? Did he keep his faith? Did he remain loyal when troubles fell upon him?"

I didn't answer. All I could think of was how disloyal I had been, how I'd practiced magic on this ship against the admiral's orders.

The admiral answered for me by smacking a pile of papers off his desk. "Job, who had promised—nay, *swore*—to heed the word of the Lord . . . Our man Job broke the rules. He demanded an explanation for his suffering. He started *questioning* the Lord. Can you imagine anything more insolent than this, de Torres? Can you imagine anything more abominable than questioning your maker?"

"No," I murmured, feeling my face go warm with shame.

"'How dare you?' God said to Job. 'How dare you question the one who made you from nothing, the one who created and bounded the seas? I am the one who created the skies and the earth! I am the one who made the sea beast Leviathan, a dragon large as a mountain, with scales of iron and breath made of fire! I created all of this! I, not you, Job!'"

Colón's face was red as he paused in his speech, and he held onto the back of his chair as he caught his breath. "Do you understand this story, Luis?" he asked me.

"Yes," I murmured, but Colón pretended not to hear.

"On this ship, *I* am your God, de Torres! *I* am the one who created this voyage! Not you, not Martín Pinzón! I am the one who makes the rules. And when I say, 'Do not use your magic,

Luis, do not use it under any circumstances,' I mean: Do not use your magic, Luis, not *under any circumstances!* And when I say, 'Do not summon one of your infernal creatures, Sorcerer,' do you know what I mean?"

"Sir, I—"

"You better believe I damn well mean it!"

Colón's anger hit me like an invisible wave of power, so strong that it pushed me back almost into the door. I waited for the blood to rush out of the admiral's face before muttering, "I know you think I summoned it. But I didn't. I didn't summon the hameh."

"What did you call it?"

"The demon. I didn't summon it. I swear to you."

"Then who did?" The man dropped into his chair with a huff. "If you didn't call the demon to these ships, why did it come here?"

"I don't know."

"And why did it focus its attention on you, and you alone?"

"I don't know!"

Colón let out another huff through his nose and crossed one leg over the other. "This is your last warning," the admiral said without looking at me. "What you did tonight might have caused a mutiny. And I have no problem with having mutineers hanged. Do you understand me?"

"Yes, but—"

"Do not question me, Job. You are dismissed."

⚜

The next day marked the seventh week of our journey, and the ships seemed to straddle two worlds. One was normal, a world where you woke up, did your duties—almost without thinking, like the ropes were part of your body. At dusk you chanted your prayers, ate your supper, dropped to sleep. Day after hazy day it was the same.

That was the normal world for us on that seventh week—but there was another world hiding beneath the surface. This world was a spirit world, one you could only see through the dead eyes of a sailor. It was a world of demons, of fear and false promises, of ghost ships cursed to roam the Atlantic forever. The bird—once a symbol of hope and nearby land—had degenerated into something more dire. Each time any of us saw a petrel or a seagull, we held onto our brooms and thought of Hell.

Before long we were eight weeks at sea, and the men had grown sick as well as weary. Scurvy had painted Antonio's teeth red, and open sores dripped pus down his legs. Every night Martín came aboard to rail at Colón for his errors, but there wasn't much the admiral could do to solve the problem. The wind around us had died down almost to nothing, leaving us nothing to do but swim beside the ships and wait. Jinniyah, afraid of the water, looked down on me from above, her boy's eyes wide and full of worry.

The wind returned to us on week nine, but it was weak and brought only halfhearted cheers. By this point even the admiral looked ill. He had turned waxy, seeming to melt anew each day under the autumn sun. And each night at dusk he seemed to droop a little more as he preached patience during our prayers at vespers.

Patience. It was the word of the hour. But there was another word too, sitting unspoken on everyone's lips—"mutiny." The threat of it worsened every night when Martín Pinzón came aboard to discuss strategy with Colón.

Week nine and a half, and I could hear Martín yelling through the cabin wall I was leaning against. It was the same speech he always made. By now I could recite it by heart.

"Why do we not turn back?" the *Pinta*'s captain challenged the admiral. "We are nearing the point of no return. If we turn back now, we'll have enough water to survive."

"You forget your place, Captain," the admiral warned. "The queen put me in charge, not you. I'll have you remember that this is *my* mission—"

"But this is *my* crew! And they are dying, Colón! Look at them! Most of these men have been sailing with me for years now, and I will see to it that they sail for many more. The time is soon coming for them to make a choice. And I think we both know where their loyalty lies."

I adjusted my posture outside the cabin door. It seemed this old play had a new scene, one I had never heard before.

"Is that a threat?" Colón said in the cabin.

"It is the truth. Tell the queen that, if you make it home to see her."

Martín exploded out of the cabin and onto the deck. "Out

of my way, Jew," he said as he blew past me. The admiral chased after him, his face peeling and covered with sweat.

"Pinzón!"

Martín stopped short in front of the gangplank leading to his *Pinta* and held up three fingers. "Three days, Colón. You have three days to find land."

"Or what? Do you actually believe you frighten me?"

Martín's thin mouth twisted up in a smile, and he answered by striding across the gangplank.

On the *Santa María*, Colón pushed his lips together so hard that I could see them shaking with rage. I felt myself trembling inside, too. Three days. In three days Martín would take over, lead the mutiny himself, and sail the lot of us back to Europe. Europe, the land that had exiled me. Europe, where the Malleus Maleficarum waited.

Of course the thought of reaching Cathay didn't ease my mind much either. There was a hameh out there, somewhere beyond the horizon, and a long-lost father who for some reason wanted me dead. And I couldn't forget about the evil being that the Baba Yaga's prophecy had predicted—but I had begun assuming he and Amir were the same person.

I dealt with the pressure the only way I knew how. I trotted over to the mainsail and said, "Hey, Antonio. I remembered something else about that flower girl, Dirty Mary. Did I ever tell you she had a twin sister?" But I felt the story wilting as I told it, and the words tasted like rot inside my mouth.

166

"Sorry, kid," the old carpenter said, barely able to hold onto the hammer falling out of his hand. "The only story I want to hear is the one about the sailors reaching the Indies."

That night as I tried to sleep, I lay on the deck of the *Santa María* feeling completely trapped. Above the stars winked at me, but they provided no comfort. They were only pallid reminders of how small I was in comparison to the wrathful black ocean.

In my hard and desolate sleep I dreamed of a dark, faceless man. A windswept beard covered his chin, and layers of robes pooled around his feet. Two corpses—my aunt and uncle—lay dumb and glassy-eyed beside him, and their mouths opened in silent cries. Then the faceless man reached out to suffocate me, and I heard the hameh's scream, and I awoke on the *Santa María*'s deck calling out, "Jinni!"

Jinniyah's human eyes fluttered open at the sound. She was lying next to me under a gauzy night sky, squished in a fetal position between me and the rail. "Hi, Bal," she said in a sleep-drenched voice. "What happened? Did we find land?"

I pushed my hands madly over my hair and looked around at the dozens of crew members sleeping around us on the deck. On my other side, Antonio muttered something in his sleep, half-woken by my outburst, but it seemed I had bothered no one else.

"No, Jinni," I whispered so no one would hear. "We haven't found land. Something's wrong." I don't know how I knew, but I knew. On an instinct I reached back and flung my bag open.

It was empty. Completely empty. My coin purse, my money—even my hat had disappeared. And the scroll, that script-covered scroll, the one sealed shut with the image of the hammer . . .

"Gone," I said, barely able to comprehend the word.

Jinniyah brought a shaking hand to her mouth. "Oh, Bal. Your money!"

"Forget the money!" I said in a panicked whisper. "They've got the scroll! The one from the Malleus Maleficarum. My whole life is on that paper! Who my father is, who I am. *What* I am."

I buried my head in my hands. They were here. Here. On this ship, hiding in the shadows. They were going to find me. They were going to torture me. They were going to—

"No, Bal!" Jinni exclaimed in a whisper. "No one knows that scroll is about you. It could be about anyone. The scroll says Baltasar Infante, remember? But everyone thinks you're Luis de Torres!"

The hairs on my arms settled slightly at her words. "Still. The scroll was in my bag. If anyone on this ship suspected me of being a Storyteller, now they have proof."

I scanned around me, studying the faces of the forty sailors sleeping on the *Santa María*'s deck. Antonio, Salcedo, Bartolome, Pérez. Any of them could have taken the scroll. Any of them.

"Bal." Beside me Jinniyah had gone rigid. "Bal, my nose is tingling like crazy."

I removed my hands from my bag, trying to puzzle out what the girl said. "You mean someone's using magic? Here?" I took hold of the girl's hands far too tightly. "Where?" I said in a harsh, urgent tone. "Tell me, Jinni! Where is it coming from?"

The fake boy recoiled from me. "That's tricky, Bal. There are so many people on this ship, and they're all so close together. I don't know if I can—"

"You have to! You have to find him! Whoever's using that magic . . ." I trailed off, my imagination racing. What if al-Katib wasn't in the Indies at all? What if he'd been hiding on this ship all along, waiting to attack? And Diego had said that, for all their talk about the wickedness of Storytelling, the men of the Malleus Maleficarum weren't above using magic when they needed it.

"Please, Jinni. I'm begging you."

Jinniyah sucked at her upper lip, her eyebrows knit with worry. At last she took my hand in hers. "Come on."

Jinniyah led me around the main deck methodically, stopping here and there to adjust her course. Nearby a few sailors watched us, wary, but only Rodrigo asked us where we were going. "Running an errand for Colón." I ran off before he could ask any more questions.

After another minute of wandering around the crowded

169

deck, Jinniyah stopped and let out a breath. "Here," she whispered to me. "I think the magic is coming from here."

We were standing in front of the cabin door.

"Colón . . . ?" I whispered. *"He's the one using magic?"* I rose up on my toes to see what was happening on the aftcastle. No, Colón was up there after all, so deep in conversation with the helmsman that he didn't notice me lingering around the entrance to his cabin.

But if Colón was up there, then . . .

I shaded my eyes as I peered through warped glass that covered the tiny porthole in the cabin door. "No one's there," I said, disappointed and relieved. All I could see inside was a blurred image of the admiral's desk, dimly lit by candles.

"Bal, let's go," Jinniyah said, looking nervously around her. "Someone's going to see us. I made a mistake. Let's go back to sleep."

But I couldn't. I had to know what was in that cabin. "You go, Jinni. I'm going inside."

Jinniyah didn't move. I steeled myself and reached out to open the cabin door.

It wouldn't budge. I jiggled the handle a few times more. Nothing. The door was locked.

"Ali Baba," Jinniyah whispered behind me. "Have you heard it?"

"You're talking about a story. A Moorish story?"

Jinniyah whispered quickly, "One day Ali Baba found a

group of thieves hiding in the woods. He tracked the thieves to this cave, which was their hideout, but it was locked. The cave would only open if you said the right word."

"You're saying Colón locked his cabin with a magic password?"

Jinniyah slapped me lightly on the arm. "Baltasar, sometimes you are the silliest person! I mean someone locked the cabin with a regular key, but you can use a magic key from the Ali Baba story to open it. I saw Amir do it once before. Ali Baba's key will open any door you want to open."

Summon a key, hmm? Tapping the sides of my legs, I paced in front of the cabin door. "I don't know." I hadn't used magic in weeks now, plus Colón was right there, mere yards from where I was standing.

Then again, it was only a key. And I had to know what was inside that cabin.

I closed my eyes.

The Ali Baba story. Though I'd never heard it before, it seemed familiar all the same. After all, how many stories had I heard over the years about magic words? Even Diego's golem came to life with the word *ameth*. And using a magic word to open a door . . . wasn't that almost the same as using a magic story to open one? I'd bet my life that this Ali Baba character was a Storyteller—or at least the person who jinxed the cave door in the first place was.

Something heavy fell into my hand, and I opened my eyes

to see the words ALI BABA gleaming in Arabic across the door. A golden key inlaid with rubies lay cold against my palm.

Aha. I stuck the key into Colón's door and turned it. With a near-silent click the lock relented. I tossed the key into the air, caught it, and stuck it in my pocket. "Stay here and keep watch, Jinni. I'll be right back."

BAHAMUT

I skulked into the cabin and let the door close itself behind me. A few lit candles warmed the room's disheveled interior. Other than the dark, the place looked exactly as it did the last time I'd been inside.

I took another step forward. No, nothing magical in here, as far as I could tell. Of course I'd have to check the desk to make sure. Maybe there was some kind of magical artifact hiding somewhere among the clutter.

I walked over and began rummaging through the admiral's papers.

A sharp pressure drove up against the small of my back. "Don't move," said a voice behind me. "That pain you are feeling is a sword. Now put up your hands and turn around—slowly."

I did exactly as I was ordered. And when I turned around, I found myself facing Pedro Terreros—and, indeed, he was holding a sword. Though the young nobleman stood perfectly

173

still, his tawny curls shivered around his forehead. Evidently the cabin boy had been hiding behind the door when I entered. He waved the tip of his sword at my face, wearing his usual expression of disgust.

"How did you get in here?" he asked me.

Conjuring up that key must have temporarily sapped my Storytelling abilities, because I couldn't think of a story, true or false, to answer Pedro's question. I backed against the nearest wall and said, "You can put down that sword, Pedro. Listen. I can explain."

But Pedro drove me against the wall. His knee pounded into my gut, and the hilt of his sword pressed hard against my throat.

"Oh, you will explain, Luis. Explain: How did you get in here?"

"How did I—? Through the door. Listen, I don't know what you're—"

Pedro applied some extra pressure to my windpipe to cut my yammering short. "I've heard quite enough of your stories, Luis de Torres! The cabin door was locked, and you know it! Now tell me the truth! What were you looking for in the admiral's desk?"

"N-nothing!"

"Liar!" the cabin boy snarled. "Who are you working for?"

"Me? *I'm* not working for anyone! You're the one working for the Malleus Maleficarum!"

Pedro's whole body jerked back at my accusation. "The Malleus . . . ? How could you possibly think . . . ?" A fearful expression contorted the cabin boy's features. "Who are you?"

I didn't have a chance to answer. Just then the door to the cabin banged open as Jinniyah barged inside. "Bal—I mean, Luis! Come quick!" When she saw that I was being held at swordpoint, her voice went quizzical. "Pedro?"

Outside, the ship had erupted into a flurry of sound. "Do you see that?" I heard someone cry.

"Salcedo! Get the admiral!"

"It's another demon!

"I told you! This mission is cursed!"

Juan de la Cosa's voice buzzed through the ceiling above us. "It is naught but a whale."

Admiral Colón, also above us on the aftcastle, added, "By Saint Fernando! Everyone back to your posts!"

Pedro tossed his head over his shoulder to get a glimpse out the cabin door. "What in the world . . . ?" he said to the voices outside, and he loosened his hold on my throat.

This was my chance. I threw Pedro and his sword off me, tossed a pile of Colón's papers at his face, and made a run for it.

"You come back here!" Pedro screamed after me. "You coward! You come back here at once!"

I raced out the door, ignoring the men gathered around the starboard rail, and galloped three steps at a time up the aftcastle stairs. Pedro followed close behind, but before he could reach me, Colón stepped between me and the cabin boy's sword.

"What is the meaning of this?" the admiral demanded.

"This boy has been spying on you!" was Pedro's wild reply. "He sneaked into your cabin when it was locked, and—"

Colón took a step toward his cabin boy. "Locked? Why was my cabin door locked, Pedro?"

Pedro stammered a few words. With his free hand he adjusted his cape around his neck. "That is beside the point, Admiral," he said at last. "That bird—that black hawk—gave chase to him, and him alone! He mysteriously speaks foreign tongues, and now he's breaking into your quarters in the middle of the night! It all adds up to one truth: This boy isn't who he says he is!"

Around us our fellow sailors looked at one another, whispering in skittish agreement. Pedro pushed past Colón. "Now you come back here!" Pedro shouted at me, and he swung his sword in a reckless arc in my direction.

I dodged out of its way.

But the moment I did, I heard a deafening *bang* as something smashed into the *Santa María*. The force of it threw me off my feet.

"*Bal!*" I heard Jinni shriek.

But before I could recover my balance I tumbled over the rail. I grasped at the air, trying to grab a hold of something. The dark waters of the Atlantic rushed up to meet me.

I crashed into the ocean. The icy water pricked at my skin. Salt clawed at the back of my throat. My mind blacked out momentarily at the sight of that infinite abyss below, and I thrashed toward the sound of the screams above me.

I broke through to the surface. In those few moments of terror, the current had carried me far beyond the reach of the ships. From back here I could see what had hit the *Santa María*: a humongous black animal, smashing its body against the ship's bow. A whale, Juan de la Cosa had called it. He was wrong.

That thing wasn't a whale at all.

"*Bal!*" Jinniyah was screaming above me. Waves were pummeling me on all sides. "It's Bahamut! Isa saw it in the story! It supports the heavens! And it's *his*, Bal! It's *his*!"

The Bahamut. Although most of its body was submerged in the raging waters, I could tell that it was larger than all three ships combined—an enormous black creature with seaweed-covered spines that shot up from its ridgy black backbone. The beast leaped out of the water so it could send a wave crashing against the *Santa María*. Before it plunged back under the surface, I could see its empty black eyes, sharp fins, and the twenty-foot-high curving needles that were its teeth.

The Bahamut.

No. Not *the* Bahamut. *His* Bahamut. Amir al-Katib's Bahamut. Now there was no question. My father wanted me dead, and I had to stop him.

"Bal!" I heard Jinniyah cry. I could barely understand her.

"Something something!" she seemed to be saying, but the waves gushed into my ears, pushing the words out before I could grasp them.

Something something.

Something something . . .

"*Summon* something," I mouthed, as the black waves pushed me up and down. I had promised Colón that I wouldn't—but Colón and the others would be dead soon, the way things were going. The Bahamut was focusing on the *Pinta* now, making smaller loops to crash into it at a faster rate. The *Santa María* swayed drunkenly beside it, looking moments away from capsizing.

Summon something. I would—but what? Titivillus was useless against a creature that large, and I doubted a golem could swim.

"Think!" I said aloud, spitting salty water back into the sea. Oh, think, you idiot, you fool!

As I berated myself, I thought I heard Colón's voice joining in: *"How dare you question me, Job? How dare you question the one who created and bounded the seas? I am the one who created the skies and the earth, the one who made the sea beast Leviathan!"*

The Leviathan.

Yes, the Leviathan! Of course! If anything could defeat a world-carrying sea-beast, it would be him, the armored dragon of Biblical times.

The Bahamut raised its barnacled tail and whacked it against the ocean's surface, sending white waves arching over the *Niña*. I took a deep breath, treading in the swaying water. If I was going to summon the Leviathan, I would have to do it now.

So I closed my eyes and thought of the story of Job. It was about a man, a Jew who questioned the Lord. And the Lord questioned him back, lecturing him about the Leviathan, a dragon.

The story was about words. That I knew. With a few words, Job earned the fury of his maker. With a few words God put Job—all questioners, really—back in their place. Colón made me tell him the Job story too, using my own words against me to scare me into submission. These words alone were more than enough to cow me, just like Gonzalo's were back in Palos. In an abandoned monastery a priest's words made me betray my family. Each time, like Job, I let myself be bullied by words.

So that was it, the moral of the story. I was Job. Job was pathetic, like me.

But I wondered.

In the story God used words to frighten Job. But why? Job was pitiful, a broken, mortal man. And God was God—omniscient, almighty. Why would God waste his breath lecturing a human? Why would the creator of all things care what one of his creations had to say?

A blasphemous thought took hold of me then. Could it be that, in the story, God was *afraid* of Job? That Job's questions made God anxious, because He didn't have any good answers?

That would explain why God ranted at Job. He got nervous, so He puffed himself up by referring to past accomplishments.

In my mind the invisible Lord transformed into Gonzalo. He puffed himself up too, tromping around Palos as if he owned it. Maybe Gonzalo was scared of me, too. After all, I had won a kiss from his precious Elena Hernández, a feat even Gonzalo couldn't achieve. In one move I had made him look a child, a fool. Stupefied, terrified, he punched me in the jaw.

My mind's image of Gonzalo morphed into the Malleus priest in the abandoned monastery. This man must have been frightened of me too. Why else would he want to burn me, unless he was scared of my Storytelling powers? Finally the priest's actions made sense. He had ordered me killed because he was afraid of what I could do to him.

In my mind the priest transformed into Colón. The gray-maned admiral was more frightened than all of them combined. He had spent so much time petitioning the queen to allow him this voyage, and now it looked like he was going to be deposed by a mutiny and a fourteen-year-old sorcerer.

I had to laugh. So Gonzalo was scared of me, and the priest and admiral, too.

Hell, why not Amir al-Katib? Why else would he send a monstrous Bahamut to kill me, his scrawny son, when any small creature would do? It didn't make sense.

Unless, for some reason, he was terrified.

Far below me the earth grumbled, and two colossal walls of water shot up in front of me. The spray hung in the air around the Hebrew word LEVIATHAN, and a metallic dragon surged out from the depths. It was the Leviathan, the serpent of Biblical times, coiled above the ships and the Bahamut.

The dragon's iron scales were locked into one another like a phalanx; they glistened like diamonds in the moonlight. Its white eyes cast a beam of blinding light down at the Bahamut sending up clouds of vapor as it burned through the water. I heard a sound like thunder as the Leviathan's belly began to swell with fire. Then it unleashed holy flames on the pitiful creature below.

The Bahamut shrieked and squirmed in pain in the water. One move, and the Leviathan had already won.

I shouted at the Bahamut, "Swim back home, you coward! Tell Amir he *should* be afraid! Tell Amir I'm coming for him!"

The Bahamut did as it was told. It surged toward the southwest, in the direction of Amir al-Katib, his master.

"I release you!" I yelled to the Leviathan, which broke into white pieces above me. Summoning the dragon had drained me, and I found I barely had the energy left to swim. I made one more attempt to get back to the *Santa María*, but my vision grew blurry as I watched someone dive off the ship. The last of my energy was gone.

The last thing I heard before I slid under the surface of the water was a *splash* and muted screams from afar. Then the current rushed back into my ears, and I could hear nothing at all. Eyes and faces with the luster of pearls loomed before me in the cloudy waters. One of those faces seemed to be Pedro Terreros, but at the same time it wasn't his face at all. That Pedro's face would be the last thing I'd see was a sweet irony. My laugh was morbid as the current took me.

fourteen

CATALINA

The first thing I was aware of was salt. I could feel it, gritty, on the back of my teeth, and it burned as it dried over my lips. Next came sand, crunchy bits stuck in my molars, between my toes, under my elbows. I opened my eyes. A sliver of a moon illuminated an empty blue shore. On one side the black ocean lapped gently against unspoiled sand. On the other hundreds of palm trees swayed in a balmy breeze.

"What the hell?" I said aloud to the ocean. No sooner had I started believing that I would never see land again, that I'd be stuck in that coffin of a ship till the end of time, than I washed up ashore on some empty beach in the middle of nowhere. I let my head sink back onto the sand.

At least I was still alive.

I didn't have much time to wonder at the thought. Because just then a mumble—a human mumble—pushed its way over the hushed roar of the wind and waves.

I searched through the blue night to find the mumble's

source. A figure was splayed on the sand behind me. I wiped the sand off my cheek and crawled over to it.

"Jin—" I started to whisper, then stopped. It was someone else. Even in the dark of night, I could see the reflective pallor of the person's skin, the tawny wet hair. I reviewed the figure's sharp chin, lightly-freckled nose, the barely-parted lips. And I had to come to an incredulous conclusion.

"Pedro?"

And it *was* Pedro. I was certain. Pedro Terreros, the wavy-haired nobleman from Burgos. He was wearing Pedro's clothes, he had Pedro's coloring.

Yet something was off. Pedro's hair had grown longer than before, and his eyebrows had mysteriously become thinner. And under the cabin boy's tangled, fur-lined cape, his chest sloped up and down in a peculiar fashion.

A sudden whack sent stinging pain across my cheek. I fell backward and howled. Pedro Terreros, or whoever *she* was, had launched upright and slapped me across the face.

"You!" the girl snarled at me.

Fearing her words more than her fists, I scuttled back in the sand. "What? What did I do?"

The girl tripped backward, her brown eyes raging. "Oh, you know very well what you did! You tried to kiss me, you bastard!" She scooped up a rock from the sand and launched it directly at my head.

I ducked to avoid her stony weapon, although I didn't really need to. The rock thumped a few paces in front of me and bounced harmlessly away. "I should have known!" the girl cried. "This is what I get for saving your life! Well, I'll have you know now, Luis de Torres: I am not some . . . *thing* to be used as you desire! I am not your sleeping princess!"

"Sleeping princess?" I asked, lost in more ways than one.

The girl swept up a thick branch from the ground and brandished it in front of me. "Stand, de Torres. Face me like a man. You want me? Go ahead and try it. But be warned! I have killed men for less."

Slowly I stood, trying to hold in my laughter. Oh, to think I had survived the Malleus Maleficarum, the Bahamut, and Amir al-Katib's hameh only to be felled by a tree branch!

I said, "Look, Pedro, if you put that down for a second, I think we can work this out. I swear I didn't touch you or even try to touch you. I swear to God, I was just looking at you."

"Looking at me?" The girl cast her stick aside and pushed me back by the shoulders. "How dare you! How *dare* you!"

I flung her hands off me. Now I was getting annoyed. "How dare I what? How dare I *look* at you?" I threw an angry hand out toward the Atlantic. "I'm not sure if you were paying attention, Pedro, but I almost *died* back there! Then I wake up on an island in the middle of nowhere and I hear someone talking in their sleep. I think it's Jinniyah, but no—it's someone else. Someone who looks awfully like Pedro Terreros but is, you know, a *girl*! So, yes, Pedro, I *did* look at you, and I'd rather not die because of it, because I've had a really bad day, actually, and I'm really, *really* tired!"

I assumed that after that feat of rhetoric the girl would offer me some kind of reply. But she said nothing, only dropped onto the sand.

At length the girl grumbled, "You really are a Storyteller, aren't you?"

"What's that supposed to mean?"

"It means you talk a lot."

I couldn't disagree with that, so I joined her on the sand. Like Pedro, the girl held herself like an aristocrat, like one of those snooty merchants who sometimes came to Palos from the north.

"Who's Jinniyah?" the girl asked me.

I let a smile rest on the edge of my mouth. Too late to lie about this one. "Juan. She's a girl too, and a genie. Or half-genie. It's complicated."

If my answer surprised this girl she didn't show it. She simply leaned back on her hands and smirked. "A genie. Well! The crew isn't going to like that. Assuming we ever see them again, of course."

I leaned back on my hands, too, mirroring the girl. "Can you imagine what they're saying now? They're probably going crazy, knowing there was a sorcerer on the ship the whole time."

The girl hmphed. "'Sorcerer?' Try 'sorcerers,' Luis. Plural. Unless you believe I don't count as one."

I knitted my brow, trying to pick apart her words. The eyes that swam through the waters of the Atlantic floated up to me then, and the silvery women's faces. I had seen Pedro's face there too, in the ocean, but at the same time it wasn't his face at all.

"It was you," I said, marveling at the thought. "You saved me." They were mermaids, those silver-faced women, and Pedro—this girl—had conjured them. It was a miraculous idea, the most miraculous one I'd ever thought. Pedro Terreros, who hated me from the instant he saw me, had dived into the ocean and cast a spell to save my life.

"I guess your name isn't really Pedro, is it?"

The girl pushed her lips together, seething out at the foamy blue shore. "You have no idea what you've done, do you?" she said in a low voice. I didn't know how to answer. I opened my mouth, but before I could get out a word, the girl banged her fists against her thighs. "You can make dragons out of nothing— the size of mountains, that can fly and breathe fire! But can you save yourself from drowning? No, of course not! You had to make *me* do it!"

"Sorry," I mumbled, rubbing the back of my neck. "I was, you know, *drowning.*"

Before I even finished the word, the girl shot up in her spot, sending sand flying in every direction. "You selfish, infan- tile . . . ! Do you have any idea what you've done? I suppose you don't even realize that I had to remove my Jeanne d'Arc spell so I could summon my sirens and save your sorry life!"

I recoiled at her tone but said, "Look, Pedro—"

"And the crew! They saw everything! The Pinzóns! Colón!" The girl paced around the beach, pushing her fingers into her eyes. Shaking her head, she muttered under her breath. I think she was trying her damndest not to cry. "Oh, God. You idiot! You've ruined everything. Everything!"

I rose behind her. "Pedro."

She shook her head and whispered, "You've ruined everything."

Not knowing what to do or say to that, I stood there watching her, listening to the hush of the ocean and the frogs twittering in the forest.

"Thank me," the girl said at last. "I think I deserve at least that much."

I couldn't bear to look at her when she said that. The way her voice shook shamed me. It broke my heart.

I didn't know what else to do. So I did as she asked. "Thank you, Pedro. Thank you for saving my life."

Huffily she dropped down in the sand next to me. "You're welcome. And my name isn't Pedro. It's Catalina. Pedro is my brother."

My mind slowly accepted this information as I sat down in the sand beside her. "So, Catalina Terreros. Is that right?" The girl shrugged in assent. "The whole time on the ship, I thought you hated me because you thought I was Jewish. But you were just avoiding me so I wouldn't notice you're a Story-teller."

Catalina Terreros rolled her eyes. "Why should I hate Jews? Half the men at court are conversos."

In my mind I was still back on the *Santa María*. "And tonight Jinni sensed magic coming from Colón's cabin. But it wasn't Colón she was sensing, or any magical item."

"Yes, yes, it was me," Catalina said, impatient. "I was *trying* to get some privacy so I could replenish my Jeanne d'Arc spell." To my blank look she went on, "The spell that kept me in disguise. Honestly! Can you at least *try* to keep up?"

And here I'd thought that the whole point of being a Story-teller was making monsters come to life. "So you're saying there are spells that can make girls look like boys?"

Catalina took my question as a personal assault. "Yes! In fact there are about a *thousand* stories that can do that. Because there are about a *thousand* stories about women dressing up as men to get the respect they deserve!"

When she was done I felt like I'd been chewed out by my Aunt Serena. I scratched the back of my neck and said, "Ah, sorry. I didn't . . . I didn't know that. But why did you need to disguise yourself in the first place?"

Catalina took her knotted hair in both hands and wrung it out over the sand. "To be frank, Luis, I don't think that's any of your concern."

I laughed as I removed my soggy shoes. The Leviathan out

of the bag, so to speak, there was no more reason to keep the real Luis de Torres's name hostage.

"It's Baltasar," I said.

"I beg your pardon?"

I pointed to my face. "Baltasar Infante. Pleased to meet you."

The girl considered me as if for the first time. "Infante?" she said with an expression of disgust. "Well! Evidently you've some secrets of your own."

Laughing, I rubbed my salt-encrusted head. "No, I'll tell you. I'm a prince in disguise. I've escaped my evil stepparents and am on my way to start a new life in Cathay. I mean, they wanted me to get married, but I didn't like the girl, so . . ."

"That's impressive."

"I know."

"I mean it's impressive that someone who is purportedly a Storyteller could come up with something so clichéd."

"I like to call it 'classic,'" I said.

"If you must."

The girl paced along the shore, rubbing one palm angrily. She unlaced her boots, pulled them from her feet, and hurled them across the sand.

I wondered if I'd accidentally touched on something I shouldn't have. Prince in disguise, evil parents, fleeing from an arranged marriage . . .

That's when it hit me. I knew exactly who this girl was. She was the sister Rodrigo Sanchez was talking about the first day on the ship. Pedro Terreros's sister Catalina. The one set to marry the Duke of Alba's son.

But the look on the girl's face told me she didn't want to talk about it, so I decided to change the subject. "What's this sleeping princess you were going on about earlier?" I asked, yawning.

The girl sagged down in the sand, softening under the weight of the exhaustion she must have been feeling. "Just a children's tale."

Ready to hear it, I reclined on my side, propping myself up on an elbow. Catalina sighed and went on, "There's not much to tell, and I'm not sure if I'm telling you the right version, since I've heard maybe a dozen over the years. It's about a witch who puts a princess under a spell so she sleeps for a hundred years. The only thing that can wake her is a kiss of true love. So along comes a dashing prince, who fights his way into the castle and kisses the sleeping princess, waking her and the rest of the court. Then they get married and live happily till the end of their days." As Catalina spoke her brown eyes grew wearier and wearier.

"You don't seem to like it," I noted.

"Your powers of observation are astounding."

"But it doesn't sound that bad, your story. It's like, you're not even awake if you haven't found your true love."

To my surprise a warm pink light formed between us, and

the salty ocean air grew flowery in my nostrils. The words SLEEPING PRINCESS bloomed pink in French before us, and a summoned prince and princess glowed up over the sand. A red, red rose formed between them.

"I release you," I said, shocked by what I'd done. The ghostly couple brought their hands together on the rose and dissolved into nothing.

Catalina exhaled a quiet laugh. "A boy's way of looking at it. To me, the princess is trapped, and she stays trapped. The witch traps her and her castle with a spell, and then the prince comes and does the same thing. Happily ever after."

As she spoke the summoned princess reappeared in front of us, but now she appeared haggard and drawn. Another rose grew in front of her, but as it grew its stem desiccated and coiled around itself, and its petals wilted to black. Thorny vines grew from the tip of the rose's stem and snaked around the princess's wrists and over her mouth, tight like ropes. Her phantom eyes darted back and forth with terror.

I turned away. Skin taut across her body, the princess writhed against the constraints. Worse were the eyes. *They look like hers.* I swallowed the thought whole.

"You're looking ill, Señor Infante. Don't you want to hear any more stories? Like the one about that flower girl you're so fond of. Dirty Mary, was it?"

Though Catalina's voice was soft, it cut me like a hameh's claws. The tale of the flower girl Dirty Mary: the girl who sold herself along with her flowers. I hadn't realized when I'd told that story on the ship that a girl other than Jinniyah had been listening to it. I said, "If I'd known you were there, I wouldn't have—"

"Oh, wouldn't you?" Catalina cut me off. "But whyever not, Señor Infante? That story was so *funny*. It must have been, or you wouldn't have told it so many times!"

I looked down at my feet, trying to avoid looking at the haggard princess she had summoned. Why *had* my story been so funny, anyway? When the flower girl had been trapped like the sleeping beauty of fairy tale, the grotesque creature writhing in front of me.

"And I can take a joke!" Catalina flew to her feet. Black rose vines whipped out from the summoned princess's wrists and sliced through the air at me. I had no way to stop them. They snapped around my arms, my legs, my chest. Every time I breathed the vines constricted tighter around my body and bit harder into my skin.

"What are you doing?" I choked out. With every breath I was suffocating. "Catalina! Stop it!"

"Once upon a time, there was a girl named Dirty Mary. Well? Go on, Infante! Go on and tell that one again!"

The vines pulled themselves tighter around me. "Please!" I managed to gasp as the black vines crept around my throat. Tears of pain were forming in my eyes. "I'm sorry. Please. Let me go. Catalina."

The girl blinked as if coming out of a dream. "I release you," she said, and the vines around me went slack. I fell backward, gasping and rubbing my arms and throat, now bruised from the vines and flecked with shallow thorn-gashes. The eyes of the haggard princess darted back and forth as the specter dissolved into nothing.

"Are you all right?" Catalina said. Worry creased into her face, contrition. She sank to the sand. "I shouldn't have done that. I was tired and upset. Sometimes I let the spells get away from me. I shouldn't have. I . . ."

But I took her hands and squeezed them. "Are you kidding?" I exclaimed. "I didn't know you could summon things to *strangle* people! That was amazing!"

"Th-thank you?"

"How long have you been Storytelling?"

"I—I don't . . . My whole life, almost. My wetnurse taught me and my brother. I was about six—"

Six! "So you must know loads of spells!"

"Well, yes, but—"

"Then you're going to teach me."

Catalina threw herself to her feet. "Now wait! You wait a second! You sit here, pelting me with demands, yet I know next to nothing about you. Now tell me! Earlier this evening you accused me of working for the Malleus Maleficarum. Why?"

I lounged back on my elbows. "Because they're after me. I'm a fugitive, you know."

"And what about that black hawk we saw? The one that attacked you!"

"A demon my father sent to kill me."

"And that black sea-beast! I suppose you know why it attacked us too!" Catalina crossed her arms over her jerkin and shook her head at the ocean. "No, you're going to have to tell me everything. From the very beginning, if you please."

I pinched both of my lips, amused. "Why, Doña Terreros!" I said. "It sounds like you want me to tell you a story!"

The girl pursed her own lips but said, "Yes, Señor Infante. That is exactly what I want you to do."

THE CURSE

An hour or so later I had finished telling Catalina my tale. As she braided her knotty hair over her shoulder, the icy moonlight gave her an otherworldly splendor. "That was a long story, Señor Infante," she said. "Would you like some water? I'm deathly thirsty."

The watery words FOUNTAIN OF YOUTH appeared in the air, and a marble pool of water shimmered into existence on the beach. Catalina picked up a large clamshell from nearby, blew the sand out of it, and used it to scoop out some water out of the fountain.

She passed me the shell and explained, "It won't make us youthful, since we're already young. And even when it works it only keeps a person young for about an hour. But the water is fresh—certainly better than the little we had left on the *Santa María*."

I sipped at the shell. Indeed, the water tasted sweet and was refreshingly cool. "I guess Martín didn't have to worry about us dying of thirst after all. In the end we could have summoned this fountain for the crew."

Catalina took the shell from me and refilled it. "Yes. Right before they hanged us for witchcraft."

After we had had our fill of the water, Catalina dismissed the fountain and sat next to me in the sand. "So you have absolutely no idea why your father keeps trying to kill you?"

I wiped the extra liquid from the corners of my mouth. "No. Why? Should I?"

"To be blunt, yes. Consider. The Baba Yaga sends your father to kill an evil being with the potential to destroy the world. Then your father tries to kill you."

"So?"

"So evidently he thinks *you're* the evil being foretold in the prophecy! He thinks *you're* the one who will destroy the world!"

"Me?" I said with amusement. "Come on. That's crazy."

"Is it?"

"You're saying that, when Amir came to my house that night in the summer, he didn't come because he wanted me to help him. You're saying he came to my house to kill me!"

"Well, no. That's not exactly—" Catalina started, but I cut her off, overwhelmed by dark laughter.

"Sure, why not? A great power travels west, who will destroy the world as we know it. What if my father knew something the Baba Yaga didn't? What if he knew the evil power was me?"

Catalina smirked at the idea. "I don't mean to offend, Señor

Infante, but you don't seem the world-destroying type."

"Oh, no?" I said, manic from exhaustion. "You saw what I just did to the Bahamut! That Leviathan I summoned could have destroyed a whole city!"

"The spell was powerful, I'll admit. But it doesn't mean—"

I barely heard the rest. All I could hear were the invisible creatures whispering behind us in the forest. Somewhere in that jungle, Amir al-Katib could be waiting, girding himself to destroy his monstrous son.

I threw an angry hand toward the forest. "Hell, maybe that's why he abandoned me in the first place! Amir must have known I'd grow up to be trouble."

"Let's not jump to conclusions," Catalina said. Needless to say I didn't listen.

"Jinni and the Baba Yaga wanted me to be the hero. But *he's* the hero! I'm the villain! Everything I go near I destroy. You said before that I ruined your life—and you're not the only one."

"Infante, please. That's enough."

"Why? Amir's right! I'm a curse! That's why the Malleus Maleficarum are after me! That's why my aunt and uncle are dead!"

"I said *enough*!" Catalina shouted. "Stop it! That's enough!"

Exhausted, I studied my sandy fingers, waiting for them to steady themselves. They wouldn't. I rolled them into fists and closed my eyes. "I'm so sick of this. It's too much. You know?"

Catalina's pitying face was draped in shadow. "Yes. I know."

I shifted my weight in the sand. "Then what do you think?"

"About the prophecy?"

"About everything."

Catalina paused, then looked me stark in the eyes. "I think you may be right. You may be the source of evil the Baba Yaga prophesied. You may destroy the world as we know it." The girl tossed her braid over her shoulder and shrugged. "Then again, you may not. Amir al-Katib may be right; you may be right. Perhaps I'm right, or all of us are wrong. We might be wrong about al-Katib, for all I know. But it seems to me that al-Katib is after you, and his actions are being determined by the way he interpreted the prophecy. So you need to be on your guard."

"You're saying that, even if we figure out who the evil being *really* is, it won't matter because my father will try to kill me no matter what."

"I'm saying that the truth, in this case, is irrelevant. It's your father's interpretation that matters."

I picked up a handful of the shadowy sand and watched streams of it seep out from between my fingers. "So I'll find him and convince him his interpretation is wrong."

Catalina tilted her head and said, "It's certainly not the worst plan I've ever heard. First you'll need to sharpen your Storytelling skills so you can better protect yourself against his attacks. Then you'll need to use your spells to break through his defenses and get close enough to him to talk." The girl nodded to herself. "Yes. Yes, it could work. Although . . ."

Catalina trailed off and breathed in sharply as she brought her fingers to her mouth. "Although . . . ?" I asked her.

"I was thinking. Ideally you'd be able to talk to al-Katib and convince him he's in the wrong. But if your father is anything like mine, he may not be open to reason. There are some who would rather die than admit they made a mistake." The girl sighed. "As much as I hate to say it, you may have to prepare yourself for the possibility that discussion won't be enough. In the end it may come down to 'kill or be killed.'"

Kill or be killed. In the back of my mind, I'd always known my story might end this way. But faced with the reality of tracking down my father, confronting him, and killing the man in cold blood . . .

"You can't be serious," I whispered. "That's . . . that's not an option. It's not even possible."

Catalina considered me, then offered me a little smile. "Hopefully it won't come to that. But it's not impossible. If it comes down to it, I think you will be able to defeat your father. He may be one of the greatest Storytellers who ever lived. He may have decades of experience on you and a horde of monsters he can summon at will."

"I've got to tell you, Catalina. This is not making me feel better."

"I said he *may* have those things, but you have something better." Under the pall of shadow, the girl's eyes glittered in the moonlight. "You have me."

❖

200

I awoke the next morning sweaty and in pain. Catalina had decided to rouse me by kicking my lower back. "Rise and shine, Infante! The sun's been up for hours."

"Watch it," I murmured, opening my eyes. Bits of sand had attached themselves to my eyelashes in the night; I found I could barely see. "What's the hurry?"

"The hurry is I don't want to live on this beach forever. I'm going to see if I can find the *Santa María* and the other ships, or perhaps some sign of civilization. You may stay here if you want; that's your prerogative. But I am leaving."

Catalina pulled on her boots and started hiking down the shore. I peeled my face off the ground, spit chunks of sand off my tongue, and slapped more sand out of my hair. "Wait!" I called after Catalina. "I thought you were going to teach me Storytelling!"

I stuck my shoes under one arm, quickly rinsed my sandy hair out in the ocean, and ran down the shore in the direction of the October sun. Catalina was currently standing on a sand dune, thumb locked into one of her belt loops as she surveyed the ocean.

"If we're lucky," she said, "someone in the crew spotted this island, and Colón's trying to find somewhere safe to lay anchor."

Spotted the island? I wondered how could anyone miss it. Shielding my eyes against the white morning, I took in the view of the verdant peaks that rose out of the forest in front of us. The sight was so beautiful I almost ran and embraced it. Oh, green, green! After nine gray weeks at sea I'd forgotten such a sublime color existed. Crowned by ocean mists, the kingly face of the mountains grinned up at cloudless skies. Three cormorants soared above us before swooping down for breakfast in the sea.

Catalina and I traveled down the shoreline, avoiding washed-up seaweed and jellyfish as we went. "Where do you think we are?" I asked her as we walked.

"Java, perhaps. Or Cipango. Although the lack of pagodas is worrisome."

"What's a pagoda?"

"A building with golden roofs stacked on top of one another. Marco Polo spoke of them in his writings on the East. Polo wrote also of an archipelago of inhabited islands off the farthest coast of the Asian continent. If we are on one of them, surely there is someone here who can direct us to the mainland." Yet I heard a note of doubt in her voice, doubt modulating into despair.

"Why'd you decide to help me, anyway?" I asked her. "Afraid I'd leave you all alone on this island?"

"Hardly! I was simply bored, that's all."

I supposed boredom was as good a motivation as any, but I couldn't help but think there was more to it than that. Maybe she really *was* afraid, foundering in the dark like I was. Maybe she was searching some heroic quest to shape her life, to give it meaning. Or maybe, after nine weeks of keeping herself distant from the crew, she was simply looking for a friend.

I raced in front of the girl and walked backward so I could face her. "What are you going to teach me? Storytelling-wise, I mean."

Catalina advanced past me, tipping her head toward the sea. "Before anything you're going to have to build up some stamina. Is it a wonder you almost drowned when you summoned the Leviathan? One must walk before learning to run, Señor Infante."

"So I should only summon small things for the time being. Got it. What else?"

"That depends. Do you know how to use more than one spell at a time?"

I thought of my attempts to do so back on the *Santa María*. "Not yet."

"I haven't been able to do it, either. But supposedly it is possible, so I thought I would ask. Do you at least know how to summon fantastic settings as well as creatures?"

"No," I said, full of wonder. "You can do that?"

The girl stopped to sigh at my ignorance. "This may take longer than I thought. I suppose we will have to start at the very beginning."

"I'm ready. Teach away."

Catalina crossed her arms and stepped toward me. "Tell me, Señor Infante. How do you summon a mythical creature?"

I took the shoes from under my arm and let them dangle from my fingertips. "To summon a creature . . . you figure out what the story means. Don't you?"

"That wasn't my question. I didn't ask how *people* summon creatures. I asked how *you*, Baltasar Infante, make a creature come to life. Be specific."

I swung my arms by my side, thinking. "I just think about what the story reminds me of. Like Titivillus reminded me of my old priest, and Job was me."

"And the golem you summoned back in the monastery?"

"The golem?" I swallowed. "The golem was my Uncle Diego."

Catalina must have noticed the sorrow in my voice when I said that, because when she spoke again her voice was milder than usual.

"That's all well and good, Señor Infante, but it's not going to help you defeat Amir al-Katib. Linking stories to your own life . . . I'll admit that's how I started out, too, when I was young. But what happens if a story *doesn't* remind you of anyone you know? What if you wanted to summon a siren, for example? I find it doubtful you know any women who have fishtails. I certainly don't."

"But you—"

"But I summoned those sirens before, to save your life? Is that what you were going to say? You're right. I did summon them, but I didn't do it by thinking about myself or people I know. I did it by thinking more abstractly. In the stories, sirens are lovely creatures that tempt sailors so they can drown and eat them. I don't know anyone who acts like that, do you?"

A pretty girl who might secretly be plotting to kill you? Why yes, I did know someone like that. Someone I was talking to right now in fact.

Without waiting for an answer, she went on, "When you consider which characters are weak and which are strong, which are heroes and which are villains, it's easy to tell what the story is about. Who is the villain in this story? The sirens, of course. And who are the tragic heroes? Why, the men, the sailors. Thus the story is about men's fears of women and the sea. It's a common theme. If you spend time looking at enough stories, you'll find that most female creatures are extremely frightening. Apparently men find us incredibly scary."

I had never thought of it that way. Smacking a fly off my neck, I said, "I'm not sure I like that interpretation."

"Why not?"

"It assumes that all men are scared of all women."

"Aren't they?"

"I don't find you scary."

Catalina broke into laughter as she continued her hike down the beach. "Oh, don't worry, Señor Infante! You will."

I followed her down the beach, up steep sandy hills, and through spiny rock formations nearly impossible to cross. An hour later Catalina bent over her knees to catch her breath.

"This humidity is going to kill us," she said, wiping her brow.

"I have a suggestion," I said. "If you teach me a new spell, I can summon something for us to ride down the beach. I learn a new spell; you get to stop walking. What do you say?"

Catalina knelt on one of the holey rocks and wiped some sweat off the back of her neck with the end of her cape. "I suppose I can teach you to summon a unicorn. It's a story for young girls, so you won't be able to think about yourself."

"A unicorn?" I said wryly. "Don't you mean a karkadann?"

"I beg pardon?"

"Never mind. Just stand back and watch."

I closed my eyes, feeling sweat dripping down my face as I tried to summon the unicorn. But no matter hard I tried, I couldn't think of anyone I knew who was as wild and elegant as a unicorn, and I couldn't think of another way to interpret the story. After a minute I cracked open one eye. "Before I start, how about you give me one tiny hint? The story's about purity, isn't it? Something like that?"

Catalina didn't say a word. Facing the forest, she reached back and put a hand against my chest, silencing me.

I followed her gaze inland, toward the edge of the shore where sand dunes started to thicken into forest. Standing there were three copper-skinned men, holding obsidian hatchets.

Sixteen

THE TAÍNO

The three men were naked but for the strings of beads around their necks. A net of braided cotton was slung over the shoulder of one man, and a second man carried a calabash. The three were taller than I was, and their bodies were thin but sinewy. Their hair was thick, very black, and parted down the middle, and their bangs obscured some of their high, flat foreheads. A red feather puffed out one of the men's noses. Another nose had a yellow feather, and the third one, blue.

"They're not wearing any clothing," I whispered to Catalina.

"I noticed. And look at those axes."

I did. The stone hatchets each of the men held looked sharp enough to cut solid rock. Vicente Pinzón's old story echoed through my head: *Barbarians, man-eaters, with bones pierced through their nostrils . . .*

The shortest barbarian fell into a crouch and began hooting with laughter. This man was less muscular than the other two, and his yellow-feathered nose bent to one side. The other two men looked at him quizzically, saying, "Arabuko? What's going on? Cousin?"

Arabuko wiped the tears of laughter from his smiling, crescent moon eyes, and showed Catalina and me his crooked teeth. "The spirits tease me," Arabuko said in a strange, mellifluous language. To his cousins he said, "Go on. Start your fishing. I will talk with them."

The other two men watched Catalina and me with suspicion as they padded down the beach to the ocean. As they went I could hear the two of them whispering—something about pale spirits from the sky.

"Good morning!" Arabuko called down to me and Catalina. Giving us a broad wave, he jogged down the beach in our direction.

"Stay back," Catalina whispered to me, and the word EXCALIBUR shimmered like a mirage through the humidity. A long sword dropped into her outstretched hand, and she stepped in front of me to protect me from Arabuko.

But the man with the crooked teeth continued to approach us. "There's no need for weapons!" he said, placing his stone ax in the sand by his bare feet. "See? I'm unarmed. Let us talk."

Catalina brought her sword closer to her chest as Arabuko looked over her shoulder at the ocean. "How did you get here?" he asked us. "Where are your boats?"

I answered, "We don't know," and immediately covered my mouth with one hand. Though I had thought every word in my native Castilian, the sentence came out in the same flowing tongue Arabuko had been speaking.

"Aha! Another shaman," Arabuko said, delighted. To my utter shock he continued talking in Spanish. "You are speaking the language of my people, the Taíno. I am Arabuko, shaman of Marién."

"Baltasar," I said carefully.

And Catalina said, "Catalina Terreros of Burgos."

"Excellent!" Arabuko replied. "And what brings you to our island?"

Catalina answered with some hesitation. "Trade, originally. But we fell overboard, and now we seem to be lost."

"I am sorry to hear that. Truly. But the spirits never do things by accident. They must have brought you here for a reason. A good one, I hope. But you must be hungry. Come! I will bring you to my village."

Before we could protest, Arabuko picked up his hatchet and jogged back into the forest. Behind me I heard a soft *splash* as the other two men threw their fishing net into the ocean. "Bring them to our village?" one of the men muttered. "After what happened with the other one?"

The other man muttered back, "The spirits have made him mad."

Catalina brought her sword down to her side as she gazed up at the forest Arabuko had disappeared into. "He's a Storyteller," she said of the man. "He must be if he can speak our language." I started to march up the beach in front of her. "Wait! Where are you going?"

"To Arabuko's village," I answered.

"Didn't you hear his cousins? They just said he's a madman!"

"A madman who has food and shelter." My thoughts then turned to Jinniyah, who I'd left behind. "Maybe someone on this island has seen the *Santa María* or knows where we can find al-Katib. Anyway, Arabuko seems more willing to answer questions than his cousins."

We looked at the other two men, who were studiously ignoring us. Catalina nodded begrudgingly.

So we followed Arabuko into the forest, where he hummed a jaunty tune over the sound of cooing doves. With barefooted ease the Taíno man skipped down a skinny, irregular path into a labyrinth of vines and crooked tree branches that scratched white lines down our arms as we passed. The stone hatchet I had thought would be used to cleave off my arms or head quickly found itself facing a far more sinister enemy: the undergrowth. Arabuko chopped through the forest easily, each *shink shink* of his ax a rebuke to my over-suspicious imagination.

A clammy mile later, our path opened into a cozy clearing. No, not a clearing—a sanctuary. Broad leaves like stained glass windows let in green light from above. Beyond those leaves, shadows of stems and palm fronds crossed over one another to create a natural spire. A choir of squawking birds echoed through the canopy, and hundreds of flapping wings created a percussive rhythm for their psalm. For a moment I felt overwhelmed with the knowledge that God's hands had reached so far to craft this paradise. The Lord's work was more mysterious than I had imagined, and more beautiful.

Arabuko brushed a heat-desiccated leaf from a moss-covered tree trunk lying supine in the black earth. He sat on the trunk and picked up a dark green fruit from beside it. He tossed the fruit to me.

"Papaya," Arabuko said in his native language. "Do you have these where you come from?"

I felt the heaviness of the fruit in my hands and squeezed it several times. "No."

"Then you are in for a treat." When I tried to bite into it, he chortled. "Make sure you peel the outside first!"

As I tried to rip off the peel of my fruit, Catalina puttered around the clearing, inspecting the undersides of the leaves above her head. They covered her face with a greenish aura. "It's like Eden," she said to herself. "Paradise."

"It is Ayití," Arabuko corrected her.

"Are we near to the continent?" Catalina inquired. "How far to India or Java?"

Arabuko reached back and scratched his shoulder blade with the hilt of the ax. "I've not heard of these places."

"Then what of Cathay? Surely you know of the Grand Khan."

"Surely! But I have not. The Cubanacan I have heard of,

but something tells me you're not talking about them. I have a feeling you are far more lost than you imagine." Arabuko breathed in deeply, laughing at the thought, and the tiny birds of the forest laughed along with him. His laughter then dissolved into another nonsense song. He stood and disappeared into the jungle.

Arabuko guided us farther inland. As we went Catalina hacked a wider path for us with her sword. After another half hour, perhaps, we emerged into a much larger clearing, on top of a hill that rolled up and down with long mounds of packed dirt. Sharp green and beige leaves stuck out of the mounds, some reaching as high as my waist. The valley below was dotted with about a hundred circular wooden houses with neatly thatched, conical roofs.

"My village," Arabuko said with pride. "Go on. I will meet you later, after I have spoken to my cacique."

"Go on where—" I started, but Arabuko ran down the hill so fast that he slid down in places. Catalina and I shrugged and followed him.

We hiked down more carefully than Arabuko did, passing a knee-high wall of flat square stones scratched with the coarse images of squatting, pregnant women. As we got closer to the town we could see the villagers—young women wearing white cotton skirts carrying howling babies with blocks of wood tied against their foreheads, and muscular men with the same coarse, parted hair as Arabuko. Some men carried sloshing buckets of water made out of gourds that hung from thick branches laid across their shoulders. Others stripped hide off the carcasses of large rodents they'd likely hunted in the forest. In the center of the village a crowd of children played on a well-swept packed-dirt courtyard, bouncing a big brown ball off their shoulders, chests, hips, and heads. We passed a group of middle-aged women with long painted skirts, some cooking over a fire and some making jewelry as they clucked over some rumor. Others took handfuls of what appeared to be some mashed starchy tuber and squeezed out its juice over a gourd bucket.

But when the Taíno noticed me and Catalina, all work abruptly stopped.

"Uh, hello," I said to the villagers in their language as we passed, but children gasped and hid behind one another when they saw Catalina's sword. "Put that thing away," I scolded her, and she released Excalibur from her service to the amazement of the crowd.

We continued walking through the village, admiring the workmanship of its massive houses. The thatch was thick, fresh, and well-woven, although it appeared this climate didn't require people to stay indoors to avoid cold weather.

Arabuko emerged from one of those houses with a shorter, paunchier young man. "Ah, there they are," the second man said. "I am Guacanagarí, cacique of Marién."

Cacique must have meant "chief" or "king," because Guacanagarí was ornamented like royalty. His ears enjoyed far more feathers than Arabuko's, and beaded red bands surrounded his waist and high forehead. A crude gold hoop formed a bridge between the man's wide nostrils, and a necklace made of pearly sea snail shells lay across his collarbone.

"So these are the young shamans," Guacanagarí said of me and Catalina. So the whole village could hear him, he announced, "In the name of the spirits I welcome you. Welcome to Marién!"

With a clap of his hands Guacanagarí ordered a feast prepared in our honor, and his subjects flitted around the courtyard to ready our meal. "I will show you our village," the cacique said. Arabuko seemed to have vanished.

We spent the rest of the morning touring Marién with its leader. We learned that the hilly area we had passed through earlier was a farm, and the stones with the squatting women showed images of one of the Taíno gods. The other end of the village was bounded by a muddy river, where people gathered to clean themselves with long leaves that looked like basil. We asked the bathers if they'd seen any large ships in the bay north of the village. None of them had.

Next, Guacanagarí led us into one of the village's cone-roofed houses. A tree trunk supported the thatched roof from the middle of the building, and the tightly-packed thatch gave us some much-needed shade. Around the circumference of the room hung human-sized slings of netted twine. What their purpose was I couldn't yet say.

Catalina directed her attention to the rafters, toward a spot near the main supporting log. There, a bundle of brown bones hung from the ceiling. From down here I couldn't tell for sure, but if I had to guess I would say the bones were human. As we passed under them, Catalina muttered, "Not very civilized, are they?"

I didn't know how to answer. Through the ever-open door I could see the village's main courtyard, where Taíno children yawped and cavorted with two yellow mastiffs and a big brown ball that made funny bouncing sounds whenever they hit it. I wouldn't call their game *civilized*, not exactly, but the children looked like they were having fun. And the Taíno had welcomed us peacefully enough.

I walked to the edge of the room and pushed one of the braided nets hanging from the ceiling. It sent a shadow dotted with spots of light swinging across the packed-earth floor of the room. "Well-made *hamaca*, no?" Guacanagarí asked me. "Our craftsmen are the best in Ayití."

"What are they for?" I asked in the Taíno language.

"Why, sleeping, of course! Please, try, try. You'll like it."

I made an attempt to climb into the hammock, a goal I wasn't able to achieve until Guacanagarí held it steady for me. After I found my balance I lay back and let the fibers of the net cocoon me. I closed my eyes and felt myself swing back and forth above the floor.

"It's pretty comfortable," I told Catalina as I sat up in the hammock. "Hey, we should use these to sleep the next time we're on the ships!"

A dreamy look passed over Catalina's face as I said that. "Then we wouldn't have to sleep on the floor."

"Whoever invented these things is a genius," I told Guacanagarí as I dismounted the miraculous invention. It was funny how even a simple net had a different meaning on the other side of the world.

The cacique said, "You will stay here. The spirits have ordained it. Arabuko and his cousins have offered their home to you. Any *hamaca* you'd like is yours. We are honored to have you as our guests in our village for as long as you need to stay."

For some reason the offer made me think of Jinni. I couldn't stay here, not as long as she was alone with a bunch of mutinous sailors in the middle of the ocean.

Catalina seemed to have had a similar thought. "We are grateful, Cacique," she said in Taíno, "but we cannot linger here. We need to find Grand Khan—"

"And our friends!" I added.

"Do not fret, young shaman," Guacanagarí said. "Our canoes are the fastest in Ayití. We will find your people's boats before long. Until then you will stay here with us. Yes? Yes."

The matter apparently decided, the cacique clapped his hands together and exited the house. Catalina muttered in Castilian, "Generous people, aren't they?"

"You don't trust them." I smirked at her. "You don't trust anyone."

"You heard the way Guacanagarí spoke to us. It's almost as if he doesn't want us to leave this place."

I did get that feeling, myself. Catalina went on, "They want something from us. Why else would they be so welcoming of complete strangers—strangers with such an unbelievable story?"

"Maybe they're just good people," I suggested. "Besides, I think we should stay here until Guacanagarí's men find Colón and the others. There's food, fresh water. And it's not like we have anywhere else to go."

"I suppose you're right," Catalina admitted, and I took my leave of her so I could locate Arabuko. Before I made it more than ten steps out of the house, Catalina called out, "Infante."

Behind me, Catalina crouched in the dirt, holding a long black feather between her thumb and forefinger.

A hameh feather. Catalina looked up at the sky. "These Taíno know more than they let on."

Seventeen

ARABUKO

That evening we feasted, served by men and women carrying wooden bowls and trays filled with about a hundred kinds of food. For the occasion Guacanagarí donned a cape decorated with multicolored feathers. Seven bare-breasted women between the ages of twelve and twenty trailed after him, all with the same black bangs as their male counterpart.

"These are my wives," Guacanagarí explained.

I tried to avoid looking at them too closely. "All of them?"

"Do not blush, young shaman! Custom on Ayití allows caciques to take as many wives as they desire. Now eat. This feast is in your honor."

The whole town gathered in a large circle in the courtyard. Catalina and I sat in the place of honor by Guacanagarí, ready to taste the many dishes his people had prepared for us. Arabuko was sitting too far away to include him in our conversation, and besides, we were too hungry to investigate the hameh feather right then. First we had some roasted, well-spiced meat of an animal the cacique called *manatí*. Then we used circular pieces of flat, starchy bread to pick fish out of a saucy, spicy pot. Over the course of the meal we tasted strange nuts and vegetables with names like *yuca*, *maís*, and *maní*. I didn't need the power of translation to know what to call these foods. What they were called was delicious.

When the meal was done, Guacanagarí wiped his fingers with some green herbs and chewed on a stack of dried black leaves called *cohiba*. "I am so pleased to have you in our village," he told me. "Is there anything else I can do to be of service?"

"Actually . . ." I pulled out the hameh feather Catalina had found. "Can you tell me what you know about this?"

The chief coughed, spitting up black saliva. He wiped it off his chin and cleared his throat. "Seems to belong to some kind of crow. Please excuse me. One of my wives is calling me."

He hurried off, and Catalina and I went to look for Arabuko, hoping the shaman might be more amenable to answering questions. He was busy at the far end of the courtyard, surrounded by a dozen boys, waving his arms as he told a story.

"And so the great Yaya killed his son Yayael, though he loved his son more than anything in the world. And he kept his son's bones in a gourd that he hung from the rafters of his house, and over time the bones turned into fish. One day the Four Twins came and climbed on one another's shoulders so they could steal and eat the fish. Then they heard Yaya returning home, and they fell along with the gourd. When the gourd hit the earth it smashed into a million pieces, and many waters flowed out of it, creating the great ocean."

The cross-legged children had clearly heard the story before. They squirmed in their seats, impatient for what would come next. Arabuko sighed, "Yes, all right, you may pick up your *cemíes*. But be careful with them. They are sacred."

Ignoring him, the boys attacked the pile of stone figurines in front of them, arguing over who got the best one. I couldn't tell the difference between one and another; each figurine was shaped like a round-eyed man with a painted red nose and a squiggly smile.

When the boys finally settled down, Arabuko said, "Let's see who can get the Four Twins to visit us." All at once the children went silent, closed their eyes, and pressed the figurines hard against their foreheads.

As the boys concentrated on their task, Arabuko came up to Catalina and me and spoke to us in Castilian. "So? What did you think of my story?"

Not knowing what to say, I looked at Catalina. She said, "It was . . . very nice. Quite fascinating."

"I apologize for ignoring you earlier," Arabuko said, "but I had promised the boys I would give them a lesson today. Whenever I have a chance, I try to teach the children to call upon the spirits so one day I can train one of them to take my place as High Shaman. We haven't had any success yet, but let's wait and see. You can try, too, if you'd like."

Never one to pass up a chance for Storytelling, I decided to take him up on his offer. But no matter how hard I tried, I couldn't understand the story: why Yaya had killed his child, why he'd kept the bones in his house, or why the bones turned into the ocean.

"Don't bother," Catalina muttered so Arabuko couldn't hear. "That story is unsummonable. It makes absolutely no sense."

Just as she finished speaking, the air in front of us began to shimmer, and a strange figure danced into view. Tall as a man, it was actually comprised of four gnomish creatures standing on top of one another's shoulders. The four gnomes had the same round eyes and wormy smiles as the stone figurines the children pressed against their foreheads.

The Four Twins from Arabuko's story. One of the boys had summoned them.

"Unsummonable, you say?" I teased Catalina, and she hmphed as the tower of gnomes began to teeter. For a second it looked like they would fall, but the top three tumbled in the air and landed lightly on the balls of their feet. The bottom twin turned a somersault and offered a squiggly smile to Catalina.

"Well done, Carabi!" Arabuko said, kneeling down beside the boy who had summoned the Four Twins. "Now we'll say good-bye and let them go home." Carabi released the Four Twins from his service. The gnomes hopped back on one another's shoulders and faded from view.

That done, Arabuko brought a hand to his chin. "What else? Ah, maybe our new friends from the east can help us learn some new spells! They are shamans too, you know." The boys in the circle looked up at me and Catalina. "Baltasar, Catalina Terreros, why don't you tell us a story from the East?"

Catalina and I blushed as we realized all eyes were on us. I stammered, "W-well, this morning Catalina was trying to teach me to summon a unicorn."

Catalina cleared her throat awkwardly before explaining the story to the crowd. "Yes. Well, a unicorn is a beautiful white horse with a horn of ivory swirling from its head. It lives in the forests, hiding, so it is very rarely seen. Fair young maidens are the only people the unicorn will approach and the only people allowed to ride one."

As I prepared myself to summon the unicorn and show Catalina what I could do, the Taíno boys stared dumbly at us, brows furrowed and jaws agape. Even Arabuko appeared baffled.

"I think you will have to explain the story again," he told Catalina.

And Carabi said, "I don't understand, Arabuko. What's a horse?"

I'm not sure how long Catalina and I stayed in the village; the Taíno had a different sense of time than I was used to. They did have a calendar—based on the movements of the moon

222

and the solstices, Arabuko told me—but they didn't measure out their days with canonical hours, and they'd never heard of the term "week." After four days I simply stopped counting the days and eased into my new life in Marién. In the mornings I would help Arabuko with his chores, harvesting vegetables from the village garden, catching fish and small birds, or gathering fruits from the forest. We gave these foods to the women of the village, who cooked them in hotpots between their weaving and stone carving. The work was hard, but not as hard as it would have been in Spain. The land here was fertile and gave up its bounty easily. Catalina was right. This land *was* a paradise, and I found myself at peace despite my worries about Jinniyah and Amir al-Katib. I kept meaning to ask Arabuko about the hameh feather, but it never seemed the right time. I felt safe for the first time in weeks, and I allowed myself to relax just a little.

In exchange for helping him with his chores, Arabuko offered to teach me Taíno magic. But his Taíno stories made as little sense to me as my European ones made to him, and I was never able to summon one of his gods. Nevertheless, Arabuko was always patient with me, despite the many questions I asked him.

"Can anybody be a Storyteller?" I asked him one afternoon as we sat in the garden outside our shared house. "A shaman, I mean. Can anyone summon a spirit?"

"Certainly." Arabuko plucked a leaf off a nearby plant,

popped it in his mouth, and munched on it. "Long ago the gods gave humans the ability to call upon them in times of need. Any human can summon a spirit, with training, although some are more gifted at calling them than others. Many people on this island fear to call upon the spirits. They believe speaking too much with the gods causes madness." Arabuko slid a nail between two of his crooked teeth, trying to dislodge a bit of green that had gotten caught in them. "Any more questions, Baltasar?"

"Actually, yes," I said, figuring this was as good a time to ask as any. I removed from the pouch on my belt the hameh feather Catalina had found when we'd first arrived. "This feather belongs to a bird called a hameh. It's a demon, and I know it was here in this village. We're friends, Arabuko. Aren't we? So tell me. What happened?"

Before he could answer, a brown ball bounced down the dirt road we were sitting on and rolled against Arabuko's leg. The shaman scooped up the ball and hopped to his feet. "Why do we sit here talking about madness and feathers? It is a beautiful day. Come! Let's play some *batey*!" And he ran off in the direction of the ball field, singing a Taíno song about a raven.

Arabuko wasn't the only one trying to teach me new magic. I had Catalina to teach me, too, every night in the courtyard after supper. Under her tutelage I mastered the unicorn, the Fountain of Youth, and even Jeanne d'Arc, though of course the spell had no effect on me. In theory, Catalina taught me these lessons in exchange for whatever fruit I could find for her in the forest, but I think she would have taught me for free. I think after all the months of keeping her abilities secret she enjoyed having someone to discuss magic with.

Our lessons were at night because during the day she was on a mission. She would leave at dawn with a gourd full of water and the fruit I had given her the previous night. Then she would disappear into the forest, on the hunt for information. Her goals, in order of importance, were finding a route to Cathay, finding a sign of Colón's ships and Jinniyah, and finding Amir al-Katib. But every day she returned having found nothing except for a few Taíno villages, rainstorms, and jungle.

Then one morning weeks or months since we had washed up on this island, I woke up to the sound of Catalina throwing herself out of her hammock. Her whole body, it seemed, was pink from sunburn and mosquitoes, and her hair had tangled beyond recovery. She scratched at the pink fly bites on her face and hands as if trying to rip off her own skin.

"I've had it," she said. "I've had it with the bugs, and I've had it with this heat. I refuse to stay on this island for a moment longer. I'm going to ask Guacanagarí if I can borrow one of his canoes, and I'm not going to stop paddling until I find the *Santa María* or Cathay."

Over the past few days she had gathered a pile of fruits in one corner; now she shoved them in a cotton bag Arabuko had given her and slung the bag over her shoulder.

I scrambled out of my hammock. No, she couldn't leave! She was the last link I had to Europe. As much as I enjoyed living with the Taíno, I wasn't ready to spend the rest of my life without hearing words like "Burgos" or "our Lord and Savior" come out of someone else's mouth. "Wait!" I cried. "Wait. I'll come with you. Just let me say good-bye to Arabuko."

It was odd that Arabuko wasn't in our house so early in the morning, and there seemed to be no one outside to tell me where to find him. Finally I found a girl and a boy around my age standing near a small house at the edge of the village. "Have you seen Arabuko?" I asked them.

The two of them turned toward me slowly. The girl's eyes were serious, and the boy's eyes full of hatred. He spat on the ground and ran off into the forest. The girl slowly turned back toward the house in front of her.

"Don't mind my brother," she said with no emotion. "He doesn't like foreigners." The girl's eyes were large and very black, and she wore a braided red cotton circlet around her forehead. Referring to the small house in front of us she said, "Arabuko is in there."

"Thanks." I took a step toward the house, but the girl caught my hand.

"You can't go inside. He's performing a ceremony."

"Oh." I remained standing beside the girl, a respectful distance from the house. Though I couldn't see through the doorway—someone had covered it with a cloth—I could hear a sound like a rattle inside, and Arabuko singing a flat, mournful melody.

"He's trying to cure my mother," the girl explained. "She was injured not long before you came here, and she's not been awake since."

I had heard of this woman. Once, when I was helping Arabuko with his chores, I had heard some men whispering about an attack and an injured woman. When I tried to get close and hear more of their story, the men noticed me and fell silent.

"I'm sorry," I said to the girl. "What's your name?"

"Mimeri."

"I'm Baltasar."

"I know."

At last the cloth door to the house swept aside, and Arabuko emerged, his face smeared with black dye. Mimeri ran inside to see her mother. Arabuko walked past her with a faraway look in his eyes, seeming not to notice her at all.

"Arabuko," I said. "Catalina and I are leaving. I wanted to say good-bye before we go."

But the shaman didn't seem to hear me. Finally he said, "Come with me to the river. I must wash."

When we arrived at the river, Arabuko walked straight into the water without even a pause. I didn't know what to make of it. I asked, "What will happen to that woman? Mimeri's mother."

"I have done all I can for her. There is nothing more to do

now but wait. The gods will give us a sign when the time comes. By nightfall she will either return to the land of the living, or she will descend into the caverns of the dead."

I nodded at his answer, but I didn't understand, not really.

The cold water must have broken whatever trance Arabuko was in, because he looked up at me more alertly and changed the subject. "So you are leaving." He rubbed the dye off his face and splashed it with some water. "Then I suppose it is time for me to be honest with you." He smiled. "Surely you have noticed I've not been entirely forthcoming. You see, before you came to this island, I called upon the great spirit Yucahú, who can foresee all that will come to pass. He told me that a great power was coming from the east—"

I was in awe. "That will destroy the world as we know it!"

"So you have heard the prophecy too. Well, not long after I spoke with Yucahú, a strange man washed up on our shores, not far from where my cousins and I found you. It was a bearded man, a shaman wearing heavy black clothes, and a black demon followed him wherever he went."

"Amir al-Katib!" I cried. "Where? Where is he?"

Arabuko waded backward and tipped himself back in the water. "When he arrived on Ayití the bearded man was very ill. He was rarely awake, and the few words he said were non-sense. Guacanagarí feared this man was the great power Yucahú spoke of, the one who would destroy all things. But I did not want to make assumptions, so I said we should wait and see."

Arabuko shook his head sadly at the water. "That was a mistake. The next morning the bearded man summoned three mighty demons. I think in his illness he thought we had imprisoned him, and he used these demons to escape. I have heard tales of shamans calling upon multiple spirits at once, but never have I seen such power. The demons rampaged through the village, injuring Mimeri's mother. We've done all we can to treat her injuries, but every day she seems to worsen. Anyway, when the demons were done the bearded man and his bird fled southeast, in the direction of Guacanagarí's rivals, the cacique Caonabó and his wife Anacaona."

I sat on a flat stone near the edge of the river and looked up at the canopy of the forest. Beyond the mesh of vines and leaves above us, I could see wispy clouds blowing across the sky. One day soon I would see the hameh streak across those clouds, darkening the sky with a black rain of feathers.

"Arabuko, why didn't you tell me this before?"

The shaman dunked himself in the river and shook out his hair with his fingers. "Do you remember the day my cousins and I found you and Catalina?"

"Yes. You looked at us and laughed."

"I did. Because the gods can be sneaky. They tell prophecies, but they never come true in the way that you expect. Yucahú had warned me that a mighty being would be coming to this island. And when the bearded man summoned those three demons, I was certain he was the evil Yucahú had warned us of. But then you and Catalina arrived. It was as if the gods were playing with me. I told Guacanagarí, and we agreed we would keep you here until we uncovered your intentions. We wanted to make sure you were not the great evil, and that you were not in league with the bearded man."

"We're not," I said firmly. "I've come here to find that man and stop him."

"Then it appears we are on the same side. Guacanagarí fears more than anything that the bearded man will ally with his rivals to the south. With the bearded man on his side Caonabó will be unstoppable."

"Then take me to him!" I jumped up from my seat. "If you know where Amir is, take me to him now, and we'll stop him together!"

Arabuko splashed up in the water and smiled. "Stop him? How do you plan to stop him?"

I hesitated and sat back on my rock. "I thought I could talk to him, convince him to stop attacking everyone." I remembered what Catalina told me and said, "But maybe that's stupid."

Arabuko came dripping out of the water and sat on the rock beside me. With a thumb he pulled one of the beaded necklaces he wore away from his collarbone. The beads tinked softly as they rearranged themselves under the light of the forest.

"You see these beads?" Arabuko said. "It is an honor to wear them. They serve as protection from illness and evil spirits."

Out of courtesy I said, "They're very nice."

"I would not use this word to describe them. The red ones represent the men I have killed in battle."

The answer jolted me to my toes. Killed? Arabuko? This Arabuko, with the gentle voice who sang silly songs and taught children? Quickly I glanced down at his necklace so he wouldn't see me counting. The red beads . . . There must have been twenty of them in that pattern! Twenty at least!

"We Taíno are a bartering people," Arabuko said. "Everything we take from the earth belongs to us all. To steal a thing from another is a terrible wrong. But to take a person? To be taken is worse than death. They took my wife, you see. A group of men from another island. But I got my revenge. I did not wish to kill them, but when the time came I found these men and delivered justice unto them." I heard those last few words in the voice of my uncle, and when I looked into Arabuko's black eyes, they seemed to ripple like the pool of hameh's blood.

Arabuko said, "To talk is good, in times of peace. But I fear this time it will not be enough." The shaman sat in thought for a moment. Then he stood from his rock with purpose, letting drops of water fall from his hair. "But I shall be hopeful like you, Baltasar. Perhaps we can stop the bearded man without bloodshed. I have decided to come with you and Catalina Terreros. Tomorrow I will lead you to Maguana, and hopefully we will find the bearded man before Caonabó does. Then, if the gods will it, we will stop the bearded man once and for all, and the world will not be destroyed."

"Thank you," I told him, and a cloud of bats billowed across the sky. Arabuko looked up at them sadly.

"There is our sign," the shaman said. "The bats carry the souls of the dead with them. Now they carry Mimeri's mother to Coaybay."

As the bats flapped by us, I thought of Mimeri. And I wondered if the bats carried the souls of others Amir al-Katib had killed, and if any carried the souls of my aunt and uncle.

Arabuko and I went off to find Catalina, but as it happened Catalina found us first. "They're here!" the girl said, running over to us. "Colón and the others are in the bay north of the village."

So Catalina, Arabuko, and I joined a small greeting party led by Guacanagarí to the island's northern shore, which surrounded a wide, gleaming bay overrun with brown waterbirds with chalky blue and yellow beaks. On the far end of the cove where the coral-darkened waters began to lighten, the *Niña*, *Pinta*, and *Santa María* waited for us. Guacanagarí directed his men to drag into the waters dugout canoes painted with reds and greens and blues. Before long Catalina and I sat in one and were rowing our way back to our floating home.

Not long later I climbed up the *Santa María*'s ladder and onto the deck, and a lithe figure swooshed into my arms. It was Jinniyah, still in the form of Juan, the servant boy. "Oh,

Bal!" she cried. "Thanks be to Allah. You're alive!" She clung to my neck as she explained what the rest of the crew had gone through.

"I told the admiral to take the rowboats and find you, but he said that it was a waste of time because you were dead. And the crew was so angry because you had summoned that dragon, and they said our mission was cursed because Colón had brought witches with him. But a couple of days later we spotted land—this island that Colón called San Salvador. And then we found another island and another, and all these strange people that don't wear any clothes! But the whole time I knew I'd find you. I knew it! I knew you couldn't be dead."

"I'm all right," I said, overcome with relief that Jinniyah was too. The feeling was so intense that it took me a moment to notice that the rest of the crew had surrounded Catalina, looking at her with murder in their faces.

"I don't see what we're waitin' for," Pérez said to the other members of the crew. Antonio de Cuellar stood behind him, avoiding my gaze. "Luis and that girl—Pedro—they're witches. It's about time we string 'em up by their throats!"

Thankfully Colón placed himself between them. "I had rather dwell with a lion or a dragon than a wicked woman—or a witch," he said to Catalina. "But we've been sailing around these islands for weeks now without a translator. Luis and the girl will remain here as our interpreters."

But Pérez insisted, "Because of them we were attacked by

demons! And don't forget that dragon—"

"All in the past," Martín Pinzón said as he climbed up from a rowboat onto the *Santa María*. "Remember we are here for trade first and foremost, and these witches of ours can help us do it. Tell me, Señor Pérez, you like gold, don't you?"

Pérez's mouth hung open under his snub nose. "Yes."

"Wonderful! Then let us trade."

And that is exactly what we did. After introducing himself to the admiral, Guacanagarí sent his men back to Marién to fetch whatever trade-goods they could carry. Before long, necklaces, flapping parrots, and balls of cotton the size of a man's head were being offered up in exchange for hawks' bells, glass beads, and anything else Colón's men could dig up from the hold. Catalina and I scurried back and forth across the deck of the *Santa María* translating for Spaniard and Taíno alike. Arabuko hung back, chewing gravely on his thumbnail. When I had a free moment, Jinni and I went over to him to ask him what was wrong.

"The way your man Colón looks at us," he said. "I heard him muttering something earlier about servants, and something about your god. I couldn't hear him well over all this chatter. But he frightens me."

What Arabuko said gave me pause, but I said, "He was probably praying. The admiral's a very religious man."

"It's true," Jinni added. "The admiral prays all the time. He was probably thanking God for allowing us, his simple servants, to find you!"

Arabuko put a hand on Jinni's shoulder and exhaled, relieved. "I'll take your word for it. You know him better than I do."

"Did you think Colón is the evil being in the prophecy?" I asked him.

"Who knows? My cacique remains certain it is the bearded man."

Guacanagarí was currently eying a pile of swords the crew had lugged out from the hold. We went over and he asked me, "What do you think we would need to offer to acquire some of these weapons?"

I translated the question for Martín Pinzón, who answered, "Spices. Or gold."

But the spices Guacanagarí offered were of no interest to Martín, and when the cacique offered his gold nose ring Martín refused to touch it. "De Torres, please inform these heathens that when I say 'gold,' I do not mean those piddling bits of wire that they pierce through their extremities. I mean this."

Martín tossed a large pouch onto the deck by the cacique's feet, where it landed with a jangling thud. Nearby Spanish sailors clustered around it to get a better look at what was inside.

What was inside was a heap of coins—all gold.

Guacanagarí scooped up a handful of the coins, some of which cascaded back into the pouch. "There is some gold on Ayití," the man said, "but I have never seen so much as this before."

"There is always Babeque," Arabuko said. "In the stories it is a land ruled by men with dogs' heads and tails. The dog-men of Babeque are so rich, they wear gold in their ears, in their noses, around their arms like this." He cupped his hand around his upper arm in illustration.

Martín's eyes turned hungry as I translated, but Colón came over and said, "I do not put much stock in stories."

Martín shot a bitter glance in my direction. "Oh, don't you? I may not be admiral, but I've sailed for longer than you've been alive, and I know this: Every story is made of truth. Myth or no, there is truth in that story, and I, for one, want a piece of it. If you remember, we once thought sorcerers were myth, didn't we? Yet you cast your lot in with them."

"The queen sent us to find spices and the Khan of Cathay," Colón said through his teeth. "She did not send us in search of fairy tales. After we've finished trading with these Indians, we will make for the continent. Cathay is our destination, not this Babeque. I do not wish to hear of it again."

I expected Martín to argue as usual. But he walked off, saying, "As you wish, Admiral."

It was only when the sun began to dip into the western horizon that the trading finally ended, and Guacanagarí prepared another feast that the Taíno brought on board the *Santa María*. This time he arranged for Marién's best poets to regale us with Taíno songs. The drumming and singing seemed to put the once-angry crew into a good mood for once, and their

236

mood only brightened as Guacanagarí's wives came on board. Soon Vicente was dancing with one and Antonio de Cuellar with two others, and Jinniyah clapped for them from the audience. Guacanagarí and Colón stood off to one side, talking to each other as Catalina translated.

I was about to ask Jinni to dance when I heard a voice behind me. "May I have a word, de Torres?"

Martín Pinzón was resting against the ship's rail. The way he stood there, holding his elbows, the man appeared more at peace than I'd ever seen him.

"I come with a proposition," he said. "I would have you on my ship as a translator."

For a second I didn't understand. And when I realized what he was saying, I was shocked by the audacity of it.

"You're planning on sailing to that mythical island, to search for Babeque against orders," I accused.

"Yes," Martín said, "and I'm sure you realize your powers of translation would be of use to me. And I would be of use to you, as well. Colón's patience with you and the girl is growing thin. He was not as happy to see you as he may appear, no matter how he needs a translator. I, however, have no compunctions about traveling with sorcerers. If you help me find gold, you can be the Devil himself for all I care."

I have to admit I was tempted. I could stay on Ayití with Arabuko, find and finally confront my father. Or I could go with Pinzón and run.

I glanced back at Colón and said, "They'll catch you. You'll be marked as a traitor. You and your crew will be sent back to Spain in chains."

"I hardly think so. I once said that wealth is my religion, de Torres, and so is Queen Isabel's. She won't dare hang me when I come back bearing a ship full of gold and jewels."

I knew what he said was probably true. "Still. You'll be betraying your admiral. Your brother! What you're doing—it's wrong."

For the first time ever I saw Martín's face soften. "Come now, de Torres. You are nearly an adult. It's about time you learn this lesson. Right and wrong? Fairy tales, that's all they are. I will buy rightness with the gold I find on Babeque. History will only call me wrong should my plan fail." Done with his lesson, Martín replaced his mask of irony to his face and said, "Now will you come with me or not?"

I glanced back at Colón a second time. Jinni was not far from him, dragging a weakly protesting Catalina to the Taíno dance. The sky above them was empty now, but the hameh was around here, somewhere, and Amir al-Katib.

"I can't," I told Martín.

"You'll be paid well, if that's what you're worried about."

"It isn't."

Martín shrugged. "That's a pity. Well, suit yourself. I suppose it will be more fun to beat Colón at his own game when he has the advantage of translators and sorcerers. Assuming he doesn't throw you all away before he has the chance to make good use of you. Good-bye, de Torres."

I barred his way back to the *Pinta*. "What about Colón?" I said. "He'll find out what you're doing. Maybe the queen won't hang you, but Colón will."

"I try not to waste my time worrying about the whims of Cristóbal Colón, Translator. Go. Tell him my plans now, if you wish. It makes no difference. The *Niña* and the *Santa María* are no match to my *Pinta* when it comes to speed. Farewell."

Martín climbed down one of the ladders that led to his waiting rowboat. As he rowed back to the *Pinta*, I did as he'd suggested. I ran over to Colón and told him what Martín was planning. But it was too late. By the time Colón decided to believe me and started to prepare his own rowboat, Martín was already on his *Pinta*. And by the time Colón started rowing across the bay, the *Pinta* had set sail and was almost over the horizon. Martín was right. There was no way to catch up with him. When Colón realized that, he retired to his cabin and didn't come out for the rest of the day.

 Eighteen

UQBA

The next morning I awoke on the deck as the wind spritzed seafoam across my cheeks. Catalina sat cross-legged nearby, sucking the side of her cheek as she pored over a piece of parchment. Beside her, Jinniyah dangled a leather string in front of Catalina's cat. Arabuko, Guacanagarí, and some other Taíno men consulted with Vicente and Juan de la Cosa across the deck.

I pushed myself onto an elbow and cracked my stiff neck and back. I said to Jinniyah, "I see you and Catalina are getting along."

"She's nicer than Pedro," Jinniyah answered. "She lets me play with her cat."

Catalina's cat pawed at Jinni's leg, asking her to continue playing. "I thought you didn't like animals," I said. "Didn't you say something about them being dirty?"

"Cats are different," Jinniyah explained. Then she looked at Catalina. "What's his name?"

"Tito," the girl said without looking up from her parchment. Jinniyah nodded to herself in approval.

I scooted over to Catalina so I could see what she was doing. She tilted her parchment toward me. "It's a map of the island," she said. "Colón's taken to calling it La Isla Española."

On Catalina's parchment La Isla Española—or Ayití, as I knew it—was a wiggly-lined island shaped like an east-facing arrow. Other, steadier lines slashed the landmass in five, and raw hatches representing mountains scattered across the interior.

"I asked Arabuko to draw it," Catalina said. "He and Guacanagarí came aboard early this morning." She pointed at the top left corner of the illustration. "This is where we are: Marién, the land of Guacanagarí. According to Arabuko, he wishes to be the foremost cacique on the island." Catalina pointed with two fingers at the two provinces below Marién. "But the warlord Caonabó and priestess Anacaona married. The marriage effectively doubled Caonabó's territory and his power." She tipped her head in the direction of the cabin, where an astonished Guacanagarí was handling one of the admiral's swords. It nicked the cacique's finger when he touched it. He sucked on his finger and laughed. "Which is why Guacanagarí wants a military alliance."

"With us?" I asked.

"Naturally. Why else do you think he's treating us to all these feasts?"

Jinniyah let Tito hop off her lap. "Maybe he's just a nice person. Storytellers! Read too much into everything."

Across from us Rodrigo Sanchez exited Colón's cabin with the admiral's arquebus in hand. He filled it with gunpowder, lit the fuse, aimed it at the sun. Finally he shot it, creating a humble explosion of smoke that Guacanagarí took in with delight.

"See what I mean?" Catalina said.

I scratched the back of my head. "Well, it makes sense that he wants to ally with us. He wants to protect his people. His village was under attack just a few weeks ago. And Arabuko said he's worried Caonabó will ally with Amir al-Katib."

The name must have lit something in Jinniyah, because she jumped from her seat like she was on fire. "Amir's here? Why didn't you tell me? What are we waiting for? We have to go find him!" She dashed across the deck to Arabuko, presumably to ask him for directions to Amir al-Katib and use of a canoe. I gave Catalina an ironic wave and followed.

On the other end of the deck Arabuko was rubbing his bare arms and arching his head toward the sky. "I do not like the feel of this air," he said in Castilian. "It feels wrong. It feels like a *huracán*."

"What's a *huracán*?" Jinniyah asked.

"A storm. The winds pull trees from the earth." Arabuko ripped the edge of his thumbnail off with his teeth. "The gods must be trying to say something, but I cannot understand what."

242

Catalina walked over and pulled her cape around her shoulders. "Should we be concerned about this storm?"

"I should not like to be at sea during a *huracán*. You use these sails to capture the wind. Sometimes the wind allows itself to be captured. A *huracán* does not."

"I'll go tell Colón," I said, but as I reached for the cabin door, I heard Colón shouting within.

"'The queen wants, the queen wants!' Is that all you can say? This may be the queen's mission in name, but it is mine in fact! And the Almighty God's!" I heard another voice—Rodrigo Sanchez, probably—though I couldn't make out what he was saying. Colón exploded, "I've had enough of your questioning! And I've had enough of traitors, thank you!"

"W-what traitors?" Rodrigo said within.

"You know very well! Tell me, Señor Sanchez, have you seen the *Pinta* today?"

"N-no . . ."

"Of course you haven't! Because that traitor Martín Pinzón has stolen one of my ships in search of some mythological island made up in the heads of savages! So I don't give a damn what your queen thinks right now! Good day!"

The accountant staggered out of the cabin, only to have the door slam shut behind him. I backed away and said to Catalina, "Maybe we should come back later. Like in a week or two."

"Oh, stop being a child. If you want, I'll come in with you . . ."

Her gaze unlocked from my face to follow something in the sky above me. "Turn around," she said in a low voice.

I did as she said. A black speck was flying from the island to the ship, completely unaffected by the raging winds that churned around it.

"Bal!" Jinniyah called from the front of the ship. "Come here! Hurry!"

Ignoring the flying speck, I ran over to where Jinni was standing. "Look!" she cried, pointing over the rail at Ayití's shore. "Can you see it?"

On the beach stood a dark, anonymous figure. The blurry edges of its black cloaks fluttered in the wind.

"It's him," Jinniyah said, her voice quivering. I couldn't tell if she sounded more relieved or terrified. "It's Amir."

I knew what I needed to do. I sprinted across the deck toward the cabin. "Where are you going?" Jinniyah screamed after me, but the only words that mattered were the ones repeating in my head: *Tell Colón—The storm—A trap—*

A black blur blasted into my side, knocking me off me feet. Above me al-Katib's hameh flapped its bloody wings and bared its claws. But what I focused on most were those eyes—yellow, like I'd once seen in my window, uncanny and surrounded by smoke.

The hameh rammed into me. I threw myself down against the deck, smashing the bird's head into the wood. Pressure and pain drilled into me as the beast's talons pierced into the muscles of my shoulder. I tossed myself onto my back and with all my strength heaved the hameh off me.

I heard a shot and felt the sting of sparks on my arms and face. The hameh loosed a rasping crow and puffed into black smoke for an instant. Too soon it returned to its corporeal form. The bird circled above the crow's-nest, dripping bloody feathers around me. It screeched and streaked back to the shore.

Colón stood before me, his arquebus smoking. He flung the gun to the ground. His face as red as the Devil's, the admiral hauled me up by my collar and shoved me against the outer wall of his cabin.

"Tell me what it is!" he shouted. "What is it? Why does it attack us?"

Jinniyah tried to tear him off me. "Let him go! Stop it! He's hurt!"

The veins in Colón's neck seemed ready to burst. "Admit you have caused this! Admit you have drawn these demons to us!"

I held my shoulder and watched the blood seep through my tunic. Though the wound was throbbing now, I could feel almost no pain.

"Admiral, it's not his fault!" Catalina told him. "He's wounded. He needs to be bandaged. He could die."

"If he does, it is God's will. This has gone on for long enough. I will have the truth." Metal scraped against leather as Colón unsheathed his sword and held it at my throat. "Who is it that attacks us? Tell me, de Torres!"

By this point I was tired of pretending, tired of lying. Perhaps it was because I felt faint, but I was ready for everything to be out in the open. "It's Amir al-Katib," I said. "The Eagle of Castile."

"Amir al-Katib?" I heard Salcedo say as if it were a curse. And Juan de la Cosa said, "That's impossible."

Colón blew air out of the corner of his mouth and let me loose. I sank back against the wall, holding my bleeding shoulder. As Catalina ran off into the cabin, the admiral strode across the deck to get a look at the dark figure on the shore. Antonio de Cuellar stood next to him, gazing out over the rail.

"It can't be him," Antonio said to the black speck on the beach. "That Moor was killed back in Granada. Everyone knows that. Luis is confused, is all. Amir al-Katib is dead."

"No, he's not," an antsy Rodrigo Sanchez said. "He can't be dead. He's just a story."

The admiral stalked back over to me, his boots thumping heavily on the deck. "Let us assume for a moment you are telling the truth. Let us assume it is Amir al-Katib who attacks us. Why? Who is he to you?"

Catalina ran out of the cabin; she'd stolen some bandages from inside Colón's desk. She immediately pressed them against my bloody shoulder, trying to staunch the bleeding.

"Who is he to you, de Torres?" Colón's voice was lower

now, and edged with fury. He took a step toward me, dragging the tip of his sword along the deck as he went. "I am warning you. You will tell me." He raised his sword.

"No!"

Jinniyah jammed herself between us, raising her skinny arms for my protection. "Amir al-Katib is his father! He's Amir's son! Don't hurt him!"

If I hadn't been bleeding, if I hadn't had to close my eyes against the dark spots winking at the outer corners of my blurring vision, I might have cared about the way the crew whispered at this new revelation. But I didn't care. I was done with secrets.

"Does anyone else feel that?" Rodrigo Sanchez said. "In the floor?" A hush fell over the *Santa María* as we listened to the deck vibrate below us.

"Admiral, look!" Antonio de Cuellar shouted.

We did. Menacing gray clouds had formed above our ship, a malevolent whirlpool of wind and vapor. Directly under the eye of the storm a creature grew out of the bay. It was a watery giant, made of wave and mounted atop a gargantuan, dripping steed. Created from the bay's churning waters, the monstrous man boasted few discernible features other than the pointed helmet atop its head and a dripping smile. Its waters drummed down on the bay, sending up clouds of mist and creating a tumult that blocked out the screams of the crew.

I took the bandages from Catalina and held them against my shoulder. From far away I could hear Jinni's voice, covered with a pillow of sound. "It's Uqba, Bal!" she screamed right in front of me. "Remember? The warrior who wanted to conquer the world!"

I remembered. "'Allah, if it were not for thy oceans, I would conquer the Earth.'"

"Amir's trying to sink the ships! We'll drown!"

The ship lurched sideways, and the mists muffled Jinniyah's screams. I clung to the rail and watched as Uqba raised a watery sword from under the ocean's surface. He swung it over us. It was longer than the entire length of the *Santa María*. Blobs of rain beat down on the crew, washing over the sounds of Colón's orders and the men charging across the deck.

"Look out!"

Jinniyah yanked me and Catalina backward. Ahead of us the foremast moaned and plunged into the roiling seas, sending waves crashing over us.

The waves sent a handful of sailors flying overboard. Jinniyah shrieked as the waters collapsed on her. "Jinni!" I cried out to her, but there was nothing I could do. When the wave receded I saw she had fallen on the deck, burnt to a crisp and gone unconscious.

"What's happened to her?" Catalina said, going pale.

"She's made of fire. The water hurts her." I shook the burnt girl. "Please, Jinni. Wake up!"

Colón shouted to the rest of the crew, "Ready the rowboats! Non-essential personnel abandon ship immediately! Someone hold that wheel!"

Arabuko sloshed over to me across the flooded deck. "You must leave. Use our canoes. I will give you time."

Arabuko removed one of the necklaces from around his neck, one bearing a stone amulet that looked like a round face with mad eyes and a whirling mouth. Around the face were two S-shaped arms also made of stone. Arabuko quickly tied the necklace to his forehead. He knelt in a graceful position as a low, droning song came from his mouth:

"I call on you, Guabancex, Lady of the Winds. With Guatabá, your herald, unleash your mighty powers!"

Storm-force winds blew from Arabuko's raised hands. They shot out in a violent gyre, whirring across the bay and up at Uqba. The watery king swatted at it with his sword-carrying hand, but the wind spell blew his arm into droplets. The winds spun back and forth around him, taking Uqba apart, piece by piece. In less than a minute, Guabancex, lady of the winds, had dispersed Uqba and his horse into formless rain.

"We must go now, Captain!" Arabuko shouted to Colón in Castilian. "My spell has weakened the creature but not killed it!" Arabuko motioned out at the bay, where the waters were slowly reassembling themselves into the form of Uqba.

Colón bellowed, "All hands abandon ship!"

Catalina hefted the unconscious Jinniyah over her shoulders. With her free hand she pulled me to my feet, and the word SIREN appeared before her. Two silver-faced mermaids with needle-sharp fingernails and golden tails burst onto the deck. "Save our men!" Catalina ordered them.

They shrieked and dived overboard into the bay, skimming across the waters. To me Catalina said, "We need to go."

But Colón cut in front of us with his sword. "No. Not you."

"What are you talking about?" Catalina cried. "You heard Arabuko. We have to go before we sink!"

"I've heard enough from you, girl! Save my men with your witchcraft, but do not question my orders. You and the Indian take the servant and go. Luis stays." Colón looked me right in the eye. "Luis will fight. He is the one who has caused this attack, and he is the one who will save my ship. You must ask yourself, de Torres, are you a coward or are you a sorcerer? Is this not why I kept you aboard my ship, despite the fact that you've brought nothing but curses upon it? Or have I sold my soul to the Devil for nothing? Save us now, Lukmani! Save us, or I will die with my ship knowing that this is the Lord's judgment!"

"He's hurt! Don't you see that?" Catalina cried. "He can't summon now! Let me do it! I will save your ship!"

I wished that she could have, but I saw the sirens heaving drowning sailors out of the water. "You can't," I told her weakly. "You'd have to end your siren spell."

Arabuko gesticulated wildly toward the rail. "We must go now! We can return for the ship later!"

I looked past him, past the few remaining sailors on the *Santa María*, who clambered down the ladders and onto the one remaining Taíno canoe. Above them Uqba was reforming.

Colón was right. If it weren't for me, none of this would have happened. I had to end this.

"Arabuko, Catalina, go," I grunted, pressing the bandages harder against my shoulder. "You have to save Jinni and the men."

Colón said to Arabuko, "Take the girl and the servant to the canoes and lead them to shore. The boy stays with me. If I am to go down with this ship, he is coming with me."

Arabuko glanced at me, looking for a different answer, but he ushered Catalina in his direction and took Jinniyah from her. Catalina scooped up Tito, who was wet and cowering inside the cabin, gave me a final look, and fled onto a canoe with Arabuko. The three of them were the last to leave the ship. Colón and I were alone on the *Santa María*.

Uqba had reformed but appeared to be weakened. He swayed over the bay, and his dripping smile had shrunk into a giant wet frown. In this state a sea creature could defeat him easily. A sea creature like the Leviathan, if I had the strength to summon him.

"Well?" Colón asked me. "Are you going to save my ship or not?"

It looked like I had no other choice. So, bedraggled as I was, I closed my eyes and thought of the story of Job. When I was a child back in church I had always pitied the poor, innocent man, a good person tormented by a bullying God. And here I was now, being tormented by Colón, my own personal god who was forcing me to do his bidding.

But I wasn't poor and innocent. Colón said I'd brought nothing but curses on this voyage, and he was right. I drew the hameh to the crew. I was the reason we were now fighting Uqba. I wasn't innocent—far from it. And maybe Job wasn't innocent either.

Job was a heretical Jew. So was I. I dared to interpret the stories of the Bible the way I wished to create my own infernal creatures. That was what the Church and the Malleus Maleficarum meant when they called magic the art of the Devil. Storytelling was blasphemy, as bad as Job's questioning the Lord. No. Come to think of it, it was worse. Job didn't create monsters—I did. Only God was supposed to have such power. Only God was supposed to create dragons.

Far below me the earth grumbled, and the Leviathan surged out from the bay. But it wasn't the same dragon I had summoned weeks ago. This dragon's scales were black and dull, and its eyes were a sallow green. A horrendous shriek cut through the air as the Leviathan bucked over the bay's surface, tormented by some affliction. The anguished dragon aimed its head at me, and a white fire formed in its open mouth.

I stumbled backward. "What did you do?" Colón shouted at me.

"Nothing! I did exactly what you said. I—" I caught myself and shouted at the Leviathan, "Don't look at me! Uqba is your enemy, not me! Destroy him! Him!" The dragon shook its head and beat its body against the bay. "Listen to me! I made you! You have to listen to me!"

Screaming in anguish, the Leviathan reared up and cast a white beam at Uqba. The ray sliced through Uqba's watery body, turning him into cloud of vapor that billowed to the sky. Bucking and keening, the Leviathan coiled around itself to face the shore where Amir al-Katib was waiting. The white ray shot through the bay, exposing shoals of sand and sharp coral. The dark figure that was al-Katib saw the fires coming. He ran and dived into the forest behind him.

I rested against the rail. The spell-casting had drained me of the little energy I had left, and my shoulder was still throbbing. But at least I had saved the ship.

Or had I? I looked up, bleary-eyed, from the rail and saw the damage the Leviathan had inflicted on the bay. Jagged sections of coral reef, now completely exposed, stuck out in front of the *Santa María*. "Admiral!" I shouted with as much force as I could muster. "Turn the ship! We're going to hit!"

Colón was up on the aftcastle, throwing his body against the wheel. "What do you think I'm doing, de Torres? You worry about that dragon! Call it off before it kills us all!"

The ship pitched sideways as Colón made a sharp swerve away from the shallows. The bow screeched underneath us as it scraped against the coral.

I hung onto the rail, shouting, "Leviathan, that's enough! I release you!"

But the dragon continued to barrel through the shallow waters, its enraged eyes aimed right at me. I stood as the *Santa María* righted itself, watching the Leviathan's fiery beam race across the surface of the bay. With a crash it carved through the front section of the ship.

A wave of faintness washed over me when I saw it, and I fell to my knees. It was going to kill me. My own creation was going to kill me.

"I release you from my service," I begged him. "Please. Why are you doing this?"

The dragon sent out a hoarse roar but did what I said. Its body disintegrated into a million glittering pieces. I closed my eyes against my weakness and sank lower on the floor.

"Admiral!" I heard Vicente Pinzón calling somewhere below us. "We have a rowboat! Abandon ship! You're going to sink!"

Sweating over the helm, Colón looked at me, then over in the direction of the voices. "So be it," he muttered to himself. He flew down to the main deck, lugged me to my feet, and threw me over his shoulder with one hand. He climbed us down one of the rope ladders and into the rowboat that was waiting for us.

When we were halfway to the shore, the *Santa María* wobbled, collapsed onto the reef, and burst at the seams. Above us, the hameh flew south.

Nineteen

ABANDONED

As soon as we hit the shore, Colón uprooted me by my tunic and hurled me onto the sand. Forget the hameh, the Leviathan, and Amir al-Katib. Forget bleeding to death from the wound on my shoulder. This man was going to kill me with his bare hands, no magic required.

"You have destroyed my ship!"

"I . . . I didn't mean to."

"You have destroyed my ship, and you have doomed these men."

A flurry of chatter rose up in alarm. "What do you mean, doomed us?" my old friend Bartolome said.

"With the *Santa María* destroyed and the *Pinta* who knows where, we've only the *Niña* to return us home! But it is too small to transport all of our crew. At least half will have to remain on this island until we can return for you."

I buried my hands in the sand. Stranded. They were stranded here at the edge of the world because of me.

Colón continued, "We must collect whatever driftwood

and supplies we can from the wreckage. De Cuellar, you are in charge."

"Driftwood?" said Antonio. "For what?"

"To build a fortress." If it was possible Colón's voice became even more bitter. "La Navidad, in honor of the birth of our Savior."

Is it already December? floated through my head, a thought so mundane it almost made me laugh.

"My men will help you," Guacanagarí said with Arabuko translating for him. The cacique's eyes were actually brimming with tears. "Not a chip of wood nor piece of string will remain in that sea. I swear to you on my honor as a cacique."

The cacique's words must have touched Colón deeply, because the admiral finally looked away from me and put a hand on Guacanagarí's arm. "Thank you, Cacique. You are a true friend." Colón then prodded me with his boot. "As for you. I gave you employment. Sheltered you from harm when others would have you destroyed. Although I suppose this is my comeuppance. I should have known the Lord would strike me down for harboring those who meddle in the Devil's arts. I should have known the first time you drew that bird to our expedition. No, not 'bird.' That *demon*."

Guacanagarí shook his head. "An ill omen."

"Go," Colón ordered me. "I cannot risk having you do more harm to my crew. Sanchez, bring some provisions. Some food and water."

I couldn't believe it. "You . . . you're banishing me?"

"What kind of captain would I be if I allowed you to stay with us? You are a curse! That much is clear. If I let you remain here, I've no doubt you will destroy us all."

I squeezed some sand in my fists. In the back of my memory, the Baba Yaga said, *A great power travels west, who will destroy the world as we know it.*

Colón continued, "After what you did to my ship, you should be grateful I don't have you hanged! Now go! Get out of my sight!"

"Admiral!"

Catalina rushed up next to me, her eyes more sunken and her hair more tangled than usual. "Admiral," she said, "let me stay here with the crew. Please."

Are you kidding? I said to myself. Wasn't she on my side?

Colón answered her, "I'll not have your kind on my ship." The admiral tapped his fingers against his side as he examined his battered crew. "But I suppose the men of La Navidad will need a translator until I return from Spain. You may stay here with them, if that is your wish."

"It is."

"So be it. As for you, de Torres, you will go now. May God have mercy on your soul."

Catalina looked down at me with pity or guilt, then pushed some hair behind her ear and walked away. "You planning on leaving me too?" I said to Jinniyah behind me. Recovered from her burns, she pulled off my tunic and the linen shirt under it, then used the shirt and Catalina's bandages to bind my shoulder. Her jaw was set. When she was done bandaging me, I put on my tunic and rose shakily to my feet. "Let's go, then."

We limped toward the forest, that clot of green before us. Rodrigo Sanchez shambled over to us and dropped a bag of food and a skin of water into my hands, mumbling something that sounded like, "Sorry, Luis." When he left Arabuko ran over.

"Your friends move about like living corpses," the shaman said. "They believe living on Ayití will be their death sentence."

"Some friends."

"They should not worry so. Guacanagarí will let your captain and the other high-ranking men stay with us in Marién. We will provide the rest of your friends with food and help them build their fortress." Arabuko circled around me to look me in the eyes. "I am sorry I cannot invite you to return to Marién with us. I suspect neither your captain nor my cacique would approve of it. But if you still plan to find the bearded man, follow the river south, and when it ends follow the sun."

"You're not coming with me?" I asked, heart sinking.

"My cacique has ordered me to help your admiral build this fortress, but after my service is complete I swear I will try to find you. If you lose your way, seek out Caonabó. Guacanagarí quarrels with him, but he and his wife are well-known for their hospitality. It will take a day or more to walk to their province, Maguana, but if you find them I am sure they will offer you shelter." The shaman handed me a small pile of green leaves. "Chew on these. They'll help the pain and stop your bleeding and protect you from bad spirits."

I stored most of the leaves in my bag and put a few in my mouth. They tasted mild and garlicky, like Serena's eggplant stew. "Thank you, Arabuko."

"May the gods watch over you."

"And you," I said. I shook his hand and watched him go.

When he was gone Antonio de Cuellar came over to me. "You're going to say good-bye to one of those naked men, but you're not going to say good-bye to me?"

I couldn't bear to look at him. "Antonio, I'm so sorry for this. If it weren't for me—"

"No, I won't hear that kind of talk. Colón and the rest can say what they want, but you and I know who's to blame. That Moor."

The conversation paused there. Antonio went on, "Don't you worry about us, Luis. I'll admit I was planning on going back to Spain, seeing the good old ladies down in Palos again. But I'm a carpenter, and here I'm getting to build a fortress! Who knows? When I get back home I might well be famous. Antonio de Cuellar: builder of the first Spanish fortress in the Indies! I tell you, I could live with that."

I tried to give him a smile as he put his hand on my undamaged shoulder. "This isn't the end, Luis. In a few days, a few weeks maybe, the admiral'll be off again, searching for Cathay or taking the *Niña* back to Europe. And then you'll come on back here and live with us. What the admiral doesn't know can't hurt him. And look, I'm sorry for avoiding you before. I don't care what the rest of them say. Witch or not, you're all right by me. Maybe when you come back, you can teach me to make one of those dragons, eh?"

I smiled, for real this time. "Absolutely."

Antonio made a move to leave. "Oh, and one more thing, lad. A bit of advice you didn't ask for, but here it is. If I were in your place I'd go into that forest and find that Moorish bastard that sent those demons to our ships. I'd track him down and end this business like a man. I know it's not in your nature to do that, Luis. You're like me—rather sit around with some pretty young ladies, tell a story, have a drink. But sometimes a man has to go against his nature and do the thing that ought to be done. You understand me, don't you?"

I did. I took Jinniyah's tiny hand in my own sweaty one and forged ahead toward the mass of forest in front of us.

"Infante, wait!"

I slowed my pace as Catalina ran up next to me, but I didn't stop. "How can you stay here? I thought you said you were going to help me."

"That was before Colón found us," the girl said, looking away.

I stopped walking, and she did too. "Come with me," I told her.

"Why?"

To be my friend. To help me. So Jinni and I won't be so alone.

But I didn't say any of those things. I said, "You can't stay here! You're a young woman surrounded by sailors who haven't

260

seen a woman for months. It's not safe!"

"Oh? And I'd be safer with you, I suppose?"

"Yes. I'll protect you."

That's when Catalina got angry. "Protect me? Such a gallant knight!" She threw her arm behind her, gesturing at the sinking wreck of the *Santa María*. "Protect me! You don't even know how to summon a spell without having it backfire!"

That volley hit me square in the chest, but if Catalina noticed, I couldn't tell. She went on, "I can protect myself, thank you very much! So go. Go off on your little quest. I'm not going to be your damsel or your lover or your mentor or whatever other role you've assigned me in this little fairy tale of yours. I have my own story, and it ends in Cathay—in a civilized land, not in some miserable jungle in the middle of nowhere!"

"Well, good luck on your happily ever after, then. I hope you enjoy it." I continued on toward the forest.

"Infante!"

But I didn't look back. My wounds were throbbing. Every step was a pain for me. Out of the corner of my eye I saw Jinniyah give a small, sad wave back to Catalina.

"Good-bye," she whispered. Then the forest enveloped us.

I hiked south, in the same direction the hameh flew. I drove myself through the knee-high sludge of the jungle, raging against it and against Colón, against Catalina and Amir al-Katib, but mostly against my own wretched body. By the time the sun began to set I was aching with exhaustion, nearly ready to give in and sink into the mire.

At some point Jinniyah had returned to her original, flame-haired form. She hovered above the mud so its wetness wouldn't bite into her skin. Neither of us had said a word since we had set out from the bay. Now she floated in front of me, blocking my way down the forest trail.

"Wait, Bal," she said, so I stopped and listened to the rain as it began to patter on the leaves above us. I couldn't stop here for long, I knew. I would surely faint.

"We need to go, Jinni," I murmured.

The girl didn't move. A few drops of rain burned into her skin as they hit her shoulders. "Go where?" she asked me, but I knew she already knew the answer.

"We're going to find Amir," I said quietly. "Isn't that what you wanted?"

"And when you find him? What will you do then?"

I didn't know. The rain fell harder on us now, beating against the wounds on my chest and shoulder.

Jinniyah flew in closer so I could hear her skin sizzling under the rain. "When we find Amir, you'll talk to him, won't you? I know that Antonio said you might have to kill him for what he did—"

"Catalina said the same thing too. And Arabuko."

"But you don't have to!" Jinniyah seized my hands. "Please, Bal. Talk to him! Convince him that what he's doing is wrong! He'll listen! Then we'll find the evil being in the Baba Yaga's

262

prophecy and fight him together!"

I removed my hands from hers. *Find him. Talk to him.* That had been my plan all along. But now that Jinniyah said it, it sounded like a joke.

Talk to him. Oh, what did Jinni know? She was nearly immortal. She could walk right up to Amir al-Katib without having to worry about being killed. But I was human. I only had my words, and I knew how they could fail. What did Jinni know about words? Words cracked like leaves! Words died!

"I'll try to talk to him, Jinni, but how do you know he'll listen? You've seen what Amir's done. He's a monster!"

"He's your *father!*"

"No, he isn't. A defector, an unbeliever, a murderer, but never a father."

"A murderer? What do you—"

"You weren't there, Jinni, but he killed a woman in Arabuko's village a few weeks ago."

Tears flew from Jinniyah's eyes as she shook her head viciously. "There must be an explanation. You don't know him!"

I gave her a dark look. "And why is that, Jinni? Why don't I know him? Because he ran off to Granada to kill my people, to become a traitor fighting on the side of the Infidel!"

Jinniyah's hair crackled under the rain, and her fingers twitched into fists. "*Infidel?!* You mean Moorish!"

"What's the difference?"

Jinniyah dug a finger into my chest. "I'm Moorish. Your father's Moorish. That makes you Moorish!"

263

"No!" I fired back. "Actually, Jinni, it really doesn't!" Words from my memory squalled through the forest: Marrano. *Coward. Traitor.* "You remember that story you told me back in Palos? The one about how your god sent warriors to kill some poor defenseless genies? If that's what being Moorish means, then I don't want anything to do with them, not ever!"

Jinniyah shoved me twice through the hammering rain. "How could you?" she cried. "I thought you were a good person. But you're just like the rest of them! You think you know everything, but you know nothing! As if there wasn't a reason for it! As if no one from Spain ever killed anyone! Those genies were evil, you know! They were torturing humans—women and children! Anyway, Baltasar Infante, Allah has every right to kill as many genies as He wants! I think when you create something out of nothing, it's within your rights to destroy it whenever you feel like it!"

She floated to the puddly ground and started to cry. Seeing her there, letting herself be burned by the rain, I felt like I might cry too.

Instead I said, "Fine, Jinni. Believe what you want. But if there's one thing we can agree on, it's this. Someone has to stop Amir al-Katib before he kills any more people. I'll try to talk to him, but if he tries to kill me—if he gives me no other choice—I'm not going to just stand there. I'm going to fight. And if the time comes, if it comes down to me or him—"

Jinniyah looked up at me and cried, "Then I'm going to stop you!"

For a few seconds we stared at each other, letting the rain fall down on us. Finally I raised my arms and let them flop against my sides. "Why, Jinni? Why do you keep protecting him? You keep saying he's a good man, but he's not. This is a man who turned his back on his country and mutilated my people. A man who this morning ripped the *Santa María* to pieces. And, oh yes, Jinni—don't forget, Jinni! This is a man who abandoned you! You protect him, you vouch for him, but what did he ever do for you? Nothing! He left you alone in a necklace for the last—oh, I don't know—how about *fourteen years, Jinni!* Fourteen years! You act like he loved you, but guess what? He didn't!"

Silence. Just the sound of the rain's last downpour before it reduced itself to a drizzle.

I heard a tiny whimper as Jinniyah's body wilted. With those hollow eyes and huddled, blackened shoulders, she looked as though I'd punched her right in the stomach.

And then she vanished.

At first I didn't completely understand what had happened. "Jinni?"

I took a few splashing steps forward through the mud. "Jinni."

Then I understood.

She was gone.

Alone with my words, I sat in the forest.

Part Three

MAGUANA

MALLEUS MALEFICARUM

I don't know how long I walked—maybe a few hours, maybe all night. I wandered through the jungle, through the rain and the heat, not caring where I was headed or why. When I couldn't move anymore I stopped. I fell to the earth and let sleep overtake me.

I awoke the next day with leaves in my hair that I didn't care to remove. Around me the jungle was alive with the chirps and hoots of unknown tropical beasts. It was raining lightly. Dawn.

Abandoned you—

I lay back in my leafy bower and closed my eyes.

Oh. Right.

She was gone.

Well, it was her fault. I had been right, after all. Her emotions got the best of her, that was all. Clouded her interpretations.

But what was it Catalina said, back on the beach? "The truth doesn't matter. It's the interpretation that's important."

Didn't I know it. One bad interpretation after another—that's what got me into this mess.

I closed my eyes. Back on the ship, things made sense. Right and wrong—what were those? Right: the knot held. Wrong: it didn't. Right: the floors sparkled. Wrong: more work and no dinner.

Or back in Spain. Father Joaquín said: Here's the Bible. The Bible is the word of God. God is right. Spain fought for God. Spain is right.

I threw an arm over my head and said to no one, "I can't believe I'm homesick for church." At least back there things were easy. At least I knew what I was doing. I felt an awful burning in my heart and closed my eyes against the pain. "Dear God," I thought, "I know how much I've sinned. I don't know if you'll forgive me. But I'm begging you: Tell me what to do. I'm sick of figuring all this out on my own. Please. Please, give me a sign."

To the north of me, leaves rustled in the forest. I raised my head and squinted against the sunlight. "Jinni?"

But a tall figure crossed over a log into my leafy enclave. "Hi! It's me. Rodrigo Sanchez."

"Rodrigo?" I pushed myself upright in my nest. "What are you doing here?"

"I followed you. You left quite a path in the forest." Rodrigo sat on the log behind him and picked up a fruit from the forest floor. "Where's your friend? Juan."

"Jinniyah," I said. My throat was so dry. "Her name is Jinniyah. And she's gone."

"Oh." Rodrigo struggled against the rind of his fruit with his fingernails. "Do you want some? These things are delicious. The trouble is opening them. Where did I put that thing?" He swiveled his head to and fro, searching for something on his belt. From his side he unsheathed a dagger and held out its shining edge to peel his breakfast. He pressed the knife with his thumb into the papaya's flesh. Then he brought the knife and the piece of papaya to his mouth.

That's when I noticed the ring on Rodrigo's finger, a ring he hadn't previously been wearing. It was gold and branded with a familiar mark: a circle enclosing the shape of a hammer.

The world swam around me. Holding onto a nearby tree I pulled myself to my feet and backed away from Rodrigo. "You're from the Malleus Maleficarum. That's why you followed me."

Laughing, Rodrigo slurped up the fruit juice that had seeped down onto his chin. "Guilty as charged."

Feverishly, I pushed my fingers through my bangs. "I should have known. From the beginning I should have known you were a spy! The way you kept falling over, the way you kept bumping into things. It was all an act."

Rodrigo burst into laughter. "If only!" He pulled up his sleeve to reveal a long red scratch. "This one's from one of the creepers." Next he pointed to a nick right above his eyebrow.

"And this one's from bumping into a tree. I'd strip down and show you the bruises I got from slipping down that hill, but it's a bit early in the morning for that!"

Faking a chuckle, I sneaked a glance over my shoulder. The forest path was clear. I could make it, if I ran.

With all my might I launched a stone at Rodrigo's head and made a run for it. I tore through the vines, not caring where I was headed. But I didn't get far. I felt shivery and weak, and in a few steps my legs gave out beneath me.

I bent over the forest floor and panted into it. *"Dios,"* Rodrigo said. He rubbed his head where my rock had hit him. "You know, you didn't have to do that."

"I thought I did," I muttered.

"Come on, Baltasar! I'm not going to kill you! Listen, we're on the same side!"

I closed my eyes, trying my hardest to keep the trees around me from spinning. "What are you talking about, Rodrigo?"

The bookkeeper knelt beside me and offered me a piece of papaya balanced on his knife. When I shook my head he sat on the ground next to me and stuffed the piece of papaya into his mouth. With his mouth full he said, "I was back in court earlier this year when the queen suggested that the Malleus Maleficarum send a man to spy on this voyage around the world. I was there because my father's the liaison between the Malleus Maleficarum and the throne, and let me tell you, he wasn't too keen on this idea. My father said the organization had no men to spare, that it had its hands full trying to track down Amir al-Katib. The queen doesn't care; she's insistent. Then my father gets an idea. He volunteers *me* to be the inspector on the voyage! He gives me this look and says, 'Rodrigo won't come back until he's done something useful for once.' *Something useful!* I think. *How am I supposed to do something useful on a ship in the middle of nowhere?* It was hopeless."

A smile spread across Rodrigo's face, and he shook a finger at me. "Ah, but then I saw you translating those documents back in Palos! And on the ship, you were always telling stories. Every day another story out of the mouth of Luis de Torres! I didn't want to get my hopes up—it was possible, after all, that you were just a good translator who liked telling tales. But I began to think there might be a Storyteller aboard the *Santa María*."

I buried my sweaty head in my hands. "So you searched my bag and found the parchment." I should have known, I should have known!

Rodrigo dug in the pouch on his belt, took out the document, and unfolded it with the tips of his fingers. "'Baltasar Infante, the only living relative of Amir al-Katib the Moor.' I could hardly believe my luck! I thought, *If I bring the queen al-Katib's son, I'll be a hero!* Even my father would be impressed by that. But before I could arrest you, you were attacked by that black bird, that demon. I wondered where it came from and why it would attack Amir al-Katib's son. It was a mystery,

273

and I decided to wait and see where it led me.

"And it led me here to this island! To al-Katib himself! He was the one who sent that bird, and that sea monster—and he sent them both to kill you! That was when I realized—you didn't sail to the Indies to *join* your father. You came here to kill him!" The smile between Rodrigo's two large ears spread wider. "I'm right, aren't I?"

I kept my mouth shut, concentrating on recovering my energy. But Rodrigo didn't mind the quiet. He continued the conversation by himself. "That's what I was trying to say before, Baltasar. I'm not here to kill you! We're on the same side! You want to kill al-Katib; I want to kill al-Katib. We can work together! The two of us will be unstoppable! What do you say?"

I answered by climbing to my feet, teetering, and hobbling down the forest path. "Your people killed my family. I say you should go to Hell."

Rodrigo Sanchez ran in front of me. "Baltasar, wait, wait! That was a misunderstanding! Those soldiers had express orders not to hurt anyone. It was an accident!"

Rodrigo blocked my way, so I paused in my trek and held myself up by a tree. "Listen, Baltasar," Rodrigo went on. "I know it doesn't seem that way right now, but I can help you. I understand you, Baltasar. You're conflicted. You lost control of that dragon back there, and it attacked you. What does that tell me? It tells me you're confused, and you could use some help. Trust me. I know."

"You don't know anything," I said, feeling guilt the weight of the *Santa María* bearing down on me.

"That is absolutely, exactly, unequivocally wrong!" Rodrigo pointed at me like he was selling me something. "No, I understand you completely! I even understand how you messed up that spell with the dragon."

"How could you possibly understand?"

"Because I've done it, Baltasar! Botch a summon? Done it a dozen times, maybe more."

"What? How could you?" I let Rodrigo's words seep in. "Be honest. Was anyone on the *Santa María not* a Storyteller?"

Rodrigo laughed. "Just you and me, I think. And the girl."

I let my head fall back against the tree trunk and thought about what he'd said. "No, that doesn't make any sense. How can you be a Storyteller and a Malleus Maleficarum spy at the same time?"

"I know. Surprising, isn't it? But here's the big secret, Baltasar. Half of the Malleus members are Storytellers. Or former ones, anyway."

I opened my mouth to call out this statement as another lie. But I stopped myself. What he said had a certain kind of logic.

"When I was a boy, no one liked me," Rodrigo said, swinging his arms as he walked around in front of me. "I was always knocking something down, making a mess. 'Rodrigo the Fool,' they used to call me. The only time I was ever happy was when the traveling performers would come to court. They'd juggle and mime and throw swords. Best of all was when they'd put on plays. There were tragedies and comedies, religious stories where the actors would dress up as things like Mercy and Gluttony and Wrath. I started thinking about the stories all the time, and eventually I was able to summon the characters from these stories. At first I was excited that I had all these new friends to play with, but then my family found out. My father was furious, of course. He was a high-ranking member the Malleus Maleficarum, and it wouldn't do to have a witch for a son. So every day he would lock me in my room and tell me how much God hated me and how sinful I was. And it worked. From then on every time I tried to interpret a story, it would always be about my wickedness, and the spells backfired."

I dug my toes into the dirt. Although I didn't want to admit it, I knew this story all too well.

Rodrigo continued, "As I got older I realized that constantly trying to figure out on your own how to interpret the stories, interpret the world—it's a waste of energy, when you come right down to it. I stopped using magic and begged God's forgiveness, and Father pulled some strings so I could join him and work for the Malleus Maleficarum. And when I joined them I found I wasn't confused anymore. Suddenly everything was simple again."

Simple. How I yearned for the days when life was simple. When I could count on Diego for a stupid joke or a story, stories that were flat and meaningless and fun.

"Life can be simple for you, too, Baltasar. I can help you find Amir al-Katib. Together, we can bring justice to a man who has brought our people nothing but pain and fear. And when it's done I'll see to it that you're initiated into the Malleus Maleficarum the minute we get back."

I lifted my head off my tree. "Get back? Back to where?"

"To Palos, naturally! To Spain! Don't you see, Baltasar? All we have to do is kill Amir al-Katib. Then we'll be heroes, and we can both go home!"

Home. I felt my breathing become more labored. For a moment I thought I could feel the earth of Europe under my feet. I could smell the smells of Palos—the stews, the perfumes, the spices. I could hear Palos's birds, its insects, its people.

But it was an illusion. "There's no such thing as home," I murmured. "My aunt and uncle are dead."

I pushed past him and hobbled south. Rodrigo raced in front of me to the log he had been sitting on earlier. "Don't do this, Baltasar," he said, pointing his dagger at my chest. "If you won't join me, then I can't let you leave."

I backed away from him. I didn't have the energy to attack him or run. "Rodrigo, don't," I said, but he stepped forward with his knife.

"Don't move! Put down your weapon."

Catalina Terreros swung her conjured sword Excalibur so its edge touched the side of Rodrigo's neck. She had sneaked up behind Rodrigo so she could stand on the log he had been sitting on earlier. "Drop your weapon," she said, "or I'll kill you."

"Catalina, don't," I said tiredly. I opened my palm in front of Rodrigo. "Give me the knife, Rodrigo. Please."

The man gulped and glanced at Catalina. "As you wish," he said, and he placed his weapon in my hand.

I shoved the dagger into my belt. "Get out of here, Rodrigo. And don't come back."

Catalina added, "Mark my words, Señor Sanchez, if I see you again, I shall kill you."

"I understand," Rodrigo said. He stumbled over the log and clambered back into the forest.

Twenty-one

EDEN

Catalina sheathed her sword and hopped off the log she was standing on. Simultaneously we dropped onto it without saying a word.

Catalina was muddy, and she slouched so much that her head was almost against my shoulder. She looked so tired. She turned her head slightly and peered at me out of the corner of her eye.

"Well, you look a mess," she said.

"So do you."

She put her hand on my cheek. "Why are you shivering? Do you have a fever?"

"It's possible." The shoulder of my tunic was torn and covered with dried blood.

"You're lucky that hameh didn't cut you all that deeply." Catalina took a breath and said, "Well, go on. Take off your shirt."

I stared at her.

"By all the saints! I'm going to change your bandages."

Wincing, I peeled off my tunic, allowing Catalina to unbind the old dressings. She touched my wounds lightly and looked at her fingers. "What a mess." Although the holes the hameh made had finally stopped bleeding, they were now covered with layers of pink and yellow pus speckled brown with mud. I chewed on some of Arabuko's leaves as Catalina removed some strips of cloth from her bag and wound them around my arm and back. When she was finished she washed her hands with some of her water, untied a pouch from her belt, and drew out a hunk of melting goat cheese with the tips of her fingers.

"About Rodrigo," she started.

"Malleus spy," I answered.

"And where is Jinniyah?"

The word cracked on its way out. "Gone."

"I see."

I reached into her pouch to get at my own hunk of goat cheese. I chewed some silently before asking, "Why are you here? What happened?"

"Nothing," she said, far too quietly.

"You can tell me. I promise, I won't try to be your protector or your lover or whatever else it was you said. Please. I just want to be your friend."

The girl looked at me, carefully checking my eyes for honesty. When she found it, she folded her hands between her knees. "I was sleeping. Last night. We were on the beach, and the men had built a bonfire. And they drank. I should have been frightened of them, the way they carried on. I know what even noblemen are capable of, and these men were far from noble. But I was so tired from building the fortress. I ignored them and went to bed. Then in the middle of the night I woke up to see some of your friends stumbling out of the forest, dragging along five Taíno women. The men were laughing. The way they laugh when—"

Catalina cut herself off and blinked up at the sky. "Go on," I said, but I felt myself shaking on the inside.

"If you had been there, Infante. If you had seen the way those women looked! There was no question of what your friends had done. And when the women tried to get away, the men laughed. The way they laughed, Infante. You knew they were going to do it again. Right in front of me. They didn't care. Not one bit."

I couldn't believe it. Antonio de Cuellar. Pérez, Bartolome, and Salcedo. On the ship we'd shared dirty jokes, lewd stories about women for fun. No matter what Catalina said, I knew in my heart they were good people. Not—

I couldn't even think the word. "But how?" I asked. "Where was Colón? He never would have—"

"Colón!" Catalina scoffed. "He was off gallivanting with Vicente Pinzón in Guacanagarí's village. He left his men to their own devices."

I rubbed my face, trying to accept this information. I didn't want to believe my friends were capable of such horrors. But Catalina had no reason to lie.

"Then what happened?" I asked her.

"I fought them. I summoned the Erinyes—the great Furies of the ancient texts. Three of them—infernal winged goddesses of vengeance with blood dripping from their eyes. They tore out from under earth as if from Hell itself. And they screamed. A scream the likes of which you've never heard and never want to hear. The men fell into the sand, holding their heads in agony. I don't think the attack killed them—but it was enough to let those women escape." Catalina shriveled then. "It didn't make a difference, though. I was too late."

"What are you talking about?" I exclaimed. "You saved them!"

"Yes. But I wasn't able to stop what your friends had already done." The girl seemed unable to look at me. In fact I was sure she was going to cry.

Suddenly I was overcome by an urge to hold her, to protect her, to take her somewhere far away from this place. When we'd first arrived on this island, she'd called it the Garden of Eden. Paradise. She was wrong. In the stories Eden was a place untouched by grief or pain or war. There, no one had to live in worry that their interpretations were right or wrong. There would be nothing to interpret at all, just earth and sun and sky and clouds.

That place appeared around us. The tangled jungle thinned

into a valley dotted with fruit trees. The drizzly rain melted into the air. The raging frogs and crickets dispersed, leaving only the low hum of the breeze that combed through our hair. The breeze was dry here, no longer humid. Under our feet the mud and rotted fruit gave way to fresh grasses, beds of wildflowers, and the sweet scent of an eternal spring.

I whirled around. Catalina and I were alone.

"Where are we?" the girl asked.

"I don't . . . I don't know."

"Yes, you do. You summoned this place. Granted, such a feat deserves some praise. It's not easy to achieve. You must connect much more deeply with a story to make its setting come to life." She dismounted the log and drifted toward the nearest grove of trees. "So where are we?"

"Eden," I mumbled, embarrassed by the admission. Then I took Catalina by the arms. "Wait, don't you see? No one can find us here! Not Amir al-Katib, not the Malleus Maleficarum. Not the crew. We're safe!"

Catalina's face softened with pity. "Infante. We can't. It's not . . ."

I thanked God she trailed off then. I couldn't bear to hear the rest. *It's not real,* she'd say. *It's just a story.*

Well, so what if it was? Couldn't she see that this story could provide us some comfort? One day free from strife, where we could be embraced by the sun's warmth! The reminder of a summer afternoon spent tripping down the cobblestones of

Palos toward a game of cards with friends, where stories of women brought nothing more than a few knowing chuckles. How I longed for the scent of stew on a fire, or a kiss from one of the girls in the marketplace. There, the only thing that mattered was the cool sensation of saliva evaporating on our lips. The pressure of her hands against my back. The taste.

I pressed my mouth to Catalina's. It tasted of Gomeran cheese, salty and familiar.

She stood there, then flinched below my touch and prodded me away. She bit her lip.

"You just wanted to be my friend, I thought you said."

I turned away from her, my face hot. "I'm sorry. I shouldn't have done that. Not now. After what happened." I stepped toward her and braced my jaw. "Go on. You can hit me if you want to."

Catalina stepped forward. Raised her hand. Dropped it.

"You're living in a fantasy, Infante," she said quietly. She lowered herself to the ground and brought her knees to her chest. "But I can't say I don't understand it. I've done it before."

I joined her on the grass. "Really?"

Catalina picked up a bit of cheese that had fallen on the ground and rolled it between her fingers. "I was not a happy child. I read stories to escape. Soon I learned to summon creatures, entire worlds. It wasn't long before I began spending more time in a false world than in the real one. But it couldn't last."

I pulled a clump of grass out of the ground. Of course it couldn't. "The story you lived in. What was it?" I knew it was a presumptuous question to ask, but I needed to know.

"The story of the sleeping princess, of course." Catalina pried the hunk of remaining goat cheese apart with her nails, letting bits of it bounce into the grass. "But summoned settings only last for so long. After awhile they fade away of their own accord, unless you keep interpreting the story to keep it going."

"That didn't work?"

"If you keep interpreting the same story over and over, you'll eventually see new things in it that you didn't see before. I had always found the story of the sleeping princess a comfort. To be able to sleep forever, until your one true love rescued you? What more could a sad little girl want? But as I kept interpreting it, I soon realized the fairy tale I thought was an escape from reality was carrying truths from my own life—truths I'd rather not discover."

An image of the ghostly princess writhing against flowery bonds rose in my mind. I remembered what Catalina had said that night on the beach. "You figured out that the prince and the witch were the same. They used the princess for her castle and her beauty."

"And when I realized that, the castle vanished. It appeared I had broken my own spell."

I thought of the women the crew had kidnapped, felt the kiss I had stolen evaporate on my lips. Felt the thorny vines of guilt wrap around my chest. But Catalina gave me a soft smile. "Not to worry, Infante. This story has a happy ending. The sleeping princess made me realize I was just as trapped as she was. It was then that I decided to escape my own castle. I sneaked onto the *Santa María* and never looked back. Bad as it can be, living in the real world is always better than spending your life stuck in one story."

She stood and wiped her hands on her hose. "Here, I'll break out of this one too." Catalina closed her eyes and murmured something under her breath. In seconds the garden faded into the muddy universe of Ayití. She had broken my spell.

I smirked at her. "Thanks for destroying my paradise, Eve."

"Paradise?" Catalina said, opening her eyes. "Being stuck with you in a garden for all eternity? Sounds like my own personal version of Hell."

"Say what you will, Doña Terreros. We both know you're dying for another kiss."

"Try that again and I will hit you."

I picked up the bag of supplies Rodrigo had given me and said, "So how did you do it?"

"Break out of your Eden? Simple. You just need to figure out why you don't belong there. I said to myself, 'This is a story made by a naïve little boy who doesn't know how to live in the real world. I, however, am an adult. I prefer the fruit of knowledge and the pain of life to cowardice and inexperience.' Do you want me to go on?"

I mumbled in the negative.

"Then we should go," Catalina said. "We have to find Jinniyah and your father. And Tito."

"You lost him?"

"When I left the fortress he ran off into the woods, and I haven't seen him since. But don't worry. Tito can take care of himself—although he prefers the company of others. And one more thing." She picked up my rolled-up tunic and tossed it in my face. "For the sake of everyone on this island, put your shirt back on."

I stuck my tongue out at her, and we continued hiking through the forest.

We wandered through the fetid heat of Ayití until it finally turned to night. Then we huddled under the trunk of an enormous tree, listening to the frogs whistle about us as the rain pounded on our heads. The next day after little sleep we trekked on, following the edge of the river, and the day after that we hiked through a valley surrounded by rolling green mountains. When needed, we ate the food in our bags and whatever fruits we found hanging above us in the trees. As we walked, Catalina stayed mostly quiet. Knowing what she was thinking about, I filled the silence with anything I could think of—talk of the weather, Jinniyah's whereabouts, or how we might defeat Amir al-Katib.

Try as I might all she gave me was distant, one-word answers, so on the fifth day I started to play dirty.

"Of all the great kisses in your life," I said, "how do you feel mine would rank? Because I can make adjustments if you want."

Catalina stopped in her tracks and said sharply, "Be quiet."

"I will not be quiet! I'm trying to gather valuable information!"

"I said *be quiet!*" Catalina shouted at me in a whisper. "Listen! There's someone out there!"

Her face tensed as she scanned the forest around us. I followed her lead. Then more than a dozen arrowheads stuck out of the trees, aimed at our hearts and our heads. The bow-wielding soldiers stepped out slowly from their hiding places. There were so many of them, yet I hadn't heard a thing.

"You will come with us, Spanish," one of the Taíno soldiers said. "On the order of Cacique Caonabó and High Priestess Anacaona. Welcome to Maguana."

Twenty-two

MAGUANA

We followed the soldiers of Maguana through the jungle. Soon the forests opened into an overcast valley filled with hundreds of thatched-roof buildings ringing a central square. It was Arabuko's village writ large, with thousands of people milling through its dirt roads and side streets. We were led down a main road that weaved through the city's houses. Black eyes peeked out at us from the doors of the shadowy buildings, and children with coarse black hair gawked at us and laughed.

At last we arrived at the town's puddle-filled main courtyard, an empty, garden-lined area in front of a thatched rectangular house about twice the size of the town's other buildings. The palace of Caonabó and Anacaona, I supposed. The dozen soldiers guarded us from the courtyard's grassy perimeter.

From afar we heard the wail of a conch shell trumpet and a tinkling melody of high-pitched drums. As the sound of the drumming came closer, I could hear a discordant chorus shouting a call-and-response. It seemed that the entire village, in three straight lines, was parading its way into the courtyard.

The men wore red paint on their faces; they dug in their heels with each step. The women here wore longer skirts than those in Arabuko's village, and their skirts were painted with images of birds and dog-faced men. Around their ankles they wore bracelets adorned with pink seashells that jangled when they moved. A cavalcade of young girls wearing white headbands followed the women, carrying yellow and green gourds. On each off-beat the girls shook their gourds, rattling the sand and pebbles inside them. Behind them came the drummers, and finally the man with the conch horn.

Then two figures were carried out of the palace on a litter: a man and a woman, both of striking beauty. On the left sat the warlord Caonabó, a flinty-eyed man, who, unlike the other men of his village, had pulled his hair into a knot on the back of his head. The few wrinkles circling his eyes reflected the man's middle age. Along with his thick, arched eyebrows, they gave him the look of an owl. So much red dye snaked down his muscled arms that I could make out little of his true coloring. His wispy, graying bangs were mostly hidden by a beaded red headband, in the center of which was a golden medallion. He had gold earrings in his ears, as well, thick golden crescents that stuck out of both earlobes.

Beside him sat the lady Anacaona, wearing a painted white skirt that cascaded over the lower half of her voluptuous body. What did the Taíno call the wife of a cacique? A queen? As far as I knew they had no word for it. With her long silky hair, pristine face, and bright almond eyes, I would say she was around twenty, if that old. From her place on the litter the cacique's wife threw her arms carelessly behind her head and tapped one foot to the beat of her musicians' drums.

The men who carried them lowered the litters to the ground as two young girls rushed to place two chairs at the head of the courtyard. Each chair had been fashioned out of a single tree trunk. They had high, reclining backs, and their legs had been formed into animal paws. At the front of each, on the bottom, a sculpted beast grinned at us cryptically.

Caonabó climbed off his litter and strode to one of the thrones, and two strongmen led Anacaona to the other. The queen wore nothing but her painted white skirt and a feathered necklace with a light-blue pendant. The strongmen held her hands as she sat on her throne and crossed her legs. Despite the informal way they sat, the cacique and his wife gave the impression of extreme power. The two held themselves as if they were nothing less than gods.

The conch shell trumpeted a last time, and at once all the music stopped. I glanced at Catalina and immediately threw myself into a florid bow. "We greet you, most noble cacique, and High Priestess Anacaona. I am Luis de Torres, son of the Duke of Burgos, and may I present to you my cousin Serena. We are here on the orders of the Spanish crown. Our queen sent us here to negotiate a trade agreement and perhaps in time, a military alliance—"

But when I looked up from my bow I could see Caonabó was racked with silent laughter, and his wife had put her hands excitedly on her knees.

"I like his style, Husband!"

"Yes, I might even believe his story if it didn't look like they've spent the last week surviving on tree-frogs and mud!"

The Taíno crowd surrounding us joined them in their merriment. Apparently we'd need to go for the direct approach. "My name is Baltasar, and this is Catalina. We got lost in the woods and beg for your protection."

Anacaona rested her chin on a fist. "Such nerve he has, Husband! Admitting he's lied to the cacique."

"They disrespect us, Wife," Caonabó agreed. "Even though they are less than scum."

Anacaona beckoned a girl of about seven standing shyly in the corner of the courtyard. "Higuamota, beautiful daughter." Anacaona gestured in my direction. "Show them how we treat foreign scum."

Two soldiers came up behind Catalina and me, so fast that we had no time to stop them. They grabbed our hair and forced us into bows on the ground. Higuamota looked back and forth between our prostrate bodies and her mother. At last the girl came forward and spat dryly in our faces.

"Let them go!" I thought I heard Jinni cry, and a Taíno girl with Jinniyah's face flew in from the crowds and landed beside me. "You get away from them!"

Jinniyah grabbed the wrist of the soldier holding onto

Catalina. The man fell backward, squealing and holding his wrist, which was now branded with a blistering burn in the shape of Jinniyah's hand. "Get back," Jinni said to the soldier holding me, threatening Higuamota with her hand. With a *whoosh,* black flames cascaded down Jinniyah's body as they had done in the inn back in Palos. The soldier holding me fled into the crowd, and little Higuamota screamed and ran crying to her mother.

"What are you?" Caonabó demanded of Jinni. "How long have you been hiding in our city?"

"Two days." Jinni transformed into her original flame-haired form. She put her hand on mine and said, "Bal, I heard one of them talking about Amir, but I haven't been able to find him!"

On the other side of me Catalina's fingers screwed into the dirt. Her fingers had gone white, and her face was bright red. "How dare you!" she said to Caonabó and Anacaona. "Do you have any idea who we are?"

For a second I thought Catalina would summon something or rush at the priestess and fight her with bare hands. But it was suicide, I knew—we were still surrounded by arrows. I squeezed her hand and whispered, "They know where Amir is. Let's try and talk."

Anacaona stood and slunk toward us. "Yes, talk," she said, her voice low and cutting. "Go on, boy. Confess. Tell all of Maguana of your crimes."

I let go of Catalina's hand, startled. "What are you talking

293

about? We didn't do anything to your people."

"Oh, no?" The queen arched her back, rising to her full height. Her long hair swished around her hips as she turned to address the crowd. "Then I shall refresh your memory. Several nights ago your people raided our northern camp and stole off with five of our women!"

The crowds around us exploded into jeers and hisses, slinging insults at us from every angle: "Savages!" "Kidnappers!" "Demons!" "Rapists!" My heart dropped into my stomach. The five women Catalina had told me about. I looked over at Catalina, but she looked away, wrought with some unknown emotion.

Caonabó raised a finger, silencing the crowd, and Anacaona looked down on Catalina. "And you," the queen said. "I expect men to allow such savagery. But a woman? To let such horrors occur in front of you?" I could see tears forming in Catalina's eyes. Anacaona's lips lifted in disgust. "Stand," the queen ordered Catalina, and two soldiers came forward to pull the girl to her feet. "Well? What do you have to say to defend yourself?"

But Catalina couldn't answer that question. She had gone pale and limp and would likely collapse if the soldiers that held her let go. I rushed to my feet. "Catalina did nothing wrong! We've cut ties with the rest of the crew. We had nothing to do with the kidnapping of those women!"

Hearing this, the crowds around us began calling for our heads. Again Caonabó silenced them and crossed one muscled leg over his knee. "The boy may not be lying, my love. It is possible they left their crew before the incident occurred."

Anacaona turned back to her husband. "Nevertheless. We cannot allow such savagery to go unpunished."

"No doubt. The question now is, what do we do with these three? Three Spanish hostages might be useful."

Anacaona returned to her seat on the throne. "Hostages are good. Severed heads are better."

"Perhaps. But we must not be rash."

Beside me, the soldiers holding Catalina let her loose. She fell to her knees. As I watched her, the voices of Anacaona and Caonabó seemed to fade from the courtyard. For an instant, I was sure she and I were alone.

Catalina. Where are you? What do you see? Right now, with her face bloodless and gaunt as a banshee's, I could have mistaken her for the sleeping princess she had summoned on the beach so many weeks ago. *Trapped,* that empty look seemed to say. *Please help me. I'm trapped.*

"Mama, look!"

A series of gasps rippled across the courtyard as I followed the line of Higuamota's outstretched finger. Ashy words reading SLEEPING PRINCESS formed in front of me. And the princess arrived: the familiar drawn cheeks, the crazed stare, the rose-thorn shackles. I had summoned her accidentally. But this time her face was different. This time she looked exactly like Catalina Terreros.

I looked back and forth between Catalina and the doppelganger I had summoned. Higuamota rushed into her mother's arms. Caonabó rose from his throne, the veins on his face and arms stressed and swelling. "What is this . . . *thing?*" he demanded. Before I could answer he grabbed a fish-tooth spear from one of his soldiers and aimed it at the Sleeping Princess. Black thorny vines whipped from underneath the summoned princess's tattered sleeves, shot out at the cacique, coiled around his spear, and threw the weapon far from his reach.

The cacique's guards moved in and aimed their spears and arrows at me.

"Don't you dare," Jinniyah warned, and she whooshed back into her black flame form. I jumped in front of her and waved my hands in front me like a madman.

"No, Jinni!" I cried. "Everyone, stop! We're not here to fight!" Not when Catalina was close to weeping on the ground. Not when we were surrounded. Not when we were so close to finding Amir al-Katib.

Amir al-Katib. Suddenly I had an idea, a way to get Catalina out of this place and finally track down my father.

I stepped closer to the Sleeping Princess and announced to the Taíno around me. "We're not here to fight, but we are very powerful shamans. And we will kill your cacique and the priestess unless they do as we say."

Caonabó shook out his hand, which had been twisted when

the Sleeping Princess yanked the spear out of his grip. "More shamans," the cacique muttered to his wife. "No wonder they speak our language."

"I don't give a damn who or what they are!" Anacaona jumped up from her seat. "They threatened us! They must be executed at once!"

But Caonabó raised a hand, stopping the soldiers from attacking. "Wait. I would like to hear what these shamans have to say."

"But they are Spanish snakes!" Anacaona sputtered. "He just summoned a spirit to murder us!"

Caonabó walked behind his wife's stool and massaged her arms. "Many of the best friendships begin with attempts at murder. I remember a young priestess, for instance, trying to kill me on our wedding night. Yet that turned out well in the end."

Easing into the massage, Anacaona pursed her lips, still angry. But underneath her scowl, I could see the beginnings of a smile. "Very well. Let us hear your terms, Shaman."

I paused, looking to Jinniyah for support. "There are rumors in the north that you wish to ally with Amir al-Katib, the bearded shaman from the east."

"Merely a rumor," Caonabó said, returning to his throne. But the way he spoke told me the rumor was true.

Anacaona added, "We had no desire to ally with the bearded one until that pitiful Guacanagarí allied himself with Colón!

This Colón is part of a prophecy—a man from the east who will destroy the world as we know it."

So they had heard the prophecy that Baba Yaga shared with me. Good. I could use this as part of my plan. I lied, "You're right. That is exactly why Colón has come here. He has come to destroy your kingdoms and take your lands for himself. And he has the power to do it. He has well-trained men, swords—sharper swords than you can imagine. And guns—hollow sticks that can shoot rocks made out of fire." Worried murmurs swept through the crowd at this statement. "He'll bring armies from Europe. Horses!" I reached one hand high over my head. "Giant beasts, ten feet tall, that can run twice as fast as your fastest man. Colón and his armies will ride atop them, shooting your people down with his guns." I cocked an invisible arquebus and aimed it at the ducking crowds. "Bam! He'll kill you before you get close."

Around me, Taíno mothers held their children closer to their breasts. Caonabó asked, "What is the point of this legend, Shaman?"

"You need the bearded man to even the sides. Amir al-Katib is the best shaman the world has ever known, and he hates the Spanish even more than you do. If you free us, I will bring you to him, and you will have your alliance."

The Taíno crowds chattered at my offer, and the wet-faced Higuamota crept closer to her mother.

"Impossible," Anacaona said. "The bearded man hides in

the Cave of the Jagua. No one may dare enter it, lest the gods frown upon us and bring us to despair."

"But *I* can enter it, with your permission, may I not? And Jinni and Catalina. We can go inside the cave and bring out the shaman. The man is my father, and I can convince him to join you—if you let us leave this village unharmed."

Caonabó leaned forward and tapped his thumb against his mouth as he looked at an emaciated older man on the courtyard's perimeter. "What do you say, High Shaman Cocubo? Can these foreigners enter the cave?"

The old shaman squinted at the ground in thought. "The stories say the cave birthed the Taíno in the days of yore. But they didn't say anything about foreigners."

"So we can go inside?" I said expectantly.

"Yes. Yes, I believe so."

Anacaona combed back her daughter's hair with her fingers. "The boy is lying. He does not know the bearded man. He only wishes to escape our punishment."

"Then we will make it so he cannot escape," Caonabó replied. "I will take him to the cave myself, with an army. He will bring us the bearded man or we will kill him. Remember, dear wife, a shaman is not invincible. Regardless of what powers he has, his skin can be pricked by an arrow."

Anacaona considered the offer and a smile spread across her face. "I *would* like an alliance with the bearded one. You heard what he did in Marién."

"Then it seems we have a deal, young shaman," Caonabó said. "Our women will prepare some food for your journey. And water."

"Wait." Catalina stood and raised a tightly-flexed hand. "The deal is not done. I have another term."

Anacaona's smile spread toward me. "Is this your way, Spanish? We give you one thing and you demand another?"

Catalina said, "Yes. If we are to have a deal, you must not attack La Navidad."

Anacaona's hair swished about her as she looked back at her husband. "She demands a truce with the Spanish? After what her crew did?"

Caonabó agreed, "They must pay for their atrocities."

"Then at least wait until we've found the bearded man," I said quickly. "With Amir on your side, Colón will be more willing to bargain. You can ask for the men who kidnapped your women, take them as prisoners. Then no one will have to go to war."

Anacaona threw her head upward, flipping out her hair. "He acts as if we fear war with the Spanish." She stood and addressed the Taíno around us. "It matters not what weapons they have. We will fight them and take their weapons by force! We have our own armies, our own shamans, and soon will have the bearded one, the mightiest of them all. We know these lands and how to protect them. These intruders who plant foreign banners on our soil will rue the day they first set eyes on Ayití!"

The Taíno crowds cheered around us, but Catalina ignored them. Her eyes blazed as she marched up to Anacaona. "That is *not* what will happen," Catalina said. "You will start a war, and my people will win. I know how the Spanish work. If you start a war, they will not stop until they have destroyed all of you. Not just the soldiers of Maguana, but everyone in Ayití. Men, women, and children. All will fall under Spanish swords. Those who survive will be worse than dead, forced into servitude. My people will not stop until Ayití is a wasteland."

Jinniyah's black flames receded, leaving her in her normal half-genie form. She hovered in the air before Anacaona. "Please. Listen to Catalina. She's right."

Anacaona looked to her husband, who offered no help. "You think this talk frightens us?" she said, but her eyes flicked apprehensively to the side.

Catalina stepped up to Anacaona so she was about an inch from the priestess's face. "Yes. And you are right to be afraid. Our queen is not as merciful as you are. Even we shamans fear her and her Inquisition. So make the right choice. You do not want to be enemies with Spain."

Higuamota ran up to Anacaona and wrapped herself around her mother's leg. "All talk," the queen muttered to herself, but she held her daughter close. "Very well. We will not attack the fortress. But go now and bring me the bearded man, or I will stop being so merciful."

THE CAVE

Caonabó and his army led us east through the jungle until the muddy forest trail hardened into a rocky path that cut through Ayití's mountains. After a half-day's march we spilled out into a rock-strewn valley covered with a gray blanket of clouds. I asked the cacique, "How much longer?"

"We're not far. And do not think about escaping. My men are ready to take you down at first order."

Escape was the last thing on my mind. I was on my way to Amir al-Katib.

Caonabó hiked past me, and Jinniyah came up by my side. "I missed you," she said quietly. "David said I was supposed to protect you. I shouldn't have left."

"No, Jinni. I shouldn't have yelled at you. What I said in the forest—I didn't mean it."

"Did you mean what you said in Maguana? About bringing Amir out of the cave alive?"

Squinting up at the clouds, I said truthfully, "I'll try. If

Amir lets me talk to him, I'll talk. But if he attacks us again, if he leaves me no choice . . ."

"I know," Jinniyah said darkly. Her body angled forward, she forged past me, to warn Amir I was coming for him.

We marched through a series of brush-covered hills with Taíno soldiers ahead of us and behind us. Soon Jinniyah was so far ahead of me I could barely see her. I slowed my pace so I could speak with Catalina.

"Are you all right?" I asked her.

"Yes. But I wish you hadn't done that before. Summon the princess with my face."

"I'm sorry. It was an accident."

"I know. But don't do it again. I'm not a fairy tale for you to interpret. I'm a person."

"I know," I said.

"Good. Don't forget."

A shriek rang out in the hills above us. Jinni.

We galloped up the closest hill, followed by Taíno soldiers, kicking over piles of stones as we went. The dirt path we were on led us up a steeper incline until we could see a wide maw fringed with rocky fangs. It was the Cave of the Jagua, where Amir al-Katib was hiding.

Jinniyah burst out of its entrance and smashed into me. "Jinni, what happened?" The girl shook her head into my chest.

A group of Taíno soldiers climbed up behind us, and Caonabó handed Catalina and me lit torches. "The Cave of the Jagua. We will wait until you return with the bearded man."

A damp breeze pushed up against me, exhaled by the cave mouth. Inside I could see nothing. Jinniyah clamped onto my arm. Together, we walked inside the cave.

We found ourselves inside a narrow tunnel. Our torches and Jinni's hair cast gold and black light over the rocky walls, revealing unreadable Taíno glyphs that seemed to glow out of the stone.

"Why did you scream before?" I asked Jinni, and the girl peeked out from behind my arm.

"I saw eyes in the dark. This place is full of magic."

When we reached the end of the passageway, Catalina lowered her torch to assay a squat hole that led into the next room. Then she raised her torch so it shone on a stone face carved into the wall above the hole. The face was about the size of a human's, with two thick horizontal gashes for eyes and a gaping O for a mouth.

So this was what scared Jinniyah. I rubbed my fingers along the top of the stone mask. It was surprisingly smooth. "Looks like a warning," I said. "Don't come in here or else." Jinni shuddered as we crawled through the hole in the wall and into the next room of the cave.

Once inside the next room I instinctively fell backward. My feet touched the edge of a cliff. One more step and I surely would have fallen into the bottomless pit below. Our torches showed us almost nothing, only the slender stone walkway that we were currently standing on. There were no Taíno glyphs here, as far as I could see. I gathered we'd gone farther than their shamans dared to tread.

Catalina lifted her torch to get a better look at the stalactites that pricked out of the ceiling above us. "Do you hear that?" She swung the torch out in front of us. A muffled sound like rushing water thundered beyond the far wall.

"Sounds like a river," I said.

While we were investigating the top level of the complex, Jinniyah was checking out the bottom. She had crawled on all fours to the edge of the cliff and pointed down into it. "Bal, Catalina, look!"

I joined her at the edge of our walkway. Far below us, deep in the chasm, a skinny scar of white light shot out of a sheer rock wall.

"Amir could be down there!" Jinni said.

Catalina knelt next to her and reached her torch out above the chasm. "Rather conspicuous, isn't it?"

"You think it's a trap?" I asked her.

"Even if it is, we have no choice but to go into it. Caonabó and his men will kill us if we leave this place without al-Katib."

"Then what are we waiting for?" Jinniyah said. She dragged Catalina down the stone walkway, leaving me to look down at the distant, blazing scar. I kicked a pebble off the cliff and into the chasm. It was several seconds before I could hear the telltale *plink* as it hit bottom.

It really was a long drop. I took a breath and followed Catalina and Jinni into the deep.

We hiked down the cave's natural path and soon reached the bottom. From down here the entrance the Taíno mask guarded had shrunk to a distant speck of light. Stalagmites stuck out in front of us, spiny teeth in the earth. It was hot, and the room smelled of animals—bats, maybe, but I couldn't see them. I didn't see further signs of Taíno shamans' work down here. All the better—I didn't want to interfere with a sacred spot.

"Some place to have a hidden lair," I said, swinging my torch in front of me.

"You stay there!" Jinni said. "I'm going to talk to Amir." She ran off, barefooted, across the rock, toward the scar in the wall she had pointed out earlier. I took a breath and slowly followed her across the field of stone. Amir al-Katib. I had finally made it.

Jinniyah was halfway to the scar now, about forty feet in front of me. She knelt and placed one hand against the floor. "Oh, no!" I heard her cry. Her fearful words echoed through the cave.

Though her tone unnerved me, I reminded myself that Jinniyah was easily excitable, and I kept my own voice calm. "What's wrong, Jinni?" I called across the hall.

"Don't you feel it?" she shouted. "The room is shaking! It's sand, Bal! The ground is turning to sand!"

She was right. I could now feel the ground vibrating beneath my feet, and a fine layer of sand seemed to be forming on the rock floor. I swept some away with my fingertips. More sand grew in its place. Something seemed to be sucking the stale humidity of the cave dry, leaving a harsh, empty heat in its stead.

"What is it?" Catalina shouted to Jinni. "What is he summoning?"

Jinniyah screamed back, "Ghuls! Arabian desert demons! They—"

There wasn't time for her to continue. As if spit up by a geyser the sand shot up to our knees. Two skeletal hands covered with coarse hair and sickening greenish-black skin ripped through the dunes and grabbed Jinniyah by the heels. She didn't even have enough time to try to fly out of their way.

"*Bal!*"

I raced across the sand and threw myself at the dunes. Too late. The sand gave no resistance. Jinni and the ghuls' hands slipped beneath the earth.

"Jinni!" I dropped my torch, fell to my knees, and raked the sandy mounds aside. Nothing.

A pull at my collar jerked me backward. "Watch out!" Catalina shouted. Rolling waves of earth sent us stumbling off our feet. Inches in front of me, a dozen more claws tore through the sand.

"This way!" Catalina wrenched me off the ground.

"But Jinni—!"

"You won't be of any use to her dead!"

We flew back the way we came, toward the path that had led us down into the cavern. But the path was gone. As we hurtled forward I saw that the cave had completely transformed. Where the rock wall used to be was now a sandy horizon and a hazy yellow sun. The stalagmites on the floor had disintegrated into more raging sand dunes, and the stalactites were replaced by an infinite red sky.

Amir al-Katib had not just summoned the ghuls. He had summoned the desert.

Claws shot through the shifting sands as we ran. Catalina cried out as one scratched the back of her calf, ripping the hose and flesh right above the top of her boot. "This way!" I exclaimed, pulling her up a tall dune in front of us. "We'll get the high ground."

Catalina and I raced up the dune, slipping through the moving sands as we did. At the top we bent over to catch our breaths. Those ghastly green arms hadn't followed us up here. They stuck out of the sands underneath us, surrounding our dune. Bending awkwardly at the elbow, the ghuls' arms pressed against the earth. Then with a final push, they hurled themselves out from underneath it.

And finally we saw them in their entirety: dozens of corpse-like women with red cats' eyes and warped grins on their faces. They crawled on their knuckles with their backs arched so their coarse black manes jutted farther out of their spines.

Panting, Catalina bent over and pressed her hand against her bloody leg.

"Are you all right?" I asked her.

"I'm fine." The she-beasts were making a slow circuit around our hill. They were in no hurry. There was nowhere for us to run.

"Should we summon something?" I asked Catalina. "A golem might sink in this sand." When the girl didn't answer, I said, "Catalina? What do you think?"

But when I turned back to her, two hands crashed into my throat and threw me onto my back. I screwed my eyes against the pain. Then I noticed who was strangling me.

"Cat . . . ?"

But Catalina's eyes were now red like the ghulahs', red as the blood dripping down her leg where the ghulahs had scratched her. She bit her lip as her fingers tightened around my windpipe. With both legs I kicked her off me, and her nails raked against my face.

I held my stinging cheek, then looked down at the lines of blood on my palm. "Damn it," I said to those lines of blood. The ghulah's scratch had turned Catalina into one of them. And now Catalina had scratched me.

I knew what would happen next.

I blinked. And when I opened my eyes again, the world changed. Everything was red now. I felt a new strength coursing through my veins. Suddenly I knew exactly what I needed to do. Amir al-Katib had been a distraction. This woman was my enemy. She had been my enemy all along! Now I knew why she had followed me all of those times before—into the ocean, into the forests of Ayití. She was using me, trying to take my glory! I would show her who was in charge here.

I would kill her.

I pounced at her. Now we were on the ground, wrestling with jaws clenched. Her teeth were gleaming with saliva as she wheezed air between them. I snatched a handful of sand from my side and threw it into her eyes. With a screech she flew off me. I smirked and buried my teeth into her neck.

Catalina threw me off her and summoned her sword Excalibur. With a drunken movement she swung the sword at me. I leaped out of the way. She growled, adjusted her grip on the handle, and came at me again. I managed to dodge the sword just as it swept past. Catalina tripped and went flying into the sand. As she made impact with the ground I stomped on her sword arm and held her head down with my elbow. I twisted the sword out of her grasp with my free hand as she thrashed beneath my shoe.

Now I had her. Slowly I raised the sword over my head. Good-bye, Catalina Terreros.

"Bal!"

My grip loosened around the sword, which wobbled behind my head as my wrist went slack. "Jinni," I said, remembering

310

where I was. The world quickly went back to its normal coloring. I swung my head over my shoulder. Below my dune, I could see Jinniyah's hand and half of her face sticking out of the sand.

"Bal, help me!" she cried. "Get us out of here! *BAL!*"

More green hands shot out of the sand around her. They smothered her and dragged her down into the earth.

I pushed Catalina over so I could see her face. Tears were streaming from her eyes—from the sand I'd thrown at her, I guessed. A ring of red teeth marks glared at me from the side of her neck. Trying to ignore them, I shook her. "Catalina, wake up! It's a mirage! The ghulahs put us under a spell! Please! I need you to get us out of here!"

Catalina kept squirming under me, her eyes inflamed, savage, and red. Oh, how had she broken out of my Eden before? If I could do the same thing, I could break us out of this desert prison.

"How did I break out of your Eden?" Catalina had said in the forest. *"You just need to figure out why you don't belong there."*

And once she'd said, too, *"You'll find that most female creatures in myths are extremely frightening. Apparently men find us very scary."*

At once I knew what the story of the ghulahs was about. And I yelled so Amir al-Katib could hear me, "This is a story told by a man who's afraid of the desert, just like he's afraid of women." I looked down sadly at Catalina and said, "Just like

311

some people are afraid of men. And I can't blame you for it."

I went on, much louder, "But it's a mirage, Amir! And I won't be afraid of mirages! Maybe this desert is your prison, but it's not ours! We don't belong here. It's only a story! It's not real! So if you don't mind, we're leaving. And next time you want to summon the desert, leave me and my friends the hell out of it!"

A whirlwind of sand spiraled up toward the sky. I covered my head and held Catalina tight. Over the sound of wind, I could hear the ghulahs shrieking. Then the wind stopped, and I fell forward onto my knees as the sand disappeared under my feet.

I stood and looked up. The red sky of the desert had given way to the rocky ceiling of the Cave of the Jagua. We were back in Ayití, in the dark.

The sound of coughing drew my attention back downward. "Catalina!"

I helped her sit. She was shaking wildly, breathing gasping, shivery breaths. "What happened?"

I held her and said, "Nothing. A mirage."

"Bal!" Jinni yelled from across the room.

"Jinni!" I cried. "You're okay!"

At the other end of the cave, Jinniyah balled her hands into tight little fists, and her hair cast black light around the room. "Bal, I *hate* ghuls!" she said. "They're dirty and ugly, and I hate them!"

I helped Catalina stand and said, "Catalina and I didn't love them, either. But they weren't too hard to deal with, once we figured out the story . . ."

I trailed off at the tail end of the word. In front of us, by the scar in the cave wall, bits of lightning were shooting out of the ground. A wind from nowhere gushed through the cave, and I felt the floor shuddering like it had when Amir had summoned the ghulahs. Over the deafening rumbles that reverberated out of the floor, I yelled, "What's he doing now, Jinni?"

The wind swept up a cloud of dust from the cave floor. But through the dust I could see parts of the beast appearing in front of us. Out of its broad, bullish face grew an ivory horn, long and sharp as a jouster's lance. The beast threw its head back and roared, revealing razor sharp, saliva-wetted teeth. It trained its glowing red eyes on us, kicked up its hooves, and came at us.

Twenty-four

KARKADANN

Catalina and I dived in either direction. The monster was pure muscle, and as it barreled past us, the earth shook with the force of a hundred horses. But pure muscle is difficult to stop. The beast plowed into the cave's back wall. It shook its head against the blow and snorted in frustration.

From my place on the floor I looked up to make sure Jinniyah had escaped being trampled by the beast. I found her about twenty feet above us, hanging onto one of the closer overhanging stalactites, wrapped around it so tightly I guessed she might have dug her toenails into the rock. I ran over while the beast was still in its dazed state.

"Jinni!" I yelled. "What is that thing?"

"It's a karkadann, Bal!"

A karkadann? Oh, yes. The unicorn with the taste for blood. But this beast looked nothing like any unicorn I'd ever imagined. This karkadann was almost fifteen feet tall with a body more bull than horse. Its fur was a coarse brown, not white, and its

314

tail whipped against the cave floor so hard that stalagmites cracked apart.

"Is there a way to beat it?" I shouted up to Jinniyah.

Jinni shook her head into the rocky spine. "I don't know! I heard some warriors killed a karkadann once, but I don't know how they did it!"

The beast was currently shaking its head and whipping itself with its tail as if to spur itself on. "Look at the wall!" Catalina exclaimed. "This cave is falling apart. One more hit like that and the whole thing will collapse on top of us! We have to summon something and stop it—quickly!"

She was right. Where the karkadann had hit the wall, a thin but ominous fissure had formed. It slowly crawled up the wall toward the ceiling.

"Golems!" I shouted back, and I quickly outlined the story for her. "Jewish protectors made of clay. *Ameth* makes them live, *meth* makes them die. Quick, Cat!"

Catalina muttered something under her breath, and a golem grew out of the earth beside her. In an instant my own golem grew next to hers. Though Catalina's golem was black and mine was the color of clay, both were thick and angry, with eyes made of burning coals.

Seeing the golems, the karkadann shook out its bull head and snuffed in anger. I climbed onto my golem's back, and Catalina's golem raised her onto his. "Careful, Infante," Catalina said. Giants though they were, our clay protectors were little more than half the size of the karkadann.

The karkadann lowered its head, trained its beady red eyes on us, and charged at our two golems. At the last second before impact my golem stepped aside, letting the karkadann smash into his clay arm. Catalina's golem added more buffets on the karkadann's other flank. One final, mighty blow sent the unicorn sliding across the cave on its side, tossing up stalagmites and stones as it whisked past.

I climbed higher on my golem's back to peer over its shoulder at the fallen karkadann. "Is it dead?" I asked Catalina.

The karkadann answered the question by letting loose an earth-shaking roar and trotting to its feet. It threw itself at my golem and smashed its horn in the golem's pottery gut.

"This isn't working!" I shouted over to Catalina. "I'm going to summon something else!"

"No, wait!" she shouted. Her golem brought down its fists on the karkadann's skull. "With *two* golems, the fight is a draw. But with three . . ."

My lips parted. "With three . . ."

Our golems barged across the cave. "Jinni!" Catalina and I screamed. "Jinni!"

I reined in my golem right beneath Jinniyah. "You have to summon a golem, Jinni! It's the only way!"

The girl shook her head and hugged her spiny rock tighter. "I can't, Bal! I'm a genie, and genies can't be Storytellers! I can't even grant wishes!"

"Exactly! You're a *half*-genie, which makes you half-human! Arabuko said any human can be a Storyteller, so you should be able to summon a golem!" Sure, he also said it would take training and work, but I had to hope Jinni could figure it out.

My own golem lumbered forward and cuffed the karkadann on the ear with one of its clay fists. Doing my best to hang on as he pirouetted around the beast, I shouted, "You already know the story of the golem, Jinni! Now just figure out what it's about!"

Jinniyah sobbed back, "Why does it have to be about anything?"

Catalina's golem rammed headfirst into the karkadann's front legs, sending it hurtling off course. The karkadann tumbled across the room and lay there, stunned. Catalina hung onto the back of the golem's neck and called up to Jinni, "You can do it, Jinniyah! Please try, at least!"

I said, "I'll help you, Jinni! It's a story about a protector. The golem and its master share a bond, like me and Diego! Or like God and the Jews!"

If anything that made Jinni despair even more. "Oh, Bal. What do I know about Jews?"

On the back of my golem, I wiped my face with one hand. "Forget the Jews. The bond the golem has with its master is the same bond you have with your god. That's the truth of the golem. That's why you have to write 'truth' to make the golem come alive. *Ameth*—"

317

Catalina's golem cut in front of me. "No, don't listen to him, Jinniyah! The story is about life and death! You write *ameth* to make it live, because the Word is life. But to make it die, all you need to do is take away the A, remember? *Ameth*: life. *Meth*: death. That's the truth of it: the truth that life and death are only a letter away from one another. And that's why the golem is made of clay: 'Dust to dust, ashes to ashes, clay to clay,' and so on?"

Typical Catalina. Of course she had to read the story in the most depressing way possible. "Not every story is about death, you know!" I shouted over to her.

"This one is!" Catalina retorted. By now the stunned karkadann had managed to get itself on its feet, and it shook its head again as if to clear it. Before long it would charge at our golems again, and this time I wasn't sure if our clay monsters would survive the attack.

Maybe Catalina's right. Life and death are *only a letter apart.*

And it hit me. "Jinni!" I shouted as my golem knelt below her. "Listen—we're both right! The story is about life and death—*and* it's about protection! The golem protects the Jews *because* they have the power of life and death over him. The Jews created him, and they can destroy him just as fast. With nothing more than a word, Jinni! Remember what you said to me back in the forest? About genies and Allah?"

Jinniyah turned slowly from her stalactite. "When you create something out of nothing, you're allowed to destroy it when you want to! Oh, Bal, you're right! It's the same! Me and the golem . . . We're the same! It's the same story!"

A beam of light shot out of the rock near Jinniyah's head. Then two more light shafts blazed out from under the two golems.

"What's going on?" I said.

Catalina pointed at the ground. "Infante, look!"

What I saw filled me with terror. Our golems were melting into pools of clay.

For once I didn't need to think. I made a mad leap off my melting golem and shouted, "Catalina! Run!"

We sprinted across cave, as the three lights surged down the floor toward a point in the center of the room. When the beams met they exploded into a blinding white flame. Shielding my eyes, I pushed Catalina behind a stalagmite.

Catalina gasped for breath. "Infante . . . you . . . listened to me. About the story."

"I know. I'm as shocked as you are."

The ground shook. Catalina peeked around the stalagmite, and her mouth fell open.

In the middle of the cave the puddles of clay that our golems had melted into combined into one large pool. The pool began to thicken and grow, first into a mound and then into a mountain of clay maybe fifty feet tall. Arms grew out of the mountain, and legs, and finally a head. It was a golem—a new, enormous golem.

"Did Jinni do that?" I asked, amazed.

Catalina answered, "I think all of us did."

The karkadann saw the new golem and snuffed with disdain. It roared, reared up, and stampeded with all its might at the golem's massive leg.

A smash rang through the cavern as the karkadann's horn shattered against the golem's foot. With one giant hand the golem scooped up the de-horned unicorn. The golem considered the karkadann for a moment before lobbing it across the cave. It smashed against the cave's back wall and shattered into a million tinkling pieces.

It took a second for my mind to accept what had happened. It was over. The karkadann was gone.

"I release you from my service," I said to the golem. The clay beast turned slowly to look down on Jinni and Catalina.

Catalina said, "Maybe since we all created it together, we all have to send it away at once. I release you, golem."

Jinniyah soared down from her stalactite and flew in front of the golem's face. "Thanks, golem! You can go home now." The golem's angry clay mouth turned up into a smile as he disappeared from sight.

"Bal, I did it!" Jinni exclaimed. "Did you see? I helped you summon that golem!"

"That's great, Jinni. Now come on. Let's go before Amir summons something else." I felt for the dagger Rodrigo Sanchez had given me and started running across the cave.

"Slow down!" Jinni said, starting to follow me. Before she could reach me, a boulder the size of the karkadann's head slammed down between us.

"Jinni!" I screamed.

"Don't worry!" she exclaimed from behind the boulder. "I'm all right!"

Catalina ran over to her and cried, "We have to go! The cave is collapsing!"

I whirled around. Through the light of Jinni's hair I could see the thin fracture that the karkadann had made when it hit the wall earlier. The fracture had widened and was currently snaking up the rock face. The floor trembled beneath me. I had a feeling that even if I did succeed in bringing my father out to Caonabó and Anacaona, they wouldn't be happy that I'd pretty much destroyed their holy place. I hoped the main part that the shamans used survived our fight with the karkadann.

"Watch out!" Catalina cried, looking up with horror at the ceiling of the cave.

I threw myself out of the path of a stalactite that fell and crashed before my feet. The fissure in the wall was growing faster and faster, zigzagging up the cave wall to the ceiling. The rocky spines that dotted the top of the cave shivered and rained down on us from above. I dodged the spears of rock as they plunged down in front of me and dived into the scar in the rock wall.

I heard Jinniyah scream, *"Bal!"* as an elephant-sized boulder fell between us, blocking the entrance to the tunnel. I could hear more falling rocks rumbling beyond the boulder, but I could no longer hear Catalina or Jinni.

"Jinni!" I called, banging on the boulder with a fist. "Jinni! Catalina! Can you hear me?" There was nothing. "You two get out of there," I called, probably to no one. I held my knife tighter and said, "I'll try to find another way out."

I swallowed and walked down the rocky passageway, in the direction Jinni said would lead to my father.

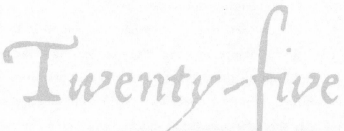

THE STORY OF AMIR AL-KATIB

I let my fingers trail along the walls of the tunnel as I made my way through. They were damp and cool. A chill breeze blew through the passage, carrying sea spray. There was a river nearby, or a waterfall. I could hear its roar.

The tunnel emptied me into a circular room crowned with spiny thorns. Dusty afternoon light filtered in from a stony window and wrapped itself around the stalagmites, shaping them.

A flapping sound. My head shot up.

Not far from me the hameh circled above a stooped figure partially hidden by the shadow of a tower of stone. The figure wore a black cloak with gold embroidered edges, which was held in place by a silver brooch. Underneath that cloak the man wore a long silk robe, with buttons leading down from a high collar to a silver belt. The hameh settled on the man's shoulder, let out a mild squawk, and ruffled its feathers to shake away the dampness of the cave.

I wet my lips. Amir al-Katib. Not a legend. A man. The cloaked man bent in shadows before me.

I had come here to talk, but what was I supposed to say? "I'm Baltasar Infante, your son. Please stop trying to kill me"? He could run me through before I could get out a word. My eyes flicked up at the hameh. There was that bird to deal with too. My shoulder spasmed at the thought. I could summon the sleeping princess, have her tie al-Katib to one of the spiny rocks. And I could take down the hameh with some flying creature. A rukh, maybe. Or Catalina's Furies. Or—

A deep voice cut through my thoughts. "Welcome."

The voice's owner lifted his head. Hameh wings masked his face except for his long graying beard. The angle of his body revealed his exhaustion. Summoning so many creatures had drained him. I could see his hands, lit by the invading afternoon light. They were dark hands, Moorish hands. Hands that murdered Spanish soldiers not much older than myself. And yet they were old hands, wrinkled hands, hands bent with arthritis. In the legends al-Katib had always been a man of perpetual youth. Only now I remembered he was an old man, old as Diego or even older.

Seeing me, the hameh flapped above its master and gave a violent shriek, announcing its attack. It was about to dive at me when the old man—the legend—said, "No. Wait."

The hameh obeyed. Narrowing its yellow eyes, it landed on a nearby stalagmite and bristled.

"Come," al-Katib said to me. "Step out from the shadows so I can see you."

I held back. That was an Andalusian accent. My accent. I had assumed a man with the name of al-Katib would speak with the lilt of a Moroccan or an Arab. In my mind I scolded myself for the thought. Of course this man spoke like I did. He had grown up in Palos, after all. Like I did.

"Come. I wish to look upon the face of my assassin."

I didn't move. I couldn't. I felt rooted to the spot, full of so many different emotions I couldn't think what to do next.

Al-Katib made the decision for me. "I understand. You will not step out of the shadows so that I, a man nearly blind from age, can see you. I had not thought one with the power to destroy the world would be so petty. Very well, so be it." The man planted his feet firmly in the ground. "You will soon see what a half-blind man can do."

The man stomped forward, making a furious motion with his hands, and the word MANTÍCORA—manticore—bled through the air before them. A vicious leonine beast with the spiny, whipping tail of a dragon began to materialize in the cave in front of the letters.

I barely noticed it. At that moment all I could focus on were those wrinkled Moorish hands.

They were trembling.

Al-Katib fell forward and caught himself. He was weak. He could die. "No." I threw my hand forward. "Titivillus—!"

A shocked expression formed on al-Katib's face as the black imp Titivillus crashed through the atmosphere. The inky creature rocketed past the summoned lion and attached himself to the letters that read MANTÍCORA. Titivillus bared his sharp claws and plucked the letters out of the air, folded them together, and tossed each one back into place. Now the MANTÍCORA read ROMÁNTICA. Immediately the manticore's snapping mouth went soft. Docile as a kitten, the beast romped over to the shocked al-Katib, licked the man's face, and rubbed up against his side. Al-Katib let out a disbelieving laugh. "I release you from my service," he said, and the manticore disappeared.

"I release you, Titivillus," I said, and the imp faded into nothing. His near-voiceless cackle followed, melting into silence.

Al-Katib touched his cheekbone where the manticore had licked him. "That was clever." His voice was soft but resonant. "Titivillus, hmm? I haven't seen that one in—heh—quite some time."

I took a few small steps toward him. "Sir, I—"

"So! Titivillus. I wonder. Have I been defeated by a monk? Or a diligent scribe, scratching away at his papers, making ink stains on his wrists between wizards' duels?"

No trace of malice lined his voice. No, no emotion at all. "Well? To whom do I owe this pleasure?"

I glanced down at my reflection in my knife. *He looks like me. Same pointed nose, same dusky skin. Same slanted smile.*

Diego always said I looked like my father. He was right.

"I'm Baltasar," I said to my reflection. "Baltasar Infante."

The old man eyeballed me. Laughed. "Impossible. Baltasar Infante is in Spain with his aunt and uncle."

I stepped farther into the light so al-Katib could see me. "No. He's here. I'm here."

There were tears in my voice, though I didn't know where they came from. The man reached back to steady himself on a stalagmite. "It is a trick. A spell. You are an ifrit. A djinn in disguise. You . . ."

For a moment he could not say anymore. The man was so weak he had to sit on a nearby stone.

Without thinking I cried out, "Father!"

But the man said, "No." And the cruelty of it cut me so deeply that my hand instinctively tightened around my knife.

"You," the old man spat. "You are not my son. You are the evil being the Baba Yaga predicted, the one who will destroy all things." His voice crescendoing, he continued, "I will give you some advice, Djinn! Kill me now, before I have a chance to recover. Otherwise I will bring down such mighty forces upon you, the likes of which the world has never seen!"

You heard him, Luis! I thought I heard Antonio de Cuellar say. *If you don't kill him now, he'll kill you and every Spaniard on this island! I know it's against your nature. But sometimes a man has to go against his nature and do the thing that ought to be done!*

I know his kind, Admiral Colón added firmly. *He has a*

mission and will not stop until he's dead.

Arabuko said, *You see these beads, Baltasar? They represent the men I killed in battle. To speak is good, in times of peace. But sometimes, to speak is not enough.*

And Martín added, *Do what you wish, Sorcerer. History will only call you wrong should you fail.*

A squawk from the hameh brought my attention back to the here and now. The bird landed on Amir's shoulder as the man returned to his swaying feet.

"Strike me down, Djinn!" al-Katib demanded. "Show me your true form!" With disgust he looked upon me and the dagger I held. "You. You pretend to be my son? My son would not stand there with a butter knife in his hands! My son would attack! He would fight! He would never grow up to be such a coward!"

Lavalike heat rushed up to my face as I shouted, "What would *you* know about me? Your *son*? I didn't even know you were my father until a few months ago! You were my hero, and you turned on us! You left! So don't lecture me on what I would or wouldn't do. You don't know a damn thing about me!" Admiral Colón, Antonio, all of them were right! I needed to end this now, while I still had the chance!

I tightened the grip on my knife and started to rush forward.

Suddenly I thought I heard Jinni cry, *Bal, no!* Her voice stopped me in my tracks. *Give him a chance! Talk to him! Please! Amir will listen!*

In my mind I shook my head at her. *Look at him, Jinni. He's made up his mind. It's over.* I paused. *He'll never listen to me.*

Anacaona did, I heard Catalina say. *And Caonabó. They were arrogant, hidebound. They didn't want to hear a word we had to say. But you spoke with them, Infante, convinced them to come to an agreement. Don't give up on your father. Try again.*

I shut my eyes, trying to be strong, trying to will the tears away. *What would you do, Diego? If you were me. You always helped me before.*

And I remembered being seven years old, and my uncle sitting on the stool by my bed. He said, *Once upon a time, there was a man named Amir al-Katib, known as the Eagle of Castile. People called him the Eagle, Bali, because he has a face like a rukh, the giant eagle of Arabia. And they say he's of Castile because al-Katib is a Spaniard, because he was born right here in Palos. You might wonder, how he could be both a rukh, which is Moorish, and of Castile, meaning Spaniard? I have asked this question many times myself.*

But then I realized: He is a Moor and *a Spaniard. A rukh* and *a hameh.*

Something clicked in my mind when Diego said that. *A hero and a traitor. A killer and a father. A protector and a villain.*

"Do not stand there, Djinn!" al-Katib shouted across the cave. "Come at me! Show me your true form!"

My true form. *I am a Marrano,* I thought. *A converted Jew, from my uncle and aunt. Half-Christian, from my mother's side, and half-Moor, from my father. I am Spanish, but Arabuko calls me a Taíno shaman. I am the jack of spades, a hero on a quest to save the world. I am a coward, a Storyteller. I'm all of the above, like you. You're a person. Catalina said it. You can't interpret a person so quickly. I've never understood you. I can't understand you. You're the one story I can't ever hope to interpret.*

His features crazed, al-Katib lunged forward, sending the hameh off him in a flurry of feathers. "Why do you stand there? Show me who you are!"

I shut my eyes, bracing myself for my father's attack. The attack never arrived. I opened my eyes.

The words AMIR AL-KATIB hung before them. I gasped as a ghostly image of a young man with a clipped beard and long black hair walked through the letters. It was as if I were seeing an older version of myself, reflected in a glass, wearing slightly old-fashioned clothing. The apparition stopped and smiled at the older version of himself. The real al-Katib staggered backward. His gaze darted back and forth from my face to the face of his younger self. I'm sure to him we looked almost exactly the same.

From behind the ghost of Amir al-Katib appeared four more figures. Serena: a young woman with a mischievous smile and thick hair pulled back behind her head. Diego: a slightly older man with thinning hair and spectacles. Jinniyah was there too, the same as always, and a fourth figure with dark hair and a tranquil expression. My mother, I guessed. I had never seen her before.

The five apparitions blocked al-Katib's path, guarding me. The old man fell onto his knees. I could hardly bear to look at him, or at the five ghosts I had summoned. I closed my eyes, thinking of my aunt and uncle as I remembered them, happy and older, before the soldiers came. And I grieved over a memory from the childhood I never had, a vision of my parents and aunt and uncle in my room in Palos, gathered together to tell me stories of their adventures.

When al-Katib next spoke, his voice was weak and throaty. "Few alive know of Jinniyah, of David and Sara, of my wife. How, Djinn? How do you know this story?"

I swallowed, trying to take control of my own voice, trying to hold back the tears that were surely coming.

But I couldn't. "I know because I'm your son." I flung Rodrigo's dagger to the side. It slid halfway across the cavern. "And I'm not a coward. I'm here to talk."

Al-Katib's lips began to tremble, and a layer of tears formed across his eyes. "Baltasar," he said at last. He rushed through the apparitions, dispersing them into fog, and finally crushed me in his arms. "Forgive me," he breathed. He all but collapsed on me. I stood there, trying not to cry. Suddenly fourteen years of heartache and loneliness poured out of me, and I held onto my father for the first time.

Twenty-six

FATHER

After a while my father looked down at me, his intelligent eyes peeking out under thick eyebrows. Up close I could see those eyes were clouded and iridescent with cataracts. He wiped his tears and spread an arm toward a low, rounded stalagmite. "Come, my son. Sit beside me for a while."

We sat. Overwhelmed and exhausted, I covered my face with my hands. "You don't know what I've gone through to get here. What you did to me. And Diego and Serena. I . . ."

I couldn't speak anymore. As I bent over my knees, my father put his warm hand on my back. "It's all right, Son. It's all right."

When I was able to compose myself, he said, "You have no idea what it means to me to have you here. I've thought of you every single day. How you were doing. If you were safe. And now you're here. Part of me wishes you had never come. My life is so full of danger, which is why I never wanted you to be part of it. But I suppose it's time for me to stop worrying about you. I see now that you can take care of yourself."

The old man smiled at me proudly. I didn't realize until that moment how much I'd yearned for his praise. He said, "I take back what I said before. You are not a coward. Throwing down your blade like that was an act of tremendous courage."

I tried to smile. "Or tremendous stupidity."

"I suppose it depends on your point of view."

"Mostly it depends on if you kill me or not."

My father laughed, but his laughs dissolved into coughs, and his coughs became tears. "No, my son. I would never harm you." Through his tears he smirked at me. "At least, not knowingly." The old man put his hands on his knees, the way Diego used to. "You said you came here to talk. So talk. What would you like to know?"

"We should probably start with why you keep trying to kill me."

My father blew out a heavy breath and brought a hand to his temple. "Ah, that. Well, it is a rather long story."

I sighed, amused. "What did I expect? Long stories seem to run in the family."

The tears in my father's eyes made them glisten. "Yes. I think you're right about that." My father cleared his throat and began his story:

"For the past ten years I'd been fighting for the Moors of Granada. Then, in January, the castle Alhambra fell. Granada suddenly belonged to Isabel and Fernando. After centuries of war, Spain was finally a united Christian nation."

"I remember," I said. "The day the news came, there were parades in the streets."

My father shook his head. "A rueful day. Many good men died. And for what? More conquest. Power. Wealth. I had seen the same thing before in Constantinople. Looking back over it all, it bewilders me, why I am known as such a glorious hero. It seems I'm always choosing the wrong side.

"After Granada, I wanted nothing more to do with Spain. After what I did, I could never return to Palos, and I knew you were safer there without me. So I decided to continue my travels, this time in Africa. There I found an entrance to the house of the prophet of many names. In Europe most know her as the Baba Yaga. She told me of a great power that traveled west—"

"That will destroy the world as we know it," I recited.

"Ah, so you know it too. I thought so. In any event, the cards' suggestion that this power was a Spaniard further sharpened my desire to conquer it. So I sailed west, alone on a runt of a ship, with spells to keep food in my stomach and wind at my sails. Well, not completely alone." My father nodded over his shoulder at the hameh, who was preening her feathers while perched on another stalagmite. "That one was with me. From time to time, I sent her out to search for another ship heading west, which I knew must be carrying the evil spirit of Baba Yaga's foretelling."

"And that's when the hameh attacked me," I said.

"Attacked you?" My father sounded genuinely confounded. "No, I sent the hameh merely for surveillance, never to attack! That is very strange. Very strange, indeed."

Almost amused, I said, "Oh, and I guess you're going to tell me the other creatures attacked me by accident too?"

My father laughed and brought my head closer to his so he could plant a kiss on the top of it. "Oh no, no! I assure you, the others were very much on purpose! You see, when the hameh returned from her surveillance, there was blood on her claws, and I knew she had discovered what I had sent her to find. There were sailors following me across the Atlantic, and I sent the great Bahamut to destroy them. But summoning such a large creature and sending it such a long distance weakened me, especially since I had other spells working at the time. Not long after, I landed on this island, half-dead and half-mad with fever. I think I attacked some of the natives in my madness. I fear I may have even killed one."

My father fell silent at the thought. Eventually he went on, "I wandered for days until I found this cave. I stayed here a long while, trying to regain my strength. And when I did, I returned to the shore, only to see three Spanish ships floating in the bay."

"And you sent Uqba to sink them," I said.

"Yes. But I was foiled." My father gave me a knowing look. "There was a powerful sorcerer on that ship."

I looked away from him. "That powerful sorcerer accidentally *destroyed* the ship."

"Your captain must not have appreciated that, my son."

"He did not."

My father considered my face for a while. I scratched my arms to avoid that look. "So Catalina was right," I said. "You *did* think I was the evil being in the Baba Yaga's prophecy. You thought I was going to destroy the world."

"Not you specifically. I only knew it was a person on one of those three ships. And when you came into this cave just now, I thought you must be that being. A man clever enough to overcome my defenses could very well have the dark powers the Baba Yaga described in her prophecy. Evidently I was mistaken."

"No," I said. "I *could* still be the evil power. Or it could be any of the people who traveled with me. Or you. Anyone who traveled west from Spain could fit the prophecy. We have no way of knowing for sure until it's fulfilled."

"You may be right." I waited for him to say more. No more came.

After a time he said, "Enough about me. Tell me about yourself! I want to know everything about you. What was your childhood like? How did you find me? How are David and Sara?"

"David and Sara," I started. I blinked away some tears. "David and Sara . . . they died."

I don't think I've ever seen someone look so shaken. "What? How?"

"The night you came to my house, you led the Malleus Maleficarum to us. They imprisoned me and killed David and Sara."

I said this with no bitterness, only an unfathomable sense of regret. As I spoke, my father stared out at nothing, then closed his eyes, put his head in his hands, and wept.

"I am so sorry, my son," he whispered. "Had I any idea that would happen, I never would have risked coming back to Palos." His sobs became stronger as he said, "I can only hope some day you will forgive me."

As he mourned for my aunt and uncle, I thought of the long months of my travels and how much I had feared and hated this man. For so long I'd blamed him for my aunt and uncle's deaths, for all the bad things that had happened to me. But right now, all I wanted was to know him, to be his son. We had lost so many years.

So I put my hand on his. "I will, Father."

"I only came to your house that night to say good-bye. I was going to face the evil being in the prophecy, and I knew I probably would not return. And there you were in David and Sara's house, safe and well. At least I thought it was you. With the dark and my poor eyesight, it was nearly impossible to tell who was there at all."

"I saw you," I told him. "And the hameh."

Under his beard the man grimaced. "And I did so much to ensure you would not. You must forgive me, Baltasar, but I used some sleeping dust on you that night. I thought if I did that, even if you saw me, you would have thought it a dream."

Ah, the glowing yellow eyes, the smells permeating my bedroom. Now it all made sense.

But there was one more thing I still didn't understand. "You said you never told the hameh to attack me. But it did. Why?"

My father wiped his wet face with his palms. "I have a theory about that. Do you know the story of the hameh?"

I thought back to what Diego had told me long, long ago. "It's a bird that springs from the blood of the unjustly murdered. A spirit of retribution that hunts its prey until justice is served."

"Well said."

"But what does that have to do with me?"

The smile on my father's face made my heart sink. "It seems to me that you must have killed your mother."

If I'd been expecting a certain answer, it was not that one. "Me? Didn't she die when I was a baby?"

"Yes. One day shortly after we were married, a man from the Malleus Maleficarum came to our door and asked if I would like to join them in their mission to cleanse Spain of witchery. I was surprised they would ask me, a sorcerer and a Muslim, and naturally I refused. They left, and I thought I was done with them. But one day some weeks later I returned home to find men in my house and your mother lying on the floor in her own blood. She had been near a curtain; I expect she was trying to hide with you. Not a very good hiding spot, I suppose. You must have cried or made some kind of sound, alerting the guards to your presence. And when they saw Marina . . ."

My father brought his fingers to his brow. So the story my uncle had told me wasn't entirely true—the Inquisition *hadn't* ever captured my mother. Perhaps Diego never got the full story.

My father went on, "You cannot imagine the state I was in after that. They had murdered your mother, and you were gone. I thought they'd killed you, too. I was so overcome with shock and melancholy that I let the soldiers take me without even putting up a fight. And in my prison cell, I wept and did not try to escape. For a moment I considered taking my own life.

"But then, the next night, a hameh appeared in my prison window. I had been thinking about the story, and I had summoned her by accident. I took this accident as a sign that I had to live so I could avenge your mother's death. I gathered my powers and delivered justice unto the men who had captured me. One of the soldiers begged for his life and told me you were alive. I tracked you down and rescued you and brought you to your aunt and uncle. Then I hunted down the man who was in charge of the Malleus Maleficarum at the time and slayed him for what had happened to your mother. I thought that, when these deeds were done, my hameh would disappear, like in the story. But the hameh remained. She blamed someone else for your mother's death."

"I don't understand," I said. "How could the hameh blame me? I was only an infant. I didn't mean . . ."

"The hameh is not like us, Baltasar. She does not see subtleties, nor can she make interpretations. She has one purpose, and one purpose only: to exact revenge. She cares not *why* a crime has occurred, whether it was due to an accident or a misunderstanding, or whether it was the fault of a child. All she knows is justice: her own simple brand of justice.

"The pull this type of justice can have on a person is very strong, Baltasar, especially after that person has experienced a loss. That is why I left you with David and Sara. There, you would be safe while I took my revenge on all of Christendom. First I offered my services to the Ottomans, then to the Emir of Granada. I fought battles in Italy, Hungary, Moldavia, Spain. I took my revenge on anyone who would fight me: old veterans, new recruits, young soldiers just years older than yourself. But I see now it was folly. I've turned myself into a ruined, bitter old man, so blinded by hatred that I nearly destroyed the only thing I have left. My son."

A squawk rang up from behind us, from the bird demon roosting on a stalagmite beside us. Wiping his eyes, my father walked up to his hameh.

"I suppose I am done with you, my shadow." With the back of his hand he caressed the creature's face. It squawked again, seeming to ignore the gesture. "I had always thought you were my servant, but it was the other way around, wasn't it? But no more. I do not desire any longer to be a hameh dressed in the garb of a man. I will live the rest of my days as a man, alone, and endure the pain that comes with such a decision."

My father took a breath and, with a sureness belied by his trembling fingers, said, "I release you from my service. I am done with you."

The hameh let out a final cry and slowly dissolved into a fine black smoke. And though he said it in a very low voice so I wouldn't hear, I heard my father murmur, "Peace be with you, Marina."

He lingered there for a while, lit in the half-light of the setting sun. I stood and took his hand with both of mine. The floor rumbled underneath us, and I could make out the sound of rocks crashing in the room where we had fought the karkadann. My father said, "We should go. It is nearly night, and a place like this is not a place to talk."

"We can't," I said. "Part of the other cave collapsed."

"No, there is another way, beyond the waterfall. Unless you wish to stay here?"

I returned the man's smile. "No, thanks. There are probably some worried people waiting for me outside."

My father put an arm around me to lead us to a path hidden behind one of the stalagmites. Spray from the waterfall hit our cheeks, and moss padded our footsteps.

"Worried people?" my father said as we went. "They doubted your success?"

"Doubted me?" I flung my father's arm from me. "If anything, they thought I'd kill *you*!"

My father chuckled. "Well, I'm certainly glad you didn't. And not only for myself. It shows you are an optimist."

We ducked under the low ceiling behind the waterfall and emerged into the spotty sunlight of the forest. I went on, "Not that I *couldn't* have killed you. I did beat all of your monsters, you know. And the Malleus Maleficarum."

"I can't wait to hear about it."

"It's a long story," I warned him.

My father put his arm back around me and hugged me close. "That's all right, Bali. We have plenty of time."

Somewhere beyond the sound of the raging waterfall, I could hear voices calling. "Infante! Can you hear me?"

"Bal, say something! Please! You can't be dead!"

My father smiled at me. "Are those your friends?"

I rubbed the back of my head. "Sounds like it."

"Then you will have to tell me your side of the story on the way back."

I returned his smile. "Sure."

We circumnavigated the lake the waterfall emptied into, hopped the stream, and followed the sounds of my friends' voices. We turned a corner and found the troop of Taíno soldiers, who were lit by the dying light and nearly a hundred torches.

In front of them Catalina and Jinniyah shouted up at the mouth of the cave, which thankfully looked like it hadn't been destroyed.

I pointed to the taller girl. "That one's Catalina," I said to my father. "Pretty sure you know the other one."

"AMIR!"

Jinni's scream was so deafening my ears popped. "You're alive!" She dived onto my father and strangled him with hugs.

"It appears so!" my father said, laughing. The soldiers in front of us watched in surprise as he swung Jinniyah around in the air and held her close.

As he hugged her, Jinniyah looked over his shoulder at me. "I knew you wouldn't kill him." She removed herself from my father and flew over to kiss me on the cheek. "Thank you."

I smiled. "No problem. I could not kill people all day."

My father smiled down at Jinni, too, seeming to grow younger by the second. "Look at you. I suppose it goes without saying, but you haven't aged a bit."

Jinniyah examined his face and scrunched up her own in her usual way. "You got *old.*"

That made the Eagle of Castile laugh from deep within his gut.

Twenty-seven

THE WAR

Outside the cave the battalion of Taíno guards parted, allowing Caonabó to approach us. The cacique examined me and my father with hard eyes. "I see you have upheld your end of the bargain, Shaman." To my father he said, "Good spirits be with you."

My father bowed in response, with a hand over his heart. "And peace be unto you."

An awkward silence followed, so I went on, "Cacique Caonabó of Maguana, may I introduce my father, Amir al-Katib of Spain—"

But my father put a hand on my shoulder. "Of nowhere," he said.

Caonabó considered the man and his answer before speaking again. "We will discuss more later. Let us return to Maguana. My men will provide for you tonight."

As we followed the Taíno troops through the forest, I told my father the story of our travels. Or I tried to, anyway. I could hardly get out a sentence without Jinniyah interrupting with commentary or Catalina saying, "That isn't how it happened at all!"

When I was done, my father said, "This is all my fault. All the terrible things that happened to you. David and Sara—"

Jinniyah interrupted, "It is *not* your fault! It was the Malleus Maleficarum. *They're* the ones who killed David and Sara, not you!"

"You're right," my father said, and he didn't add any more.

I said to my father, "There's so much you have to tell me. About your adventures with Diego and Serena. And Mother. And Jinni!"

"But I told you all about me!" Jinni argued.

"Maybe. But how do I know you were telling the truth?"

Tired as I was, I felt so much lighter now. My quest was over, and I was standing beside my father. I said to him, "Everything's going to be different now. Tomorrow I'll bring you to La Navidad, introduce you to Arabuko—and Colón! He's our admiral. He shouldn't be angry anymore, now that I defeated the evil sorcerer who was attacking us."

"Let's not be too hasty, my son. You may recall that I'm still considered an enemy of Spain."

"Then I'll tell them it was a big mistake. They'll understand. I'll make them."

It was wishful thinking; I knew that. But I kind of believed it anyway. Nothing was impossible now, not with my father by my side. Starting tomorrow, he would teach me everything he knew so I could become a great Storyteller, and he'd go back to being the hero Diego always said he was.

My father looked up at the darkening trees, his face golden under the lights of the soldiers' torches. "And Colón, the leader of this expedition. What kind of man is he, I wonder?"

I thought back to what Titivillus had written about the admiral months ago in the *Santa María*'s hold. Admiral Colón: icon or lie? "I can't say the two of us always got along so well. But I don't blame him for anything he's done. He was caught in a bad situation. Underneath it all, I think he's a good man."

"My son the optimist. And what do you think, Señorita Terreros? What is your estimation of the man?"

Catalina blinked. Clearly she had not expected my father to speak to her directly. "I'm not certain *good* is the term I'd use for him. I don't know many people I would label *good*. But in my interactions with him he has been . . . principled. I may not always agree with those principles, but . . ."

My father put his hand on Catalina's shoulder. "Good enough, young lady. Good enough."

By the time we reached Maguana, night had long since fallen. The villagers crowded around us in a dumbfounded throng. The soldiers led us to one of the circular houses, where bowls of food and fresh water awaited us on the floor, and lean white hammocks hung from the rafters. We sat on a mat made of woven palm fronds and enjoyed our dinner. The whole time Jinniyah and I tried to force new Taíno foods into my father's mouth, saying, "This is really good! Try it!"

When we were done Jinniyah jumped into one of the house's hammocks and said, "Amir, come sleep near me!"

"In due time, little one. I should like to speak to the chiefs of this village and thank them for their hospitality."

"Can't that wait until morning?" Jinni said, pouting.

Catalina said, "We should come with you."

My father put up a hand. "Don't bother. You've done enough for today. Sleep. We will have plenty of time tomorrow. You sleep too, Baltasar."

I smirked. "More stories tomorrow, old man."

My father gently pushed me down in my hammock. "Yes. But now you must sleep."

"I guess I am pretty worn out. I mean, ghulahs, a karkadann, and Amir al-Katib all in one day? Even great heroes need their rest."

"Undoubtedly. Good night, my son."

"Good night, old man."

That night under the chirps of the crickets and frogs, in the balmy air of Ayití, I dreamed like a child.

It was quiet when I woke up the next morning. The sun already hung high overhead. It must have been near noon. Calm.

Well, I deserved calm, after everything. A day to sleep in, wrapped in a hammock, rocked by the wind of the tropics.

"A drink would be nice too," I mused, rolling over on my side. Why not sleep in? What more was there to worry about, with Amir al-Katib at my side? My father—

I shot up. Amir al-Katib, my father—

"Gone," I said aloud, stunned by my own declaration. Only Catalina and Jinni remained with me in the room. Tangling myself in my hammock, I stumbled onto the floor and out the door. Nothing. The town was almost empty. Only old people and a few young mothers and their children remained. Other than that, completely quiet.

I ran back inside and shook the others from their sleep. "Catalina! Jinni!"

"Mmph," Jinni said, draping an arm over her head. Catalina sprang up in her hammock, tense.

"What's wrong?"

"All of the men are gone. My father—"

Jinniyah bolted out her hammock. "Amir?!"

Catalina brought her fingers to her mouth and fell into thought. "Damn it," she whispered.

I reached out to her. "What? What's wrong?"

She closed her eyes and said, "We've been so stupid! We were so caught up with finding your father. We forgot. *I* forgot."

"What? What did we forget?"

"I should have known. This is what I get for letting my guard down!"

I grabbed her upper arm, probably tighter than I should have. "Catalina, *what* should we have known?"

"Pay attention for once, Infante!" she snapped. "We should have known they'd attack La Navidad!"

No. Attack La Navidad? It was impossible. They wouldn't.

"That doesn't make sense. Like you said, it wouldn't be in the Taíno's interests to attack the fortress. They'd lose trade with Spain. They'd make enemies of Guacanagarí. And King Fernando and Queen Isabel would hunt them down to the ends of the Earth!"

"Didn't you notice, Infante?" Catalina said bitterly. "We *are* at the ends of the Earth."

I couldn't believe it. But if Catalina was right . . .

If she was right—

"They could start a war!" I said, shaking her in her hammock.

"Honestly, Infante," Catalina murmured. "You just figured that out?"

I paced around the room, cursing myself for oversleeping. On second thought, maybe that wasn't my fault. I could smell a spicy scent on the air, the same scent I'd smelled back in Palos the night the hameh visited.

Sleeping powder. My father had drugged us.

That was when I caught sight of Jinniyah. She finished pouring our water into pouches and gathered our leftover dinner into my bag.

"Jinni, what are you . . . ?"

"I'm going to find Amir. He could be hurt. He could be— He could be—" She stopped herself and continued packing.

"I'm going." She flew out the door.

"Look," Jinni said once she was outside. She pointed at the vegetation behind our house at the edge of the village. An army hundreds strong had cut a clear trail through the forest. "They're going northwest, to where the ships were! We have to follow this trail!"

I said, "Jinni, it took us days to walk here from the bay."

Catalina slung her own bag over her shoulder. "Yes, but we wasted a lot of time, and we didn't know where we were going. We had no path, and I know we were walking in circles. If I had to guess, I'd say the distance from here to there is probably less than a day's march." She looked up at the noontime sun. "The problem is that we slept late."

I said, "If they left last night, Caonabó's troops are probably half a day ahead of us."

"So what?" Jinni snapped. "We have to stop them! You're sorcerers! Summon something!"

Catalina said, "Jinniyah, we mustn't be headstrong. We could be walking right into a war!"

"I understand that. I'm not a child!"

I prodded Jinniyah to the ground with my palms. "Calm down for a second. Catalina's just being careful. Not all of us here are immortal, you know."

"But Amir—!"

"Can take care of himself." I saw Jinniyah's despairing expression and took her hands. "Besides, I never said we weren't going to go." I turned to Catalina. "Would you like the honor, or should I?"

Catalina spread her arms, and light radiated from her hands. A minute later, we were charging through the forest on the back of an enormous unicorn.

With Catalina and Jinni clinging to the ivory mane in front of me, I watched as the world whizzed by us in a haze of green. The path Caonabó's armies hacked away followed a river that soon led us through a stretch of hills flanked by mountains on either side. Another hour sent us plunging back into the forest. The shafts of light that broke through the canopy dimmed as clouds formed above our heads. It was going to rain.

Our unicorn galloped forward. We had traveled west from Europe, and now we were making our way to the most wester-ly tip of the most western island any Spaniard had ever known. West, where the sun went to die. Catalina was right. This really was the end of the Earth.

We could be walking into a war. Catalina's words repeated in my head. Caonabó, Anacaona, Antonio, Arabuko, Colón: They could be dead already. My father, too, was old, bent, weak. On the battlefield who could say what could happen?

Faster! Unless we stopped this war now, there would be no end to it. Spain would hunt the Taíno, or the other way around, until the other was annihilated. One way or another the world would never be the same.

A great power approaches in the West: a power that will destroy the world as we know it. Baba Yaga's words rang clear against the thunder of hooves. That prophecy had started it all. My father thought I was that dreadful power; at times, I thought it was him. And that misunderstanding almost led to father and son dying at the hands of the other, for no reason.

But what if the Baba Yaga wasn't talking about either of us? What if, after all that, she was talking about Colón and his men? What if the battle between Spaniard and Taíno was the first of many, the start of a war that would change the course of history?

"And here I thought I was the main character," I thought. "Maybe I wasn't even part of the story."

Under the rain clouds Catalina drove our steed forward.

"Do you smell that?" Catalina said at last. In the hours we had been traveling, not one of us had spoken a word. I was sure Catalina would say something snide about how she hadn't thought me capable of keeping my mouth shut for more than a minute at a time. Later, maybe. If later ever came.

"Smoke." Jinniyah brought her hand to her mouth in horror. "Smoke! Something's on fire!" Jinniyah vaulted from the unicorn. "Come on! We have to find Amir!" she said, and she flew through the vines to the north.

"Jinni, wait!" I leaped off our mount, staggered forward, and clawed my way through the undergrowth.

"You are free, Unicorn," I heard Catalina say behind me, and she ran behind me down the path through the forest.

Free of the deafening hoofbeats of the unicorn, I could now make out the sounds of the ocean ahead of us. The air reeked with smoke, more bitter than those dried *cohiba* leaves Arabuko's people so enjoyed. I tripped as the ground beneath me gave way into sand. I gave a final push and tore out of the jungle to the open shore.

A thread of black smoke connected the dark clouds above to a blazing fire below. La Navidad Fortress—little more than a walled village of shacks made of driftwood salvaged from the *Santa María* in the few days we'd been gone—sat aflame on a bluff flanking the east side of the bay. A battle had raged around the fortress earlier, it seemed, but now the battle had moved down to the beach. Not fifty yards in front of me, arrows and wobbling spears flew toward the bay. I cried out as they completed their arcs, taking down my old friends Bartolome and Pérez, who had been running through the sand with crossbows. Bartolome and Pérez fell forward. The Taíno warriors who killed them hollered past, running to the east.

I had barely a moment to experience any grief. Catalina ran up behind me. "Where's Jinniyah?" she asked me. In the chaos of battle I could see no sign of Jinni.

"We have to find Caonabó," I said, taking Catalina's hand. "He's the only one who can stop this."

I dragged her down the shore in the direction of the bluff.

Below it, toward the eastern end of the bay, the waters were rising into the shape of Uqba. That meant Amir was that way. Maybe Caonabó was there too.

Flocks of bats soared above us as we ran through the arrows and spears. As we neared the eastern end of the bay, the beach became littered with blackened, desiccated remains of corpses that crackled like cicada skins. A shaman I didn't recognize knelt in the sea foam, the figurine of his wind goddess tied around his forehead. Like Arabuko on the *Santa María*, he called up the hurricane winds and dashed Uqba against the bluff. This shaman must have been from Guacanagarí's tribe, because one of Caonabó's men fell on him, beating him with a club. "No!" I shouted, but it was too late for the shaman. Caonabó's men rushed past me.

Catalina brought a shaky hand to mine. "Infante. Look."

I looked down next to her, where another bloody Spaniard was lying. "De Torres," the body said. Antonio. I flew to my fallen friend, who was black with soot and caked-up blood. Two arrows had pierced his side, and sand stuck to his blood-stained beard and dried lips. He tried to sit, then winced, and lay back in the sand.

I reached out, ready to pull the arrows from his side. "Should I . . . ?" I started.

"No, no," he said in a hoarse, gurgling voice. His breath rattled in his chest between each word. "In a bit. Let me rest. Just for a minute."

I bent my head in my hands, temples pounding. "Where's Colón?"

When Antonio laughed, blood spurted from his mouth. "Colón! Lucky bastard. Got out yesterday on the *Niña*. Some Indians in boats said they saw the *Pinta* in a river not far from here. So Colón, Vicente, and some others ran off to find him. And then back to Europe!" Antonio laughed, spitting more blood onto his lips. "But don't worry. They'll be back soon, they said. To pick us up, heh."

"What about Arabuko? My friend. The one who spoke Castilian."

"Admiral took him. He'll fetch a nice price at market, I'll expect. Not that any of us decent, hardworking folk will see a penny of it . . ." Antonio dissolved into another fit of gurgling coughs.

I removed my hands from my head. "What do you mean, 'price at market'?"

"Servants, Colón says. Slaves, more like. Colón took a half-dozen or so. They'll get a good price, too, if they make it to port alive. Skinny things like that might not do so well on a sea voyage."

I stared dumbly at Antonio's wounds. Arabuko had told me once, *"Better to die than be taken. To be taken is worse than death."* And he'd once said, *"Your man Colón . . . he frightens me."* I closed my eyes, praying for my friend the shaman, and cursing myself for being too late to save him.

"Too bad the women ran off." De Cuellar let out a rattling breath, remembering. "They would have fetched a pretty penny, back east."

The five women the crew had kidnapped. I looked over at Catalina. She was looking away.

"Hey, Luis," Antonio rasped, looking out at nothing.

I barely paid attention. "I introduced Arabuko to Colón," I said. "I told him we were trustworthy. We *were* trustworthy. I—"

It was then that I noticed that Antonio had turned his head toward the ocean. His eyes were glassy, and his chest no longer seemed to move. I bent over, put my head against my friend's stained body. No heartbeat. Dead.

I clenched my teeth against the tears and smashed a fist against his silent chest. "I trusted you!" I said into the man's shirt. "You were better than that! I trusted you!"

"Infante," Catalina said. "Come on. We have to go."

Catalina put her arms under mine and pulled me to my feet. I flung sideways out of her grasp and sent her stumbling backward.

"No, Cat! You don't get it! I trusted them! You don't understand!"

"I do," she said.

"You don't."

"I do!" She closed her eyes against her tears. "Please, Baltasar, I do."

My legs gave way then, and I collapsed into the sand. "He was my friend."

And there was nothing more to say. Catalina put her arms around me, and I cried without sound for some time.

Twenty-eight

LA NAVIDAD

A squadron of Taíno men raced across the beach carrying spears and spear-throwers. As they rushed past us I recognized some of them from the courtyard in Maguana. Otherwise the beach was mostly empty, except for the dead. The battle, it appeared, was almost over.

Catalina wiped tears from her cheeks and said, "I'm going to look for Jinniyah."

I didn't answer. Only focused on Antonio's broken body. Catalina's face creased with worry. "You'll be all right here?"

"Yes."

She watched me for a moment longer, then stood. "Take cover. Caonabó's men probably won't attack you for fear of breaking the alliance your father. But be careful. I'll only be a moment. I'll bring Jinniyah, and your father, if she's found him."

She waited for me to say more. I didn't. She left. I listened to the breathing of the sea.

"My son."

I lifted my head. Not far away, camouflaged by the forest behind him, my father sat on a rock. "Baltasar." He stood. Stumbled. Fell back to his seat. All of his summoning had weakened him.

I scrambled to my feet. "Don't move! I'll come to you! Don't move!"

I tripped across the beach. Buckets of sand shot out from under my feet as I ran. "Father."

The old man's breathing was shallow. He seemed to be supporting his entire weight on one arm. "It seems I have overexerted myself," he said. "Your mother always told me never to summon more than one story at once. I never listened."

"Jinni was looking for you."

"I saw her. It was only just now that I had enough strength to call out to anyone."

I scanned over the perimeter, searching for Jinni. All I could see was fire and sea and corpses. "How could you do this?" I said to my father. "How could you join Caonabó?"

"I didn't have a choice, Bali," he answered patiently.

"Of course, you did! I thought you'd given up your old ways. You said in the cave fighting for revenge is folly!"

"It didn't do this for revenge. I did it because of the prophecy. The cacique and I agreed, these Spanish men are the ones the Baba Yaga spoke of. They are demons with the power to destroy the world."

"They are my friends. You murdered my friends!"

"I am sorry, Bali. When you are older, you will understand."

Understand? I would never understand this. Never!

I was about to rage against my father more, rail against him for all the evil things anyone ever did to me, and for all the evil, stupid things one man ever did to another, when a funny thing happened. I heard a quick, blunt noise, and my father's eyes went blank. He reached up near his heart. When he removed his hand, it was covered with a wet maroon stain. He fell sideways off the rock.

I stared down at him. A figure was standing behind him in the forest. There, Rodrigo Sanchez held Colón's arquebus. "The admiral left his gun at the fortress," he said. "Lucky I found it before one of the Indians, eh?"

Immediately an arrow flew across the sky and hit Rodrigo in the neck. I cried out as he made a strangled noise and fell down in the sand.

I heard the sound of running behind me. Catalina and Jinni were racing over.

"Amir!" Jinniyah threw herself down beside him.

"Was that a gunshot?" Catalina exclaimed.

I dropped to the ground and took my father's hand with both of mine. It was shaking like mad. A fine layer of sweat embalmed the man's face, and I could hear him wheezing through his teeth.

Amir raised his arm feebly toward Jinniyah. "Baltasar, you must do something for me. Before—"

I shut my eyes against the word. "Tell me what you need me to do."

He brought his free hand up to Jinniyah's tear-burned face. "This girl. This wondrous girl. You must help her. Otherwise when I die she dies too."

"What do you mean?" I looked from my father to Jinniyah, who seemed to be growing transparent. And I understood. "You summoned her," I said, full of wonder.

My father caressed Jinni's cheek as she wept into it. "Yes. She was one of the first creatures I ever summoned. I was a small child, and I had so wanted to summon a genie to grant me wishes. But a true genie is a being of incredible power, and I did not know how to control him. He would not do a thing for me, just stood there and looked at me like I was nothing."

Exactly the same thing that happened to me when I'd summoned my own genie on the *Santa María*. My father continued, "But then I read about the creature called the half-genie. A being half-spirit and half-human, who could not fit well in either world." The man blinked back some tears. "That was a story, my son, that I could understand all too well."

By now Jinniyah had faded so much that I could see almost right through her. My father's breathing was becoming more labored. He squeezed my hand tighter and said, "You must keep the spell going, Baltasar! I need to know that when I'm gone, that girl will live on. That she and my son will live on, together!"

"I will, Father," I said. I closed my eyes and thought of the story of the half-genie, and of Jinniyah. Back in Palos I'd misunderstood her, doubted her. A genie without the power of wishes? What was the use of that?

But now I understood what her power was. There was power in being from two worlds at once. Someone like her might understand both the spirit world and the world of man, though neither race would accept her. There was power in that—a different kind of power, but a power all the same.

"You silly boy," I heard Jinniyah say. I opened my eyes and watched as the fading Jinniyah pressed herself against my father. "If you wanted a genie to grant you wishes, you should have summoned King Suleiman's ring."

It took me a moment to grasp what she had said. "Jinni, what did you say?"

The girl looked up from my father, her face almost completely black from her tears. "Bal, don't you know any stories? King Suleiman had a ring that gave him power over all genies, and he used it to force them to grant him wishes."

I looked up at Catalina, who was hanging back not far from my father. "Catalina," I ordered, "summon a genie—*now.*"

Catalina seemed to understand my urgency. She closed her eyes and the word IFRIT appeared in Arabic before her. The black spirit she summoned was as tall and muscular as the one I had summoned back on the *Santa María*, but somehow hers looked angrier. I closed my eyes and thought of the story of King Suleiman's ring, which quickly appeared and dropped into my hand. I forced the ring onto my finger and ran in front of the genie.

"I have Suleiman's ring," I said. "So you have to do as I say. How many wishes do I get?"

The genie was impassive. Slowly, he raised one finger.

"Fine." And without thinking I said, "This is my wish. No one else is going to die today—not my father, not anyone. Save him, Genie. Save them all!"

The genie looked down on me and folded his arms, but nevertheless he lowered his head in a nod. I noticed Rodrigo's body glowing blue on the ground not far from me. He sat up, yanked the arrow from his throat, and looked up at the genie. His mouth opened in terror as he looked upon the spirit. He fumbled for his gun and hightailed it into the forest.

"Amir?" Jinniyah said, and I saw my father's body glowing too. Jinniyah helped him to a seated position, and he rubbed his once-wounded stomach.

"It appears I am healed," my father said, and he chuckled at the thought. "You are a smart one, my son. Your mother called you Baltasar so you'd be wise."

Behind Catalina, dozens of dying sailors and soldiers were rising from the ground. They felt around their bodies for their wounds, and—finding nothing—began attacking one another again. Each time they died, they glowed blue and returned to life, but they still screamed in agony when hit by a spear or an arrow.

"Stop!" I yelled at them, but they didn't hear me or wouldn't listen. I asked my father, "Where are Anacaona and Caonabó?"

He answered, "Last I saw them, they were up at the fortress. Why?"

"Stay here," I told Catalina and Jinni. "Make sure my father doesn't move." I began running across the beach toward La Navidad.

"Wait, Bal!" Jinni cried behind me. "Where are you going?"

"To stop this."

I crossed the beach and climbed up the cliff where the remains of the fortress smoldered. Taíno men roamed about the cinders, picking up bits from the wreckage. A backlit figure with its hair tied high on its head in a warrior's knot oversaw the looting. "Useless," the figure said, tossing away some half-burnt junk from the *Santa María*.

"Anacaona," I said to her.

The Taíno queen turned around and beamed at me. "Why, if it isn't our young shaman!" With her face smeared with a swathe of deep crimson—dye or blood, I wasn't sure—she might have been a hameh. The priestess clapped her hands together to remove the ash from her palms. "You came to gaze upon our glorious work?"

I looked over the hundreds of bodies that still lay around us and below us on the beach. The genie was able to save those who were dying, but not those who were already dead.

"Call off your men," I told the Taíno priestess. "This battle is over. I've made it so no one else will die today."

"Oh, have you?" Anacaona said, and she looked over her shoulder to see a half-burned sailor from the *Niña* staggering out of the fortress wreckage. Anacaona whipped the bow off her back and let an arrow fly at the sailor. I almost cried out as it pierced through his skull. The man's body glowed momentarily. Then he removed the arrow from his head.

As the sailor ran off, Anacaona exclaimed, "Very nice, little shaman! I suppose this battle is over." She stepped over to the edge of the cliff and shouted to her troops, "Put down your weapons! We have won!"

Below the soldiers of Maguana cheered. They gathered their loot and ran off into the forest. I saw Guacanagarí there, too, limping as he ordered his troops to return to Marién. Anacaona was about to go home when I snatched her hand and pulled her backward.

"Why did you do this?" I demanded. "Why did you burn the fortress? You made a deal with Catalina. You said there would be a truce!"

Anacaona tossed her chin upward. "I'll not deny it. But the truce ended when you returned to our village with your father. We had no choice. Not only did the Spanish kidnap our women, they invaded one of our sacred caves, killing one of the shamans inside."

"It could have been an accident!"

"It was an act of war. We had no choice but to strike back."

"You promised you would talk!"

"Talk! What good would talk do? The world doesn't work that way, Shaman. We have tried to talk before, when others stole our women, attacked our lands. Talk is useless."

Maybe she was right. I thought of the women the crew had kidnapped, and Arabuko enslaved on the *Niña*. I said, "I agree that what my people did was wrong. But a war won't help the Taíno. If you had waited, I could have helped you negotiate with Colón. You could have built an alliance based on trade, done something in the self-interests of both our people. And maybe we could have avoided any bloodshed."

"Be sure, Shaman, we Taíno do not seek out conflict. But we must defend ourselves." With a bare foot Anacaona prodded one of the dead on the ground next to her, the corpse of my old friend Salcedo, the musician. "People like this do not listen to reason. Your people and mine are too different. The only language they understand is the language of spears and blood."

Thunder crashed above us, and Anacaona shielded her head with an arm. The crimson band of paint streamed down her cheeks under the rain. "Enough talk. We will return to Maguana. You and your father may stay with us for as long as you desire."

I fixed my gaze on the charred bodies by her feet. "My thanks," I murmured. I had nowhere else to go.

The young queen rubbed my wet head and picked up my chin with a finger. "Buck up, little shaman! Tonight we will feast." Anacaona grabbed a sack of booty from her side and hoisted it over her shoulder. I watched her as she made her way down the path to the bay across the beach, a sprightly red figure hiking through a maze of black bodies.

"They'll be back, you know!" I called down to her. "Colón and the others. There will be a war!"

"I hope so!" she called back. "They deserve it."

I watched Anacaona for another minute until she disappeared into the forest. As it started to rain, I made my way back down to the beach, where Jinni and Catalina were helping my father stand. "I'm fine," he said to their fussing, and he looked it too. Rotating his shoulder in its socket he said, "I haven't felt so good in a long time." He looked over at the genie I had summoned and said, "I will have to remember that trick."

Catalina and I released the genie and ring from our service. I told my father, "Anacaona invited us to stay with her in Maguana."

"Then we should go," he said. "I think I could use some rest."

"You go. I'm going to stay here for a minute."

Jinniyah clung to my arm, and my father said, "Very well, Bali. Then I will see all of you in Maguana."

As angry as I was that he had attacked the fortress, as I watched my father leave the battlefield I felt mostly relieved. At least my father was still alive, because of me. I would have time to argue with him later.

As Amir followed the rest of the Taíno into the forest, I took Jinniyah under a palm tree to protect her from the rain. Catalina joined us and said, "What are we going to do now?"

Before us the high tide crept up over the corpses of those the genie had been unable to save. I said, "We're going to bury them. All of them."

And we did. Even using golems to carry the bodies and dig the plots, the burials took most of the evening. As we worked, Anacaona's words beat on my mind: *It is a sad truth. They do not listen to reason. Your people and mine are too different.*

In the forest I added a last pile of dirt to the grave of my friend, Antonio de Cuellar, and wondered if she was right. I wiped my hands and sat with Catalina and Jinni at the edge of the woods. We watched the ocean as the rain began to thin.

Something flat, maybe a leaf, struck the side of my face and lay against my cheek. I took it off. It was a playing card, one of the old cards Antonio and Pérez had played with long, long ago. It was burnt around the edges, almost unreadable. I wiped off the soot and raised the thing in front of me.

The king of spades. *A dark man, full of wisdom.*

A light wind, filled with drizzle, brushed past us, bearing a rank smell of fire and death. "Wisdom," I thought. "What a joke." I flung the ashy card into the wind and let it tumble away.

There was no wisdom here in this graveyard. In the old stories, the hero would go from a child who knew nothing about the world to a warrior full of strength and insight. It wasn't supposed to happen the other way around. But now I felt more childish and useless than I had ever felt before.

"It didn't have to be like this," I said, looking back at the graves we had made. "They could have talked. They could have listened. They could have—"

Catalina, sitting beside me, talked into her knees. "That's not the way things work in the real world, Infante."

At another time, maybe, I would have let that be the last word. Now I shot to my feet. "The real world, the real world! I am sick of the real world! If this is the way the world works, then it's not one worth living in! The whole time we thought we were trying to stop an evil power that would destroy the world. Well, maybe a world like this needs to be destroyed! I'm done with it! I'm sick of it! I'm sick of it all!"

Jinniyah tugged at the bottom of my tunic, her eyes sparkling with new tears. "Bal, don't say that!" Next to her, Catalina bit her lip, looking like she was about to cry.

I knelt down next to her. "Don't look at me like that. I didn't mean it."

"Please don't say things like that, Infante," Catalina said in a small voice. "When you say things like that, you sound like me. I hate it."

I sat next to her and said, "Why? What's wrong with sounding like Catalina Terreros? I'd have to work on sounding more pompous, but . . ."

"Something tells me you could handle it." With a finger she began drawing circles in the wet sand. "I never trust people. Not for a second. But you do."

I picked up a rock I found in the sand and threw it out into the bay. "And look where it got me. I trusted Caonabó, Anacaona, my father. I trusted Antonio. I trusted Colón." I buried my face in my knees. "I'm a fool."

"You're an optimist. Your father said it, and I wasn't sure I believed it at the time. But it's true. Underneath the stupid stories and the jokes and the sarcasm, I see it. The way you interpreted my sleeping princess story the first time; the way you talked Anacaona out of killing us. The way you talked to your father instead of killing *him*. I wish I could be like that. Like you and Jinniyah. You have faith in people. In the world. That's why I like you."

Under the drizzling rain, I felt my face grow hot. Catalina must have seen me blush, because she scowled and said, "For goodness' . . . ! I didn't mean it *that* way!"

I stood and took a couple of steps toward the sea. A cool breeze was blowing in from the west. "All right. I don't want the world destroyed. That's the wrong word. A long time ago, Antonio said we'd be going to a new world. And a new world can be, well, new, can't it? Different, I mean."

"I think, after this, everything's going to be different. For everyone."

Jinniyah suddenly leaped up pointing in the direction of

La Navidad. "Hey, look. It's Tito!"

Indeed a raggedy shape was stumbling down from the bluff. Jinni flew over to the scraggly cat, scooped him up in her arms, and flew back to dump the heap of sand and muddy fur into Catalina's lap.

"Here's your kitty." Though tear-burns lined her sooty face, Jinniyah wore a tentative smile.

Picking him up by the scruff, I said, "I think he's lost some weight."

The cat grumbled, and Catalina frowned. "We'll feed him when we get back to Maguana. Or I suppose we could find him a tree frog or something."

Jinni scrunched up her nose and took Tito from me. "You shouldn't eat frogs, Tito. Dirty, dirty animals."

Catalina scratched behind Tito's ears. "Honestly, I don't think it matters to cats."

Jinniyah brought Tito's face close to hers. "I don't know. Tito's picky. Like his owner."

As the two girls continued fussing over the cat, I felt a warmth growing within me. On the bluff, Anacaona had said people were too different, that they could never understand one another. And I certainly didn't always understand Jinni or Catalina. All the stories in the world wouldn't give me the power to read their thoughts or understand what it meant to live every day as a genie or a girl.

But as I watched the two giggling together, I couldn't help

but hope that Anacaona was wrong. "We can still stop this," I said to myself.

Catalina looked at me oddly. "What did you say?"

"Sorry. I was just talking to myself again."

Catalina kept scratching Tito and said, "You never can stop talking, can you?"

"No," I said, standing. "And I won't. Anacaona said we're welcome to stay in Maguana. We can keep talking to her and Caonabó, convince them to end this war. Antonio said Colón'll come back; when he does, we'll talk to him. We'll talk to Guacanagarí, to my father. We'll—"

"But Bal!" Jinni cut through my speech. "You saw what the Baba Yaga's cards said! Someone's going to destroy the world as we know it. That's the future, and you can't change the future!"

I plucked up the king of spades I'd tossed into the sand and showed it to Jinniyah. "That's the thing, Jinni. We don't know what the Baba Yaga's cards said. Maybe this war is going to destroy the world—"

Catalina finished for me, "Or maybe the Baba Yaga wasn't telling the future at all. Perhaps she was trying to trick Infante and his father into traveling west for some reason we don't yet understand."

"Exactly. The Baba Yaga said it herself. The cards have different significances—different interpretations. So I'm going to interpret them my way. I say they mean that *we're* going to destroy the world. We're going to destroy this awful world and replace it with a new one—a better one." I threw my hand out at the makeshift graveyard behind us. "We're going to make sure this never happens again. Never."

"You make it sound so easy," Catalina said.

"Sure, I do. I'm the hero. For me, everything comes easy."

While I grinned, Catalina rolled her eyes. "I think you need to start paying more attention to what goes on around you, Infante."

I put my hand out in front of her. "So, you going to help me or not?"

"I suppose I could find the time in my busy schedule to help you." She put her hand gently in mine and let me help her to her feet. "What kind of recompense are you prepared to offer?"

I scratched the back of my head. "I'll let you stay with me in Maguana."

"I accept. At least until we can find a route to Cathay or Cipango."

"Jinni?"

Jinniyah smiled up at me from her place on the ground. "We're a team," she told me. "Always."

"Then let's go!"

I guess Tito understood what I said, because he jumped out of Jinniyah's lap and sped off into the jungle. "Tito, come back!" Jinniyah yelled. She let go of my hand and chased after him.

As she went I looked back toward the ocean. Good-bye,

Arabuko. I turned back to the forest graveyard. Good-bye, Bartolome, Salcedo, Pérez. Good-bye, Antonio.

"I wish we knew how to give them a proper funeral service," I said.

Catalina opened her mouth, closed it, and sighed.

"What?" I said. "Did I say something wrong?"

Catalina sighed again and made a cross with her fingers in the air. And she sang in Latin, *"In paradisum deducant te Angeli. In tuo adventu suscipiant te martyres . . ."*

And as she sang I understood her words: "May the angels lead you into Paradise. When you arrive, may the martyrs receive you and lead you to the holy city of Jerusalem. May the angels receive you, and with the pauper Lazarus may you have eternal rest."

"Amen," I said.

We watched the ocean and the sun sinking into the west. Bats swooped over the shoreline and into the forest.

And I laughed. "What's so funny?" Catalina asked me.

"I'm a little shocked, that's all. I thought I'd figured out all your secrets."

"What secrets?"

"Like . . . how did you learn to sing?"

Catalina rolled her eyes at the memory. "I lived in a convent for a while. Singing was unfortunately a requirement."

A convent! The word set my Storytelling heart aflutter.

"Ooh, let me guess! You were in love with a dashing young

man—dark, not too tall, but handsome—but your parents didn't want you to marry him because he was too far below your station. So they sent you to a nunnery and arranged for him to be sent to a monastery far, far away."

Pretending to ignore me, Catalina walked into the forest toward the sound of Jinniyah's voice as she yelled some incomprehensible commands at Tito. "Don't read too much into this, Infante."

I ran to catch up with Catalina as she entered the brush of Ayiti. "Your parents sent you away—but they didn't realize the convent was actually a front for a witch's coven! And every Sunday night there would be virgin sacrifices, and demonic rites, and . . . and orgies . . ."

Catalina swatted away a vine hanging in front of her. "You have a very active imagination, Infante. But—and please pay attention so I don't have to say this again—this isn't one of your fairy tales. I lived in a regular, unmagical convent with regular, unmagical nuns. Sometimes, if we were particularly fortunate, a regular, unmagical bishop would come visit us. There is no hidden meaning in this story. I promise."

I laughed. Somewhere in my memory, I heard my Uncle Diego say to my aunt through a dream, *It is just a story, my love. Meaningless.*

I understood now that he was lying. After all, there was magic in a story, wasn't there?

I said, "You know, my uncle told me something when

I was younger. Once there was a poor family that was forced to move to a faraway land. They lived in a house on a large field, but the field was barren and they nearly starved. And to make matters worse, one day their house was struck by lightning and it burned to the ground."

"Lovely," Catalina said in a dull voice.

"No, listen! Even though the family was all but ruined, they didn't give up. They decided to build a new foundation and a new home. And when they were digging in their barren fields to start on the foundation, they found gemstones buried in the earth. There was a hidden treasure there for generations, and no one even knew it. The family became rich and generous, and they were happy for the rest of their days."

Catalina said, "I'm sorry, Infante. I'm still not following you."

I wrapped an arm around her shoulder and said, "What kind of Storyteller are you, anyway? I'm saying there's a whole world of fields out there. Let's go dig up some treasure."

Author's Note

Some of you may be wondering, "How historically accurate is *Hammer of Witches*?" Magic aside, I'd say, "Reasonably." Cristóbal Colón was of course a real person, as were the Pinzón brothers, Antonio de Cuellar, Juan de la Cosa, Rodrigo Sanchez, Anacaona, Caonabó, Higuamota, and Guacanagarí. Colón's Jewish translator, Luis de Torres, and his cabin boy, Pedro de Terreros, also existed, though I'd venture to guess they weren't actually wizards.

The cultural diversity in *Hammer of Witches* is based in history. Before 1492, Spanish Catholics, Jews, and Muslims lived and worked side by side, often grudgingly. Then, as Baltasar mentions, the Muslim emirate of Granada fell to Spanish forces, marking the end of the Spanish Reconquista, a series of wars battled over the course of several centuries to "take back" Spain from Muslim rule. In Granada, King Fernando and Queen Isabel signed the Alhambra Decree, expelling all non-converted Jews from the country. At least a hundred thousand Jews were displaced, and those who converted faced a more aggressive Inquisition. Hundreds of thousands of Muslims left Spain at the time of the fall of Granada, and the Moriscos (Muslims who converted to Christianity) would be banished not long later. But Spain would remain diverse in other ways. Walking through the streets of fifteenth century Valencia, for example, you'd see Spaniards, Berbers, Arabs, Genoese traders, Eastern European and Greek slaves, and a substantial population of Africans (both slave and free). Palos, as a small harbor town, would not be as diverse as a large city, but it also wouldn't be completely white.

When writing about the events that unfolded in Ayití (Hispaniola) during the last weeks of Columbus's first voyage, I strove to be as historically accurate as possible and to describe Taíno culture with as much precision and sensitivity as I could, given my own non-native background and the dearth of reliable primary sources from the period. No written language existed in the Caribbean in pre-Columbian times, so most of what we know about fifteenth century Taíno culture comes from a few contemporary Spanish writers (all of whom had their own agendas) and more modern archaeological and linguistic research. What these resources make clear is that Taíno civilization was and is significantly more complex than high school history textbooks give it credit for, and I hope my humble abilities as a writer were enough to illustrate the richness of fifteenth century Ayití's culture. At the same time, Baltasar is a somewhat unreliable narrator who sees the Taíno through young, Eurocentric eyes. Throughout the book he swings back and forth between seeing the citizens of Marién and Maguana as "barbarians," noble savages in a Garden of Eden, wise mentors, warlike villains, victims in need of saving and, sometimes, actual human beings. He's learning—slowly. His beliefs are his beliefs and not my own.

No one knows exactly what happened at La Navidad, so the final two chapters of this book are based on my own educated guesses. Primary sources tell us that, in the beginning of 1493, Columbus left thirty-nine members of his crew in a fortress cobbled out of timber from the *Santa María*, which had run aground on Christmas day. When Columbus returned a year later, the fortress was destroyed, the crew was gone, and the Spanish objects inside the fortress taken by the Taíno. Guacanagarí told Columbus that Caonabó had burned the fortress, killed some or possibly all of the Spanish men, attacked his village, wounded him, and stolen one of his wives. Columbus believed this report. I'm inclined to believe it too.

If Caonabó *had* attacked the fortress, the attack may have been spurred by his discovery that some of the Spanish were taking three or four Taíno "wives" apiece (according to Guacanagarí). There were also reports of Spanish men being killed after they had trespassed on Taíno mines either before or after the destruction of La Navidad. Whatever his reasons, Caonabó probably did attack the fortress, because, when the Spanish captured him during Columbus's second voyage, the cacique admitted to burning the fortress and killing between eleven and twenty of the thirty-nine men. However, it is also possible that the crew themselves burned the fortress after some internal conflict, though I've personally seen no evidence for this theory.

So in general I'd say that the history in *Hammer of Witches* is reasonably accurate, but you might want to think twice before using it as a study guide for your next history test. Here's why:

THE TIMELINE

Hammer of Witches is a work of fiction, and fiction has its own rules which don't apply to history. For one thing, history doesn't follow a schedule. Events can happen gradually over a long period with many lulls in between. Fiction, on the other hand, must keep readers' attention, and climaxes hopefully arrive when expected. For this reason I compressed the timeline of Colón's first voyage, cutting out his layover in the Canary Islands and some of his wanderings around the Caribbean so I could focus solely on his time in Ayití, where more of the dramatic events occurred. Unfortunately that meant readers didn't get to see the Bahamas or Cuba in this book, and here, Martín Pinzón separated from Colón near Hispaniola and not off the Cuban coast.

THE SPANISH INQUISITION

The Malleus Maleficarum witch hunters in this book are an invention and should not be confused with the historical Spanish Inquisition. As horrific as the Inquisition was, the real Inquisitors of Spain would not have kidnapped Baltasar under the cover of night with no warning, nor would they have resorted to torture so quickly. The Inquisition was far too legalistic for that. They would have first formally accused Baltasar of heresy and given him a month or so to confess and repent. If he didn't turn himself in at the end of the month, he would have been arrested and taken to a relatively nice prison, in comparison to other Spanish prisons of the time. (Still, he might have to wait there for a few years before his case was heard.) The Inquisitors would have seized his and his family's assets to pay for his imprisonment and trial—and perhaps more importantly, to line their own pockets. At the trial, Baltasar would have faced a tribunal of learned men, had a defense attorney, and likely be defended by character witnesses. The tribunal would rule for torture only rarely; the seizure of assets and threat of torture were usually more than enough to get a confession. Afterward Baltasar would face execution, hard labor, public shaming, or freedom.

In contrast, the fictional Malleus Maleficarum in *Hammer of Witches* is more of an organization of spies, renegade priests, and bounty hunters than an arm of the Spanish legal system. The book *Malleus Maleficarum* did exist in the 1400s and was somewhat popular in Europe. However, both the Church and Inquisition condemned it.

THE CHARACTERS

I did not live in the 1490s, nor did I have any personal interactions with Christopher Columbus, Martín Pinzón, Caonabó, or Anacaona. No one can know exactly what these people were like, although we can make guesses based on our primary sources. That said, *Hammer of Witches* is a work of fiction. At times I flashed my poetic license and changed the characters for the sake of plot. Here's the breakdown:

Things we know about Christopher Columbus: He made some over-the-top demands of King João of Portugal and Spain's King Fernando and Queen Isabel and finally was able to make his first voyage; he seemed to be a religious Catholic; he got along with Guacanagarí; he took between six and ten Taíno back with him to Spain after the first voyage; in later voyages he attempted to establish a slave trade and forced the Taíno to pay tribute to him in the form of gold, under penalty of death; he was eventually arrested for his mismanagement of Hispaniola.

What we don't know about Christopher Columbus: where he came from (his son and contemporaries said or strongly suggested Genoa); if part or all of his family was Jewish; if he was a good captain and navigator; if he liked or hated Martín Pinzón (or both); why he immediately believed Guacanagarí when he said he didn't attack La Navidad; whether he was a nice guy to be around. During the second voyage, rumors of Columbus's cruelty to the Taíno (cutting off heads, hands) began to spread, but it's unclear how true these rumors were.

Things we know about Martín Pinzón: He was from Palos; he was an excellent mariner; he was famous for his efforts in the War of Castilian Succession; he had a couple of brothers who were also involved in the first voyage; he was initially so confident about Columbus's plans that he put up his own money to help fund it; for some reason he sailed off without Columbus while in the Caribbean; eventually they found each other again and returned to Europe, where he quickly died.

What we don't know about Martín Pinzón: if he had syphilis when he was on the first voyage, and if it had any effect on his decision to separate from the other two ships; if he died of syphilis at all; if he separated from Columbus on purpose or by accident. For the purposes of this book I decided he left on purpose, because nothing happens in a fantasy book by accident.

Things we know about Caonabó: Bartolomé de las Casas said Caonabó was not from Hispaniola, but one of the Lucayan islands (the Bahamas or Turks & Caicos); he was married to Anacaona and was cacique of Maguana; he was older and sharp-witted, and Columbus respected him; after the second voyage he and others attacked some Spanish fortresses Columbus had ordered built; he was captured by the Spanish and died in a shipwreck on the way back to Spain.

What we don't know about Caonabó: if he really burned La Navidad (see above); if he really stole one of Guacanagarí's wives; if he really was captured when the Spanish tricked him into putting on a pair of handcuffs by calling them bracelets. That last story sounds particularly fishy to me.

Things we know about Anacaona: She was from Hispaniola; she was the sister of the cacique of Jaragua; she was married to Caonabó and was the mother of Higuamota; she was well-respected as a composer of areitos (Taíno ballads); the Spanish thought she was beautiful; toward the end of 1496 she and her brother made a treaty with Columbus, after which she was friendly with the Spanish; she eventually became a cacica (female cacique); later, during a feast, Spanish Governor Nicolas de Ovando burned down her meeting house and had her hanged.

What we don't know about Anacaona: if she agreed with her husband's decision to attack the Spanish. In *Hammer of Witches*, I decided the answer was "yes" to make her a more active character. However, there's no proof either way.

THE STORIES

Most of the stories recounted by the characters in *Hammer of Witches* are retellings of real folktales, fairy tales, myths, and religious stories. But I've taken some liberties. The prologue's hameh story is mostly my own invention, and I decided to keep the Ali Baba story in there even though there's no evidence it was being told at the time. Then again, there's no evidence it wasn't.

THE MAGIC

Storytelling is an invention of mine, so I had to make guesses about how it would affect the world if it did exist. In the 1300s and 1400s, Spain increasingly disapproved of differences of religious belief and interpretation; for this reason, I assumed there would be a "Magic Inquisition" to eradicate the heresy of Storytelling. In Ayití, such inquisitions did not exist, so I concluded that Storytelling would likely be more accepted there. In the fictional world of *Hammer of Witches*, the best Taíno Storytellers (like Arabuko) would become the village shamans by virtue of the fact that they could apparently call upon and talk to spirits. That said, I do *not* want to suggest that real Taíno people are magical or that real Taíno shamans were witches. In reality, the Taíno shamans (*behiques*) were religious leaders and doctors who used medicinal herbs, *cemíes* (religious icons), ceremonial fasts and purging, songs, and hallucinatory drugs to perform their sacred rituals.

THE LANGUAGE

Some readers have asked me why Baltasar's narration in *Hammer of Witches* doesn't sound more "medieval." Put simply, *Hammer of Witches* is a young adult novel, and I wanted it to be accessible to young adults. Beyond that, Baltasar is neither a member of the church nor the aristocracy, so there's no reason to believe he would have written or spoken in a formal manner. If I wanted to write in a historically-accurate fashion, I would have written *Hammer of Witches* in Old Castilian (which Baltasar would have spoken), Renaissance Latin (the language in which he probably would have written), or very very Early Modern English. If you'd like to see some very very Early Modern English in action, I encourage you to read "The Tree of Common Wealth" (1509) by Sir Edmund Dudley, which begins, "fforeasmuch as euy man is naturallie bounde not onlie moste hartelie to praie for the prosperous contynuaunce of his liegue Soueraigne Lorde . . ." I could have certainly written *Hammer of Witches* in such language. Something tells me, though, that my editor wouldn't have been too happy with me!

So there you have it. If you want to learn more about fifteenth century Spain, Columbus's voyages, or Taíno culture, please visit my website hammerofwitches.com to find a suggested reading list and other special features. Thanks for reading!

Pronunciation Guide

Unless otherwise noted, all names should be pronounced as if one were speaking Spanish, specifically late fifteenth century Andalusian Spanish, which not-so-coincidentally sounds like the Spanish used throughout the Americas. Taíno words sound like Spanish words, except GU sounds like a W. Put the stress on the capitalized letters, and roll your Rs if possible! It's fun.

Baltasar Infante	bahl-tah-SAHR een-FAHN-teh
Amir al-Katib	ah-MEER ahl kah-TEEB (or the more Arabic AH-muhr ahl KAH-tuhb)
Anacaona	ah-nah-cah-OH-nah
Antonio de Cuellar	ahn-TOHN-ee-oh deh KWEH-yahr
Arabuko	ah-rah-BOO-koh
Bahamut	bah-hah-MOOT
Bartolome	bahr-toh-LOH-meh
cacique	kah-SEE-keh
Caonabó	kah-oh-nah-BOH

cemíes	seh-MEE-ehs
Cristóbal Colón	kree-STOH-bahl koh-LOHN
David	thah-VEETH (the "th" sounds like the "th" in "this," not "thick")
Diego	dee-EH-goh
Elena Hernández	eh-LEH-nah ehr-NAHN-dehs
golem	GOH-lehm
Gonzalo	gohn-SAH-loh
Granada	grah-NAH-dah
Guacanagarí	wah-kah-nah-gah-REE
hamaca	AH-mah-kah
hameh	HAH-meh
Higuamota	ee-wah-MOH-tah
huracán	oo-rah-KAHN
Jagua	HAH-gwah
Jinniyah	dzhuh-NEE-yah
Joaquín	hwah-KEEN
Juan	HWAHN
Luis de Torres	loo-EES deh TOH-rrehs
Maguana	mah-WAH-nah
Malleus Maleficarum	mah-LAY-oos mah-leh-fee-KAH-room
maravedíes	mah-rah-beh-DEE-ehs
Marién	mah-ree-EHN
Martín Pinzón	mahr-TEEN peen-SOHN
Mizrahi	meez-rah-CHEE ("ch" sounds like a less-harsh version of the ch in "Chanukah")

mudejares	moo-deh-HAH-rehs
Niña, Pinta, Santa María	NEE-nyah, PEEN-tah, SAHN-tah
	mah-REE-ah
Sara	SAH-rah
Serena	seh-REH-nah
Shana Mlawski	SHEY-nuh muh-LAU-skee
Taíno	tah-EE-noh
Titivillus	tee-tee-VEE-loos
Uqba	AHK-bah
Vicente Pinzón	bee-SEHN-teh peen-SOHN
Yucahú	yoo-kah-OO

For more information about these pronunciations, please visit hammerofwitches.com.

Acknowledgments

There are many, many people I'd to thank. First, Jessica Regel, the best literary agent who ever lived, and Stacy Whitman, my wise and eagle-eyed editor: you both are brilliant. Thank you for everything. My deepest gratitude to all the wonderful people at the Jean V. Naggar Literary Agency, Tu Books/Lee & Low, and Audible for bringing this book to life and putting it out into the world. A hearty thank you to everyone who read and gave me notes on my mediocre early drafts, including Jordan Stokes, Adriana Vallejo Kreger, Leslie Root, Carlos Hann Commander, Daniel Hayes Kahn, Selena Liao, Wes L. Miller, Laura Biagi, Kiffin Steurer, and Julia Johnson. Special thanks to Jorge Estevez at the Smithsonian's National Museum of the American Indian for his kind words and helpful insights into Taíno culture. Andrew Mar and Isaac Stewart: you are amazing. I can't imagine a more beautiful cover than the one you created for this book. Much love and thanks to all of my former English and writing teachers, especially

Barbara Aronowitz and John Crowley, and to my friends and family for their unflagging moral support. I am humbled and honored to have you all in my corner.